Alex Gray was born and educated in Glasgow. After studying English and Philosophy at the University of Strathclyde, she worked as a visiting officer for the DHSS, a time she looks upon as postgraduate education since it proved a rich source of character studies. She then trained as a secondary school teacher of English. Alex began writing professionally in 1993 and had immediate success with short stories, articles and commissions for BBC radio programmes. She has been awarded the Scottish Association of Writers' Constable and Pitlochry trophies for her crime writing. A regular on the Scottish bestseller lists, her previous novels include *Five Ways to Kill a Man*, *Glasgow Kiss*, *Pitch Black*, *The Riverman*, *Never Somewhere Else*, *The Swedish Girl* and *Keep the Midnight Out*. She is the co-founder of the international Scottish crime writing festival, Bloody Scotland, which had its inaugural year in 2012.

Alex Gray

ONLY THE DEAD CAN TELL

sphere

SPHERE

First published in Great Britain in 2018 by Sphere

1 3 5 7 9 10 8 6 4 2

A CIP catalogue record for this book
is available from the British Library.

Hardback ISBN 978-0-7515-6845-5
Trade Paperback ISBN 978-0-7515-6844-8

Typeset in Caslon by M Rules
Printed and bound in Great Britain by
Clays Ltd, St Ives plc

Papers used by Sphere are from well-managed forests
and other responsible sources.

Sphere
An imprint of
Little, Brown Book Group
Carmelite House
50 Victoria Embankment
London EC4Y 0DZ

An Hachette UK Company
www.hachette.co.uk

www.littlebrown.co.uk

This book is dedicated to
Dr Jenny Brown, my dear friend
and agent extraordinaire

Love the sojourner therefore; for you were
sojourners in the land of Egypt.

Deuteronomy 10:19
Revised Standard Version

PROLOGUE

Dorothy Guilford spent a lot of time thinking about death. Her own death. That it would not take place when her body had suffered the decrepitude of old age was something to which she was resigned. Especially now.

The letter had trembled in her hand as Dorothy read it for the second time. To her it showed clear proof of her suspicions. But others might not see it that way, of course. A duplicitous character like Peter Guilford with his easy charm could explain away almost anything; the bruises on her arms, the black eye that he claimed was a gardening accident. No difficulty for a man like Peter to tell his family and friends that Dorothy wanted to increase the premium on her life insurance.

She could imagine him, eyes downcast, voice breaking with feigned emotion, telling how much his dearly departed wife had wanted to be sure that he was looked after in his later years.

She longed to screw up the letter in that moment but then he would know she had read it, guess that she had an inkling of what he was about to do.

Bastard! The word stuck in her throat, making the woman choke for a moment. Then she gasped aloud, panic setting in.

Would that be what Peter had in mind? Suffocation, a pillow over her face? Or would he fake yet another *accident*, injuring her in a way that meant a slow and lingering death? What if he were to push her over a cliff? Run her down in the driveway? Bash her head in and pretend it was the work of an intruder?

Dorothy clutched at her heart as the sound of buzzing filled her ears and her eyelids began to flicker. She backed into a chair and slumped down, head spinning as the dizziness began again. Palpitations, the doctor had told her. Nothing to be overly alarmed about.

But what if Peter had already begun his deadly scheme? What if he had put something into her food . . . ? A red mist appeared before her eyes as the beat of her heart intensified. Was she about to die? Here and now?

CHAPTER ONE

Dr Rosie Fergusson gave a tiny gasp as she felt the kick in her womb. Her mouth curved into a smile, glad of the timely reminder of new life, aware of the irony as she bent to examine the body lying on the kitchen floor. Life and death. The smile faded, replaced by a frown as Rosie bent lower to scrutinise the position of the woman's hands grasping the knife.

At first glance it would appear that the victim had been trying to pull it out of her chest. But what if the fatal wound had been self-inflicted? Rosie had seen cases before where there was a dubiety in the cause of death, sometimes having to argue across a courtroom as the evidence began to tell her a different sort of story from the one that seemed most obvious.

The pathologist narrowed her eyes. There had been another case, early on in her career, one Rosie preferred to forget, but she had to admit her interpretation of the evidence in that case had caused a whole lot of grief for the family of the deceased. They'd been so certain their father had taken his own life and Rosie had wanted to believe that too. But the police investigation had shown a different scenario and a man was still languishing in prison, convicted of murder. Yet he'd been at large for so much longer than he might have been if she'd made the correct judgement.

'Time of death, doctor?' A voice behind her made Rosie turn to see DC Kirsty Wilson, her young friend and sometime babysitter for Abby, her four-year-old daughter.

'You know I can't give anything but an approximation, Kirsty,' she said, swivelling on her heels. 'But I'd say the victim died some time after three o'clock this morning. Rigor is incomplete,' she added, nodding towards the body on the floor. 'You say she was found at seven-fifteen, that's right?' Rosie glanced towards the scene-of-crime manager who, like the others, was clad in the regulation white forensic suit.

'Aye, the husband found her lying on the floor here,' DS Jim Geary replied. 'Said he came downstairs and heard the radio on. Thought his wife had got up to make breakfast.' Geary's eyebrows rose under his forensic hood as though to indicate his scepticism.

'Strange that she didn't clear up from the night before, isn't it?' Kirsty observed. 'Even I do the dishes before I make breakfast. And the rest of the kitchen looks spotless.' She turned to cast a glance over the dark granite worktops and gleaming stainless steel oven and hob.

Geary nodded, eyeing the sink full of dirty dishes and pans, grease congealing in the cold water. 'Have a look at that, Wilson,' he said, nodding towards the sink. 'See if there's anything worth noting before the SOCOs and DI McCauley get here.'

Kirsty moved towards the kitchen sink, light from a window shining on the utensils. There was a large griddle pan immersed in the water, a single plate leaning against it. Fishing in the water with her gloved hand, Kirsty found a fork and a non-stick spatula under the pan. To one side of the sink lay a black plastic container, its label rolled back. Careful not to disturb the evidence, she lifted it between her finger and thumb.

'Looks like she cooked a sirloin steak for her supper,' Kirsty remarked. 'Just one plate, unless she cleared up after herself and left her husband to do his own dishes. But there's no sign of a knife,' she added.

'Laguiole,' Rosie told her.

'What?' Geary asked.

'French steak knife. We've got a set at home. Look for a flat wooden box somewhere with one missing,' she added.

'That's what . . . ?'

'I can say with a degree of certainty that the weapon in the victim's hands is a Laguiole knife, yes,' Rosie agreed grimly. 'But whether or not she actually ate that steak needs to wait until we carry out the post-mortem and see her stomach contents.'

Rosie looked back at the body, concentrating on the hands clutched around the heft of the knife. She would examine the wound more thoroughly once the weapon was withdrawn, see what its shape and depth could tell her. But meantime there was something she could offer to the detectives hovering above her.

'Cadaveric spasm,' she muttered, her gloved fingers touching the dead woman's own.

'What?' Geary repeated.

'Her hands have stiffened up considerably,' Rosie replied to the detective's question. 'Could mean one of two things. She may have been trying to stop the penetration of the blade . . .' The pathologist tailed off.

'Or?' Geary persisted.

'Or it was suicide,' Rosie said quietly.

'Really?' The detective sergeant's voice was tinged with disbelief. 'Wouldn't it have been easier to take an overdose? Can't think that a middle-aged woman would thrust a knife into her own heart . . . '

Rosie swallowed hard, the memory of her mistake coming back with an unwanted force.

'We'll know more once we have her in the mortuary,' she replied stiffly. 'One thing is quite certain, though. Mrs Guilford was clutching that knife at the moment she died.'

'I can't believe it,' the man moaned, rocking back and forwards on the edge of his chair. 'I just can't believe it. Why would she do something like that?' He looked up at the two officers who stood over him, his eyes flitting from one to the other.

'When did you last see your wife before she died, Mr Guilford?' DI Alan McCauley asked.

Peter Guilford shook his head, frown lines appearing between his brows. 'I . . . I don't remember,' he faltered. 'Some time last night, I think. She was in bed asleep when I turned in. Don't know what time that was . . . ' His mouth fell open as he glanced beyond them to the door that separated the lounge from the kitchen area. 'I didn't hear her get up . . . Sound sleeper.' Guilford attempted a shrug but his shoulders did not relax and both officers could see the telltale signs of tension in the man's body.

'And before that,' DI McCauley persisted. 'When did you last see Dorothy awake?'

Peter Guilford licked his lips nervously before replying. 'I . . . ' he stuttered, 'I think it must have been around teatime. Dorothy, my wife, hasn't . . . ' he swallowed before continuing, ' . . . *hadn't* been feeling very well lately.' He looked up at the two officers in turn. 'She went to bed straight after I'd finished dinner.'

'Would you mind telling us what you ate, sir?'

'What?' Guilford frowned.

'It would help us if you could, sir?' McCauley persisted.

'A steak and some microwave chips,' Guilford replied. 'What's that got to do with—'

'You ate alone?'

Guilford nodded. 'Dorothy said she didn't want anything.'

'And did you cook your own dinner?'

The man shook his head, still frantically gnawing at his lip. 'She always cooked for me,' he began then sniffed, running a hand across his nose. 'It's what she was like ... good wife ... ' He bent forwards, burying his head in his hands.

The two detectives glanced at each other as the man sobbed quietly. Was this all an act? Or was the manifestation of grief a genuine reaction?

'What did you do for the rest of the evening, sir?' McCauley asked.

Guilford sat up, pulling his dressing gown sleeve across his eyes before replying. 'Went down the pub. Quiz night, y'know? Had a few pints with the lads ... Usual thing,' he said. 'Dorothy didn't like drinking. She ... she never minded me going out of an evening, though ... '

'And she was in bed when you returned?'

The man nodded, seeming too full of emotion to utter another word.

'Okay, we'll leave it there for now, sir, but you need to get yourself dressed, come down to the station with us to make a formal statement.'

Peter Guilford's mouth fell open in silent protest.

'A necessary formality, in such circumstances, sir,' he was told. 'And if you don't mind putting your nightclothes into this plastic bag ... ?'

The expression of fear on the man's face might have been

fleeting but it was something that the officers would remember to log later in the day.

DC Kirsty Wilson gave a sigh as the last of the scene of crime officers trooped out of the front door. A small breeze rippled across the plastic tape that cordoned off the garden gate but Kirsty reckoned that it would probably be taken down pretty soon. Poor woman had killed herself, wasn't that what the pathologist had told her? But what if Rosie was wrong? Wasn't there the possibility that Peter Guilford had committed this act? There were no signs of a break-in, the front and back doors having been locked, according to the weeping husband, something that the officers packing up their van had all but confirmed. There was plenty of trace evidence to process and no definitive answer to the puzzle of the woman's death could be given until that and a post-mortem was done. She locked the door with gloved hands then placed the keys in a plastic bag before thrusting them into the pocket of her raincoat. She would follow McCauley, Geary and the others in her own little car to Helen Street, where she was based, another day's work just beginning.

All over the city commuters were struggling through the traffic, nose to tail, the M8 a snake full of moving vehicles. It had been lucky that this call-out was fairly local, a nice house along St Andrew's Drive. The detective looked up and down the road, noticing the schoolchildren heading towards Craigholme, the private girls' school nearby. As she drove away, she saw their uniform, kilts instead of skirts, swinging as they walked. For the kids this was just another ordinary Wednesday but for the family of Dorothy Guilford, this would surely be the day that would be burned into their memory for years to come.

CHAPTER TWO

Aberdeen. The granite city, home for decades to the oil industry, a place where hard men thrived against North Sea winds and sharp-tongued women. Once it had been part of the fishing trade, the coastal waters teeming with herring, the 'silver darlings' of legend. Women had worked these shores, back-breaking toil, fingers raw from gutting and filleting the catches their men had brought in from the swelling seas, danger rife in every sailing. There lingered still a defiant attitude in this northern city, a determination to defeat any odds stacked against it. And yet the decline in the oil trade had meant falling house prices and a lowering of morale as workers left in their thousands.

The city was looking at its best as Lorimer drove along Union Street, early morning sunlight glinting off the grey stones, sky washed clean after the shower that had swept along the coast. Who would guess that these fine buildings were a front for something darker? Like a stage set where the actors were hiding in the wings, he thought. Ready to come out and show what really went on behind this façade of respectability. And he would be there to see it happen, guaranteed a front row seat.

The Major Incident Team from Glasgow had been here for days now, the final tip-off culminating in the raids that were scheduled to take place throughout the city centre. A network of trafficking in human misery had been uncovered, the gang-masters largely identified, the premises where the illegals worked already under surveillance. It was a highly structured operation, the Aberdeen police committing officers to various locations, Lorimer himself taking control of each and every movement.

His driver slowed down and turned along a side street, the vehicle's tyres juddering over the cobbles. A workman in dark trousers with a hi-visibility jacket strode along, head down, bent under the weight of a backpack, never giving their car a single glance. He might be a genuine workman heading home after a night shift or he could be one of their own; it was impossible to tell and that was all to the good. Their undercover officers had infiltrated this illicit business in several ways, relating snippets of intelligence back to the MIT, culminating in this morning's business, Operation Fingertip. The name had come from one quick-witted DI back in Glasgow who had thought up the tag. *We've got a few of them fingered already*, she'd explained with a grin and a wiggle of her own painted fingernails. *And that's just the tip of the iceberg, right?*

Several nail bars in the city had been targeted and the girls who worked there identified, many of them illegal immigrants suspected of having been trafficked. There had been pressure from Immigration to swoop on them all but the MIT's operation had taken precedence, the need to catch those responsible for trafficking of far greater importance. A few of the girls were regular employees of the salons, mostly teenagers who were doing City and Guilds courses with the hope of furthering their careers in the beauty business. None of them knew that their journeys to and from home had been carefully monitored by police officers, nor that their Eastern European handlers were being watched day and night.

Night-times had been the hardest for the surveillance team, knowing that some of these young women were being used for prostitution and yet until today they had been helpless to do much about it, secrecy being paramount. Most of the men who had frequented the dark alleys and tenement buildings had been identified and now, as the clock ticked towards five-thirty, each and every one would be brought to account.

Lorimer felt the tension in his chest, the familiar adrenalin rush that always came at moments like this. One false move and the entire operation could collapse, leaving officers scrambling to capture whom they could. But it wouldn't go wrong. Everything had been put into place and all were waiting now for one word from the detective superintendent, who sat silently staring up at the row of windows beneath the dark grey slates.

He saw the man next to him turn his head, a question in his eyes. Lorimer nodded and reached for his radio.

'Foxtrot One to all units . . . Go!'

The once deserted street was immediately teeming with men in riot gear, booted feet racing up the tenement stairs, the detective superintendent watching them go. He would wait here a little longer, see that every device was in place, then make his way up the three flights of stone steps to the brothel at the top of the building.

Somewhere in these pale forget-me-not-blue skies a drone was hovering, watching and recording all that was happening in the city street. Later, many eyes would inspect its footage but right now he was part of its creation.

The sound of the battering ram reached Lorimer's ears as he

climbed the steps, looking upwards, noticing an officer placed at each landing door, keeping the other residents safe from the disturbance.

A splintering of wood, a crash, then screams ... his feet hurried up the remaining flights of stairs, grim-faced officers nodding recognition as he passed them by.

The door hung off its hinges as he slipped into the darkened hallway, voices yelling from different areas in the house.

'What are you doing to me?' a man's voice protested as Lorimer walked along the corridor. Two officers had hold of a skinny wretch of a fellow dressed only in trousers and a dirty vest, his arms pulled behind him and fastened with handcuffs.

'Who's he?' The man stopped struggling, jerking his head towards the detective superintendent.

What did he see? A tall man in a raincoat, no helmet, no black clothing but clad in something that even this stranger recognised as authority.

Lorimer's mouth curled in the semblance of a smile.

'Let him get a pair of shoes and a jacket,' he said. 'It's cold outside.'

Then, ignoring the man's open-mouthed gape, he moved into the first room off the hall where a girl sat sobbing on the edge of a bed, a crumpled sheet hardly covering her naked body. Dark hair hung over a pale face and he could see her bare shoulders shaking.

Lorimer bent down beside her till his eyes were level with hers.

'It's all right,' he told her. 'We're from Police Scotland. We're here to take care of you. Keep you safe.'

But the brown eyes that met his were still filled with fear and now the girl's entire body was trembling with shock.

He made to pull the duvet across her shoulder but the girl gave a yelp of alarm, pulling back as if bracing herself for a blow.

'Dear God, what have they done to you, lass?' he murmured as she tried to make herself as small as possible, cowering against the pillow. 'I'm here to help you,' he said once more, his voice calm and gentle.

She looked at him again, head tilted to one side as though she were absorbing his words then she shook her head.

'No En-gleesh,' she said at last.

Lorimer nodded his understanding. God alone knew what nationality this shivering girl was. He looked around for something to cover her nakedness, saw a dressing gown hung on a hook behind the door and grabbed it.

'Put this on,' he told her. 'You're safe now, child. Whatever nightmare you've had, it's over.'

The tone of his voice must have reassured her as much as his kindly gesture of turning away for a few seconds to allow her to wrap herself in the gown because when he looked back, she was standing before him, arms hugging her body, resignation etched on her features as if something like this had happened before. Had she been dragged from place to place against her will? Used as no young girl ought to be used? The thoughts were fleeting as he led her out of the room and handed her over to one of the female officers who were now in the flat.

She turned and looked at him for a moment, eyes solemn as though assessing this man who had entered her room and yet failed to touch her like all of the others. Then she put out a hand and he took it, shaking it briefly. As he let it go, he noticed the red nails, perfectly curved and polished to their fingertips. How would her story end? He might never find out but, as she let the officer take her along the corridor, Lorimer wished her a silent good luck.

*

13

Afterwards, there was the inevitable sensation of anticlimax tinged with relief. In his imagination Lorimer had seen other officers ramming doors, catching hold of screaming, frightened young women, cuffing their captors' wrists. All over the city the same scenario had been played out. Girls from different ethnic origins were taken, bewildered and scared, to Aberdeen's Divisional HQ; men were bundled into cars and vans; the dingy apartments where the girls had been kept examined by the forensics team. Already reports were being typed up, the police press officers readying themselves for the first conference where the man from Glasgow would make a statement.

By nine o'clock it was all over, interview rooms and cells full of the men taken from these premises, calls from interpreters being swiftly answered. And hundreds of daily commuters now ready to begin their day's work were blithely unaware that their journey across the Granite City had been preceded by such drama.

CHAPTER THREE

'Why on earth would she do it?' Rosie muttered to herself. 'Doesn't make sense. And yet ... ' She pursed her lips in the determined manner to which her husband was accustomed. Sometimes, he had told her gently, she needed to step back from things a little more, consider the options. Well, as a consultant forensic pathologist, Rosie had done that all through her career. Nothing was ever set in stone; there were always statements made that considered likelihoods and possibilities. Only the dead could ever really tell what had happened. But the options here frightened her. They resembled far too closely that other case, the one she thought she'd put behind her a long time ago.

Rosie heaved a sigh. Perhaps the PM would show a little more, or maybe the toxicology results might give an indication of what had been happening prior to death. If there was a large enough amount of drugs in her system then perhaps they could indicate a certain state of mind. Perhaps, perhaps, perhaps ... Rosie frowned, irritated by the word drumming in her brain. She was tired already and there were hours to go till her working day ended.

Baby appeared to have settled down again, his kicking spell over for the moment. Rosie's hand circled the bulge under her smock, a gentle touch to let her child know she was thinking of him. She was so sure that this was a little boy; the pregnancy had been quite different from her first. And yet she and Solly had chosen not to find out . . . the mystery of birth was something too special for each of them. Besides, Abby had been talking about wanting a wee brother; Chloe, her best friend at nursery, had a baby brother and it seemed logical to Abby that her own sibling should be a little boy. Well, she would have a while yet to wait, Rosie thought, moving the cushion on her chair to make herself a little more comfortable.

Dorothy Guilford . . . She wrote the heading, wondering what words would follow once everything had been examined, tagged and dissected.

'He's got previous,' DI McCauley told the offices standing outside the interview room.

'Peter Guilford?' Kirsty Wilson's eyebrows rose in surprise. 'But he's . . . '

McCauley nodded. 'I know who he is. Owns Guilford's, the truck rental outfit. So what? Like I said,' he repeated, 'previous. Assault to severe injury. Did a spell inside years back.' He looked at her sharply. 'Been clean since then, but . . . ' He shrugged and made a face. 'Doesn't mean to say he's changed, just been clever enough or fly enough not to get caught beating up a woman.'

'You think he killed his wife?'

Kirsty saw the DI's eyebrows lift as he gave her a knowing sort of look. 'Don't you?' McCauley replied. 'Statistically it's the partner that does it; you know that and I know that but it's proving it that makes our job so interesting, eh?' He grinned.

'No signs of forced entry,' Kirsty agreed. 'What are you going to ask him?'

'Come in and see,' McCauley offered, indicating the interview room. 'Having a woman in there might help him open up a bit more anyway.'

Despite herself, Kirsty gave a shiver of apprehension. Sitting in on an interview was not something she had done very often, and never here in Helen Street with a suspected murderer, though she'd already met some of those in her short career. Maybe DI McCauley was singling her out for special attention, saw some sort of promise in his detective constable?

Yet it was a different thought that made Kirsty feel a little nervous: what if this was a genuinely grieving husband and they were about to accuse him of murder?

Peter Guilford was sitting on his own, the polystyrene cup empty on the table. He looked up at the two figures entering the room, an expression of dismay on his face.

'Do I have to be here long?' he asked, shifting uncomfortably in the plastic chair. 'Only I should be back home. Or at the office to let them know. So much to do . . . ' He ran his hand across hair that had once been light brown and was now streaked with grey.

'This shouldn't take too long, sir,' McCauley replied with a wintry smile. 'We simply need to clarify what you told us earlier on, take a written statement from you.'

Kirsty saw the relief in the man's face, though the signs of strain were there: that furrowed brow and the downturned lips. His shoulders were high with tension, too, she noted as she tried hard to remain objective, battling against the natural inclination to empathise with his pain. Her eyes fell on the hands clasped tightly on the table, noting the thick gold linked chain on his

17

wrist and that expensive watch. These hands could have thrust that knife into his wife's heart, she reminded herself.

She remained silent as McCauley began his questioning.

'Mr Guilford . . . Peter,' McCauley began. 'This is hard for you, I understand, but we need to know a bit more about Dorothy at this stage of our enquiries, okay?'

The haggard-looking man opposite them nodded, licking dry lips nervously.

McCauley rubbed his wrist where he had taken off his own watch earlier and placed it in front of him as if to indicate that time was an issue here. Was this some sort of device he used in questioning a suspect? Kirsty wondered, reminding herself to ask afterwards.

The DI began with the usual preliminary questions, routine stuff that was both necessary and helped to calm down the distraught man.

'Could you describe for us what your wife's state of mind was like in recent days?' McCauley asked at last, his eyes staring intently at the bereaved husband.

The detective inspector's words appeared to have settled Guilford somewhat, his shoulders easing a little.

Guilford leaned forward as though to share confidences.

'She was always such a worrier,' he told them. 'Worried about her health, that sort of thing. Not that there was any need . . .' He tailed off, glancing between the two officers as if to affirm that he had their attention. 'Dorothy was afraid all the time,' he added. 'Ask anyone. They'll tell you how nervous she was, how she used to imagine things.'

'Are you trying to tell us that your wife had a mental health problem?' McCauley asked.

Guilford sat back a little before answering. 'Don't know if I'd

18

go as far as calling it that ... ' he mused thoughtfully. 'Let's just say she was a bit of a hypochondriac.'

'She attended her local GP?'

'A lot,' Guilford confirmed. 'She was always imagining that the least wee thing was something serious. Terrible bad with her nerves, she was.' He nodded again and this time Kirsty recognised a certain satisfied look on the man's face as if he had scored an important point. Did he hope that they would assume from this statement that Dorothy Guilford was of unsound mind and had taken her own life? *With a kitchen knife?* Kirsty realised, for the first time, despite the pathologist's claim, how absurd the notion really was.

'Did Mrs Guilford have any prescribed drugs from her family doctor?' McCauley went on.

'Aye, she did,' Guilford told him, a tone of confidence returning to his voice. 'Painkillers, sleeping pills, that sort of stuff. I think sometimes the medics gave her what she wanted just to please her.'

McCauley frowned for a moment.

He's deliberately pausing, Kirsty decided, watching her boss's face and listening intently as he went on to pose his next question.

'How had Mrs Guilford's ... behaviour ... been recently?'

Guilford shook his head and gave a sigh. A real sigh or was this a bit of theatre for the police officers' benefit? Kirsty wondered.

'Worse than usual,' he told them. 'Really nervy and irritable. Said she wasn't sleeping well at night. That's how I didn't worry when she went early to bed, y'see.'

'Was she a difficult woman to live with, then?' McCauley asked.

The question surprised Kirsty. Should the DI be asking such

19

a leading question, making the kind of assumptions that might be to the husband's benefit?

Again, that long sigh and then Guilford slouched back a little in his seat and shrugged silently as though to demonstrate how hard done by he was, having this awkward person for a wife.

A wife who was lying in the mortuary, Kirsty thought to herself. Where was Peter Guilford's compassion? Was this what McCauley was trying to do? Get onside with the man to figure out his real feelings for Dorothy?

'How would you describe your relationship with your wife?' the DI asked, the answer to the previous question still hanging in the air between them.

'Och, we got along just fine,' Guilford said at once, sitting up once more. 'Anybody would tell you that.' He glanced once more between McCauley and Kirsty. But there was tension back in those shoulders and Guilford had not looked directly at either officer, shooting a glance instead to the doorway.

A sign that he was lying? Maybe, Kirsty decided. And maybe they would be doing that very thing; asking around friends and family to ascertain how Guilford had really treated his wife.

'So you would describe your marriage ... how?' McCauley crossed his arms and looked at the man before him, his eyes still demanding answers.

'Well, how's anyone going to describe their marriage?' Guilford lifted his hands as though to protest his innocence. 'Ups and downs like most couples, I suppose,' he continued when McCauley did not reply, his hands now grasping the sides of the plastic chair. 'Like I said, she could be a difficult woman at times.'

But you didn't say that, Kirsty thought silently. It was McCauley putting words into your mouth.

'She wasn't the easiest of people to get along with, but, see,

20

I'm a patient sort of man, don't make a fuss about things, you know ... ' He shrugged again but now he seemed less sure of himself, biting his lower lip. 'Dorothy imagined things ... ' He tailed off suddenly and shifted in his seat as if he had run out of things to say.

'You told me earlier that you came back late last night. Was the door locked when you came home?'

'Yes, Dorothy would never leave it unlocked. Far too paranoid—' He broke off, glancing at Kirsty for a second.

'So you had your own front door key?'

'That's right,' Guilford replied, nodding, his shoulders relaxing under the routine question.

'Anybody else have a key to your home, sir?' McCauley's voice remained detached, aloof, but Kirsty noticed a change in Peter Guilford's face at once. He licked his lips then shot a glance to one side.

'No, nobody,' he told them. 'I mean, nobody special,' he added, wiping a line of perspiration from his brow. 'I ... I think maybe ... the ... the cleaning lady has one,' he stuttered, swallowing hard.

That was a lie, Kirsty thought suddenly. There was more than just a cleaner who had a key, she decided. Whose identity was this man trying to conceal?

McCauley thought so too, she noticed, watching as the DI sat back and crossed his arms, his gaze never faltering as he regarded the man across the table.

'Did you kill your wife?'

The question came like a bullet, making Guilford gasp and sit back suddenly, one hand clutching his chest.

'What ... ?' The word was a hoarse whisper, Guilford's eyes widening in disbelief.

'Did you kill your wife?' McCauley repeated, making no change to the tone of his own voice.

'No, no, of course not, I ... I wouldn't hurt her ... ask anybody ...'

'I'm asking you.'

'No,' Guilford said again. 'I did not.' Then, looking at McCauley's impassive expression he added quietly, 'I think I would like to call my lawyer.'

'Guilty as hell,' McCauley told her as they strode along the corridor. 'You just need to know what signs to look for.' He grinned down at Kirsty. 'Plus what we know from his record, of course.'

'There'll be forensics ... ' she began.

'Course there will,' McCauley snorted. 'Wait till you see. My bet is that this'll be wrapped up before you go home, Wilson. Wee word with his lawyer and he'll tell us everything. Another bloody domestic.' McCauley shook his head wearily. 'Seen it all before.'

Then glancing down at her, the DI grinned. 'What d'you think, Wilson?'

Kirsty kept in step with the man's stride. 'Don't know, sir ... his body language ... ' She hesitated as he came to a halt and regarded her with a gleam in his eyes.

'You saw that too, eh? Well done.' He gave her a friendly slap on the shoulder. 'Nice to see an officer that shows promise.' He winked at her and then nodded towards the muster room a little further along the corridor. 'Now let's report back to the rest of the lads and lasses, let them know there won't be much more to do here.'

'What if he doesn't confess, though, sir?'

For a moment Kirsty saw McCauley hesitate and she began to

wonder whether the senior detective was as confident of an easy end to this matter as he was making out.

'Well, if Peter Guilford refuses to cooperate then we will be asking the Fiscal to issue a search warrant.' His smile returned again. 'There'll be something in that house that proves he murdered his wife, wait and see.'

CHAPTER FOUR

It was hard to be sure, Rosie had told her colleague, John, stripping off the rubber gloves and flinging them into the bin. Post-mortems did not always give the entire answer to questions of how a person might have died. The pathologists were accustomed to dealing with possibilities and not stating that anything was definitive in their profession but this particular case had them baffled.

Her colleague, who had been taking notes during the PM, had offered little in the way of an opinion, though Rosie had caught a questioning glance in the younger man's eyes when she had mentioned sucide.

The stomach contents were still to be analysed but in truth there was very little to see, suggesting that the deceased had not eaten for several hours prior to her death. The senior investigating officer, Alan McCauley, had told Rosie that the husband was in custody, pending further investigation into the woman's death, something that had made her feel rather queasy. Was it the idea of an innocent man being accused of something he did not do? Or was she simply more fragile these days, the pregnancy giving her so many fluttery sensations and sleepless nights?

There was no denying the historic injuries, however, and that did chime with what McCauley had revealed about Peter Guilford's criminal record. The pathologists had recorded several areas of the woman's body that showed scar tissue and X-rays had proved conclusively that she had suffered broken bones at one time in her life. Rosie had seen it before, the results of a battering at the hands of a vicious partner, a woman's life snuffed out in a moment of drunken rage. So why should she be so hesitant with this one? Wouldn't it be easier by far to admit that there were signs of injury having been inflicted in the past? To agree that, yes, it looked like he'd plunged that steak knife into his wife's heart?

Yet there was other evidence that told a different story. The woman's rigid hands clutching that weapon looked to the pathologist as if she had taken the knife and inflicted the fatal wound deliberately. *Why* was not the question she ought to be asking so much as *how* it had happened. That was her professional remit. Though the why might be explained if the victim's GP could enlighten her by supplying details from Dorothy's medical records. It was worth finding out, when she could spare the time. Things had piled up in the department recently, the shortage of qualified staff making her own schedule busier than she would have liked. A lesser mortal might have been tempted to let the policeman pursue his theory and leave well alone. Yet she was not made like that, her tenacity keeping her from giving up on what she saw as the truth. Still, as Rosie Fergusson turned away from the post-mortem room, she experienced a distinct sense of foreboding that she was not going to agree too readily with Alan McCauley.

There was a light rain shower as Kirsty ran towards the car park from the sanctuary of the Govan police office, sunshine breaking through the racing clouds. May had been warm and sunny up here in Scotland but it looked as if the prolonged dry spell might be coming to an end now. *Flaming June*, her mum, Betty, had always sighed whenever the rains began in early summertime. Kirsty opened the car door and waited for the DS to arrive, smiling at the thought of her mother's voice. Mum and Dad were both enjoying their retirement now, happy that their only child was settled into her career in Police Scotland. Settled, too, with James, though Mum often picked up Kirsty's left hand and gave her a meaningful look as though to ask when an engagement ring might be forthcoming. She was right about James's intentions, though, Kirsty knew that. But his finances would not stretch to making a significant purchase like that, let alone a wedding ring, for a good time to come yet, his savings put aside meantime. He was on the hunt for a job now, his years of academia over at last.

Her mum was always letting her imagination take her forward to the day when she would be weeping tears of joy as Mother of the Bride but Kirsty wasn't fussed about a big splash. Oddly enough, James had talked about it only recently, how he'd be 'making an honest woman' of her, one of these days, hinting that he, too, would like to have a big day to remember. He wanted to compensate, that was all, she told herself wryly; just because she was the one with a salary right now didn't mean he had to feel he owed her anything.

The thoughts about weddings vanished as Jim Geary entered the car and pulled on his seat belt.

'Right, Wilson, off we go. Let's see what's to be found at the Guilford residence, shall we?' He turned and grinned at her, rubbing his hands together in a gesture of glee.

'Yes, sir,' she said, returning his smile, and drove out of the car park, turning towards the leafy avenues beside Bellahouston Park, the short journey that would take them to St Andrew's Drive. What would they find there? A suicide note, perhaps? Or would there be something more sinister that gave credence to McCauley's insistence that Peter Guilford was guilty of his wife's death?

Across the city the man who had been in Kirsty's thoughts picked up the day's mail from the dark shadows of the hallway. The usual flyers, James thought with a grimace; more rubbish for the recycling bin. But these flimsier papers concealed a proper letter, a long white envelope that felt quite thick. He extracted it from the rest and turned it over, his eyebrows rising as he noted the US postmark. For a moment he just gazed at the envelope, wondering what it contained, knowing that one way or another he would have something to tell Kirsty when she came home from work.

He had to read the letter twice to make sure. But when he did understand its contents, James gave an enormous grin that made his face glow. This might be the beginning of something really great, he thought, heart thumping with excitement. If he were selected from the possible candidates then he could do everything he'd ever wanted ... He'd tell Kirsty later, but first he had to ring his mum, let her know that he'd been given an amazing chance to join a bank like the Federal Reserve Bank of Chicago. *The position for an economist*, the letter read, *is open to candidates with a PhD or Doctorate in macro, micro and/or international economics*. He scanned it again. He had the relevant qualifications, including his dissertation that had been already published in *The Economist* magazine. James Spencer was not given to flights of fancy, his northern upbringing keeping the young man well grounded, but for a few moments he did indulge himself, imagining a big house with kids playing in the garden, Kirsty and he happy together and financially stable, their lives blossoming in a place far away from this tiny flat with its rented furniture.

'You need to be careful,' the DS told her as they pulled on their gloves. 'Locard's principle: every contact . . . '

' . . . leaves a trace,' Kirsty finished for him.

She was rewarded with one of the detective sergeant's grins and then he turned the key in the lock and they stepped inside the silent house.

'You take the bedroom, Wilson, I'll look in their study. Bound to find papers there. And we'll take any computers back with us,' Geary told her.

The stairs up to the first floor wound in a gentle curve, reminding Kirsty of the scenes from American movies she'd watched as a child when the heroine would glide down, wearing some diaphanous creation. Bit of a change from her size six sensible shoes, she grimaced as she clumped up each stair, glancing at the passageway above. It was a huge house, she realised, once she had reached the first floor landing and saw yet another flight of stairs stretching upwards. They'd be ages here unless a suicide note or something that might incriminate the husband was found.

A quick recce along the passage gave Kirsty access to what must have been the couple's own bedroom, the drawn curtains still barring any daylight, giving her the initial impression that everything seemed to be shrouded in pale muted tones of cream or beige. She moved towards the window to draw aside the heavy silk curtains, hearing them swish as she tugged a cord to reveal a large airy space looking out over lawns and flowerbeds so immaculate that it seemed as if an army of gardeners tended them. Someone wanted things to look good from the outside. Lots of money here, she told herself. But she had found out a long time ago that no amount of money brought real and lasting happiness to a person's life, and certainly not in this home. The desolate thought cast a gloom over Kirsty's mind as she walked slowly around the unmade bed, its covers thrown to one side as the man must have leapt out of bed. Leapt? Why had she assumed that? He might have sat up slowly, rubbing sleep from his eyes then stood up to face what he thought would be a normal day.

She was making up a story, Kirsty realised, and that was bad. *Never think yourself into a theory; always let the evidence tell the tale.* Now who had told her that? Lorimer, she grinned, had to be him. Maybe she would catch a glimpse of him back in Govan, though their paths rarely crossed these days now that Kirsty was back in CID and Lorimer was heading up the Major Incident Team whose officers were quartered upstairs from her own domain.

Her gloved hands searched underneath the bedding, below the deep mattress of the king-sized bed, as Kirsty made a few observations. This great monster of a bed would have allowed the woman to slip away quietly in the night without disturbing her husband and that was what it looked like. Her side of the bed was neatly smoothed down, as if she had drawn one hand over the duvet before leaving the room.

The bedside cabinet was an ornate piece of white-painted furniture with spindly legs and two tiny drawers, more for show than practicality, a single candlestick lamp on its bare surface. No book, no clock, and certainly no note propped up to explain this final goodbye. The first of the little drawers held an assortment of pills, all of them with the chemist's label attached. Prescription drugs, Kirsty noticed. Loads of them. They would be matched with the contents of the woman's stomach later on, she guessed, slipping them into a plastic bag and sealing it. And this was just what Peter Guilford had told them. So far, so truthful. But McCauley needed to find something that might tell them if Guilford's words were simply hiding the real facts and it was her task to seek that out. The lower drawer was full of bits and pieces, more like the sort of junk that everyone kept: a half open packet of paper tissues, an old address book (she took that out and laid it on the carpet), a pair of glasses in a leather case, then a pack of old airmail letters bound in a single elastic band. That was interesting, she thought. Why keep these things unless they were of some sort of sentimental value? She picked up the bundle and frowned at the date. Wasn't that postmark one that was only used by the military? She pulled out a plastic production bag and placed the letters inside. They would keep till she had time to go through them properly, though goodness knows what they contained. Far too old, surely, to be anything to do with a suicide, if that really was what had happened here. Folk emailed nowadays, letters almost a thing of the past.

Kirsty swept her glance over the rest of the big room; there was a dressing table and two sets of matching chests of drawers in the same fancy white. Her taste or his? Surely it was a woman's style, Kirsty told herself. James would have laughed at any suggestion of buying stuff like this. But had the couple bought it? It was old-fashioned enough to have been inherited, perhaps, and now that she had dropped to her hands and knees beside the dressing table, Kirsty saw telltale scuff marks on the bowed legs where a vacuum cleaner may have bumped them over the years.

The surface of the dressing table was almost bare apart from a hairbrush and comb and a large bottle of eau de cologne still in its wrapper. A gift for someone? Or had she never opened one of her own? Kirsty hesitated for a moment then pulled out her phone and took a quick photo. There were no male toiletries on the other side of the dressing table, just a small white vase. She picked it up carefully in her gloved fingers and turned it over, noting the Royal Denmark crest, then placed it back. The contents on this side were of little interest; packets of tights in one drawer, cosmetics in another, all neatly zipped into bags, some for lipsticks, others for eye shadows, still others for nail polish. So well ordered, Kirsty mused; in fact, everything was scrupulously neat and tidy. That was something she could say about the woman's personality now, at any rate, she thought, rising to her feet and proceeding to rake in each and every drawer in the two chests.

Nothing to show how or why she had died, Kirsty sighed a few minutes later, but she had begun to have an inkling about Dorothy herself from the dead woman's predilection for sensible white underwear with not a trace of lace or a thong in sight. Even her nightwear had been old-fashioned, more suitable for a hospital stay than a boudoir, not at all what she imagined a person of forty-eight to have worn. Her own mum favoured pretty matching nightdresses and negligées and she was way older than that. Aye, Kirsty told herself, Dorothy Guilford had been a strange one, right enough. The clothes hanging in the wardrobe were all hers, suggesting to Kirsty that Peter Guilford had his own dressing room elsewhere and that this was principally Dorothy's room. All of the clothes were dark shades, camel or drab green. Kirsty frowned. Not one of the clothes showed familiar High Street labels. Were they expensive stuff, then? She'd have to check but her first impression was that these garments spoke of quality. However, they were all pretty much out of date, nothing looked as though it had been purchased recently, even the rows of low-heeled leather shoes were well worn. Had she been stuck in a fashion rut? Or were these things a sign that she had not been allowed to spend any money on herself in recent times? Kirsty could see that this was a place that smelt of money but none of it had been lavished on the dead woman's clothes, a fact that she stored away to be taken out and examined later on. Peter Guilford had been wearing that thick gold chain and a good watch, she remembered. He wasn't slow to spend cash on himself, was he?

Kirsty stood up and gazed around her. There was something odd about this room, she felt. As though it was already empty, the woman long gone. A couple of flower prints on the walls but no framed photos. Perhaps the downstairs lounge would throw up more clues as to the characters of the Guilfords. She was curious to see if the DS had made any progress.

That room was in some ways a mirror image of the huge bedroom, its French windows looking out at the gardens. Kirsty tried the lock but it was shut fast, no sign of a key. Looking around the room, she gave a shudder. Bland? No, bleak, she decided, noting the out-of-date beige sofas, the fawn and brown carpet, the magnolia painted wallpaper. She could see a few old-fashioned picture frames containing images of flowers, and a rather nice dark still life that made her stop and stare a little longer. But there was one framed photograph on a small side table next to one of the armchairs and she picked it up, eyebrows raised for a moment.

The man in the picture was handsome, right enough. Peter Guilford had certainly scrubbed up well for someone to take a photo on his wedding day. And Dorothy was gazing up at him, a posy of flowers clutched in both hands. No long white dress, Kirsty noticed, but a pale pink coat that hid her figure and a satin Alice band across her wispy hair. The newly married woman's expression was unmistakable, she thought. Adoration. Only word for it. Would she look at James in such a way if and when they were to be wed? Kirsty gave a little smile. Though she loved her boyfriend dearly, she doubted whether such an expression of worship would cross her face, no matter how radiant she might appear. This husband and wife seemed to have been happy once upon a time, at any rate.

Putting the photo down, Kirsty began to walk around the room, her eyes intent on finding a note. But there was nothing. If Dorothy Guilford had decided to take her own life then it didn't look as if she was leaving a goodbye letter explaining why. Geary was still in the couple's study, quietly working through piles of papers, so Kirsty retraced her steps upstairs. Perhaps she would have left a note in the husband's dressing room.

It was much smaller than the master bedroom, with a single bed flanked by two side cabinets. One of them showed ring marks where glasses or mugs had been laid down. She picked up an empty crystal glass and sniffed. Whisky. So, this was where Peter Guilford took his ease, she thought. Was McCauley correct? Had the husband killed her in a moment of drunken madness?

There was certainly no trace of a suicide note, she realised, opening the sliding wardrobes where several rails of gentlemen's clothes hung, a row of well-polished shoes lined up with military precision. Kirsty thought of the airmail letters. Was there an army connection here, then? That was something else to find out back at headquarters, she decided, returning to the big room and picking up the packet of letters where she had left it.

The sound of feet on the stair made her turn around.

'Anything up here?' Geary was standing in the doorway, looking around. 'Fancy,' he said, eyebrows raised. 'Dead old-fashioned, though. Think this lot's been here since the ark.' He snorted derisively. Then he shook the plastic bag he held in one hand. 'See what I've found.' He grinned, pointing at the papers inside the bag. 'Reckon our pal Mr Guilford has some explaining to do.'

Kirsty drew up in the Helen Street car park and heard the click of Geary's safety belt being unfastened. The DS was in a hurry to take this new evidence back to show the boss, and no wonder. It certainly looked from these recently signed insurance papers as if Peter Guilford might have had a good reason for killing his wife. Geary's discovery certainly trumped anything she had found in the dead woman's bedroom. She followed him into the building and they headed straight for the CID room and the far-away cubicle where the outline of McCauley's seated figure could be seen through the frosted glass.

One quick knock and the pair were called into McCauley's tiny sanctuary.

'Boss, look what we've found.' Geary thrust the plastic bag into McCauley's hands and both watched his face for the inevitable reaction as the DI read the papers within.

'Bullseye!' McCauley exclaimed at last, looking up at his two officers. 'Dated just last week, an' all. Didn't waste much time, did he?' He tapped the insurance papers that showed the pre-mium on the life of Dorothy Guilford had been increased to more than a million pounds. 'Whew, that's a lot of money!' He turned the pages of the Will. 'And that's not all. See?' The DI's finger pointed to a sub section of the document.

McCauley looked up at the pair in turn to see their reaction. Both officers were silent, their faces expressing astonishment as they read the paragraph.

'The business was in Dorothy's name?' Geary shook his head in disbelief.

'Inherited from her parents, by the looks of things,' McCauley agreed. 'One more reason for Guilford to take things into his own hands.'

'She's signed it,' Kirsty noted, as McCauley turned the final page.

'Do you have a sample of her handwriting?' the DI asked.

'Right there, boss,' Geary told him. 'Under these insurance documents there are a couple of letters with her signature. Found them in the study.' He leaned forward and gave the papers a little tug.

Kirsty had been on the point of mentioning the airmail packet but held her tongue. That particular production would no doubt be sent downstairs to languish amongst other recorded evidence bags, not required unless new evidence came to the fore that made reading them necessary. She had learned that much from other cases. Geary was obviously one step ahead of her.

McCauley spread them out on his desk, lining up the position of all three signatures for comparison.

'Doesn't look much like her real signature on this will, does it?' he murmured.

'No, sir,' Kirsty agreed. 'Bit shaky, maybe,' she added, imagining a woman signing this document under duress. 'A handwriting expert could verify if it's a forgery, you think?'

'Bound to be.' McCauley grinned. 'Guilford is going to go down for this, just you wait and see.'

'Are you going to charge him, then?' Kirsty asked, wondering for a moment if there was actually enough evidence to do so.

'We'll certainly hold him for as long as we can,' McCauley said, rubbing his chin thoughtfully. 'Need to see the PM report, of course, but I think another chat with Guilford might actually produce a confession when we confront him with this.'

CHAPTER FIVE

Lorimer glanced at his sleeping wife and smiled. She'd left the window open again so that they might waken to the early sound of birdsong. It had been a beautiful evening after the earlier rain showers, the sunset dusky pink, fresh green leaves on the beech trees glowing in the twilight. Only a few more weeks and Maggie would be finishing the school session then they could make their way north to the island of Mull where Leiter Cottage awaited them. The detective superintendent sighed with pleasure at the thought of the whitewashed house nestling in the foot of the hill. A boat was at their disposal this year, pulled up on the shores of Fishnish Bay so they might enjoy a bit of fishing once in a while, or take a trip further along the coast. Lorimer rolled onto his back and stared at the ceiling.

He'd need to climb a hill or two just to get back into condition after spending more time behind a desk in recent months than he would have liked, though he had to admit that the new job in the Major Incident Team was demanding in so many other respects. With the success of the Quiet Release case had come some welcome plaudits from his colleagues, an affirmation that his selection for this top job was a popular choice. Since then he had been busy

37

appointing new officers to replace those recently retired, as well as overseeing some major incidents, like Operation Fingertip, across the country.

Ever since Police Scotland had changed from several regional operations to one single force, William Lorimer had travelled to different areas throughout the country where serious crimes had occurred. The recent deaths of three immigrant men in Aberdeen had left a trail of fear in their wake but happily his team had made the necessary arrests of the perpetrators although there was still suspicion that gangmasters from Eastern Europe continued to operate elsewhere within Scotland. Cheap labour in the form of illegals had resulted in a collaborative exercise with the Immigration Services, keen to root out the criminals that exploited these desperate people. Promises of work in fish factories had been lure enough for the young Slovakian women they had rescued. Of course, they had never seen inside a factory of any description, their destiny a hovel in one of these Aberdeen tenements where they had been used as prostitutes. Operation Fingertip had been a success so far, but there was still a lot to do.

For it was not only to the north-east that the MIT's eyes were turned; intelligence had provided some clues that the gangs had been operating in the Glasgow area and Lorimer knew that it was only a matter of time until some serious crime was committed against one of the vulnerable folk whose slave labour was used to fill the pockets of unscrupulous men and women. Sometimes it was a case of selling a girl to an Asian bent on getting his European passport the quickest way possible: a sham marriage for which these men were prepared to pay as much as £10,000. Ten K, Lorimer thought: the price of a hired assassin's hit. Was that all human life was worth to those on the wrong side of the law?

The detective superintendent sighed again, this time because his mind had turned inevitably to work instead of lingering on the edges of a vision of his beloved Mull. Yet, he had to admit, being in Govan and heading up the MIT was the best job he'd ever had. And if he could clear up this hidden gang it would be all the sweeter.

A glance towards the bedroom window showed that darkness was falling at last, a sweep of deeper blue covering the skies. Tomorrow promised to be another warm day, rain or no rain, as the days crept towards midsummer.

Rosie turned on her side, stifling a groan. It was the law of natural cussedness, she supposed, that this baby preferred to frolic around during the night rather than in daytime. Definitely a boy, she told herself, feeling what might have been a tiny foot kicking within the safety of her womb. A wee footballer, perhaps? She smiled at the thought, wondering if a son would bring a new dimension into their family. Abby was growing up so quickly, starting school in just a couple of months, and the little girl had begun to draw scrawling pictures at nursery of herself with a smaller person holding her hand. Already Rosie was looking forward to time away from work and she had promised herself that she would take the maximum amount of maternity leave possible.

Dr Jacqui White would take over as consultant in her absence, her younger colleague, John, away on loan to Northern Ireland, and Rosie was recruiting for another pathologist to help in the department as her replacement had the additional load of being a media darling, frequently attending television studios for a series of documentaries about forensic medicine, something Rosie had also been asked to do but had declined.

Tomorrow would bring the final candidate to her Glasgow office, a woman she had never yet met but whose CV had impressed enough to allow this interview for a position as locum. Dr Daisy Abercromby's career had been mostly in her native Australia but her letter had expressed the hope that she might settle in the UK, something that had given her the edge over other candidates. The need for practising pathologists was greater than ever and if an Aussie were to come here instead of their own graduates heading Down Under, then the department of forensic medicine would be in a much better shape.

Dr Daisy. Rosie smiled, running the name in her head. Well, if she was as good as her CV suggested, the young pathologist's name was of no consequence, though at present it brought to mind a friendly cow in one of Abby's favourite picture books.

She turned onto her side and began to take deep breaths, one hand across her abdomen. Soon the baby appeared to have settled, the warmth of her hand soothing the little child. Not time yet, Rosie told the baby silently. A few more weeks and you and I will see one another.

Rosie closed her eyes in the hope that sleep would come. But the image of a woman lying on her back, both hands clutching a dark-handled knife, was enough to keep her awake, thinking hard, wondering just what had happened two days ago on that short summer's night.

The object was one of six that were kept in a flat wooden box, the remaining five now in a production bag back at Govan CID. It was a remarkable thing, this Laguiole knife, really, the pathologist mused as she turned it over in one gloved hand. The bloodstains had darkened now to a dull rust colour, the curved handle blotched with fingerprint dust. Now it was back on her desk, Rosie examined it in a detached manner. The French had a way of creating things that had an aesthetic appeal as well as being practical. These knives had started out as simple pocket knives, probably carried by artisans all over the country before their use in the kitchen became popular. Nowadays, a set of the handsome steak knives could be found in any decent iron-mongers but the design had remained faithful to its original, the emblem of a bee set onto the stainless steel shaft before the flowing line of the blade tapered to a point. She traced her finger along the decorated line of steel that ran through the knife, the wooden shaft pinned into place on each side. It was, Rosie admitted, a little work of art and as far as she knew each knife was still hand-crafted, the maker's signature stamped onto the thickest part of the blade. The word *Laguiole* was partly obscured by the bloodstain, making Rosie wonder yet again about the state of mind of the woman whose body lay in her mortuary.

Had Dorothy Guilford thrust this into her own heart? Or was the husband a murderer and the woman's clutch merely a sign that she had struggled for her life? Some strange cases had come her way in the past so she was never too ready to assume what looked like the most obvious explanation was actually the truth. The blood spatter had not been conclusive and Guilford's clothes were still being examined for possible traces since there had been nothing visible to the naked eye on his pyjamas and dressing gown. Had he disposed of any bloodstained garments? The scene of crime officers had taken pictures of the blood spray and it seemed to indicate that nothing had impeded the pattern. In other words, no person had been in front of the woman as the knife had been plunged into her heart. But was that right? Had he taken care to cover any traces? So many people were forensically aware and this man had form. McCauley was determined to prove that Guilford was his wife's killer on what evidence they had so far.

But there had been no sign of any struggle, Rosie thought gloomily. On the contrary, the kitchen where the body had lain showed nothing to indicate that a fight had taken place. What could she add to this? Simply that the knife had not moved around, one nice clean cut matching the weapon perfectly. It didn't seem as if the woman had struggled to remove the blade and, even without the classical hesitation injuries it looked like one self-inflicted wound. She picked up the scene of crime photos of the body, noting the way that the woman had fallen, mouth open, eyes screwed tightly shut as if she had ... what? Summoned up one final moment of courage to end her life? And, to Rosie's eyes, that was what this looked like. Not a murder. Not a domestic fracas where a blade had been taken in a moment of drunken anger. She sighed heavily.

Maybe she was wrong. Perhaps it had happened so quickly that the woman had no time to react, simply fallen down, any attempt to remove the blade defeated as she gasped for breath? The pathologist frowned. DC Wilson had retrieved the cutlery from the kitchen sink, but if the husband had tossed them there after his meal, who had then taken the knife out, dried it and used it as a weapon? If Dorothy had washed it then why leave the rest of the dishes and cutlery? It didn't make sense, Rosie told herself. But then, none of this scene of crime appeared to have any logic to it. She must find time to contact the victim's medical practice, make a request to see Dorothy Guilford's files. One more thing she must remember to deal with, she thought, cursing her memory. It was true what the old wives' tales said, right enough; Mother Nature wanted you to concentrate on what was happening to your body so she cast a cloud over your mind. Rosie sighed, determined to think things through.

The SIO had decided that it was a murder scene and Peter Guilford was still being detained. He'd be charged if any further evidence were to emerge, taken to one of the local prisons on remand till such time as his trial came up. Unless he got bail. She shivered suddenly. What if the man was completely innocent? Rosie remembered other cases where a man had been incarcerated for weeks until evidence showed that the police had got it all wrong. It happened sometimes.

She would write out her report highlighting the facts as she perceived them from a pathologist's point of view. McCauley wouldn't like it but then it was not Rosie's job to curry favour with the police but to interpret the evidence in terms that would be clear, succinct and balanced when brought before a court of law. It was her opinion that Dorothy Guilford had taken her own life, possibly while of unsound mind (given the amount of prescription drugs in her bloodstream, that was a reasonable deduction), and that no further action ought to be taken.

Rosie sat for a moment, hands folded as she looked at the blank screen. Words would appear there shortly that would create a dilemma for the Crown Service. Would they take her report and decide that she was correct? Or would Alan McCauley insist that more investigating was required that would overturn the pathologist's findings?

'She's mental!' McCauley thrust himself back in the chair, bumping against the filing cabinets that took up almost an entire wall of his tiny office. 'Pure mental!' He stared at the computer screen, an expression of disgust on his face, then eased himself back towards the desk, wondering what his next move might be.

Gillian had been all over the place during her pregnancy, he recalled, thinking of his ex-wife. At times a complete headcase. He ran the tip of his tongue across his teeth as he contemplated his way forward. Surely that was what was going on here, a woman whose hormones were creating havoc, obscuring her better judgement? For a moment McCauley sat still, thinking about the diminutive blonde who was now director of the department of forensic medical science, top pathologist this side of the country. She'd come a long way since they'd first met, he remembered, whereas he was still just a detective inspector and more than likely to remain in this post until retirement. It rankled a little, though in fairness he had never seen himself in any of the top jobs, preferring to continue as a hands-on detective.

But Rosie Fergusson hadn't always been the star that she was now, he thought. Her face had appeared on the front cover of glossy magazines, comparisons made between the real-life pathologist and some of the TV actresses in crime dramas. Hadn't there been some mistake she'd made way back in the early days? McCauley tapped a pencil against his teeth as he racked his brain. Nope, nothing was coming to the surface. But perhaps if he were to ask around, even look up some of her past cases ...

The DI grinned to himself. He was right about Peter Guilford, he just knew it.

'Always could tell a murdering bastard from an innocent man,' he muttered to himself. And he'd prove it, sure he would. Just as he'd try to discredit the pathologist who was making life difficult for him right now.

The young woman swept her hair back over her shoulders and grinned, showing a set of perfect white teeth against a suntanned face.

'Hi,' she drawled. 'I'm Daisy.' She thrust out a hand and gripped Rosie's for a moment, keeping the senior pathologist fixed in her gaze.

'Glad to meet you, Dr Abercromby.' Rosie smiled back, preparing to settle down and ask the questions that she had prepared for all the candidates hoping for a locum job during her maternity leave. Dr White had been too busy to come and sit in on the interviews despite the fact that she would be in charge once Rosie was on maternity leave, something Rosie would explain during this session. But, before she could utter another word, the Australian edged her seat forward.

'Wow, that's some bump you have there. Girl or a boy?'

Rosie's eyes widened in surprise at the frank question.

'We've chosen not to know till the birth,' she murmured.

'Really? Say, that's cool. Real *traditional*,' she added, making the word sound synonymous with old-fashioned to Rosie's ears.

'How long you expecting to be off?' Daisy continued.

Rosie opened her mouth to protest but could think of nothing to say to this forward young woman who had breezed into her office and was already taking control of the interview.

'Long enough to let you have a decent page or two in your CV,' she said briskly. '*If* you're selected,' she added, receiving only another grin from Daisy Abercromby. None of the previous candidates had shown much spark and Rosie had to admit that there was something rather appealing about this fresh-faced young woman who had no qualms about asking personal questions of her own. She'd not be browbeaten by anyone, Rosie decided, suppressing a smile as she lifted the page of questions, wondering if she had already made up her mind.

CHAPTER SIX

'It's just one single spot,' the woman murmured, gazing into the lens. 'Need to see what it can tell us, though.'

She lifted her head from the microscope and began the test that would show exactly whose blood was on the sleeve of this garment, an old worn denim jacket that had seen better days. DI McCauley had insisted on a scrupulous inspection for every one of the husband's articles of clothing. The technician frowned. Didn't look as if this had been worn in years, the folds dusty and stiff with age. And yet, there it was, a tiny speck of blood that might signify a great deal to the future of its owner. If it was the dead woman's blood, then this might just be enough to charge the husband with her murder, though additional forensic work would likely be sought by the defence to see if the stain was too old to be of any value to the case. If it had degraded sufficiently then its DNA might tell them it was not a recent stain.

The technician sat back and thought for a moment. *Why not find that out now?* Then, with a smile, she began the analysis that would give a definite answer to this question.

There was something thrilling about the search and a small satisfaction obtained when the stain did indeed seem to have landed on this garment quite recently. She needed to forward her report to the SIO, wondering, as she did so, what the eventual outcome would be for the man whose jacket she had subjected to such scrutiny.

DI McCauley grinned as he put down the phone. 'Gotcha!' he said softly. 'Knew there'd be something that proved me right!' He pushed open the frosted glass door of his office and swaggered out into the room where several faces lifted from their computers. They'd be curious to know what had made their DI appear with a grin on his face and he couldn't wait to tell them.

Peter Guilford sat, slack-jawed, as the charge was read against him.

'No,' he muttered, throat suddenly dry, the word sticking in his mouth. 'No, that's all wrong.' He swallowed, eyes darting from the grinning DI to the other officers whose faces remained totally impassive. 'You're wrong,' he croaked. Then, as the handcuffs were fastened around his wrists, he knew that it was useless to make such comments. This man had decided that he was guilty and Peter Guilford knew that once the police had made their minds up it was practically impossible to wriggle out from their grasp.

The corridors loomed cold and blue as the uniforms escorted him along, their hands strong but not brutal since there was no resistance. No fight.

His body felt heavy and useless as they turned into the cell, the click of the handcuffs opening, the shuffle of heavy feet the only sounds as they left him. Then a dull clang as the door shut and the unmistakable ratcheting of a key in the lock.

*

Hours had passed, how many he couldn't be sure. The man slumped onto the narrow plastic-covered bed, head sunk into his hands. It was just a bad dream from which he would waken. Surely this wasn't real?

Peter could not stop thinking about the words that resounded in his head, words thudding like nails being hammered into his coffin.

Charged. Charged with *murder*.

This was all wrong. Nothing like this should be happening to him. He breathed out a long sigh, trying to recall the lawyer's words instead. An appeal for bail was being made but meantime he would be kept here in this cold cell, the bars shutting him off from the rest of the world when all he wanted was to go home. Guilford raised his head for a moment and glanced up at the tiny barred window, remembering. He'd been inside a prison once before and had vowed never to let it happen again.

Everything had happened so quickly after those long hours of uncertainty. One minute he was in that interview room, expecting his lawyer, Frank Dawson, to utter words that would get him out of this place; the next he was being escorted down that corridor by two uniformed officers who'd ushered him inside this cell. They'd taken his things away, too. His phone, his belt, even his goddamned shoelaces as if they expected him to do something stupid.

Peter Guilford felt hot tears prickling his eyes and he sniffed them back, cursing himself for such weakness. He'd not give them the satisfaction of seeing him emotional, he told himself, grinding his teeth together. Yet, despite his best intentions, the accused husband felt the moisture trickle down his cheeks as a wave of utter desolation swept over him.

This was not the way it was supposed to happen . . .

CHAPTER SEVEN

'He's been kept inside,' Dawson told her with a sigh.
'What? But how can they . . . ?'

'There was a spot of Dorothy's blood on one of his jackets,' the lawyer explained. 'Probably something from an old accident . . . ' He broke off, leaving the silence between them to tell its own tale. Each of them knew well that Dorothy self-harmed but the lawyer suspected that several of the dead woman's injuries had been inflicted by Peter Guilford, something that Dawson would not easily reveal as he sought to protect his client from prosecution.

'She was a nasty little cow!' The woman spat out the words, her face a mask of rage.

'Come on, now, Cynthia, bad luck to speak ill of the dead.' Dawson shook his head, attempting a feeble smile.

'You don't know what she was like, Frank. A bitter, twisted woman with an overactive imagination,' she insisted. 'Peter told me—'

'Hush.' Dawson laid a finger to his lips. 'I don't want to hear this, Cynthia. Anyway,' he shifted in his seat, gathering up the light raincoat and the tan attaché case, 'I shouldn't really be here.

Just a favour to Peter.' Then, standing up and fixing his gaze upon her, the lawyer leaned forward. 'Don't even think about trying to contact me. Understand? No telephone trails. No emails. And we won't meet again like this unless I instigate it.' His voice was low but there was no mistaking the threat in Dawson's tone.

Cynthia Drollinger sat back, her face white and tense as she watched the man turn on his heel and leave the crowded cafeteria. Dawson had insisted on meeting here, a city centre student hang-out, instead of at the office and she suddenly wondered why. He'd come to do her a favour, he'd insisted, pass on the message from Peter, but even as she told herself that Dawson was on their side, the woman asked herself if the lawyer actually believed the words that his client had asked him to relay: *Tell her I didn't kill Dorothy.*

When the telephone rang Shirley made a face. Always a cold call at this time of day, she thought, heaving herself slowly out of the squashy armchair, the battered leather cushions protesting under her weight.

'Hello,' she began wearily, listening for the background noise of a call centre, the giveaway of so many nuisance calls. But it was the voice of an educated man who asked, 'Am I speaking to Mrs Finnegan?'

'Ye-es,' Shirley replied, doubt crowding her thoughts. Who was this? And why had a shiver suddenly run down her spine?

'My name is Frank Dawson, Mrs Finnegan. I'm a solicitor. Sorry to ring you unexpectedly but I'm afraid I have some bad news.'

Shirley leaned back against the wall, telephone handset still clutched between her fingers. It couldn't be true. Peter arrested on suspicion of Dorothy's murder? The solicitor's words rang in her ears. *Was* it true? Or was this some sick bloke calling her up to torment her with the sort of story that her sister had whispered in her ear often enough?

Peter isn't good to me, she remembered Dorothy telling her time and time again, the words at odds with the sort of lifestyle they enjoyed in the big house in St Andrew's Drive. Tales of being held down and beaten were all parts of her sister's desire for drama, Shirley had told herself over and over. If any of these bruises *were* ever inflicted by Peter Guilford, why hadn't her sister reported it to the authorities? She'd never been afraid to stir up trouble in the past, after all.

Spite, that was what Dorothy had delighted in, sheer spite. Taunting Shirley with these stupid lies, making stuff up the way she always had. Even as a child Dorothy had delighted in playing the martyr, pretending that other kids had picked on her. *Sticks and stones may break my bones but names will never hurt me*, little Dorothy had chanted, as if to show how impervious she was to any harsh words her elder sister might utter. And it was always Shirley who had been given into trouble, any tales told readily believed by their parents.

An image came back then, a memory of seeing her younger sister pinching her own wrist to make it bleed then shouting, *Daddy! Daddy! Shirley cut me!*

Always the favourite at home and teacher's pet at school, something that had always rankled since, after all, it was Shirley who was the prettier of the two Pettigrew sisters. And then, after the disgrace that had banished Shirley from their home, for Dorothy to land a husband like Peter Guilford! How had *that* happened? She'd been nothing but a drab, dowdy wee spinster till Peter had swept her up and taken possession of Dorothy's life.

Shirley clenched her teeth as she staggered back to the comfort of the huge armchair. She had to remind herself that Dorothy was dead now, dead and gone for good. Not here to inflict any more harm. She sighed, closing her eyes, memories of the younger woman's sneer as she'd waved the lawyer's papers in Shirley's face. *Mine, all mine*, the gleeful, gesture had told her. No need for angry words that day. No need for words at all after the funeral, though there were plenty that burned like acid inside Shirley Finnegan's brain.

It still stuck in her craw how Dorothy had managed with her usual cunning to hold onto the family home and business, cutting her sister out of the will before their father had died, senile and insensible, Dorothy the good girl who'd stayed with him right to the bitter end. And look what had it got her. A property worth well over a million, even in these days of fiscal uncertainty, then, soon after, a good-looking husband with an easy charm that endeared him to everyone he met. No wonder Guilford Vehicle Hire had become such a household name.

Well, now she was dead. And her husband in prison. *Serves her right*, a small voice whispered in Shirley's ear, a voice uncannily like her own.

Would the police come and speak to her, like this solicitor had mentioned? They had contacted him to find out her address so perhaps they would send one of those family liaison officers. Shirley struggled to her feet, the extra weight that she carried making her lumber across the worn carpet. If they did, then she had best make herself presentable, ready to put on a show of grief, something that was going to require a great deal of effort.

CHAPTER EIGHT

'Peter Guilford?'

Rosie nodded. 'Do you know him?'

'I know *of* him, certainly,' Lorimer replied, raising the whisky glass to his lips. 'And not just because of the van hire business.' He turned to Rosie, giving a nod. 'Guilford did time for assaulting his first wife. I wasn't SIO in that case but I remember some of the details.'

'How badly was she injured?' Rosie asked, shifting a cushion on the wooden seat, the weight of the baby pressing on her bladder, making her feel uncomfortable. It was nice sitting out in the Lorimers' garden, the late-afternoon sun warm, and the soothing sound of bees foraging in the lavender that edged Maggie's herbaceous border.

Funny to be talking about this case, Rosie chided herself, when all she really wanted was to sit back and relax, something that was increasingly difficult in this advanced state of her pregnancy.

'Oh, he'd broken her arm and a couple of ribs. Did some internal damage too, as I recall. Poor woman was in surgery afterwards. It was a pretty straightforward case.'

'Go on.'

Lorimer's dark eyebrows lifted a fraction as he regarded Rosie.

'He put up his hands to it, did time and was out in less than two years.' *Why d'you need to know?* The unspoken question in these blue eyes that had seen so many bad things in their past.

Rosie sighed. Dorothy Guilford's X–rays had shown a once-broken arm and bruising to her spine, historic injuries that would surely be recorded in her medical notes. But if she had been another battered wife, then she had never alerted either friends or family to the situation, let alone the police. The Fiscal had sanctioned that Dorothy Guilford's medical records be made available to the police as well as to the pathologist and Rosie was interested to see just what they might reveal.

'How long ago was that?'

'Must be ten years or more, now. Maggie's mum was still with us ... I could look up his file if you wanted.' He frowned. 'But surely DI McCauley is keeping you in the loop?'

Rosie made a face. 'Alan McCauley and I aren't exactly singing off the same hymn sheet on this one,' she told him.

Lorimer's puzzled frown faded as Maggie appeared at the back door, a laden tray in her hands.

'Here we are.' She beamed. 'And don't tell me you aren't famished, missus!' she teased Rosie. 'Long past the throwing up stage, right?'

'Aye, thank goodness,' Rosie agreed, stretching out to take a couple of her favourite egg and cress sandwiches. 'I'll be glad when I can get back to a wee tipple as well.' She smiled. 'No worrying about heartburn any more.'

She looked up as her husband strolled out of the house. Solly glanced her way, a fond expression on his face, then sat on the garden bench by her side.

'Hope you two aren't talking shop?' he asked mildly, glancing from Lorimer to his wife, the faint rebuke making Rosie remember that this was meant to be a social occasion. It was the weekend, after all. She put out a hand and felt it being given a reassuring squeeze. He was looking after her, as he always did. Rosie gazed at her husband and smiled. To have found such a man, such enduring love ... and it had all begun in the unlikeliest of ways.

She had met Solly during an investigation when Lorimer had been SIO in a case of multiple murders, Solomon Brightman the bearded psychologist brought in to assist as a profiler. Some might have thought them a mismatched couple, the feisty Glasgow girl whose profession made her battle-hardened against any sort of gore, and the gentle Londoner whose face turned pale at the least sight of blood. Perhaps it was because of their very differences that she had found him attractive. Though it had to be said that his dark eyes and twinkling smile could melt the most resistant of hearts. His was not an easy, practiced charm, however. Sometimes Solly would break off speaking halfway through a sentence, his pause indicative of some thought that had taken hold and required internal examination. At first it had been mildly irritating but nowadays Rosie was well used to her husband's musings. She'd found strength in his gentleness and kind manner, something that less perceptive mortals might take for weakness. It was never a good idea to underestimate the man, she knew; something that criminals had sometimes learned to their dismay.

He was still regarding her with a knowing look, expecting an answer.

'Well, sort of.' Rosie shrugged, not wishing to provoke even the faintest rebuke on this sunny afternoon, a Sunday when she had promised to rest and relax with her friends.

But then Lorimer rose from his seat and beckoned Solly over to the path that meandered around the lawn.

'Time we had a wee chat about things, too,' he announced with a wry smile. 'Need to pick your brains about something, Solly.'

'How are you finding His Nibs' new job?' Rosie asked her friend as Maggie came and sat beside her.

'Not a lot different, to be honest.' Maggie made a face. 'Still works long hours and sometimes away overnight but, hey, it's nothing new. And to be honest, I'm getting plenty of things done in his absence.' Her voice dropped to a conspiratorial whisper as she grinned at Rosie.

'Oh, aye, what sort of stuff? Things for school?'

Maggie shook her head. 'No.' She glanced at the two men who were wandering around the garden, chatting.

Rosie watched the expression on Maggie's face. It was guarded as though she were half afraid of saying more.

'Come on,' she coaxed. 'What are you up to? Sounds mysterious.'

Maggie sat back and sipped from the long-stemmed wine glass before answering. 'I don't want to say too much,' she began. Then, with a shy grin she added, 'I'm writing a book.'

'For school? A text book?'

'No, nothing at all to do with school,' Maggie replied. 'It's a children's book. Something that Abby might want to read one day.'

'Really? Well, goodness me.' Rosie's eyebrows rose, showing her surprise. 'That's lovely. What's it about?'

Maggie paused for a moment and looked into the distance. 'Hope you don't mind,' she said, 'but I'd rather not say anything about it.' She made a face and turned back to Rosie. 'It's ... it would be like telling the story out loud and I want it to stay on the page.' She shook her head and shrugged. 'That sounded rude, it wasn't meant to, it's just ... it's like you not wanting to know whether you're having a wee boy or another girl. It's hard to explain ... ' She gave a chuckle. 'I'm maybe being daft, but it's all so special to me ... I would share it with you but ... ' She raised her shoulders again in a gesture of apology. 'I hope you'll get to read it some day. In fact, I have an agent looking at it right now.'

'Maggie!' Rosie's mouth opened in delight. 'That's great! What does Bill think?'

'Shh.' Maggie laid a finger to her lips. 'I haven't told him yet. Want to wait till something comes of it. And it can take months, years maybe.'

'Goodness,' Rosie replied. 'Maybe you'll be famous some day, like J.K. Rowling.'

Maggie gave a laugh. 'I'll settle for seeing it on the bookshelves,' she said. 'Now, promise you won't say a word.'

'Promise,' Rosie agreed. 'But why so secret?'

Her friend was silent for a few moments and Rosie noticed the rise and fall of Maggie's chest as she heaved a sigh. 'Not sure, really. Maybe I want to have it as a fait accompli before I start to say anything about it. I'd hate if everyone was full of expectations and nothing came of it.'

Rosie nodded, beginning to understand. Hadn't Maggie Lorimer been through that before? So many pregnancies, so many expectations for this lovely woman beside her and none of them had resulted in a surviving child.

In her eyes Maggie Lorimer was a successful person, a secondary schoolteacher of English who commanded the respect of pupils and staff alike, but perhaps that was not enough for the detective superintendent's wife? Unable to have a family of their own, the Lorimers were fond godparents to Abby and were as excited as she and Solly about the forthcoming birth. Perhaps this writing project was a sort of substitute for what she had lost.

Across the garden, William Lorimer had stopped, looking up into the branches of a huge beech tree and pointing silently at the hidden blackbird that was regaling them with his evening song.

He looked down at the dark head of the professor and smiled. 'Nothing quite beats this, does it?' he murmured. 'Quality of light, blackbird, the peace ... '

Solly nodded. The tall detective was well known for his passion about birds.

'No matter what might happen in the world, the sun will still rise and the birds still sing,' Lorimer added thoughtfully.

'Sounds like something is happening in your world, then,' Solly offered.

'Always something,' Lorimer murmured. 'Humankind being what it is.'

The psychologist waited, hands clasped behind his back, content to listen to the liquid song of the bird, knowing that he was going to be told the sort of dark things that often came their way.

'You know I was away in Aberdeen there for a bit?'

Solly nodded but remained silent.

'There's a lot of nasty stuff about these days. Brutal. People trafficking has become a huge concern with gangmasters using illegal immigrants, keeping them under cover, making small fortunes out of their misery.' He turned to his friend. 'It disgusts me, Solly, but strange to say, that's why this job is one I love, you know?'

'Because you can make a difference,' Solly continued. 'I understand that now but as a youngster it used to puzzle me why so many fine human beings ended up in the police force seeing the rotten side of humanity.'

'There's good and bad everywhere, shades of grey in between most of the time too,' Lorimer mused. 'But I'm guessing we've got a grade one psychopath amongst this lot. Not a bit of empathy for these poor people, treats them like cattle.' A note of bitterness crept into his voice.

'You got them, though. In Aberdeen?'

'We swept up most of the gang,' Lorimer admitted. 'A few Slovakians as well as Scots. Enough to keep the tabloids buzzing for the next few months. But we didn't get them all.'

Solly glanced at the tall man beside him as he heard him sigh.

'They're here, Solly. Some of the most dangerous individuals you can imagine. Right here in Glasgow.'

'Are you going to arrest them?'

'Ha! Once we find them, we will,' he exclaimed. 'Intelligence has given us indications that their work has begun here in the city but so far they've kept out of sight. And,' he turned to look at Solly with a familiar expression in his eyes, 'I think they are going to be very hard to find.'

'You want me to help?'

'I think profiling one particular individual might give us the break that we're looking for, yes,' Lorimer agreed. 'D'you want to come over to Govan tomorrow? If Rosie can spare you?' He glanced at Rosie and Maggie sitting together, the sudden sound of laughter easing the worry lines around his eyes.

'Tomorrow, yes,' Solly replied firmly. 'But today is too nice to spoil. Don't you agree?'

*

59

It was hard heaving herself out of the garden chair to take their leave, and harder still to keep quiet about the reason she'd wanted to talk to Lorimer. Peter Guilford was an enigma, all right. An apparently successful businessman, his history of violent behaviour did not seem to have repeated itself over the years since his one and only spell of imprisonment. And yet now he was languishing in jail, accused of murdering his second wife. Had he just been lucky? Had the pattern of brutality gone undetected for that length of time? Perhaps. Anyway, it wasn't her job to judge the man. But, even as she shifted uncomfortably behind the wheel of their car, Rosie frowned.

Something wasn't right about this case and she would love the chance to find out more about the woman whose body currently lay in the City mortuary.

CHAPTER NINE

Detective Superintendent William Lorimer gave a rueful smile as he scrolled up the screen of his office computer. Peter Guilford's name appeared at last and, with it, a list of those whose business interests had overlapped with the owner of Guilford Vehicle Hire. It was too much to hope that Guilford would be the link he had sought since coming back from the north-east but there was no denying that the trail to Scotland's largest city took in both the innocent and others who crept across the wrong side of lawfulness.

The report included the police raids on a chain of nail bars that had exposed the plight of dozens of young girls from Eastern Europe, whose lives were made sheer hell at the hands of their gangmasters. From their arrival in Scotland with an expectation of work and prosperity, they had been taken into squalid premises then forced to appear bright and professional at the salons by day. For the prettiest girls, nights were punctuated by other demands, prostitution running rife in the darker areas of Aberdeen. But things were changing all over the country, oil prices fluctuating wildly and thousands of jobs being lost. And, where the money went, so too did these entrepreneurs in human misery.

Peter Guilford's connection was tenuous to say the least but Lorimer knew better than to reveal even this to the pathologist, despite their friendship. The man might be involved in the trafficking business in some small way but it didn't look as if it that had anything to do with the death of his wife at this stage. Better to keep each case separate and let McCauley deal with Rosie's thoughts on the subject. Guilford dealt in commercial vehicles these days, though his background as a car salesman was something Lorimer had discovered. His second marriage certainly seemed to have been the catalyst for a change in his fortunes and Guilford's was a well-known name in the truck rental business nowadays. What would happen to the business now that the boss was in prison for murder? Perhaps some digging could be done to see if anyone there could shed a light onto that.

Odd how coincidences happened, he mused, thinking about Rosie's anxiety over the murder case. *If it was a murder*, a little voice murmured in his head. Guilford had supplied vehicles to one of the firms in Aberdeen; that was all. Nothing remarkable about that but every single little thing was being investigated by the team at the MIT, nothing too small to be overlooked as unimportant. And now his wife was dead, a kitchen knife through her heart.

Lorimer sat back for a moment, fingers clasped against his lips as he considered the options. Budget constraints were always a big factor in making any decision: could Police Scotland afford the services of Professor Brightman? Could he spare officers to dig more deeply into this case without treading on CID's toes? He was also curious to know more about this man and the wife whose life had suddenly come to an end. And sometimes a combination of coincidences and curiosity had given the detective superintendent remarkable results.

DC Kirsty Wilson had been involved from the start, of course.

And, as one of DI McCauley's team, she would be writing up her own version of the case. Perhaps it was time to see the young woman who had chosen a career in the police after her own traumatic experience of finding a murdered woman in their student flat.

He'd give her a call before she left for home tonight but first there was an appointment to keep with the professor from Glasgow University.

Solly paid the cab driver and slipped the receipt into his wallet. Driving a car had never been high on his list of things to do, even as a teenager, and only lately had he wished for the skill he'd allowed to pass him by. Rosie drove them everywhere but now, in the later stages of her pregnancy, he'd like to have taken that task over from her. He gave a rueful smile, recalling his wife's words. *Not in a million years, Solly*, she'd said firmly. *I'm far safer behind the wheel.* And she was probably correct about that, he admitted to himself, given the tendency he had to let his attention wander.

Today he would be focused, however, the MIT team relying on his expertise to analyse the data they had on their quarry. Building a profile was not an easy matter, though the various TV shows made it look as if a brainy man or woman could sum up a criminal mind in a flash. It took time and effort to sift through all of the available intelligence about a person, usually someone nameless whose activities alone were the evidence he could use. Would that be the case here? Or had the arrests made up in Aberdeen provided more? He would soon find out.

The big room was warm, sunbeams making swirls of dust motes visible against the glare. Sounds of traffic from the busy street drifted through the open windows, mingling with the officers' voices as Solly stepped into the room.

'Professor Brightman. Welcome.' Lorimer stood up and stretched out a hand, beckoning Solly to an empty seat next to him at the head of the table. 'You all know Professor Brightman,' Lorimer announced to the room, 'so let's begin, shall we?'

There were murmurs of welcome and some friendly smiles from the team of officers as Solly sat amongst them.

'Now, then,' Lorimer began. 'We are looking for the profile of the gangmaster behind this entire set-up.' He paused for a moment. 'Intelligence has us believe that he may have origins in Eastern Europe, possibly Slovakia, and we've had several lines of enquiry open between police forces in different countries through Europol.'

There was a small silence that prepared Solly for Lorimer's next words. 'Nothing. Not a thing. Nobody on their radar that would match the sort of person we're looking for.'

'And that would be . . . ?' Solly asked gently.

'A gang boss with form. A known criminal who's used to surrounding himself with thugs. Someone who'd wanted to make himself scarce in a different country all of a sudden. On their wanted list. Or so we'd assumed.' The detective superintendent gave a sigh.

'Couldn't be a British national?' Solly queried.

'We still don't think so,' Lorimer replied. 'But at the moment anything's possible. And that's where you come in, my friend.'

He glanced around the sea of expectant faces before pushing a thick folder full of papers towards the psychologist and giving him a rueful smile.

'What we need right now is for you to tell us what sort of person is capable of the things you are going to find in this dossier.'

*

It did not make for pleasant reading, Solly reflected, grimacing, some hours later as the sun filtered through the blinds of his study. The girls were mainly of Eastern European origin, their hopes of finding a better future in the UK dashed the moment they had handed over their passports to the men who had taken charge of their destinies. The lucky ones were being repatriated but several brave souls were still in protective custody, awaiting a time when their testimony might put several people in prison. He leafed through the photographs again, lips narrowing in disgust at what these young women had been forced to do. Raped, tortured, forced into positions of the utmost degradation as if they were less than human ... The images were explicit and someone behind a camera lens had enjoyed taking these photographs. It sickened Solly. And yet it was a necessary part of his job, to try to understand the depth of depravity that one person had sanctioned. Thuggery, brutality and degradation were all there like three wicked brothers from a Grimm's fairy tale.

'The evil that men do ... ' Solly whispered under his breath. And, of course, it had been ever thus, since Cain had taken out his spite against brother Abel.

'Knowledge of good and evil,' he murmured sadly, turning the last photograph face down onto the pile. It was always a matter of choice, wasn't it? A choice to do a good or evil deed with all of the motivation that such choices have at their back. Most good citizens were motivated by a desire to stay at peace with their fellow men, or at any rate to avoid the punishment that came from being on the wrong side of the law. Sometimes choices were taken on the spur of a moment, a life snatched away as passion overtook reason. Had that been what had happened with Rosie's victim? he mused, his mind temporarily distracted by the Guilford case. Perhaps. At any rate there were grey areas in every life and most folk would be appalled to know how easily they might cross the line between doing good and doing evil when passions were sufficiently aroused.

But, of course, he was looking for a different sort of person here altogether, a person whose choices had long since been made. He was someone who saw human beings as a source of income. He? She? Solly shook his head and dismissed the notion of a gangmistress. There was just too much brutality here, for one thing, and he did not find it credible that those men already in custody were the sort to kowtow to a woman.

No, they were looking for a man, someone hardened by his own life experience, no doubt, possibly brought up in a climate of violence and now inured to any sort of compassion. Or even a psychopath who had never been capable of empathising with other human beings and therefore had no qualms of conscience about inflicting the worst that he could upon them for his own ends.

How many thousands of men did that describe? The aftermath of so many conflicts must have produced boys who'd had to fend for themselves, survivors who had climbed ruthlessly over their peers in the struggle to find some hope for a future. And what then? A career devoted to crime of one sort or another, amassing enough money to travel without disturbing any border authorities and fetching up on Scotland's shores to exploit the tail end of the oil boom that had generated so much for the north-east. Was that the sort of story he had? It was possible, Solly mused. Whoever they were seeking was no amateur and he doubted whether he was a man still in the first flush of youth. No, this person had lived long enough to see the worst of humankind and not to be sickened by any of it. Quite the reverse, if his theory was to stand up.

Had his choice of girls shown anything? A preference for one sort over another? But, no, there were girls from several parts of Europe: a few from Romania and Serbia, but most from Slovakia ... He read on and then frowned. Each girl had been asked about her ethnic origins and most of them could tell a lot about their family background. Solly's thoughts turned to those young Serbian women who had been caught up in chaos as children.

The Yugoslav wars had lasted over ten years, the bloodiest and most brutal conflicts that had afflicted some of their young lives. Entire families had been wiped out, several of the girls being brought up in care or by distant relatives. He read their testimonies again and again, information filtering through the horn-rimmed spectacles into a brain ready to process the slightest fact. They had all been born during these conflicts. That was only to be expected, of course, though the youngest had only been months old when the final tanks had rolled off their streets.

It was something that Rosie never spoke about, her part in volunteering to help identify victims from these mass graves after the Srebrenica massacre that had horrified the Western World.

He ran a hand through his dark curls and sighed. Surely there was something he had missed? Once again Solly reread the files, pencil in hand to make ticks against the suggestions that he had thought helpful.

What if ...? He knew it was good to look for different shapes and sometimes the space between shapes, as his art teacher back in London had been fond of telling her class. It was an idea that Solly brought into his own world of studying human behaviour.

Pencil in hand, he stopped as he put down the final page of testimony.

There were no Muslim girls whose families had originated in Bosnia. Solly heaved a sigh. Did that even amount to a clue? Was the man they sought an ethnic Bosnian, for instance, who refused to employ girls from his own background? A few of the girls who had worked the nail bars had come from Muslim families but admitted to having left both family and faith behind them on entering the brave new world that was the UK.

Solly pushed the glasses up onto his forehead and rubbed his eyes. He was trying too hard to find correlations. The man they were looking for could be a Scottish psychopath, plain and simple. And yet how had he managed to inveigle so many people from Eastern Europe into his various schemes? Besides, most of the women were Slovakian. No, his tired brain insisted. He was looking for someone who could speak several languages. A clever man, perhaps, not necessarily educated in the way that Professor Brightman had been, but on the streets of Sarajevo, in the melting pot that had once been Yugoslavia . . . Someone who had been here, in Britain, long enough to communicate fluently and to command the authority that graduating from the school of hard knocks with honours might well bring as its reward.

And, his age? Would he have been a child in those early days of war-torn Yugoslavia? An impressionable ten-year-old in 1991? By the end of the conflicts had he even seen action? Solly pursed his lips, refusing to contemplate what sort of action a man like this might have considered necessary. Well, it was 2018 now, so maybe he was somewhere in his late thirties?

He sighed again and closed his eyes. Maybe he should be concentrating on the Slovakian women instead? Sometimes, Solly knew he could tell himself a story that sounded attractive only to abandon it when further intelligence pointed in a different direction. After all, it was just conjecture. He was weaving a story around what scraps of information he had been given by Lorimer. Yet, if this tenuous theory was correct, where had the boy gone after 2001? Seventeen years had elapsed since the end of that horrific war and many Bosnian refugees had gone back home again, disillusioned by life in Britain. He remembered a paper that had come out some years back from a fellow psychologist showing that Bosnian refugees had suffered significant traumas after arriving in the UK. Many had found conditions here poorer than in pre-war Bosnia, certainly their lifestyles and income were worse here than they had been back home. And the majority had been Muslim Bosniacs.

How many had stayed? And, among them, had there been a young man ruthlessly determined to make his own way in life? It was an idea formed from very little substance, he knew, but it was a start, and the longer he thought about it the more he could see a profile forming in his mind. Was this a man who had been robbed of something; his childhood, his innocence or just his faith in humankind?

CHAPTER TEN

'What d'you think, Kirst?'

She looked at his face, the expression both eager and hopeful. A face she loved, wanted to see smile, always. But this ...?

'America?' she asked eventually.

'Aye, Chicago. Hot summers, cold winters.' James grinned. 'But if they decide they want me we can plan on exactly whereabouts we want to live. It doesn't have to be in the city centre. Plenty of good suburban areas, I'm told—' He broke off and took her hands in his.

'I know it's a big step, Kirst, but it doesn't have to be for ever. It's just a beginning,' he told her. 'A real chance to establish myself in the business world, make some decent money ...' He tailed off at the sight of her sudden frown. 'I didn't mean ... your job pays fine, lass, we know that, and I'm so, so grateful for all the support you've given me, but now I feel it's my turn.'

'What about *my* job?'

'You don't need to work again, if you don't want to, not with the sort of salary they'd be paying me,' James countered. 'Anyway,' he slid one hand up her arm, 'I thought maybe ... in time ...?'

'Aye?' Kirsty reckoned that she knew where this was going but she was determined to make James spell it out.

'Och, lass, you know I want us to be together. All our lives. Properly together ...' He folded her into his long arms and she relaxed against him in a sigh, part of her glad for this moment.

'Will you marry me, Kirsty Wilson? Let me carry you off on an adventure?' he murmured into her hair.

Safe and secure within his grasp, Kirsty wanted nothing more than to look up, smile and say the single word that would seal this question.

I want to, she thought, I want to so much, but ... Images of the house she had visited, the victim on the kitchen floor, the DI's warm words of approbation promising a future with Police Scotland stopped her giving him an answer.

'I've sprung this on you too soon, haven't I?' James said at last, drawing apart and looking down solemnly into her eyes. 'Sorry. Just been so excited ever since I opened the letter.'

'Can I see it?'

'Course you can. Here.' He picked up the letter and handed it to her. 'I'll make us a cuppa. Then, how about we both get togged up and go out for a meal? I feel we should celebrate, even if it's just me being given a chance, eh?'

Kirsty nodded and returned his grin. Her boyfriend's mood was infectious and she had to resist the temptation to succumb to it too soon. What was she thinking of? Wasn't this the sort of opportunity that every young couple grabbed if they could?

Yet one half of every young couple did not necessarily include a detective constable keen to work her way up the ladder in Police Scotland, a little voice reminded her. No way did she want to be a part of an American police force, however. But, if she did

71

go along with James's plans, if he did get this job, what would she do with her own life?

Kirsty slumped into the settee, smoothed the sheets of paper in her hands then began to read.

She had to admit that it did sound more than hopeful. With all of the other stuff about housing and additional benefits (a car, health insurance, resettlement allowance ...) this bank really did sound as if they wanted to employ James Spencer. With a postgraduate degree under his belt, James had attractive qual-ifications, after all, and this was a big organisation, the Federal Reserve Bank, one that even Kirsty Wilson had heard of. So, why did she have this funny feeling in her stomach?

'Hey, don't look so upset. Is it the thought of leaving Scotland? The police? Your mum and dad? They're retired now, bet they'll want to come over for Christmas and everything ...' James beamed at her as he set down the two mugs of tea on the table.

'No, it's not that ...' Kirsty picked up the mug. 'Thanks for this. Like you said, it's all so sudden, you know ... takes a bit of getting used to ...' she admitted, letting the real reason for her hesitation remain unsaid.

'Okay. I get that,' he replied, sitting next to her, one arm slung around her shoulders. 'Let's have a nice meal out and we can talk about this later. After all, I don't need to reply till tomorrow. And I may not even get past the next interview stage.'

The evening sky was bright as they strolled along Great Western Road, hours of daylight still remaining as midsummer approached. It was a time of year that Kirsty loved, she realised, her hand clasped in James's, the pavements dry and warm, the river a mere gurgle over piles of stones as they crossed Kelvin Bridge. It reminded her of the carefree days between leaving school and beginning her university course, a degree she had abandoned in favour of joining the police. Back then in the summertime anything had seemed possible, long days ahead, mornings radiant with promise. In a way, she had managed to recapture that feeling now. The idea of moving to a new country, settling down with the man who wanted her to be his wife, held the same sort of appeal. It was like the ending of a really good movie where you just know everything is going to be okay.

She glanced up at James and he caught her eye and grinned, the squeeze on her hand making her feel warm and safe.

Then she looked away, across the main road at the pedestrians on the far side. A woman was pushing a baby buggy, a man by her side, and they were arguing about something, that much was evident from their body language. Had it been the woman's shouting that had made her look at them?

Suddenly the man jerked the buggy out of her hands and made to cross the road but the sound of a car horn and a scream stopped him as he edged over the kerb.

Gasps came from several of the people around Kirsty and James as they all stood still, shocked at the almost accident, the driver of the car gesticulating at the young father, his vehicle slewed at an angle, the traffic behind him forced to stop.

'Stupid idiot!' Kirsty heard James exclaim. 'Could've got that baby killed.'

For a moment Kirsty hesitated, watching and waiting to see if there was anything to be done, her warrant card ready to be pulled out if necessary. But it was soon all over, the buggy back on the pavement, the woman snatching it from her partner and marching determinedly ahead. A quick V sign and the man scurried after her, leaving the driver to concentrate on straightening up his vehicle and heading off towards the city centre.

She was still quiet as they entered the cool interior of the restaurant, the magic of her sunny moment spoiled by that little incident.

As if reading her thoughts, James put out his hand and stopped her with a rueful smile. 'Glasgow,' he said, cocking his head as if to indicate the stupidity of the young father. 'Chicago can't be any worse, surely?'

And Kirsty grinned, in spite of herself, knowing that what he said was true.

But I don't know Chicago, she told herself silently. And this has become my city.

CHAPTER ELEVEN

Rosie smiled as she walked beside her husband, their sleepy daughter curled into his shoulder. It was a perfect night, collared doves cooing from the leafy treetops, kids out playing in the park, several other couples having a final stroll with their little ones before bedtime. She'd be glad when the baby came, months of maternity leave ahead when she could stay home, watch over her newborn and forget all about work. Though, she admitted, that was not strictly true. There were several cases that might demand her presence in court, including this latest. If Guilford pleaded not guilty and went to trial then she might well be called to testify, perhaps, this time, for the defence?

'Time this little girl was in her bed,' Solly murmured as they crossed the road to their home in Park Circus. 'She's becoming quite a weight, even for me.' He smiled, shifting the child in his arms.

Rosie nodded. Once Abby was settled she needed to talk to her husband, ask his opinion about the Guilford case. She'd come close to it before but they had never managed to discuss it properly. Now, she told herself, if he had no other pressing matter, she'd see what Solly made of it all.

*

'You know, of course, that the human psyche is wired for survival,' Solly began, glancing sideways at his wife. She had expressed her misgivings about the case already, insisting, however, that there was sufficient forensic evidence to suggest the possibility that Dorothy Guilford had taken her own life.

'Yes,' she nodded, 'I know that. And I also know that those unfortunate souls who do commit suicide have gone way over what is "normal" in the way of human behaviour.' She lifted her fingers to create quotation marks in the air. 'Dorothy Guilford took all sorts of stuff to help her sleep. I've seen her medical records. Makes for grim reading.'

'Do you think her husband had ever attacked her? He has got previous, after all.'

Rosie sighed. 'There was never anything like a charge brought against him. The medical notes suggest Dorothy may have been injured by something other than an accident but her practitioner evidently had insufficient proof of that to take it any further. Besides, the onus is on the victim to report any such injury to the police.'

'Which she never did.'

'Right.' Rosie nodded. 'Anyway, apart from her injuries there appears to be a history of mild depression. She was still taking prescribed drugs. Her husband said that she hadn't been well recently.'

'It would be to his advantage to point that out, though, wouldn't it?' Solly asked, continuing in his role as devil's advocate. 'And, if she did take her own life why would she choose to thrust a knife into her heart rather than overdose on pills she already had to hand? Hm?'

Rosie sighed. She could imagine the prosecution's argument already.

'Okay, say she had planned it all down to the last detail. Was there anything about her death that she was trying to say?'

'Like?'

Rosie thought for a moment. Could she express the ideas that had been circling around her head? All those what ifs? Like, what if the woman had been deranged enough to have wanted to frame her husband for her murder? She had killed herself in a horrible way. What if she had placed that drop of blood on his jacket, secretly beforehand? Then plunging in that knife in a fit of rage and spite? Oh, to say these things out loud would sound so stupid! So, looking up at her husband, she shrugged instead.

'Oh, I don't know. A broken heart?' She looked at Solly and saw the sympathetic smile on his face. 'I know, it sounds pretty feeble, doesn't it? I just wish I knew a bit more about the woman. About her past. Anything that would give me an idea to help me understand what happened that night.'

'It was during the night?'

'Aye, some time around three in the morning. The death hour,' she said darkly.

It was a fact that they were each aware of, the hour between three and four o'clock in the morning being one when the human spirit seemed to be at its lowest ebb. As a psychologist it was something that Solly took into consideration whenever he had to lecture on the subject of depression, and for Rosie, it was a wonder she hadn't written a paper herself about the number of sad souls who had taken their own lives at this gloomy hour.

'You won't be doing yourself any favours, you know,' Solly murmured. 'You'll be taking the stand for the defence and the evidence McCauley has gathered could easily sway a jury against Peter Guilford. Particularly if the press get hold of it and print anything about his previous jail sentence.'

'I know that,' Rosie snapped. Then, taking her husband's hand she shook her head. 'Sorry, I know you're only trying to help but I just have this strong feeling that McCauley wants this all done and dusted without looking into the background a bit more.'

Solly smiled and squeezed her hand. 'That's all right. Don't think about it right now. The case won't come to trial for months anyway and by the time it does you'll be so glad to escape into town from a demanding little baby that you might even enjoy it.'

'Demanding?'

Solly stroked her belly gently, feeling the ripple of movement within. 'This little one is making his presence felt already. I suspect we are going to have plenty of sleepless nights once he arrives.'

'You think it's a boy too, then?'

Solly nodded and smiled. 'But I won't mind if we're proved wrong about that.'

CHAPTER TWELVE

The door was unlocked, making Kirsty Wilson step back in alarm. There was no sign of any forced entry and no one else was meant to have a key apart from the ones that Guilford had handed to the police.

She fingered her mobile, ready to make a call should there be an intruder within the big house in St Andrew's Drive. But not yet. Not until she knew for certain what was happening.

Pushing open the door Kirsty saw dust motes dancing in the brightness of the air, the sunshine from the street creating a wedge of light in the reception hall.

She stood silently, listening, wondering if her own arrival had been noted and already a figure was hiding behind a door, cosh in hand, ready to give her a thump.

Then, despite her beating heart, she gave a wry smile. Faint sounds of a familiar tune came from somewhere beyond the left-hand corridor that led into the kitchen where the woman's body had been found. The strains of '*Fur Elise*' . . . She frowned, wondering who was listening to the music.

More curious now than brave, Kirsty crept quietly along the

corridor, hugging the wall so that she might not be spied as she came to the kitchen doorway.

Her fears vanished at the sight of a large woman on her hands and knees, wiping the laminate floor with a cloth. A radio on the countertop nearby was filling the room with music.

'Hello?' Kirsty stepped forward, warrant card held out so that the woman would know she was a police officer.

The woman jumped back onto her heels, one hand clutching her bosom.

'My Gawd, lassie, you gave me a fright!' She wiped the sweat from her brow as she sat on the floor. 'Thought me heart wis goin' tae stop, so ah did!'

'Who are you and why are you here?' Kirsty asked, though the answer to the second question seemed obvious. She was the Guilford's cleaning lady, if Kirsty's guess was correct.

'Ah'm Magrit. Mar-gret Daly. Who're you?' The woman struggled to her feet, dishcloth still grasped in her hand so Kirsty helped her up, letting her see the warrant card more closely.

'Detective Constable Wilson,' she told her. 'This is a crime scene.'

'Aye, I heard,' Margaret blustered. 'But the lassie from the office telt me it was okay to come in again. This is my day to clean, see?'

'So you know what happened here?' Kirsty said, steering the woman away from the place where the body had lain.

'Terrible, jist terrible.' Margaret shook her head. 'And that awfu' man in the jail now.'

'You mean Mr Guilford?'

'Aye, right bad lot so he was. Led that puir wumman an awfie life. I could tell ye things that'd make yer hair staun on end, so ah could.'

'Really?' Kirsty murmured, eyebrows raised. Perhaps this wasn't a bad idea; the telling, at any rate. 'Mrs Daly, do you think you might make us a cup of tea? Then we could have a chat about . . . things?'

Kirsty watched as the woman moved away towards the other side of the kitchen, her slippered feet stepping gingerly over the still damp patches on the floor. There was nothing wrong with asking a few questions. She would make sure that everything was relayed back to DI McCauley, of course, but the fact was she had come here this morning primarily at the behest of a different person altogether. And Lorimer would be very interested to know that permission for the cleaner to resume work had come from Peter Guilford's office.

Kirsty's eyes followed Margaret Daly as the older woman set the cups and saucers on to a tray, filled a small jug with milk and made space for a sugar basin and a plate of chocolate biscuits.

'Strong or first out the pot?' Margaret asked, bending over the kitchen table where Kirsty now sat.

'As it comes.' She shrugged, well used to all sorts of tea from pale beige scarcely brewed to builder's tea that resembled a fake tan.

'Hm.' Margaret Daly poured the tea into two cups then sat down heavily opposite the detective constable. 'Right, what's going on?' she asked.

'I think that was going to be my question to you,' Kirsty countered wryly. 'As far as I was aware the house was to be kept locked up meantime.'

'Not what Cynthia telt me.' Margaret pursed her lips in a defiant gesture. It was evident that the presence of the police did not worry the woman in the slightest, something that Kirsty found rather intriguing.

'Cynthia?'

'*His* secretary.'

She would pursue that in a moment but first Kirsty needed to wheedle out more information about that blunt statement concerning Peter Guilford's treatment of his late wife.

'You said he had been bad to her . . . ' she began.

'Aye, and surely they'd have seen a' the bruises an' that? There wis a post-mortem, eh? Like on *Silent Witness*, Gawd that's a brilliant programme, so it is!' Margaret Daly exclaimed, lifting a chocolate teacake and popping it into her mouth.

'Yes, there was a post-mortem but I cannot comment on its findings,' Kirsty told her.

Margaret gave her a sideways glance, narrowing her eyes until they almost disappeared into pockets of wrinkled flesh. 'Bet they learned a lot, though. Ye cannae hide broken bones and the kind o' bruises wee Dorothy Pettigrew had oan her body. Ah seen it,' she added nodding. 'So did her GP, nice wee wumman, cannae mind her name. Aye, ah seen it often enough an' ah heard his rages as well. Had that puir wife o' his like a tremblin' wee jelly, so he did.'

'What sort of things had you heard?' Kirsty prompted, noting that the cleaning woman had used Dorothy Guilford's maiden name, a sign that she had worked for this family for many years.

Margaret Daly leaned forwards, her bosoms straining across the table top. 'I c'n tell you they weren't nice things, not nice at all. I swear tae God I wance heard him tell her he'd kill her if she didn't do what he wanted.'

'And would you also swear to that in a court of law?' Kirsty asked.

The woman sat back again, a shadow of doubt crossing her face.

'Don't know about that,' she mumbled. 'Don't want to inter-
fere, you know?'

'It wouldn't be interfering,' Kirsty insisted. 'If what you say is
the truth then it would give the Crown Prosecution more reason
to tell a jury to convict your boss of murder.'

'*He* wisnae ma boss,' the big woman replied. 'It wis her. Ah've
been with that family since I wis a girl. Kent them all. Young
Shirley afore she wis sent away, auld Mr and Mrs Pettigrew when
they both ran their business frae here.'

Kirsty looked down at the bottom of her cup and gave a smile
as she handed it over for a refill. 'Would you mind? I'd love
another please?' she asked winningly. Inside, she felt a sense
of triumph. She'd struck gold here, if she was not mistaken.
Everything this woman might tell her could be passed on to both
McCauley and Lorimer for their different interests. But first she
had to gain the woman's confidence sufficiently to ensure she
would give a full and frank statement back at Govan.

For a moment Kirsty knew the satisfaction that came from
a real breakthrough. But then she remembered James and his
proposal, a question that still remained unanswered. Would she
really be able to choose her boyfriend over the job she loved so
much? And yet, how could she bear to let him go?

Then, dismissing her own preoccupations, she looked straight
at the woman across the table once more.

'Tell me more about the Guilford business,' she asked. 'And
why would Mr Guilford's secretary give you permission to come
back here?'

The woman dropped her gaze and Kirsty saw that the question had made her uncomfortable.

'Didn't know who else to ask, did I?' she said, squirming a
little on the kitchen chair. 'And someone has to pay my wages,

don't they?' Her chin jutted up again as though that were the correct answer to give.

'You were paid as a private cleaner. Not through an agency, then?'

'Aye ... all above board. I pays my taxes like onybody else, you know. Not that it amounts tae much wi' me on a widow's pension ...'

The trembling lip and the way she turned her head as though to avoid Kirsty's eyes told a little story of its own. She was probably paid by the hour and didn't declare it as income at all, Kirsty guessed. Happened all the time, older folk trying to eke out their pension any way they could. And who was she to make a fuss about that?

'I'm sure that is all above board, Mrs Daly,' she soothed. 'But I really think it would be wonderful if you could repeat all of this for my boss. He'd be so pleased to hear it from you and use it as a proper statement, if you know what I mean?'

The older woman looked doubtful again. 'They'd jist want tae know stuff I'd heard, is that right?'

'That's right,' Kirsty agreed. 'By the way, have the front door locks been changed in all the years you've worked here?'

The woman shook her head. 'Naw. Same keys, same lock. Same front door. Ither folk changed theirs tae wan o' thae fancy double glazing wans but this is the original,' she remarked with a tilt of her chin as though she was proud of the fact.

'So it's not just you who has keys? All the family would have had them?'

The cleaning lady shrugged. 'S'pect so. That Cynthia has wan, too, I bet,' she added darkly.

Kirsty nodded. Was that why Guilford had been so eager to say nobody else had a key? There was certainly someone he'd been trying to protect ... or conceal.

84

'Mine's always bin the same, see?' She sauntered over to the back door where a pink poplin jacket hung. Rustling in a pocket she produced a bunch of keys with a huge key ring that bore the Rangers FC logo.

'Thanks. I'll make sure you are allowed to keep them but meantime I better check with my boss in case he would rather the house is kept empty. Is that okay?'

Margaret Daly nodded doubtfully and Kirsty was reminded that the older woman probably depended on this regular income.

'I can take you back with me just now, if you like. My car's outside and Govan station's not far away. I'd make sure you got home afterwards too. Where is it you live?'

Margaret Daly shrugged. 'Paisley Road West. Just up the road frae Helen Street. Oor Geordie wis a cop till he got his bad leg,' she added. 'I know fine where you lot are.'

And, with a look of resignation on her face, she heaved herself to her feet and began clearing the tea things away.

'Jist let me do these the now then I'll get my bag and come wi' ye, lass.'

Kirsty watched as Margaret shuffled across to the sink, her worn slippers making padding sounds across the clean laminate floor exactly where the body of Dorothy Guilford had lain.

'Good work, Wilson.' McCauley slapped her on the back. 'Lorimer told me he'd asked you to take a look into Guilford's business dealings with regard to that matter up in Aberdeen. Bit of luck finding the old biddy in the house though, eh?' He gave her a grin. 'I won't let this be forgotten, you know. Between you and me I think you've got a long way to go. One of these bonny days someone will be calling you "Ma'am",' he winked.

CHAPTER THIRTEEN

It was an automatic gesture to cross his hands over his genitals as the shadow stopped outside the shower.

'I won't be long,' he began, his words lost in the torrent from the overhead spray beating against the floor tiles.

The cubicle door opened and the shadow became a thickset man, one hand raised menacingly.

Peter tried to squirm sideways as the man lunged at him, the chib that had been concealed in his fist striking his neck.

For a moment they grappled, the soapy floor making both men slip and slide.

'No! No! Help!' Peter screamed as the man grabbed hold of his testicles and began to twist.

Peter felt the blow on his face as the bigger man struck him with his forehead. He screamed as another blow landed in his stomach, then his knees buckled and he felt himself slither helplessly into the pool of slimy water.

'Stop! Stop!' he yelled, but his voice was lost in the steam and drilling of the jets as they washed red streaks from the Perspex walls.

He tried to call out again but another blow to his head made him fall forward, his chin impacting on the hard floor.

For a moment there was nothing but the drumming and gurgle of water, then he froze, eyes tight shut, fearing the slash of that sharp weapon. He sensed the shadow coming closer, heard the deep irregular breathing as his attacker bent down beside him.

'Tell Dorothy hi when you see her on the other side,' a voice whispered.

Then Peter felt blow after sickening blow as a sharp-booted foot thudded into his body.

The buzzer rang insistently, its noise half drowned by the sound of running feet as prison officers scrambled to the shower block.

A couple of young men dressed in denims stood back, arms hugging bare chests as they waited to be questioned.

Inside the shower they could see a prone figure, his body curled into a foetal position as he had attempted to resist the attack.

'Turn that damn thing off!' the voice from a dark-suited figure barked and another officer stepped forward, one arm stretched out towards the shower switch.

The interior of the cabinet was streaked with blood, though much of it had been washed down the drain hole by the spray.

'Is he deid?' one of the young men hugging the corridor wall whispered.

The prison officer who had issued the order was now kneeling down, one hand feeling Guilford's limp wrist.

'There's a pulse. Get an ambulance. Now!' he ordered. 'Either of you two see what happened?' He stood up and glared at the young men, his face darkened in rage, making them take a step backwards.

'Naw, we jist came along and seen the mess . . . Joseph here,' he indicated the other lad, 'ran tae get help and I stayed wi' the man. Are you sure he's no' deid?' he asked again, looking at the twisted shape lying face down in a pool of water that was now gurgling into the drains.

'Not yet,' the officer replied, giving both of the men a hard stare. 'Get some clothes on. You'll both be wanted for statements when the police arrive.'

'Is he dead?' McCauley unwittingly echoed the question that the prisoner in the remand block had asked.

'No, but he's very badly injured,' the voice on the telephone told him. 'We won't know for a while if he'll pull through.'

'So where is he now?'

'The Queen Elizabeth. In the operating theatre, as far as I know. He'll be taken to a secure room afterwards and we'll need a round-the-clock police presence. We don't have the staff available to do that right now.'

'Okay,' McCauley sighed. 'I'll come over and bring a couple of officers with me.'

He put down the phone and ran a hand over his head. 'Bloody Guilford!' he exclaimed. Why on earth should the prisoner on remand be targeted in such a vicious way? Barlinnie ran a tight ship, everyone knew that, but someone had managed to evade the prison officers long enough to inflict some serious damage to Peter Guilford. McCauley shrugged. It might save the courts a whole lot of expense if Guilford karked it. And yet as a detective he was curious enough to want to know who had organised this attack. And why.

*

Kirsty walked along the corridor beside DI McCauley, two uniformed cops in their wake, conscious of the faces turning to stare. It was obvious that something was happening in the hospital and natural human curiosity was making these patients and visitors want to know more. It would probably not be long before the newshounds began sniffing around, she thought.

And just when she had thought that her coup this morning was bringing her a modicum of kudos, here she was, landed with the task of waiting probably for several hours until Peter Guilford woke up. *If he ever did*, a small voice murmured gloomily.

'Wait here,' McCauley ordered and Kirsty sat down in the plastic seat outside the room where Peter Guilford would be brought once he was out of surgery. She watched as her boss strode along the corridor and through a set of swing doors. The officers in uniform, two young men who were unknown to Kirsty, began a muttered conversation, ignoring her for the time being.

It was hours since the incident had occurred in HMP Barlinnie and daylight was beginning to fade now. This pair had probably just come on duty, Kirsty surmised, brought in from a city division. She stifled a yawn. Well, at least she was earning overtime, one advantage of being a lowly DC. And, sitting here gave her time to think. Why would anybody want to attack Peter Guilford? He'd been accused of murdering his wife, just another domestic, as far as anyone could see. Stats showed that a crime like this happened with horrible regularity, so why a revenge attack? Or was it about something else? Something to do with the business?

Kirsty chewed her lip as she let her mind wander amongst the possibilities. If it had been an attack by another inmate then it had been planned beforehand since a makeshift weapon had been used, the old-fashioned chib left where it had fallen in the shower. Was there anybody from that trawl of people traffickers who had been remanded in Barlinnie? McCauley had already asked for a list of names but it was someone from Lorimer's team who needed to cross-check that to see if there was any sort of link.

If Guilford did survive this horrendous attack there were definitely questions he would be compelled to answer, even for his own safety.

The whine had disappeared and his ears were filled now with low voices, murmurs that ebbed and flowed in waves of sound. Everything was like a haze; white shifting to palest blue, sudden lights dazzling his eyelids, then that dull red as he slipped back into the welcoming darkness.

A beeping noise made his eyelids flicker and Peter blinked, not sure if what he was hearing could have come from the machines by his bedside.

Where was he? And what he was doing lying on this white bed, his hands flat against the sheets, cannulas with tubes snaking out of sight? Above him hung a bag with yellowish liquid, its slow drip, drip mesmerising him for a few seconds.

He felt no pain, just that dullness behind his eyes and a metallic taste in his mouth.

Something had happened. Had he been the victim of a road accident? Had one of his vans crashed? Peter blinked again, only this time he was aware of another movement, a figure sitting quietly to one side, a woman. Had she come to tell him what had happened? There was no telltale lanyard, no stethoscope around her neck, so maybe not a doctor . . .

'Peter?' The woman had a nice voice, gentle, Scottish with an

accent he couldn't quite place ... not broad Glasgow ... somewhere else ...

He tried to swallow but there was something wrong with his
throat and he began to croak.

'D'you want some water?'

She stood up and brought a plastic cup to his lips and he took
small sips, grateful for the liquid easing the harsh gritty feeling
in his throat.

'Thhhh ...' His tongue made a feeble noise as he tried to
thank her.

'It's okay, don't try to talk just yet,' she soothed. 'I'll be here
when you can speak again. Don't worry.'

'Who ...?' He wrinkled his brow, aware for the first time of
the padding that encircled his head.

'I'm Detective Constable Wilson, Mr Guilford. I'm here to
take care of you. Okay?'

He saw the smile, noted the dark glossy hair and keen eyes.
She looked as if she meant it, Peter thought. Though why anyone
needed to take care of him he could not understand.

Kirsty watched as the man's eyes closed once more and she
waited until she was certain he had fallen asleep before rising
from her chair and stretching her arms above her head.

Outside it was dark now, the city lights twinkling like myriad
golden stars across a velvet backdrop. The consultant had come
and gone, checking on the vital signs, his mouth a straight line,
giving nothing away. That Guilford had come round was nothing
short of a miracle; his subsequent drift back into unconsciousness
something that seemed not to have surprised the doctor. If the
man survived the night there was some hope that he might make
a recovery, he'd informed the detective constable, but it would

be a goodly time, if ever, until he was fit to be returned to any of HM prisons to await trial for murder.

Across the city James would be waiting, anxious to know how she was, wondering no doubt if a night like this had sickened her for the job she was doing. He would be disappointed to know, however, that on the contrary, Kirsty Wilson was finding this turn of events more fascinating than ever.

CHAPTER FOURTEEN

Guilford Vehicle Hire had several depots scattered around Glasgow but its main office was in the city centre, a short walk from George Square. Kirsty had left the car at the underground station in Govan and was walking alongside DS Geary, past the Millennium Hotel, glancing across at the beds of summer flowers blooming in the square and tumbling out of planters outside the City Chambers. It was a pretty spectacular edifice, she had to admit, gazing up; its neoclassical style pleasing to the eye even in this day and age of mirrored glass and steel. She remembered her history teacher at school telling the class that Glasgow City Chambers was a testament to the city merchants of old whose money had been spent on so many fine buildings, though in modern times the elected councillors who worked there had a lot less in their coffers to spend on luxuries like this.

The lights changed to green and they crossed the road, heading along George Street in the direction of the older part of town. Her face lit up in a smile as she passed the University of Strathclyde, where she had first met James. She'd been conducting a little bit of an investigation of her own back then, before she had even considered a career as a police officer. It seemed so long ago now, she realised. The memory faded as Kirsty turned into Albion Street and slowed down to check the address she'd been given.

'Your show this morning, lass,' Geary told her with a smile. 'I'll just watch and listen, okay?'

Kirsty nodded her agreement. One of these days she would be up for her sergeant's stripes and she knew that Jim Geary was only too well aware that his young colleague needed all the experience he could give her.

The office was at street level, tucked between a restaurant and the old Press Bar, a haunt for journalists from decades ago. There were no big illuminated words to tell her that this was a part of Peter Guilford's empire, simply a number etched onto the glass lintel and a discreet brass plaque set into the stone wall: *Guilford Vehicle Hire.*

Kirsty pushed open the door and found herself in a modern reception area that was bigger than she had expected. Two grey plush settees sat at an angle either side of a square glass-topped table, several glossy magazines artfully fanned out on its surface. A pale wood desk held a slim vase of white lilies, their heads not fully opened, as though they had been put there that very morning.

'Nice,' Geary remarked, picking up one of the magazines then letting it fall back again.

Behind Kirsty the muted sound of traffic blurred against strains of music that she recognised as the theme tune to the old TV adaptation of *The Railway Children*, a film she'd loved watching with her mum. It was a nice place to be waiting, she decided, wondering whose inspiration had been behind this particular interior.

'Hello, can I help you?'

A tall young woman wearing a tight black skirt and a short-sleeved white blouse appeared from a side door into the reception area and took her place behind the front desk, a frown of annoyance on her face.

The lines on her forehead only deepened when Kirsty held out her warrant card for inspection.

'Detective Constable Wilson, Detective Sergeant Geary,' she announced. 'I'm here to speak to Peter Guilford's secretary. I did telephone.'

'Cynthia?' The young woman laid her well-manicured fingers protectively across the desk. 'Oh, well, she didn't tell *me*,' she said crossly.

'Would you be so kind as to tell her we're here?' Kirsty asked sweetly, the receptionist given the benefit of her brightest smile. It never failed to disarm them, she'd learned. A polite word, a smile, could elicit far more cooperation than an authoritative command.

'Oh, of course. What did you say your names were again?' The girl seemed suddenly flustered, twin points of real colour heightening her sharp cheekbones, under sweeps of peachy blusher that looked newly applied.

'DC Wilson. DS Geary. Police Scotland,' Kirsty added, just to add a little gravitas to the situation.

She looked around the place more intently as she waited for the secretary to arrive. It was not luxurious by any means but money had been spent to make it calm and welcoming and Kirsty suspected that the classical music floating from a speaker set high on one wall was designed to give the impression of a superior establishment. She'd taken note of the company's annual turnover and been impressed by their profitability. Dorothy Guilford had been married to one of the city's more successful businessmen and could easily have afforded a wardrobe full of designer gear, not the drab stuff she'd found after the woman's death. It was a puzzle Kirsty was still trying to understand when a woman emerged from the same door as the leggy receptionist.

'Miss Drollinger?'

'Yes.' The woman was about the same height as herself, dark hair drawn back into a knot that accentuated her gaunt features. She extended a hand to Kirsty then took it back abruptly as their fingertips touched, as though contact with a police officer had scalded her.

'Please come through to my office, will you?' The tone was clipped.

Cynthia Drollinger stood aside to usher the detectives into a short corridor that led to an open door, giving Kirsty no time to scrutinise the woman further. But her first impression had been interesting nonetheless. Hostility seemed to waft from Peter Guilford's secretary as though she was seething inwardly and finding her emotions hard to control.

Seated on the other side of the secretary's desk, Kirsty took note of the clenched jaw and the cold stare and immediately felt a stab of sympathy for this overwrought woman whose morning she was about to spoil.

'I'm afraid I have some rather bad news, Miss Drollinger,' she began, before adding gently, 'I thought it better to come here in person than to let you know over the telephone.'

Cynthia Drollinger stiffened up, her hands clutching the edge of her desk.

'What sort of news could be worse than hearing that Peter . . . Mr Guilford was in prison?' she retorted. Then a hand flew to her mouth. 'Oh! You can't mean . . . ?'

'Mr Guilford was attacked by another inmate yesterday,' Kirsty told her, watching closely as the colour faded from the woman's cheeks. 'He's been in surgery and his condition is still considered to be critical.'

She saw the secretary's mouth open in a moment of disbelief.

'Why . . . ?' she whispered at last.

'That's what we are trying to find out, Miss Drollinger. And I hoped that you might be able to help us.'

'Me?' Cynthia slumped back, clearly in shock. 'Why do you think . . . ?'

Spots of pink flooded back into her face, telltale signs of emotion. Or embarrassment?

'We wondered if Mr Guilford had any enemies in the business world?' Kirsty asked. 'We are following this line of enquiry for the moment.' She noted the sudden sigh of relief from Guilford's secretary. What had she been expecting? Something closer to home? Did Cynthia Drollinger's reaction say something about her relationship with her employer, perhaps? Or was that a fanciful notion on her own part? Kirsty wondered fleetingly.

'No, of course not.' Cynthia Drollinger was brisk and businesslike once more. 'The firm runs smoothly, our accountants assure us that we are well in the black with no creditors demanding payment . . . Why on earth should you think that Peter had enemies?' She shook her head. 'The very notion is absurd,' she added, clasping her hands firmly on top of the desk.

'There were several vehicles rented out to a client in the north-east,' Kirsty said, drawing out her notebook and flicking over the pages as though looking for some details. 'A client whose personnel included several men who have subsequently received prison sentences for people trafficking,' she added, her eyes on the pages.

'That's preposterous!' Cynthia exclaimed. 'Are you trying to say that we provide transport for bringing in illegal immigrants?'

'That is something that the Crown Prosecution Service may well be asking, Miss Drollinger.' She exchanged a glance with Geary who nodded encouragingly. 'But I'm sure you have nothing to worry about.'

'What our clients do with the vehicles they hire isn't any of our business!' the secretary snapped. 'We hire out vehicles daily all over the country. All we require is payment in full and a clean vehicle on return.'

'So, I suppose they could have been used for an illicit purpose?'

'What? You're not seriously suggesting that Peter had anything to do with . . . with something like this?' The woman had leaned forward now, clearly agitated.

'We need to follow every line of enquiry,' Kirsty replied smoothly. 'If your boss's attacker was nothing to do with his business life then we have to assume it may have been to do with the crime he has been charged with,' she said, her eyes never leaving the woman's for one second.

'He didn't kill his wife,' Cynthia hissed. 'I know that.'

'Oh?'

'I mean . . . I know the sort of man he is,' she blustered. 'I've worked for Peter long enough to know him incapable of murdering anyone.'

'And Mrs Guilford? Did you know her, too?'

Kirsty saw the change in the woman's expression immediately, the coldness as she narrowed her eyes, the slight shake of her head.

'Dorothy Guilford was a mean woman, Detective Constable.

98

She led Peter a terrible life. Pretending to be so ill and yet all the time she was doing everything in her power to make his life a misery.'

'What sort of things . . . ?'

'I . . . ' Cynthia faltered for a moment. 'I only know what he told me,' she said at last, glancing sideways to avoid Kirsty's stare. 'Peter used to confide in me. Said he had no one else to talk to.' She bit her lip. 'A secretary in a firm can often see more of a person on a day-to-day basis than a wife at home,' she added at last, flicking a glance between Kirsty and the silent DS who had remained impassive all through the conversation.

'I suppose that's true. And did Mr Guilford also tell you that his wife had suffered several injuries?'

Cynthia Drollinger gave a frosty smile. 'Attention-seeking. I think there's a name for that. It's a sort of illness, I suppose,' she added grudgingly. 'Dorothy was forever self-harming. Had been since she was a child, I believe.'

'Really?'

Cynthia nodded. 'Ask her sister if you don't believe me. As I said, she led Peter a dreadful life. Always demanding that he be there, never trying to make the best of herself.' She broke off, unconsciously stroking one perfectly manicured hand with the fingers of the other.

And had he found consolation with another woman? Kirsty thought to herself, looking intently at Cynthia Drollinger.

'More fuel to add to the DI's fire, don't you reckon, Wilson?' Geary asked as they headed back through the city centre. 'That one was just biding her time to become the next Mrs Guilford, if you ask me.' He raised his bushy eyebrows as he smiled at Kirsty. 'Think her boss killed the wife?'

99

Kirsty gave a sigh and shrugged. 'I don't know, sir,' she replied truthfully, though the conversation with that bitter woman had revealed more than Cynthia Drollinger had probably intended. She was a woman who had clearly despised Dorothy Guilford. And had she, perhaps, had a reason for wanting her dead?

CHAPTER FIFTEEN

Barlinnie Prison was a place that William Lorimer knew well, having been there countless times to interview its various residents, yet it still made him grimace as he walked along the corridors beside a prison officer, bunches of keys at the man's belt. The interior had been modernised to an extent but outside, its high grey walls were the stuff of Gothic nightmares, looming darkly over stone pathways, blotting out the summer skies. 'Harsh' or 'bleak' were words he would have used to describe the architecture of the place but within these walls the regime was the same as every other Scottish prison. The governor sought to keep a tight rein on the inmates whilst delivering a programme of rehabilitation. The attitude of 'lock them up and throw away the key' had largely died out although some of the more extreme experiments in turning around their more violent inmates had also fallen by the wayside. The Special Unit was now a thing of legend, a story to be told of how creativity might affect a person's whole life and change it for the better, reformed Glasgow gangster turned artist Jimmy Boyle its most famous example.

Lorimer waited for the next door to be unlocked then followed the officer along yet another corridor lit only by artificial light towards the door of the man who was currently in charge of over a thousand prisoners. It was some responsibility, Lorimer knew, running this, the biggest of the prisons in Scotland, several of the inmates known for horrific crimes that had made tabloid reading for months. Despite this, there was rarely any trouble within these massive walls and the attack in the shower block could indeed be described as an isolated incident.

The man behind the desk rose to his feet and came around, one hand outstretched.

'Lorimer, good to see you, though perhaps I shouldn't be saying that under the circumstances, eh?'

Martin McSherry waved his visitor into a chair and nodded towards the officer who was still standing in the doorway.

'Coffee? Tea?'

'Coffee, thanks, Martin. Just black, no sugar,' he added, turning to the prison officer who merely nodded and disappeared along the corridor, closing the door behind him.

'Sorry you've had to come over here, Lorimer. Pretty bad thing to have happened but there was no way we could have foreseen anyone in that block presenting a problem for Guilford.'

McSherry gave a sigh, steepling his fingers together thoughtfully.

'He wasn't in the secure block, then?'

McSherry shook his head. 'No reason why he should have been. No known addictions, not a vulnerable prisoner of any description.' He shrugged. 'A prisoner on remand is, as you know, kept amongst the regular inmates but doesn't follow the same sort of work programme. Guilford had been assessed by our resident psychologist and deemed to be of no risk to himself or to others.'

'Any idea who might have carried out the attack?'

'Hm, difficult to say. We've got plenty of blokes here capable of that but nobody saw a thing, as you'd expect.' He gave Lorimer a sardonic grin. 'And if they did they wouldn't grass up a fellow inmate anyhow. You know the score.'

'Our forensics people have found no trace of anything that might be useful in identification. So far,' Lorimer added.

'All down the drain,' McSherry sighed. 'It's what usually happens if someone wants to attack another prisoner. Showers leave practically no trace and if you jump them fast enough they won't have time to retaliate.'

'So, no new superficial injuries on any of your lads?'

'Every last one of them checked out,' McSherry assured the detective superintendent.

The prison officer entered the room once again and laid down a tray with two mugs and a plate of biscuits then, with a perfunctory nod at the two men, left quietly, closing the door behind him.

'You said on the telephone that there were a couple of the inmates serving their sentences here who had been arrested in Aberdeen. Chaps who might have had dealings with Guilford,' Lorimer began, coffee in hand.

'Aye.' McSherry scratched his ear. 'A long shot really. Both of them are from Slovakia, seem to speak very little English.'

'But could they have attacked Guilford?'

'Perhaps if both of them had had a go, but not as individuals. They are wee guys and not exactly wiry types. I wouldn't have thought that Guilford went down so easily to a pair like that. Still ... '

'Still, I would like to talk to them,' Lorimer finished for him. 'Even if it wasn't them, they may know who did carry out the attack.'

'We've got an interpreter coming here,' McSherry thrust back his shirt cuff to examine his watch, 'in about five minutes.'

There were several officers to whom he could have delegated this particular task but Lorimer knew his own capabilities, one of which was an ability to wheedle the truth out of even the most reluctant suspect in an interview situation. He had decided that a face-to-face interview with the two men was to be his particular task and there were two prison officers on hand not only for corroboration but to ensure the safety of the interpreter and the senior officer from the MIT.

Lorimer watched as Pavol Ferenc sloped along the corridor to the interview room. The man clearly suffered from some sort of disability, one leg trailing. As he shuffled into the seat Lorimer noted the tremble in the man's hands, something far more than stress or nervousness; maybe a sign of something like Parkinson's disease.

It was going to be hard going, he realised as he introduced himself, the middle-aged interpreter careful to enunciate each word in a loud voice as though Ferenc was deaf.

'I want to talk about *Peter Guilford*,' he began, stressing the name to see what reaction the Slovakian would give. But there was none, not even a flicker as the name was repeated and Lorimer knew then that this was a waste of time as far as the attack on the vehicle-hire boss was concerned. Still, there was a secondary reason for his presence here today and he would not let the opportunity be wasted.

'How long have you been in Scotland?' he asked, waiting until Ferenc had heard the question in his own language then the reply, nine fingers held up and a grin that revealed gaps in the man's discoloured teeth.

'Nine years or nine months?' he asked and discussion between the prisoner and interpreter ensued.

'Months,' the interpreter told him.

'And where did you come from, Mr Ferenc? Whereabouts in Slovakia?' he added, glancing at the interpreter.

A conversation ensued where Lorimer noted the frown on the old man's face, a sigh then a shake of his head, his hand gestures making Lorimer wonder if he was sad to be so far away from home. Or was there something else? He had seemed to listen intently as Lorimer asked the questions. Did he have a better grasp of English than he was letting on? That was something that the detective had come across before; foreign nationals hiding behind the pretence of not understanding what was being said.

'He's a Romany, a gypsy,' the interpreter explained. 'They're from a little village in the east of the country near the Ukrainian border called Streda nad Bodrogom. They call it Gypsy Town.' Lorimer guessed that the man had not been given that information from the old man beside them. Ferenc was not the only one from that village, Lorimer pondered; some of the young women rescued during Operation Fingertip had also lived there. How much did this gypsy know about the gang master? And would he tell them more than the facts they had gleaned so far? He could imagine the scenario: the offer of working in the UK, a pretty girl lured away from her country village and the expectation that she would provide for her impoverished family back home. That was what he wanted to stop, he and hundreds of other professionals like him across Europe and beyond. But until they caught the people behind it there would always be a continuing rise in this trade in human flesh.

'Who was the big boss in Aberdeen?' he asked then, sitting back and smiling as if this was a casual question to ask.

The interpreter spoke in the same tone of voice, unhurried and measured as Lorimer locked eyes with the prisoner. But the old man blinked then looked away, head bowed. What was he trying to hide? The identity of this man? Or something more personal?

'Who was the boss in Aberdeen?' Lorimer repeated.

At first he pursed his lips as though considering the question then shrugged as if to say that he did not know. Or did not understand?

'Who brought you to Scotland, Mr Ferenc?'

The question was again relayed through the interpreter and this time Ferenc nodded and spoke aloud. 'It was Max.' He nodded, a grin on his face as though delighted to be able to answer in the few English words that he knew. 'Max,' he repeated.

'Was he a friend? Someone known to you?'

The old man shook his head as he listened to the question in his native tongue. *Not a friend, a person come to offer help to us poor Romanies*, was the answer, given with a pitiful look and a gesture of entreaty. *He tricked us.* The old man scowled.

'And where is Max now?'

This time there was a shadow of doubt flitting across the older man's face before he answered.

'He says he does not know but thinks that Max returned home,' the interpreter told him.

'To Slovakia?'

Ferenc grinned but Lorimer noticed that he had also shrugged his shoulders, as though uncertain how to respond. Also, he was avoiding eye contact with the detective, who was beginning to think the old man knew fine what he was asking.

'And Max was like you, Slovakian?'

The conversation between the old man and his interpreter

106

produced frowns then scowls, accompanied by a fierce shaking of the head.

'He says, no, Max was not from his country. He was a British citizen but spoke many different languages.'

Lorimer tried not to show his surprise. This was something new and put quite a different complexion upon things. Solly Brightman would need to know, too, as he had been profiling a mystery man they had all supposed to be from Eastern Europe, not their own shores.

'Was it Max who paid you to look after the girls?' Lorimer asked, knowing quite well that the Slovakian had been no more than a guard in the tenement building where they had discovered scores of young girls kept as virtual prisoners, rented out as prostitutes by night and nail-bar girls by day. He had given the name Max a tad too readily. Why? Did he want the gang boss caught? Had he a reason of his own for being in Aberdeen, playing nurse-maid to a group of teenage girls? The thought began to play out a possible scenario.

'Max,' Ferenc nodded eagerly.

'And did you like the work?'

Once the question was repeated, Ferenc sat back, uncertain, avoiding Lorimer's blue gaze.

'Why did you come to Aberdeen? Was it to find a girl you knew, perhaps?'

This time, when he had heard the question, a change came over the man's face. His neck reddened and colour suffused his stubbled cheeks. Ferenc blinked and dashed a hand against his eyes, the sudden emotion impossible to disguise.

'Did she get away safely, Pavol?' Lorimer dropped his voice and the old man nodded even before the translation could be uttered.

'She safe now,' he nodded. 'My Juliana safe.'

Ferenc stumbled in his heavily accented English to explain his concern for his only niece, Juliana, who had disappeared with the family's hard-earned savings to begin a new life in Scotland. She was like a daughter to him, Ferenc told them; the parents had died in a terrible tragedy, leaving their boy and girl to be brought up by Uncle Pavol. Promises of riches that would be sent home never materialised and so Pavol and his nephew Mario had travelled to Aberdeen, the last known address of the young girl. There they had fallen in with other Slovakians in a dockside bar and by sheer luck had been offered work that had brought them into contact with Max, the Slovakian-speaking gangmaster who had evaded all of Police Scotland's attempts to find him. Then the pair had come in contact with Juliana and it was during one of the police raids that they had managed to set her free.

'It was you and Mario who blew the whistle, then?' Lorimer asked and the old man had nodded, a rare smile twitching at the edges of his mouth. Both uncle and nephew had pleaded guilty to being part of the gang, but this new information would certainly help once their trial came to court, something that Detective Superintendent Lorimer would urge the Crown Prosecution to take into consideration. And now he had a name. Max.

'Max has another name?'

Another shake of the head.

'What does he look like, this Max?'

What followed in fit and starts became only a sketchy description of a big man, 'a little younger than you, Inspector. Shaved head, dark eyes and a dangerous man in every way', Ferenc shuddering violently as he gave the description. 'His face was strange, smooth and shining like the skin was put on too tight. Gave young Mario nightmares . . . '

Lorimer blinked, his imagination forming a picture of a man who had been subjected to intensive surgery, possibly a victim of some horrific accident. That would be something at least for the psychology professor to think upon.

'Thank you, Pavol, I will see that you are treated well here and I hope that you might return home before too long,' Lorimer said at last, taking the two trembling hands into his own and rising to his feet to signal that the interview was at an end.

The interpreter spoke softly, though there was perhaps no need for translation, both men watching as tears began to fall down Pavol Ferenc's sunken cheeks.

'*Ďakujem*. Thank you, sir,' the old man said as he was helped to his feet by the prison officer and led back out of the room.

Mario Ferenc, the younger Slovakian, had sat on his hands throughout the interview, eyes flicking between the interpreter and the tall detective superintendent, evidently scared to death. But after questioning Juliana's brother about the time of the attack on Guilford, Lorimer found that the young man had been with the prison psychologist for a counselling session. Through the interpreter and from what McSherry had been able to tell him, Lorimer realised that Mario was under the additional stress of being unable to communicate with his fellow inmates, his English practically non-existent.

Satisfied that the attack on Peter Guilford had not been at the hands of either of those men, Lorimer knew it might still have been carried out on the orders of someone within the illicit organisation. Had Guilford been a knowing part of this trafficking scheme? And had he been targeted on the orders of the gang boss, this Max? Whoever had beaten Guilford had meant him to die. And there was every chance of that happening still. But if

109

Guilford survived and could identify his attacker ... well they might just be in with a chance to nail the bloke as well as ferret out the mysterious Max.

It was lunch hour by the time Lorimer drove away from HMP Barlinnie, a frown creasing his brow. Neither of the Slovakians had been able to give coherent statements regarding any knowledge of Peter Guilford and he was certain that the man lying in the Royal Infirmary had never laid eyes on them. They were small fry, each of them too far down the line of command to have had anything to do with Guilford or hiring his vehicles. No, that would have been left to a local man, someone with a good command of English, more likely. Their main concern had been to find Juliana and set her free from the clutches of those traffickers. Or so they said. But he had instinctively believed the two men. His respect for them rose as he drove through heavy traffic along the M8. To keep their true identity hidden and still manage to sneak into the operation had been a mixture of luck and sheer bravado.

One thing he could not get from either of them, however, was the present whereabouts of the girl and he could only hope that she was indeed safe from the menaces that had imprisoned her in that den in Aberdeen.

CHAPTER SIXTEEN

'He said what?' Alan McCauley bunched his fists by his side as he faced the detective constable.

'Detective Superintendent Lorimer said that he doesn't think the men he interviewed had anything to do with the attack on Guilford,' Kirsty told him.

'Two Slovakians locked up in the Bar L and he doesn't think they had anything to do with it? Come on, who's he kidding?'

Kirsty handed her boss the email she had printed off and he scrutinised it, his face creasing in a frown.

'Okay, I can see what he's saying. Right,' McCauley sighed. 'Any word from the hospital? Can he be questioned yet?'

'No word yet, sir.'

'Best get back over there, Wilson, and see what's happening. Don't want him dying on our hands, even if it would save our precious courts a lot of bother in trying him for murder.'

There was no change, the nurse told her, shaking her head and giving Kirsty a sympathetic look. She sat in the same chair as before, watching the drip, listening to the machines as they ticked and hummed, the sounds so hypnotic that Kirsty found her eyelids drooping several times, jerking herself awake to stare at the inert figure under the crisp white sheet. A half-finished cup of tea lay at her feet, one of several that a kindly auxiliary had brought the detective constable as she waited and watched, watched and waited, the afternoon slipping by.

Now it was dusk and well into her overtime. Problems with staffing were particularly bad during the summer months as officers sought holiday leave, but she had hopes that someone would come and relieve her before too much longer.

At last a familiar figure stepped into the room and DS Geary gave her a nod.

'I'm doing the night shift tonight, lass, you get on home now,' he told her quietly, tapping the paperback in his hand. 'Plenty to keep me going till the morning.' He grinned.

Kirsty stood up and stretched then glanced back at the bed.

'Don't know if he'll wake up again . . . just that once and he couldn't speak properly . . . Oh well.' The sigh turned into a yawn as she gathered up her jacket and bag then crept out of the room, glad to be leaving the confines of the place and to be heading homewards at last.

Across the city Lorimer was sitting on his favourite armchair, Chancer the marmalade cat on his knee, purring softly.

'That man's still in a coma?' Maggie asked.

'He woke once but slipped back into some sort of deep sleep,' Lorimer told her. 'They suspect brain injury, that's why he's in the Queen Elizabeth and not the Royal, so even if he does wake up there's no guarantee that he will remember anything at all about his attacker.'

'I don't suppose there was anyone in Barlinnie who would have been trying to avenge his wife's death?' Maggie mused.

'Who knows? It's unlikely. No one in Dorothy Guilford's family appears to have a criminal record.'

'Not family, then, but maybe a friend? Someone who liked her?'

Lorimer's eyebrows rose. 'It's a thought,' he agreed. 'But so far nobody has mentioned Dorothy Guilford having any friends.' He stopped and considered his words. What a bleak epitaph for anyone to have! But someone had attacked the husband and he had to admit that Maggie's question raised the possibility that this was revenge for Dorothy's death. Maybe someone had been close enough to the woman to care about her. But if that was the case, what would they be doing in Barlinnie Prison?

CHAPTER SEVENTEEN

'He isn't dead.'

    'Not yet. Rumour here says just a matter of time.'

'You told me he'd be finished . . . '

'Shh. Watch what you're saying.' The big man standing at the telephone cubicle shuffled his feet uneasily, aware of a shadow passing behind him. Several inmates were waiting, impatiently, for their turn at the payphone. It was an added nuisance, but no mobiles were permitted inside a prison, the discovery of one resulting in severe consequences for the user.

'Thought you said they don't listen in . . . ?'

'Who knows what they do in here,' the reply came, a bitter edge to its tone.

'Well, keep your head down and say nothing.'

There was a pause before the man leaned further towards the wall and whispered, 'What about your part of the bargain? Remember you still owe me, big time.'

The sound of a person clearing their throat made him fidget. Was the call about to be cut?

'I can make things difficult for you,' he warned. 'Remember that.'

'Sure you can, sure.' Was there a hint of mockery in that voice? Was he being reassured or laughed at?

Then, as he pressed the receiver closer to his ear, the faint sound of traffic in the background filled his head, reminding him of a different world where people walked along city streets while the men waiting behind him were in this hell-hole day in, day out.

'Might have another job for you if you're interested. Money will be where you want it. Once we know he's finally gone,' the voice told him at last.

This time he heard a definite click, all sounds of the outside world vanishing in an instant. The big man hung up with a sigh, staring at the grey painted wall, wondering if he'd been played for a fool.

CHAPTER EIGHTEEN

Solomon Brightman was an expert in the study of human behaviour. Nevertheless, he had some qualms about applying his own theories when it came closer to home. There was no doubt in his mind that Rosie's job was causing her stress and that this latest case had caused her blood pressure to rise significantly. Bed rest, he'd told her, knowing even as he'd spoken that this would fall on deaf ears. Rosie could be described as 'thrawn', one of his favourite Scots words – far more powerful to Solly's mind than simply 'stubborn'. She went her own way despite loving him to the ends of the earth. But it was not just his wife he had to think about but also their unborn child. If she could only relinquish this case to someone else, but, no, she had carried out the initial checks and the post-mortem examination so she would see it through to the trial, should one be forthcoming.

Perhaps the man in the Queen Elizabeth University Hospital would not survive. And, if he did, would he be fit to plead? Solly was not the type of man to wish another person's life away but the thought that this could help his wife crept into his mind right now. McCauley had made it quite clear that he was set against the consultant pathologist's interpretation of the case and so she would be acting for the defence if Peter Guilford ever stood trial for murdering his wife.

Now that he had time to consider it, Solly sat at his desk in the bay window overlooking University Avenue, pondering the big question. Was Rosie right to think that Dorothy Guilford had taken her own life when there was evidence to suggest murder? Might her judgement be impaired by the effect of hormonal surges caused by the pregnancy? This was something he had tried to discuss but she would have none of it, outraged at the very suggestion, and he didn't blame her. It was not as if he was being dismissive of his wife in any way, but Solly had the tendency to look at things from every angle, playing devil's advocate when the need arose. And he suspected that McCauley would not be backward at making similar hints to the Crown Prosecution about her capabilities. Even in these enlightened times the knife could be pushed in and turned to a counsel's advantage.

With a sigh, Solly reread the paper he had printed off from a recent medical article on the subject. Really, there was nothing to worry about. Rosie had shown no signs of depression or over-anxiousness; her job involved stressful situations all the time and he had seen at first hand how well she coped with even the most terrible crime scenes. The one in St Andrew's Drive was almost run-of-the mill compared to some others she had attended. True, she did weep easily, but over silly, sentimental things and if he were to be honest, his wife had become more whimsical as her pregnancy progressed, taking time to sit with Abby and read her stories. It was as if she relished these moments with her little girl. Was she afraid that their new baby would take her away from Abby's attention? Did Rosie have underlying worries she had failed to communicate to him? It was hard to say but one thing Solly was sure of was that Dr Rosie Fergusson took her work extremely seriously and would be furious if she did not have his support over this matter.

But could he promise that? Was Rosie correct to make the assumption that she had? And, if she were proved wrong in a court of law, how would that affect her self-belief? Rosie had wept into his shoulder the other night as she'd recalled that old case where she'd made such a mistake, something that had happened long before they had met. It had obviously made a huge impact on her and now the raw pain she'd felt all that time ago was back. Solomon Brightman was wise enough in the ways of the world to know that it was useless to try to shield the woman he loved from any mistakes that might be of her own making. To do so would be to belittle her professional ability, something he knew could cause a rift between them. And yet, his instinct was to love, to protect, to be a good husband, all the things he knew that Rosie valued. Still, he was a psychologist, too, with a psychologist's awareness of how certain human behaviour might be played out. So, he told himself, let's examine the facts and see where they might lead.

Peter Guilford seemed to be guilty of murdering his wife. And someone in Barlinnie Prison had tried to kill him, Lorimer had said. Why? Was this an avenging angel? Some man who had been close to Dorothy Guilford? Solly sat stroking his beard thoughtfully, wondering about the sort of passion and strength that had been required to batter the man senseless. And yet and yet . . . if Rosie was correct, why would anyone target an innocent man?

There were two possibilities, perhaps three if he were to include a random act of violence from some crazy inmate. Perhaps Guilford had an enemy within the prison who felt sufficiently vengeful about Dorothy's death to want to eliminate her murderer. He paused and sat back, tapping his beard with one forefinger. Was it possible to find out if one out of more than a thousand prisoners had been known to the dead woman? That was surely something the police would be asking right now. He sighed and shook his head. What if . . . He closed his eyes for a moment, considering the other option. Here was a scenario that was far murkier, someone wanted rid of Peter Guilford because of what he knew or had seen up in Aberdeen. There was the renegade gangmaster, Max, a man who was not, after all, Slovakian, a person of interest to Police Scotland. And it was Guilford's vehicles that had been rented by his henchmen.

Max. Solly savoured the name, wondering if it was an alias or the man's real name. A man with a face that could have been burned in an accident, disfiguring him for the rest of his life. The psychological implications of that were interesting in themselves, of course. Fury at what had happened, pain and suffering, having to look in the mirror at a different image from the one he'd known till then . . . what sort of changes might these things have wrought in a personality? He'd terrified not just the illegal immigrants whose lives he had wasted but also the men who had been on his payroll. Only the older Slovakian on remand in Barlinnie had let the name Max slip from his eager tongue. The others in the remand wing had nothing to say at all. Fear did strange things to people, as Professor Brightman well knew, the most frequent being the tendency to keep their mouths clamped shut.

If he could find the girl, talk to her about her journey from home to Scotland and the eventual rescue by her brother and uncle . . . Solly frowned. Why on earth had she escaped when the two men had been taken by police? Surely they would have wanted to accompany her away from the tenement brothel? See that she was safe? Something didn't make sense and for the first time he began to wonder if Juliana Ferenc really had escaped the clutches of the gangmaster.

CHAPTER NINETEEN

They'd given her money, rolls of banknotes fastened with rubber bands, that she had pulled apart with fumbling hands, terrified to lose any of it, knowing that she had to part with enough to get her to Glasgow.

Juliana's memory of Scotland's biggest city was of being pulled out of the back of a van into dark streets then hastily shoved into a minibus with the others. At the time she had been excited, eyes wide as she looked out of the window at the Christmas lights around the huge square, its statues looming out of the darkness. A glimpse of golden stars, a net against the night sky, rows of offices, alleyways, twisting and turning through the city streets. Then the vehicle had gathered speed and the motorway lay like a magic carpet carrying them away to the north where she hoped to make her fortune.

They had all been well-treated back then, not questioning the need for their passports to be taken from them, eager to begin their work in the beauty salons, a real step up from the less glamorous work in fish processing plants. The little she had seen of the city was just a distant memory and now, as the coach drew into a huge parking bay, the girl wondered where she should go next.

There was already a queue of travellers waiting to board the bus as she climbed down, grasping the handrail to steady herself and looking for the exit. Following the signs, she came to sliding glass doors that led onto a wide paved area. Juliana blinked as her eyes fell on a strange piece of modern art, metal legs running under a clock face. What was it meant to signify? That time was running out? She shuddered, hoping that this was not a bad omen. Then, looking across the street, she saw a huge building that was surely a department store.

What few possessions she had were still in that place in Aberdeen, so it was important that she find somewhere to buy new clothes. Stopping only to look for an opening in the traffic, she hurried across and entered the store.

It was important not to look conspicuous, so her first purchase was a backpack in which to store her subsequent needs. She wandered from one area to the next, fingering the soft cotton fabrics, looking at price tags that meant nothing to her except if she could afford to part with more of these folded up banknotes.

It was less than two hours later, bag bulging, that Juliana sat in the ground floor café eating a cheese toastie, her first meal of the day. Her head was spinning from the array of goods in John Lewis's store, floor after floor of dresses, shoes and cosmetics, all so tempting to try on. Back home there had never been shopping expeditions like this, money too scarce for anything new, hand-me-downs gladly accepted, some of her older cousins' frocks coveted for years until they'd been outgrown and ready to pass on to little Juliana. The girl smoothed down the creases in the new jeans, relieved to be wearing fresh underwear, her old things stuffed into a bin in John Lewis's toilets.

She swallowed the final piece of crust, savouring the taste of melted cheese, watching the people coming and going, strangers all.

'Anyone sittin' here, doll?' A man loomed over her, indicating the bucket chair opposite, and Juliana started in surprise.

He carried a small tray with a mug of something and a plate with a couple of pastries, and, she realised with a tightening in her chest, he was regarding her with more than a passing interest.

'No.' She shook her head. 'Just going,' she murmured, bending down to retrieve her bag and avoiding his stare. All men tended to look at her like that, she thought bitterly, leaping hurriedly to her feet and making for the exit, not looking back to see if he was following her with those hungry eyes.

CHAPTER TWENTY

It was not the first time that William Lorimer had dealt with illegal immigrants nor, he suspected with a degree of resignation, would it be his last. Memories of a young Nigerian girl waving them farewell as their Land Rover drove along a dusty African track made him smile for a moment; one story that had ended well, at least. The world was a seething place of change, displaced people streaming across it in search of somewhere new to call home, refugees in their millions lost for ever to the lands of their birth. In his grandfather's day there had been the unspeakable cruelty of the Holocaust, millions of Jews exterminated on the orders of a madman who had created terror across Europe and beyond. Brave men and women had resisted that wave of anti-Semitism, helping some to escape the tyranny and find safe refuge. Solly might not be here today had it not been for folk like that, he mused. Even now there were other threats to the safety of ordinary folk, their race or faith marking them out as targets for murder.

He sighed as he sat at his desk in Helen Street. How lucky he was to have been born and raised in a small country where nothing much had changed in centuries; certainly no civil wars or threats to eliminate sections of society. Recently he and Maggie had attended a church service where one of her colleagues had married an Afghan refugee, a Christian woman who had fled her homeland and settled here, finding work as a teacher. Lorimer recalled the pastor's words as he had delivered a short homily after the marriage ceremony: 'Love the sojourner therefore; for you were sojourners in the land of Egypt.'

The word had stuck with him then. *Sojourner*, a traveller passing through or a person trying to find a place to call home? Surely these Slovakian men were sojourners of a sort? Languishing now in prison but hopefully soon making their way back home once more.

His thoughts were cut short by a knock on the door.

'Come in!' he called out, then the door opened and DC Kirsty Wilson stood, smiling at him.

'Kirsty, come on in, take a seat,' he told her, standing up and coming around so that the desk was not between them. 'Any news?'

She shook her head. 'Not about Mr Guilford,' she said, shaking her head. 'Still asleep. Strange that he should've woken up just that once when I was there, though. Maybe I frightened him back into a coma?' she joked.

'But you do have some news for me?' Lorimer saw the gleam in the young woman's eyes that told him she was eager to share some new information.

'Yes.' Kirsty drew her chair a little closer to the man whom she'd known since childhood, her father's boss for so many years. 'We went to visit the office and I spoke to his secretary, Cynthia Drollinger,' she began. 'The secretary,' she repeated with a thoughtful look. 'I think she's more than that, though. Her reaction

124

to the news about her boss was … well, I'd say it was *personal*.'
Kirsty looked up at Lorimer.

'You think she and Guilford … ?'

She shrugged. 'Who knows? Bit of a cliché, the boss and his secretary, isn't it? But DS Geary and I got that sort of impression, you know? She was defensive about him, absolutely adamant that he hadn't killed his wife. Not very complimentary about Dorothy Guilford either, come to that.'

'Any way of finding out if they'd been having an affair?'

'It would certainly give some grounds for disposing of a wife that was in the way. Is that what you're thinking?'

'A bit extreme, don't you think, in this day and age of quickie divorces?' Lorimer countered. 'Though her death would mean that the entire business became Guilford's. Plus that sweet million from the insurance policy. And he'd be free to remarry, of course.'

'Well, she was very much on Guilford's side,' Kirsty repeated. 'And she mentioned a sister. Dorothy's sister. Something about Dorothy having self-harmed as a child. A bit weird, but maybe Dr Fergusson is on the right track after all?'

'I wouldn't express that opinion to DI McCauley,' Lorimer told her. 'And I have to say that so far the evidence suggests that Peter Guilford did take that knife and stab his wife.'

'A moment of madness,' Kirsty murmured.

Lorimer did not reply. Who could really tell what had happened that night? Was Guilford guilty of murder? The alternative was bizarre to say the least. But, in his dealings with human beings, William Lorimer had come across many strange things that defied belief.

He was floating high above the city, arms outstretched, the cold wind making him want to sneeze.

125

Maggie paused as she reread her words and picked up the warm cinnamon muffin, munching it absently, thinking about the suspension of disbelief. Would small children believe in her young ghost, making his midnight way across the skies? She did, at any rate. Gibby had become a character she wanted to write about more and more even though it was hard to know just how a small ghost would really feel, but she had allowed her imagination to take her on a journey with him.

The idea for her story had come from a dream, as so many of her ideas did these days, and gradually the fragments had taken shape and become *Gibby, the Ghost of Glen Darnel.* There was no such place in Scotland, as far as she knew, she'd simply made it up thinking that it sounded authentic enough to pass for real in the eyes of a child. Gibby, though, was a little person in Maggie Lorimer's mind, a child himself whose life had been cut short in a way that need not be mentioned in any of her stories. *Keep the mystery*, her agent had advised and Maggie was happy with that as it chimed with her own instincts.

She had not examined too closely the reason for creating a ghost rather than a small boy with whom children could identify. No doubt Solomon Brightman would have told her that it originated from a desire to bring back to life at least one of her lost children, possibly David, the son she had cradled in her arms for oh such a short time. But Maggie pushed any such thoughts to the furthest recesses of her mind, concentrating instead on her little ghost, the boy floating above the city of Edinburgh, and wondering how she might describe the view of the castle from way up there. Her book was almost finished now, with just a few things left to change before her agent declared herself satisfied with the story.

Maggie looked down as a soft paw tapped her bare ankle.

'Oh, Chancer, did I forget to give you some dinner?' Maggie stood up, brushed the crumbs from her skirt and walked across the open-plan room to the kitchen area where the ginger cat's bowl lay empty. The big cat watched as she opened the cupboard where his food was stored, eyes fixed on the sachet as it was emptied into his dish.

A quick glance at the clock told her that it was well past her own dinner-time and that her husband might walk through the door at any moment.

'Here you go, pet.' She stroked Chancer's fur as he gulped down the cat food and then walked back to her desk by the bay window, ready to close down her file for the day. Gibby would still be there in the morning, she thought to herself. That was one of the advantages of creating a ghost for a lead character: he was immortal, unchanging, and ever ready for new adventures with his creator.

There was something radiant about her tonight, Lorimer thought as he finished stacking the dishes and closed the dishwasher. Summer, he supposed, and the approaching holiday when Maggie Lorimer would put school behind her for a few weeks and enjoy her garden and the long balmy evenings out of doors. Just need to finish this job, he told himself, compressing his lips together as he realised how often he had made that same observation, work coming before his own holidays. But perhaps he could delegate matters to others in the team. DCI Niall Cameron was easily capable enough when it came to heading up the MIT in his absence and besides, he knew it was better to have a decent break away from it all and come back refreshed, ready to see it all with a keener eye.

'Let's go outside,' he called. 'Fancy a drink?'

'Why not,' Maggie agreed. 'So long as we can burn some citronella candles. The midges are awful now that the weather's so warm. And, d'you know what,' she came closer to look into his tired eyes, 'it might relax you a bit after dealing with that case. Slave trade, that's what it is,' she added bitterly. 'A modern slave trade.'

Maggie caught her husband's eye, as if trying to divine his thoughts. This was not an evening for talking about such things, however important they were. Sometimes, she told herself, they needed to stop and put aside their workaday lives.

She smiled as he selected a bottle from the fridge. The dusk was settling over the treetops, a haze of apricot light melting into the burnished skies. They would sit companionably together until the first star sparked, fingers touching lightly, knowing the value of such precious evenings. She pulled a cardigan across her shoulders as she settled down on the garden bench, eyes gazing upwards as a thrush trilled its liquid notes. Live in the moment, she thought, breathing in the sweetness that wafted from the night-scented stocks.

Who knew what tomorrow might bring?

Rosie laid down her glass of sparkling water and looked around the room where people were chatting before the formal part of the evening began. She had made her little speech, told the necessary jokes and now she could relax for a while in the company of her peers. The annual dinner for the Scottish Medico-Legal Society was one she normally enjoyed but this evening baby was being particularly active, pressing on her bladder, necessitating frequent trips to the hotel's bathroom.

'Excuse me,' she murmured to the man on her left, a high court judge whose easy charm and ability to make her laugh had made the evening far more pleasant than it might otherwise have been.

The ladies' lavatory was cooler than the banqueting suite and Rosie was glad to spend a little time touching up her lipstick before heading back. She rummaged in her beaded evening bag and found a small bottle of perfume.

Just as she turned her head, the fine mist touching her bare neck, Rosie caught sight of another woman's reflection in the large gilt mirror, staring at her curiously.

'Dr Fergusson?'

'Yes?' Rosie smiled at a woman, wondering who she was. Wife of one of the lawyers, perhaps? Her first impression as she turned around was of a smartly dressed woman about her own age with an enviable figure. At last someone who wasn't afraid to wear red, she thought, admiring the slim-fitting gown and the attractive dark-haired woman wearing it. So many women stuck to black, as if the costume for their day jobs had spilled over into a night out.

'Jane Loughman,' the woman said, holding out her hand.

'A pleasure to meet you,' Rosie said politely, taking the other woman's hand for a moment. 'Are you enjoying the evening?'

'I wanted to talk to you,' the woman said abruptly, moving slightly towards Rosie as if to block her way out of the powder room.

'I'm sorry, do I know you?' Rosie frowned. Her mind was playing so many tricks on her these days.

'*Dr* Jane Loughman,' the woman said then waited as though Rosie ought to be responding to the name.

In the silence that followed Rosie watched as the woman's hazel eyes regarded her thoughtfully.

'You really don't know who I am?'

'Sorry, I don't think we've met ...' Rosie bit her lip, watching the half-amused expression on the woman's face. The name was vaguely familiar. As current chair of SMLS, Rosie had read the list of attendees earlier that evening. But was there something else she was meant to remember about this stranger?

'I was Dorothy Guilford's GP,' Jane Loughman told her. 'I think we need to talk.'

The after-dinner speech was a mere blur as Rosie sat impatiently, wishing that it was over. All around her men and women in evening dress were laughing at the jokes, looking intently at the after-dinner speaker who held their attention. But Rosie's eyes strayed instead to the table across the candlelit room for a glimpse of a red frock, the neat dark head turned sideways, attentive to their celebrity speaker.

More than once she thought that Jane Loughman had glanced away, searching the room to catch her eye, but it was hard to be sure under the flickering candelabras.

At last it was over, the applause and hoots of approbation filling the room, the speaker making his bow and the SMLS secretary coming forward to present him with a very good bottle of twenty-five-year-old malt whisky.

There she was, her red skirt swishing as she walked across the room, evening bag clutched in one hand.

'We have to go,' Jane apologised. 'But perhaps you could call me tomorrow?' She thrust a card into Rosie's hands. 'I know you will have read her medical file but there's so much I want to tell you about Dorothy Guilford. Nobody's approached me personally ...' she glanced around at the crowded room where medical folk mingled with the cream of Scottish law, as well as representatives from Police Scotland, '*yet*,' she added meaningfully. 'So, the sooner we talk the better.'

Then she was gone, leaving Rosie to look at the retreating figure in that elegant red dress. As she turned the GP's card over in her fingers Rosie knew she was unlikely to sleep through the coming hours, already wondering about what the morning would bring.

CHAPTER TWENTY-ONE

Life at Helen Street was different from any other job that William Lorimer had ever done inasmuch as he was solely in charge of the operations, answerable to nobody when a sudden decision had to be made. His previous divisional headquarters at Stewart Street in the city centre had given him several years of experience dealing with major crimes, but all the time he had been aware of the need to refer to someone more senior than himself. Not that he could carry out everything with impunity here in Govan, Lorimer told himself, flicking down the list of emails that had come from the Deputy Chief Constable, Caroline Flint. There would always be more senior officers on whom he could rely but at this point in Lorimer's career he felt a freedom that he had not enjoyed in any other situation. With that freedom came responsibilities, of course, and those did weigh heavily upon his shoulders at times.

The current investigation into the slave trade, as Maggie had called it, was claiming the bulk of his time. Somewhere in his city a man allegedly named Max was operating a gang that might comprise illegal immigrants as well as local hired thugs, and he had several undercover officers searching out the likeliest places where they might be found. So far these men and women had little to report other than a few notions that there were some Asian workers in the back kitchens of restaurants in and around Glasgow whose immigration papers were less than satisfactory. He was feeling the pressure from the immigration authorities, of course, despite having explained the delicate situation of trying to trap the men they were after. Eventually, if the surveillance turned up the right people, there would be a large number of illegals detained and possibly returned to their homeland. The political climate was difficult in the world they lived in, liberal sympathies vying with the fear of terrorism. But most of the young men and women who would be leaving these shores had come seeking genuine work, in the belief that Scotland would be their ever-after paradise.

Then there were the others, often with criminal records back in their own countries, who had arrived to find a new place to exploit these hopeful young folk, robbing them of their freedom as well as their hopes and dreams.

A knock at the door disturbed his thoughts.

'Sir,' DCI Niall Cameron entered the room, 'just had a call from DC Newton,' he said, a small smile tugging at his mouth that Lorimer recognised as good news. Molly Newton was one of their best undercover operatives, an unremarkable-looking young woman in uniform but one who could alter her appearance chameleon-like for any situation. Right now she was trawling several employment agencies on the pretext of finding work as a manicurist.

'Right?' Lorimer clasped then unclasped his hands.

'She thinks she's found a place in Hope Street. Two floors up above a print workshop.'

'So it's what we suspected. Same scenario as in Aberdeen. They're hiding in plain sight for the most part.'

Cameron nodded his agreement. 'Molly reported that there are several girls that look as though they could do with a better night's sleep, if you get my understanding. And one of them is quite new, a Slovakian girl.'

'Any names?'

'Not yet. She's hoping that they take her on by this afternoon. Molly had an interview and they wanted to know if she needed digs or had her own accommodation. They also asked if she had a valid passport.'

Lorimer frowned. 'Sounds odd. Why would they do that?'

'Think DC Newton must have decided to fake an accent,' Cameron laughed. 'Making them think she was from Eastern Europe is my bet. You know what she's like.'

Lorimer nodded. Newton had specialised in languages before joining the police and was fluent in several.

'What's her cover name?'

'The passport she's using has the name Sasha Beltacha.'

'Okay, let's see if this is one of the places we should know about then we can take it from there. I guess we will be having a spate of new manicures amongst the female officers this weekend?'

Cameron grinned. 'Only those that are on the team, sir. Molly is very careful to keep a low profile.'

Lorimer's face was thoughtful once his DCI had left the room. Things had been moving very slowly since the Aberdeen raid but perhaps this was the beginning of the breakthrough that they needed. Peter Guilford was still languishing in the big new hospital not far from the police station but should he awaken and be fit to talk, Lorimer wanted to be at his bedside, asking questions about the mysterious Max and just how much Guilford had known about the use that had been made of his vehicles. Was the man a killer? Had he crossed that line by stabbing his wife to death? Or had he already spent time operating in that shadowy land where life was cheap and violence an everyday occurrence?

The first thing he noticed was the smell. A hint of disinfectant.

Peter blinked, feeling a gritty sensation under his eyelids, seeing the pale walls split between sunlight and shadow.

There was a rhythmic sound coming from his left and he turned his head a fraction to see a monitor with bright lights illuminated on its screen.

The perspex mask felt stiff across his face, and for a moment he was aware of just his own breath coming and going, his chest rising and falling.

If he lay very still then the figure in the chair might not notice that he was awake, her head partly obscured by a glossy magazine she was reading. The cover was familiar. Didn't Cynthia keep these sorts of magazines at the office?

Cynthia.

He blinked again, remembering how she had sounded the last time he had spoken to her before ... before what? Guilford felt a change in his chest. A feeling of tension, his breath coming in gasps.

'Nurse!'

He heard the cry as the woman dropped her magazine and then there was the sound of footsteps and a second person by his bedside, hands feeling for his wrist.

'It's all right, Mr Guilford, everything's all right,' the nurse soothed. 'Doctor will be here shortly.'

Then, as she came closer he saw her face; those clear grey

eyes looking down on him, a sweet smile as the nurse opened her mouth to speak.

'Welcome back to the world,' she said softly, then gave his arm a reassuring pat.

Rosie's working day ended at last as she shut down her computer and leaned back with a sigh. Two post-mortems dealt with and reports written up as well as the beginning of staff appraisals, something she was determined to carry out thoroughly before her maternity leave began. She licked her lips, wishing not for the first time that she could head home to a large glass of chilled Chablis, but the resulting heartburn wasn't worth it and besides, she valued her unborn child too much to take any risks with his health.

She smiled as one hand circled her belly fondly. A wee boy, she was sure of it. A glance at the clock on her office wall told her that she had time to cross the city and find Dr Jane Loughman. *Come at the end of my surgery*, the woman had texted back after Rosie had sent a text to ask when would be a suitable time to meet.

She flipped over the *in* notice to *out* as she left the building, a mandatory requirement for all pathologists to ensure that staff could call on them as and when an incident required their presence at a scene of crime. Happily she was not on call this evening but a really big emergency could negate any of that, as she knew from experience.

The journey across the city was slow, rush-hour traffic making her drive at a stop-start pace. At last she turned the Audi off the slip road and headed towards Pollokshields and the surgery where Jane Loughman was waiting for her.

The car park was half full as Rosie arrived and she hoped that the remaining cars were those for staff and not lingering patients.

However, she saw three people still sitting in the waiting room as she lumbered forwards to the reception desk.

'Yes, can I help you?' A tired-looking woman in her late fifties stood behind the Perspex screen, regarding Rosie with a sigh, eyes settling on the swelling beneath her maternity dress.

'I'm here to see Dr Loughman—' Rosie began.

'Name?'

'Rosie Fergusson.'

The woman frowned at her between glances at her computer screen.

'You aren't down for an appointment and antenatal isn't till next week.' The woman scowled.

'I'm not here as a patient,' Rosie explained and rummaged in her bag. 'Here,' she said, handing her card to the receptionist. '*Dr Rosie Fergusson.*'

'Oh.' The woman's face brightened as she read the pathologist's details. 'Sorry, I just thought . . . ' Her gaze fell onto Rosie's bump. 'Sorry. I'll see when she's finished, shall I?' Then she bustled off to leave Rosie standing, looking across at the remaining patients and hoping fervently that none of them were expecting to see Dorothy Guilford's GP.

The woman reappeared and smiled at Rosie. 'Just take a seat, please. She's with her last patient of the day. Says she shouldn't be long.'

Rosie sat down, aware of the glances directed her way. A pregnant lady aroused curiosity, perhaps even sympathy on this warm June day.

One by one two other patients were called, the third sitting determinedly behind his newspaper.

Then a door opened, an elderly woman emerged and immediately the man folded his paper, striding to her side.

'Okay, Mum?' he asked, and Rosie watched as the old lady smiled nervously and nodded. There was a story there, she thought, reading the patient's body language. Had she not wished her son to accompany her into the doctor's surgery, fearing some bad news?

'Dr Fergusson?' Jane Loughman was there, standing in the doorway. 'Won't you come in?' she asked. Rosie pulled herself up and lumbered slowly towards the surgery door.

'You look tired,' Dr Loughman began, glancing across the desk at Rosie. 'Glass of water?'

'Thanks. It's been a long day. I'll be glad to pack away my scalpels and take a few months off,' Rosie admitted.

As the doctor turned to fetch the water, Rosie bit her lip. How easily she had succumbed to the desire to spill all of her woes to this woman. It was a natural reaction, she supposed, to become like a patient, defer to the professional across the desk. But she was the GP's equal in this situation, something she must remember.

'Thanks,' she said, breathing a sigh of relief after taking a long draught of the cold water. 'Now, I must say I am curious to know what you wanted to talk to me about.'

'Well, Dorothy Guilford, of course,' Jane Loughman replied, a slight frown between her eyes as though Rosie might have forgotten.

'There was something you wanted me to know, though,' Rosie pressed. 'Something that wasn't in her medical notes, perhaps?'

Jane Loughman nodded. 'Yes,' she said. 'It's often hard to put some things into words when describing a patient. Dorothy was ...' She broke off and stared to one side, considering. 'She was a very strange woman,' she concluded at last. 'I'd only known

138

her for a few years and even I began to wonder about her mental capacity. She was a real hypochondriac. Always imagining that something was seriously wrong with her. And that was despite no family history of terrible diseases.'

'She was attention-seeking?'

'Definitely. Though there were the genuine injuries, of course.' Jane Loughman shook her head. 'Made me feel guilty whenever she had that broken arm or a badly bruised eye. But if you had been here to see her then . . .'

Rosie saw the woman's face flush. 'What? What is it?'

'Oh, it isn't something you can easily write down in medical notes. It was her attitude.' The doctor sighed again. 'It's hard to explain. She'd come in looking like the typical browbeaten wife, dowdily dressed, bent over as though she expected someone to give her a slap, and then there would be a sort of triumphant look in her eye, as though she revelled in being injured.'

'My husband's a psychologist. Professor Brightman. I think he would be able to say a good deal more about Mrs Guilford.'

'I'm sure he would,' Jane Loughman replied, raising her eyebrows slightly at the name. Solomon Brightman was well known in both academic and medical circles these days, his books on the vagaries of the human condition having attracted a good deal of media attention.

'So, you're really Mrs *Brightman*, then? We both kept our maiden names for professional reasons. I may be Dr Loughman to my patients but my married name is McDougall.'

'It helps to maintain one's identity as much as anything,' Rosie remarked.

'Well, I have more than one reason to keep the name I qualified with,' Jane began. 'You see, Dorothy Guilford was a patient here long before I joined the practice. It was my father-in-law who treated her for years, well before her marriage to Guilford. I wanted to keep a little distance from Dad. Never does to let folk think it is all nepotism.' She made a face and Rosie wondered if the doctor had in fact been brought into the practice because of that very relationship.

'Anyway, I thought you might want to talk to him, see a little more of the sort of person Dorothy really was.'

'Well, yes, I would. Is he local to the area?'

'He lives with us,' Jane told her. 'He's long retired, plays golf when his rheumatism allows and lectures us both on how the medical profession's gone to the dogs!' She gave a rueful smile then laughed. 'My husband is an orthopaedic surgeon,' she said. 'We listen to all of Dad's rants and tell ourselves that life really wasn't better in his day. But maybe it was,' she sighed. 'Ten minutes for each patient and home visits only in emergencies nowadays. I ask you!'

'So you think he would like to talk about Dorothy Guilford?'

Jane Loughman smiled. 'I know he would. He asked me to invite you for tea. Would you like to come back with me just now?'

Rosie thought for a moment. Abby was off for a swimming lesson with Solly and wouldn't be back for at least another hour.

'Okay. Let me text my husband to let him know when I'll be home.'

'Good. We're not far away,' Jane told her. 'Springkell Gardens. Just beside Maxwell Park.'

Rosie nodded. It was a short walk from there to St Andrew's Drive and the big house where she had first seen the body of Dorothy Guilford. As she rose to leave she was conscious of the weight of the baby within her and suddenly Jane Loughman was by her side, a friendly hand on her elbow, a concerned look on her face.

'Are you sure you're up to this, Dr Fergusson?'

Donald John McDougall was a man in his late seventies, a thatch of thick white hair above his tanned forehead and a pair of faded blue eyes that looked out shrewdly from beneath bristling brows. Though he leaned on a stick, the hands that clutched it were large and strong, more like the hands of a farmer or a craftsman despite being flecked with age-spots and thickened at the joints from rheumatism.

He gazed up at the sky, watching the mackerel clouds against a pale blue that betokened more fine weather in the days ahead. As an island boy he had learned early to tell the weather from the signs around him, though these days there was no sea to watch or faraway horizon on which to gaze. Several trips back to Islay each summer dealt with the yearning to see his home again but mostly Donald John was content to live here in the city with his son and daughter-in-law.

The old man turned at the sound of a car door closing and then he stood still, hearing a second slight noise. So, they had both arrived, then? Jane and that pathologist lass. Well, he'd be interested to see what she was like, this Dr Fergusson he'd heard so much about.

She was heavily pregnant, that was his initial impression, his years of medical experience making him look at her closely, noting the smudged mascara and the sloping shoulders that told him this woman was tired and ready for a decent rest. So why was she here? That very fact was interesting and told Donald John that the case of Dorothy Guilford's death was of more importance to the pathologist than any routine post-mortem.

*

'Dr Fergusson, please meet my father-in-law, Dr McDougall,' Jane said by way of introduction.

'Donald John, please.' The old man smiled at Rosie. 'My medical days are long gone,' he said, a twitch of a smile on his mouth as he drew a cynical look from his daughter-in-law. 'Please come into the conservatory. It's cooler than you might think at this time of day,' he continued, leading the way through the house.

'I'll stick the kettle on. Tea? Coffee?' Jane asked.

'Too early for a wee malt? Aye, well, a pot of tea please, m'dear,' Dr McDougall replied, chuckling at the face that Jane had pulled at the mention of whisky.

'Oh, just a glass of water for me,' Rosie said, stopping for a moment to glance through a doorway at a large open-plan kitchen in shades of grey and white. It was scrupulously tidy, a contrast to her own kitchen where Abby's toys were frequently strewn around and the fridge door covered in drawings from nursery. No kids, she thought to herself. Then: what a shame, as she remembered the pain of childlessness her friends the Lorimers had endured over the years.

'Here, take this chair, you'll find it gives you a decent support,' Donald John told Rosie, ushering her towards a deeply padded rocking chair with patchwork cushions arranged artfully on their points.

'Take off your shoes if you want to, lass,' he murmured, leaning forward and giving Rosie a sympathetic grin. 'Nobody will mind.' He cocked his head in the direction of the kitchen.

'Thanks,' Rosie replied, grateful to slip off her shoes and flex her toes.

'Now,' the old man began, 'you did the PM on Dorothy, that's right?'

'Correct. I was present at the initial scene and examined her body before it was taken to the mortuary,' Rosie replied. Then she hesitated.

'What?' A pair of intent blue eyes met hers. 'What did you find when you were in that house?'

'Her hands were grasping the weapon that killed her,' Rosie told him. 'And they'd stiffened up a lot.'

'Cadaveric spasm, you think?'

Rosie nodded. 'That was my conclusion at the time and still is. And I also concluded that there was a higher probability that the deceased had taken her own life than that a second person had been responsible for inflicting the fatal wound.' Rosie never took her eyes off the old doctor as she spoke, aware of his rapt attention.

'But the newspapers reported that Peter had been taken into custody as the police's prime suspect?'

'That's correct. And I'm not exactly flavour of the month with the SIO, I can tell you,' she said ruefully.

'So . . . ' Donald John paused for a moment then leaned back in his recliner chair as Jane appeared with a tray of drinks.

'Here you are.' Jane laid down a tea tray then handed Rosie a large glass of cool water. 'I'll just be through in the kitchen if you need me. Leave you two to talk,' she added with a nod to Rosie.

'She's a good lass,' Donald John murmured once Jane was out of earshot. 'Works far too hard, of course. They all do these days. But between you and me she'll be taking it easier in the months to come.' The creases around his eyes deepened as he waved a hand towards Rosie's bump.

'She's expecting?'

'Oh, I think she'll tell me any day now but I know the signs,' he chuckled.

Rosie took a long drink of water then heaved a sigh of relief. 'Hope she'll be fine,' she said at last.

'Och, Jane's younger than she looks,' the old man told her. 'She'll do all right when the time comes. Now, let's get back to Dorothy. Never wanted to be a mother, that one,' he muttered. 'What else can I tell you about her?'

His smile faded as he poured himself a cup of tea, adding milk and just one spoonful of sugar. 'Aye, Dorothy was always an odd one,' he began, taking a sip of the tea and cradling the cup against his chest. 'She was the younger daughter of elderly parents who kept a tight rein on their girls. Too damn tight, if you ask me. It was no surprise when Shirley went off the rails but Dorothy never showed any sign of rebellion. Which is strange for a teenager, don't you think?'

'I'll live to find that out,' Rosie said. 'Our daughter, Abby, starts school after the summer so we have a while to wait for that time in our lives.'

'Well, Dorothy was a quiet wee girl but the sort that folk sometimes describe as "sleekit". Good Scots word, that,' he added. 'Not like the "wee, sleekit, cow'rin tim'rous beastie" that Burns described, no, not that. She was sly, that one, watched you with these eyes of hers, solemn as you like but you always felt that she was plotting something, plotting and planning, waiting to catch you out.'

'Even as a child?'

'Especially as a child, I would say. I could tell you a lot about that family. Her parents believed in the "children should be seen and not heard" philosophy and Dorothy stuck to that, at least as far as outward appearances were concerned.'

'But not the elder sister?'

'Ah, no. Shirley was quite different. Loved bright clothes and dyeing her hair, going out with boys, all the things her parents found to be abhorrent.'

'They were strict for a reason?'

'Fervently religious.' Donald John nodded. 'Wouldn't allow the girls to wear make-up but Shirley defied them at every turn. It was little wonder they threw her out in the end.'

'They did that?' Rosie raised her eyebrows in surprise.

'Aye. Poor lass came to me weeping one day. Found she was pregnant by a lad who had no intention of leading her to the altar. Wee brat scarpered off to join the army, leaving poor Shirley to fend for herself.'

'And Dorothy? Didn't she help her sister?'

'Help?' Donald John gave a derisive snort. 'Dorothy revelled in her sister's misfortune. *She* was the good one, the favoured child who could do no wrong.'

'But she got married to Peter Guilford. Did the parents approve of that?'

Donald John gave her a solemn look as he sipped more tea. 'She married that one long after her parents died,' he said. 'Not while they were living. And,' he sighed heavily, 'it was rumoured that Guilford only married Dorothy for her money. She inherited everything; house, car-hire business, the lot. Shirley didn't get a penny piece.'

'Then the vehicle-hire business wasn't Guilford's but Dorothy's?'

The old man nodded. 'It came into her possession but he may have persuaded her to sign it over to him. Who knows? There were a lot of things that he forced her to do,' he muttered.

'I've seen her injuries,' Rosie admitted. 'There were several that might be construed as signs of abuse.'

'Well, maybe she was an abused wife and maybe she wasn't.

Dorothy never ever accused him of anything like that. We were all shocked when the husband was arrested for her murder, you know, though perhaps I shouldn't have been.'

'Oh?' Rosie looked up at the retired doctor, the shake of his head and the deep sigh both signs that he was feeling some sort of remorse.

'There was never any proof that he had hurt her and Peter Guilford would have given anyone the impression that he was a charming man.' Donald John paused, his eyebrows raised as though he now had some doubts about the matter. 'Let me give you some idea of what Dorothy was like as a patient *before* her marriage, eh?'

Rosie sat back, enjoying the comfort of the rocker as much as the old doctor's tale.

'Dorothy was an attention-seeker,' the old man went on. 'Though why she needed anybody else's attention when her parents doted on her is anyone's guess. She was adept at self-harming in such a way that you knew fine she'd done it but her reasons for the injuries were always just plausible enough to make us write them down in her case notes.'

'What sort of things did she do?'

Donald John regarded her steadily before answering.

'She'd cut herself,' he told her. 'And always with a kitchen knife to make out she'd been busy doing chores. Parents swallowed her stories every time but we knew better,' he said, his lips compressing into a grim line of disapproval. 'And after their death she was regularly at the medical centre, fussing about a wee mole on her breast or a dark vein on her leg, things that she had decided were sufficient to merit the attention of a consultant. Things that might require a surgeon's knife,' he added darkly. 'Then, more recently, in between the real injuries that, with

146

hindsight, *might* have been inflicted by the husband, she'd try to persuade me that she was suffering from some obscure disease or other.'

'Really wanting to draw attention to herself.'

'Oh, absolutely. I can just imagine her bent over her computer screen, looking up as many odd symptoms as she could find. We began to dread it every time she made an appointment,' he sighed. 'And I was jolly glad to hand her over to poor Jane on my retirement.'

'Dr Loughman said that Dorothy continued to be a regular at the surgery,' Rosie said.

'Aye, but things changed towards the end. Did she tell you that?'

'No,' Rosie replied.

'She would call me up here at home, usually in tears.' The old doctor shook his head. 'Maybe I should have taken her more seriously than I did,' he said.

'Why?'

Donald John McDougall heaved a sigh once more. 'She kept insisting that she was going to die.' He bit his lip and avoided Rosie's stare.

'You see, Dr Fergusson, Dorothy was convinced that Peter Guilford was going to kill her.'

CHAPTER TWENTY-TWO

Being dead might have been preferable after all, Peter decided as he glanced at the tall man sitting staring at him from the visitor's chair, a pair of keen blue eyes giving him the impression that this fellow could see right into his soul.

But then the man spoke and everything changed.

'We're so glad that you've come through this, Mr Guilford. The doctors tell me that you are still pretty weakened by these injuries but it looks like you'll make a full recovery.'

The voice was soothing, the words sounding genuinely sympathetic, and Peter felt himself relax a little under the crisp white sheet.

'My name's Lorimer,' the man told him. 'I'm with a team of police officers who are trying to find out who attacked you, sir,' he said gravely.

Peter blinked. 'Why . . . ?'

'Mr Guilford, Peter, we're looking at the attack as attempted murder. As a prisoner on remand you are seen to be quite innocent of any crime until a jury decides otherwise. We look for justice on your behalf, no matter what you stand accused of.'

Peter looked away from the blue stare. It was hard to believe that any outcome would see him a free man again, but perhaps this police officer could help him?

'I need to ask you about the attack, Peter.'

He looked back at the man. He was smartly dressed in a suit and tie, hair a little tousled perhaps and with a face that had seen a lot, Peter reckoned, examining the firm jaw and the deep cleft between those startling eyes. Here was someone who didn't suffer fools gladly. Even Peter was better off telling the truth: this guy would know a lie in a heartbeat.

'I don't know who he was,' Peter began. 'Didn't really see his face. He was a big fellow, broad ... ' He broke off, closing his eyes for a moment, the scene vivid once more. 'Had something sharp in his fist.' He took a deep breath, a sudden pain from the broken ribs making him bite his lip. 'Couldn't see what it was for the shower spray ... ' He clenched his fists as the image became clearer.

Then he opened his eyes and looked straight at Lorimer. 'Don't know who he was,' he repeated, 'but I know it wasn't another inmate.'

'A prison officer? You're saying that a prison officer attacked you?' Lorimer tried to keep the astonishment out of his voice.

Peter Guilford nodded then began to cough. 'Wore a uniform,' he added. 'Could it have been someone in disguise? I've had time to think about it since I woke up, you see.' He broke off, his voice becoming hoarse.

'Here, have some water.' Lorimer stood over him, a plastic cup in his hand, helping the man to take sips.

At last the policeman sat down again and Peter turned with a yawn. 'Sorry, still so tired ... '

'That's all right. We will have officers nearby at all times, Peter. If there's anything else you want to tell them I'll know about it, okay? Now, take some rest and I will be back another time to let you know how this matter progresses.'

Peter watched as the man gathered up a slim notecase and ran his fingers through his dark hair. He was even taller than he'd imagined. A good height for a goalkeeper, that random thought coming from nowhere.

Lorimer was about to leave when he turned back again and smiled.

'Oh, just one other thing. Do you happen to know a chap called Max? Might have done business with your company recently?'

Peter froze. His head felt heavy under the bandages but he wanted to shake it fiercely.

'No idea,' he croaked at last, receiving a long look from the detective.

'Oh, well, just a thought.' Lorimer smiled again then left the ward, leaving Peter Guilford pulling up the sheet to his chin as he began to shiver.

'He is probably quite correct,' Mr Ahasan, the consultant neurosurgeon told Lorimer. 'The injuries we saw were more than likely inflicted by someone wearing steel-capped boots. We even had an imprint on his ribcage,' the man said, raising his dark eyebrows to underline his point. 'I've seen things like that before in the aftermath of a fight. Sometimes the patient doesn't survive a brutal kicking like that. Our man was a little luckier, however.'

Lorimer nodded. After almost two weeks in a coma, nobody had expected the man to pull through. He had taken steps to keep everything about the prison attack from the press whilst the police had been interviewing every single inmate in an effort to establish a link between Guilford and any of the prisoners in

Barlinnie. The neurosurgical team had kept them pretty much at bay until Guilford had recovered sufficiently to talk to the police but now it seemed as if much of the man hours spent interviewing these men had been in vain.

'You cannot and must not breathe a word of this to anyone,' Lorimer warned the consultant. 'I don't want the papers getting hold of the story. It could jeopardise not just the inquiry into the attack but quite a lot more.'

'*We* also have patient confidentiality to think of,' Ahasan told him with a steely smile. 'You can be assured that nothing we have discussed will venture outside this room, Superintendent Lorimer.'

Barlinnie Prison was generally safe and secure although there had been incidents when inmates had managed to access mobile phones and spread their malice out into the world again. The very suggestion of Peter Guilford's attacker being a prison officer would send shudders through the entire prison service.

So it was with a heavy heart that Lorimer drove up to the prison and parked in front of the entrance.

The usual security routine was undertaken, no exception made for a senior police officer of his rank. All mobiles had to be left with the officers behind the safety screens or not brought into the prison at all, identities checked at every visit. Lorimer's warrant card sufficed to identify him and a security badge was thrust through the grille then he made his way through the airport-style body scanner and was met by a prison officer at the foot of the stairs.

'Detective Superintendent. Welcome. The governor is waiting for you, sir. Another smashing day, eh? What a month we're having.' The prison officer grinned as they made their way up the flights of stairs that led to McSherry's office.

151

This man was burly, quite tall, and Lorimer found himself scrutinising the fellow. Could this be Guilford's attacker? Was every officer fitting the prisoner's description going to be a possible suspect?

'Yes, it's been grand, so far,' he answered politely, his eyes lifting as another prison officer stepped swiftly down past them, bunches of keys dangling from his belt. Another big man: another possible suspect? Lorimer stifled a sigh as he was led along the corridor to the governor's office.

It was mercifully cool inside as McSherry stood up to greet him, the man's shirtsleeves rolled up past his elbow, a fan whirring gently in one corner.

'Lorimer, what news?' McSherry was on his feet and grasping Lorimer's hand.

'Well, Guilford appears to be making a good recovery so far,' Lorimer told him, sitting down in the chair that the governor indicated next to his desk. 'He'll be in that ward for a while longer, however, not just because his condition is pretty fragile but the security situation is better if he remains there meantime.'

'And? Was he able to remember anything that happened?' McSherry leaned forwards close enough for the detective superintendent to see beads of sweat on the man's brow. Was it a sign of anxiety? Or simply the heat of this summer's day?

'Yes, he can,' Lorimer began, watching the other man's expression. 'His head injury was particularly appalling. Lesions to the brain that were thought to have triggered that peculiar coma he drifted in and out of.' He frowned. 'But no permanent brain damage done as far as the neurosurgeon can see. And yes, he recalled the attack.'

McSherry sat back. 'You're going to tell me something I won't like,' he said suddenly. 'I can see it in your face.'

152

'It wasn't an inmate that attacked Guilford,' Lorimer told him. 'The man he described was more than likely one of your prison officers.'

McSherry shook his head, his jaw working silently. 'No, not possible. I don't believe it!' he exclaimed. 'That wee scrote is lying through his teeth! Must be another prisoner! He's just trying to make trouble for us!'

'I don't think so,' Lorimer said slowly. 'I've spoken to his consultant and he agrees that the assailant was someone wearing heavy steel-capped shoes or boots. And that isn't possible if it was a prisoner, is it?'

McSherry slumped back in his chair, wiping his brow with the back of his hand. 'What do we do now? Can he identify the man?'

'Possibly. Best thing to do is to show him mugshots of every one of your officers. See if he recognises his assailant.'

'I can't believe this is happening,' McSherry said, shaking his head again. 'Every one of these men is vetted scrupulously. Are you sure he isn't making it all up?' He looked appealingly at Lorimer then sighed. 'No? Dear Christ, what a hell of a mess!'

'Don't say a word about this to anyone else,' Lorimer warned him. 'There could be far bigger things at stake than just finding out who attacked Peter Guilford.'

McSherry gave him a curious look and nodded. 'You're heading up the MIT now,' he said slowly. 'Of course. So it's something major going on, right? And Guilford is just a small part of that?'

Lorimer raised his eyebrows slightly and smiled knowingly. No more needed to be said right now and McSherry would just have to wait until such times as he could fill him in with the whole story.

CHAPTER TWENTY-THREE

'Mrs Brightman?' a cheerful female voice called out as Rosie took the first step onto the staircase that led to their top-floor flat.

Turning, Rosie saw a woman wearing a pretty flowered dress and carrying a large tote bag over her shoulders.

'Oh, it is you! So glad I caught you,' the woman gushed.

'Sorry.' Rosie frowned, stepping down and walking stiffly towards the stranger standing in the reception hall. 'Do I know you?'

'Sheila Barnard.' The woman smiled widely, showing perfect white teeth against a slick of bright crimson lipstick. 'I'm features writer for the *Gazette*,' she explained. 'I've been asked to do a little story about you.'

Rosie took a step back. This was odd, surely? Coming into a person's home without so much as a telephone call or an email.

'I don't think there's been any advance notice from your paper . . . ' Rosie began.

'Oh, we just had to run with what we were given.' The woman grinned. 'You know, see if it was really true or not.' She gave Rosie a knowing look.

'What on earth are you talking about?'

'Oh, the Guilford murder, of course. Is it true that you are claiming she committed suicide? Just like that case back in 2001? You must remember that?' The woman edged forwards and this time Rosie noticed the slim mobile clutched in the woman's palm. She was actually recording this conversation!

'I have nothing to say while the case is ongoing,' Rosie replied. She turned sharply away, feeling a sensation of giddiness as she climbed the stairs once more, clutching at the banister for support.

'I'll just print that then, shall I? Pathologist refuses to revisit botched case?'

Rosie clenched her teeth, a surge of anger coursing through her. Then, a movement within reminded her that she had more to consider than the nasty attempts of the press to discredit her. She continued to climb the stairs, heart thumping. As she rounded the corner, the sound of the main door closing with its customary bang made her stop and sigh with relief.

'Here, what on earth?' Solly took his wife's arm and led her through to the airy lounge where the linen curtains were blowing in the breeze from the open window. 'You look terrible. What's happened?' he asked as Rosie pressed her face against his shoulder and began to sob.

Bit by bit the story emerged of the stranger from the *Gazette* and the way she had caught Rosie off guard.

'She must have followed me in,' Rosie wept. 'Th-thought she was so clever . . . addressing me as Mrs Brightman!'

'Here.' Solly handed her a clean white handkerchief and watched as she blew her nose. 'Look, sorry to say this, but I think it was only a matter of time before something like this happened. That SIO has no love for you, my dear.'

'You think Alan McCauley leaked information to the *Gazette*?' Rosie's mouth fell open in astonishment.

'It's possible,' he sighed. 'He'll feel threatened by your refusal to go along with his . . . ' he paused for a moment, trying to pick the right words, 'interpretation of the facts,' he said at last. 'Come on, darling, sit down and I'll make you some tea. Camomile. No caffeine,' he added with a mock stern expression.

Rosie let herself be led to the chair with its plumped up cushions that Abby had taken to calling 'Mummy's chair'. She slumped down, head still ringing with the woman's words. How could she! Rosie raged. Then, feeling another flutter inside, she closed her eyes and began to take a few deep breaths.

Today was supposed to have been a day off. The appointment at her antenatal clinic had been fun, chatting with the other expectant mums and enjoying the frisson of excitement that always came from realising their babies were that much closer to being born. How did that Bradford woman know she was going to be at home? Had someone been following her? The thought sent shivers down her spine.

But then the image of the woman's body and the stiffened fingers clutching the Laguiole knife rose unbidden to the surface of her mind. She would be under oath one of these days to tell the truth, the whole truth and nothing but the truth and by golly she was going to have her say, no matter how much the press would try to discredit her.

'Here, drink this up,' Solly said gently, handing her a porcelain mug with violets printed on it, a Valentine gift from their early courting days.

She smiled up at him, seeing the concern in those deep brown eyes, their long lashes a feature inherited by their little daughter. 'I'll be all right. It was just a fright, I suppose . . . '

'She had absolutely no right to be in this building,' Solly remarked, his tone serious. 'I think a word in the right quarters ...' He tailed off thoughtfully.

'You want to tell Lorimer?' Rosie looked up, eyes widening.

Solly knelt down beside her and began to stroke the wayward curls back from his wife's face. 'Actually, I was thinking of someone nearer home,' he murmured. 'Kirsty.'

A day off at last! Kirsty strolled hand in hand with James through Kelvingrove Park, watching the mums wheeling baby buggies along the paths. And not only mums but a few dads too, stopping with toddlers to point out the waterfowl on the pond. And there, with a group of small folk gathered beside him, was the Bird Man, hands outstretched as finches fluttered down to peck at the grain.

Kirsty watched intently as the thin man spilled more seeds into the cupped palms of the children and saw them copy his silent stance. Gradually the birds returned and she smiled, hearing the exclamations of glee as they landed on a child's hand. Squirrels hopped at a safe distance, ready to pounce on any of the spilled grain, and wood pigeons too, cooing as they waddled closer to the group, unafraid of the many pairs of feet.

She felt her hand being squeezed and looked up at James with a grin.

'Us, one day?' he murmured and she nodded, conscious of the unfamiliar diamond solitaire on her left hand. *A family heirloom*, he'd murmured that morning as he'd slipped it on her finger. *Just till I can afford something better.* But it had turned out to be a perfect fit. She sighed happily. It was good right now to know how much she wanted a future with this man, someone to share her dreams with; dreams that included children of their own, something they talked about in the wee small hours.

Then, as they continued to stroll along towards the bridge that spanned the River Kelvin, Kirsty felt the vibration from her mobile phone.

James raised his eyebrows and mouthed 'Work?' But she shook her head.

'Hi, Solly. Yes, we're just in the park right now, as it happens.'

She turned to look up towards the terrace of houses that sat overlooking the park, eyes fixed on a top flat window. There was something in the psychologist's voice that made her listen carefully. 'Of course we can. Not doing anything special? Are we?' She turned to James who shook his head and shrugged. 'Fine, be with you in a few minutes. Have the kettle on!'

'Invitation to tea?' James asked, turning back with her and clasping her hand once more.

'Aye.' Kirsty frowned. 'But I think it's more than that. Solly sounded . . . I don't know, kind of worried.'

She'd been in two minds about sharing the information that Dr McDougall had given her but now that James and Kirsty were about to arrive, Rosie made up her mind. There were things that still bothered her about this case and perhaps DC Kirsty Wilson was the very person to do a little bit of digging on her behalf.

'Where's my favourite girl?' James asked as they breezed into the flat.

'At a little friend's birthday party,' Solly told them as they entered the lounge. 'All afternoon. She'll be dog-tired by the time she comes home, I bet. An early night tonight for Miss Abigail Brightman!' He grinned.

'Come on in,' Rosie called from her customary place by the bay window. 'I was watching you cross the park. What a heavenly day!'

'Aye,' Kirsty agreed. 'Nice to have a bit of fresh air instead of being stuck in Helen Street or the Queen Elizabeth.'

'He's woken up, I heard,' Rosie remarked. 'Any further news?'

Kirsty bit her lip, not sure just how much to divulge. The rumours that had reached CID claimed to involve a prison officer but that was all she knew and they'd been warned not to talk about it to any enquiring journalists.

'The press . . . ' she began.

'Don't talk to me about the papers!' Rosie snapped. Then she explained about the visit from the *Gazette*'s features writer.

'That's shocking,' James growled. 'Wish I'd been there. I'd have marched her off the premises double quick!'

'You think she'd been following you?' Kirsty asked.

'No way of telling but how else would she have known where I'd be at that particular time? Unless she'd been sitting in a car waiting for me to appear? Anyway, there's a lot more I want to talk about besides this nasty stuff,' Rosie said, brushing biscuit crumbs off her smock top and into her hand.

'Okay, I'm listening,' Kirsty told her, settling down on the rug by Rosie's side.

'It's about Dorothy Guilford,' Rosie began. 'I think you ought to know a bit more about her medical background. I visited her old GP, and he said there was a lot he could tell me about that family, and he did, especially about Dorothy.' And she went on to relate the visit to Dr McDougall. 'So, there you have it. "Sleekit", he called her. An interesting choice of word.'

'That does chime with another person's viewpoint,' Kirsty said slowly. 'Cynthia Drollinger, Guilford's secretary said that

Dorothy had a history of self-harming. And she mentioned the sister.'

'Did she say anything about where this sister is now? Shirley?'

Kirsty shook her head. 'But I could find out,' she offered. 'DI McCauley hasn't seen fit to instruct a visit to her. Thinks it's all done and dusted since the husband's arrest, I guess. But from what you tell me this sister is someone else who had no reason to love Dorothy Guilford.'

Even as she spoke, Kirsty could feel the pathologist's eyes on her. Rosie was so determined that the woman had taken her own life. But, what if that wasn't true? What if someone else had plunged that steak knife into the woman's heart? Someone with a long-standing grudge, perhaps?

'Would you do a little digging for me, Kirsty? Find out what you can?'

'Even if I come up with answers you don't want to hear?' Kirsty rejoined.

Rosie looked at her young friend and nodded. 'Even then. If I'm mistaken then I'm mistaken. It's the truth I'm after. I just feel there are too many things wrong about this death.'

It was only fair, Solly reasoned, that he too did some digging of his own. Dorothy Guilford's was an interesting personality to profile and no mistake, he thought, gazing out over the faded blue of the afternoon sky. From an early age she had been the favoured child, the spoiled one. But was that right? As the daughter of fervently religious parents, had she been denied the sorts of things she actually craved? Nice clothes, make-up and cheap jewellery, stuff that seemed part of the trappings during a rite of passage for young teenage girls. Shirley, now, she had had the gall to step across the line drawn by these parents but

Dorothy had succumbed to their rules and regulations. Was there an innate fearfulness in the girl's character that had come with her into womanhood? Had she been programmed to obey, like the children from a bygone era? That was one thing to consider but the self-harming was quite another. Did she crave attention so badly? Probably, was his honest answer and he felt a twinge of pity for the dead woman who had cut herself repeatedly since childhood. Nobody would ever know the whole truth but Solly could imagine a scenario where the little girl had been in hospital and shown kindness from the nursing staff there, given treats perhaps that had been denied at home. Had she learned that sort of behaviour might result in the petting she undoubtedly craved? And, was her gloating over her sister's misfortune, the status conferred on her of 'the good daughter', enough to satisfy her for a time?

And yet, if that was so, she would have wanted the satisfaction, the glow that came from being fussed over after yet another accident. Had that plunging knife been a cry for yet more attention that had gone disastrously wrong?

Why had she killed herself? That was the question he came back to again and again. An accident seemed unlikely on the face of it; pills by her bedside would have given her that last deep sleep drifting into oblivion had she really wanted to end it all with less pain and less drama.

Solly sat up suddenly. That was a word that agreed with the profile he had in his mind. She'd been a lover of seeking attention, creating little dramas . . . had she any reason to have made this her final exit? His head spun with the possibilities. Dorothy Guilford had claimed that her husband was trying to kill her. Had she, in a mood of revenge, sought to rob him of that desire?

He sighed. It was all so nebulous. If Rosie was correct in her assessment of the cause of death, no one would ever really know the answer to such questions, would they? For only the dead woman could have revealed what was in her mind at the time when the knife entered her heart, cutting off her breath for ever.

CHAPTER TWENTY-FOUR

It was the way she'd always looked at her, a determined stare in those large eyes, mouth closed but with the feeling that next time she spoke it would be to sneer or put her down in the clever way that Dorothy had with words. *Sticks and stones may break my bones*, she'd chant, knowing fine well that it was Shirley who felt the sting from her taunts. The photo was an old one, no clues to tell the story of the woman Dorothy Guilford had become in the end.

Shirley put down the newspaper with a slap. It was curled at the edges now but she had been unable to bin it with the other papers. Was she gloating, perhaps? The thought came into Shirley's mind as she reached for the pack of cigarettes, regarding her chubby hands with disgust. Dorothy had always had nice hands, stretching them out to blow on her perfectly curved fingernails as she carefully painted them in shades of palest pink. Never the brassy reds and magentas that other teenagers their age had favoured, the woman thought, curling her own bitten nails out of sight. No, Dorothy always had to be the little lady, that mouse-brown hair tucked behind her ears, school uniform tidy and smart, *her* waistband never turned over and over again to create a miniskirt like Shirley's. *A parent's pride and joy*, she'd overheard their father telling someone as he'd drawn the younger daughter to his side, Dorothy smirking at Shirley before looking up at Dad with those big cow's eyes. She could have stabbed a knife into the little bitch right there and then! Shirley ground her teeth in a rage, the memory as clear as though it were yesterday.

Then she let the newspaper fall with a cry. It was stupid to dwell on such things. Besides, now that she was dead why should Dorothy still be troubling her thoughts?

The doorbell ringing made her heave herself out of the chair and waddle down the hallway, cursing whoever was on the other side of the door. If it was the man to read the electric meter she'd have to let him in, but the last bill had only just been paid.

Through the spyhole Shirley could see a smartly dressed young woman. She frowned then set the chain and opened the door so that she could see the person to decide if it were friend or foe.

'Mrs Finnegan? I'm Detective Constable Wilson,' the woman told her, holding up her warrant card so that Shirley could see it clearly.

'Is this about Dorothy?'

'Yes,' the police officer replied. 'I'd like to talk to you about your late sister.' She paused, regarding Shirley with the sort of expression that people reserved for addressing the bereaved. 'I'm sure Family Liaison have been to visit but I wanted to ask you some questions. May I come in?'

'S'pose so,' Shirley mumbled, taking off the chain and turning her back on the detective so that this DC Wilson had to close the door after them. 'In here, place is a mess. Find a seat if you can.' She nodded towards a chair that had a pile of folded towels waiting to be put away. 'The lawyer called to tell me all about it.' She drew a hand across her nose and sniffed. 'Peter finally had enough of her, then?' She hadn't said anything like that to the sympathetic officers who'd doorstepped her after Frank Dawson's telephone call. It had been hard to act like the grieving sister then and she wasn't about to keep up the act any longer.

The detective placed the pile of towels to one side, sat down then looked at her sharply. 'Did you know he was attacked in prison?'

'Saw it on the telly, didn't I?' Shirley shrugged, her massive shoulders straining the washed out white top that was at least a size too small for her now. The woman sitting opposite was one of those skinny types, probably went to the gym five times a week and lived on rabbit food, Shirley told herself, a tinge of envy creeping into her mind as she regarded the detective's shapely legs and fine cheekbones. There was an engagement ring on her finger too, a promise of good things to come, no doubt. Shirley ground her teeth, disliking the detective already.

'I'd like to ask you about your sister, Dorothy Guilford. Did you see one another regularly?' the young woman asked.

Shirley gave a mirthless laugh. 'See her? Not on your nelly! We weren't on social terms, her and me,' she said. 'Hadn't been for years.'

'When was the last time you saw Dorothy?'

Shirley's eyes fell unbidden to the fallen newspaper. She'd looked at that monochrome photo hundreds of times now, memorising the plain features, the superior expression in those eyes. 'Can't remember,' she said at last. 'Why? Is it important?'

DC Wilson regarded her thoughtfully. 'The house in St Andrew's Drive, where Dorothy and Peter lived, that was your family home, wasn't it?'

'Ye-es,' Shirley drawled, wondering what the point of this question could be.

The woman smiled then, a rather coy smile, Shirley thought, then asked, 'I don't suppose you happen to have a key for your old home, Mrs Finnegan?'

Shirley stared at her for a moment. 'Why?' she blustered. 'Why should you think I had a key for that place?'

'Oh, it was the cleaning woman, Mrs Daly, who gave me that idea,' Wilson replied cheerfully.

'Well, suppose I do?' Shirley answered defiantly. 'What about it?'

'The door keys are still the same ones you had when you were living there as a family,' the detective said. It was a statement not a question so Shirley simply nodded.

Then the woman's face changed and became more solemn, making Shirley fidget in her chair.

'Where were you on the night of Dorothy Guilford's death, Mrs Finnegan?'

Kirsty waited in the filthy living room, listening to the unmistakable sounds of retching that came from the bathroom. Shirley Finnegan had rushed out of the room as fast as her fat legs could carry her and was now being thoroughly sick. What on earth had prompted that? Kirsty's head was spinning with possible answers. Was she guilty of something that had made her nauseous? Had she been instrumental in the death of her own sister? No sooner had Kirsty asked where Shirley had been on the night of her sister's death than the woman's face changed to a ghastly white and she had put a hand to her mouth, ready to throw up.

Up until now the conversation had been fairly predictable but the woman's reaction was completely unexpected.

Kirsty stood in the hallway. 'Are you all right? Mrs Finnegan?'

There was no reply, just the sound of a toilet flushing and a tap being run in the bathroom sink.

A few minutes later Shirley Finnegan crept out, a threadbare towel in one hand, mopping at her mouth and eyes.

'Okay? Can I get you a glass of water?' Kirsty asked, anxious now that there might be some repercussions for herself. Nobody had authorised a visit to this woman's home and there was the possibility that Dorothy's sister could make a complaint. What would McCauley say if he found out she'd been moonlighting for Rosie Fergusson?

'I'm all right,' Shirley said, walking slowly past Kirsty, not brushing off the younger woman's hand as she as guided back into her chair. 'Got a problem. Stomach acts up. Just happens without any warning.'

'I'm sorry,' Kirsty replied. 'Do you need anything? Tablets? A cup of tea?'

Shirley Finnegan shook her head and Kirsty was astonished to see tears in the woman's eyes.

'It was Dorothy's fault,' Shirley began. 'All of this.' She swept a hand around to indicate the untidy room with its chipped furniture and flyblown windows. 'She got everything, didn't she?'

Kirsty heard the bitterness in Shirley's voice.

'Threw me out on my ear. Didn't even take me back when I'd had the kid, did they? Then she inherited the lot!'

Kirsty watched as Shirley fumbled in her skirt pocket and pulled out a pack of chewing gum then stuffed several pieces into her mouth.

'Takes away the bad taste,' Shirley sniggered. 'That's what I was to them, you know, a bad taste in their mouths. Didn't want anyone to know about their *other* daughter. It was all Dorothy this

167

and Dorothy that and then she ends up owning the house, the business then gets a husband into the bargain.'

'But you . . . ?'

'Oh, aye, I did get married. Finnegan was a decent enough bloke at first but kept bad company. I think you know what I mean, *officer*?' The final word was spoken as a sneer. 'In and out of jail, on benefits. Threw him out eventually, didn't I? Spending all our money on booze and the dogs.'

Kirsty glanced around, expecting to see a couple of small animals, but the woman threw her a withering look. '*Greyhounds.* Gambled it all away at the dog track and left me with nothing for the rent.'

Not all Dorothy Guilford's fault, then? Circumstances afterwards had dictated the ruined face and figure of Shirley Finnegan. But there was no denying that she continued to blame her younger sister for the way her own life had turned out. And, thought Kirsty, she still hadn't answered her question.

'Sorry to harp on about it, Mrs Finnegan, but we just need to know the facts so we can eliminate anybody that might have had access to the house in St Andrew's Drive. So, where were you that night?'

Shirley Finnegan looked straight at Kirsty without blinking. 'Here,' she said. 'On my tod. With nothing except the telly for company.' She folded her arms defiantly across her heaving bosoms. 'So?' she added, cocking her head to one side as though to ask *what are you going to do about that?*

'Anyone able to verify this?' Kirsty asked, knowing that the question was hopeless.

'Nope,' Shirley retorted. 'Why are you asking? Do you think I hated her enough to stick a knife into her guts?'

Kirsty blanched at the venom in the woman's tone.

Shirley unfolded her arms and leaned forward. 'I hated her enough to do that, Detective Constable, oh, yes I did. But someone else got there before me!'

Kirsty heaved a sigh as she turned the ignition key and glanced automatically in her rear-view mirror. Something would have had to prompt an act of murder that particular night. After all, hadn't she simmered with resentment for decades without attacking her sister?

Suddenly she wished that William Lorimer was here instead of a mere detective constable. He'd have known what to say, used his keen blue eyes to his advantage and maybe even found clues in that ramshackle flat. She sighed again and for a moment the notion of escaping to Chicago actually seemed a most attractive option.

As the car drove off, Shirley twitched back the grey net curtain that kept any nosy neighbours from peering into her ground-floor flat. Thank God it hadn't been a patrol car and a uniformed cop! But just the one officer – wasn't that a bit strange? Didn't they always work in pairs like those Family Liaison ones? Shirley Finnegan watched as the car disappeared around a bend then she picked up her mobile phone and tapped in a number that she knew off by heart. The call rang out, then, hearing a familiar voice, she sank back into her armchair with a sigh of relief.

'It's me,' she said. 'I need to talk to you. Can you come round here now?'

CHAPTER TWENTY-FIVE

Peter was propped up on a bank of pillows, the man by his side watching intently as he took up a pair of spectacles in one trembling hand.

The sheaf of papers had photographs of every single one of the prison officers in HMP Barlinnie. Each page held six different faces, mugshots really.

Detective Superintendent Lorimer frowned. He'd have preferred the images to be printed on single sheets but McSherry had sent them over like this, probably to save himself time if they'd simply been pulled from office files. He'd glanced through them, noting the scowls and wondering if these men had been hand-picked for their intimidating looks. Maybe he was being unfair; weren't they all supposed to have unsmiling passport pictures these days? Perhaps it was the same in an institution like a prison.

Give him his due, Guilford was looking carefully at each sheet, his eyes examining the faces. It would take just one flicker of recognition, Lorimer knew from experience. Then they could apprehend the prison officer who had carried out this heinous attack.

One by one, the pages were turned over and laid on the

counterpane, the detective never taking his blue gaze from the patient for a single moment.

Sometimes Guilford stared a little longer at one sheet of photographs then gave a small shake of his head before discarding yet another page.

The bundle was almost spent, Lorimer gritting his teeth in frustration, when Guilford's manner changed.

He could see the man's pupils dilate, the jaw tighten as he focused on one particular face.

Gotcha! Lorimer thought triumphantly.

But then, Guilford laid that page aside too, though the fingers that resumed their search were trembling.

The final page was scrutinised then Guilford sat back on the pillows, the strain on his face easy for anyone to see.

'Who was it?'

Guilford closed his eyes and did not reply.

'Peter, I saw how you reacted!' Lorimer pulled the pages towards him, extracting the last but one and holding it up in front of the man.

'Look at it!' he commanded.

Guilford's eyes opened briefly to glance at the sheet of faces then he looked away and shook his head.

'Nobody I can recognise,' he said at last.

But Lorimer knew a lie when he heard one.

'Peter,' he continued, 'we need to find this man. He'll never harm you again, you have my word for that!'

Guilford looked at him for a moment, a faint smile playing about his lips. 'McSherry's deputy came in to see me this morning,' he said. 'I won't be going back to Barlinnie.'

Lorimer frowned. 'But, once you're well enough you must be returned to custody,' he told the man.

Guilford's smile broadened a little. 'Aye, but they're sending me to Low Moss, aren't they?'

It had not been a complete waste of time, Lorimer told himself as he sat in the Lexus outside in the hospital car park. At least he had one page of faces that had produced a reaction from Guilford. One of those six faces belonged to the officer who had carried out that attack, he was sure. He just needed to find out which one.

Damn McSherry! If Guilford had suspected that he'd be returning to Barlinnie surely he would have revealed the identity of his attacker? But why hide it? The prison officer was someone that Guilford knew, Lorimer told himself; someone close enough to instil fear into the man. For that was the expression that Lorimer had seen flickering over Peter Guilford's face.

He looked at the faces on the sheet once again, reading the names below each shot. *Fairley, Grimshaw, McTaggart, Thomson, Raynor, Whitehead.* It had to be one of those men. He drew out of the car park, grim faced, and turned in the direction of the M8, already calculating how long it would take to arrive at Barlinnie.

'I'm sorry you didn't find him more cooperative, Superintendent,' McSherry said, his tone clipped, no offer on this occasion of tea or coffee for his unexpected visitor.

'I'm telling you, it was one of these men!' Lorimer insisted, slapping the page with the back of his hand.

'But you haven't been given a positive identification, have you?' McSherry's eyes were steely.

'I saw his face. That was enough for me.'

'Wouldn't stand up in a court of law, though, would it?'

The two men glared at one another and Lorimer knew a rare moment of defeat. The governor was bent on protecting his

172

officers. At all costs? Perhaps he was protecting a lot more than that though. The reputation of his prison mattered since every slur against it would rebound on McSherry himself.

He glanced down at the sheet still in his hand.

'I'm not finished with this,' he told the governor. 'If you aren't prepared to give me detailed information about each of these six men then I will be asking the Crown Office for a warrant to search their homes.'

CHAPTER TWENTY-SIX

The sunshine that had warmed the city for several balmy weeks disappeared behind a skein of clouds, its rays beaming down on the horizon like a benison from an unseen deity. Maggie Lorimer looked up at the sky and smiled, clasping a hand to her chest. It was more than she could have wished for. *An exceptional way of storytelling*, this particular editor had written to her agent; *more please*!

And she would write more, her little ghost taking on a sense of reality in Maggie Lorimer's imagination. *They want to publish, I think*, her agent had written. *Just a matter of finalising the offer. Will be in touch soon. Might even come to a bidding war!*

Maggie thought of the agent's email once again, scarcely able to believe the words. Little Gibby might appear on the bookshelves of her local library one day, she thought, eyes sparkling. Her wee ghost boy! Only Rosie had been taken into her confidence; even her best friend at school, Sandie, was not aware of the English teacher's project. And, once a publisher had been found, a contract drawn up and signed, she would present Bill with her story as a fait accompli.

The evening was still and Maggie watched as clouds of tiny

flies hovered above the table in the garden where she sat, her glass of white wine half finished. A salad was already prepared and waiting in the fridge, some cold chicken and home-made coleslaw ready for their meal once Bill was home. Chancer strolled out and stretched then flopped onto the warm slabs of the patio. Somewhere in the shrubbery a blackbird called its warning but the old cat did not respond, happy to lie and doze, his hunting days pretty much at an end.

Maggie smiled fondly at her pet. They had no real idea of how old Chancer might be since he had appeared one day as a stray, wandering into their lives and deciding in the way of cats that this was his home. Their next-door neighbours were kind enough to feed him whenever holidays took the Lorimers away, Maggie reciprocating by looking after their aquarium full of tropical fish.

Perhaps she could write a different series of stories, Maggie pondered. Tales about cats, using Chancer as the main character? As if he had read her thoughts, the big cat looked up and mewed before flopping back down then rolling this way and that. Maggie bent to tickle the fur on his tummy, trying to think what life was like for the cat, imagining the world from his perspective. Wasn't that what she had been teaching her seniors today? Keats' 'Ode to a Nightingale' demanded a sort of understanding of how the poet empathised with the bird. Should she be trying to do the same with Chancer the cat?

Maggie raised her eyebrows speculatively. *Chancer the Cat.* The alliterative effect pleased her. After all, he had been a cat given a second chance, hadn't he? she thought, a story forming in her mind already.

'Hi, I'm home!'

Maggie shook herself out of her reverie in time to stuff the agent's printed email into her skirt pocket and turned to see her husband coming through the open kitchen door.

'Hey, beautiful,' he murmured, bending to kiss her neck. 'Any of that left for a poor, hard-working cop?' he asked, glancing towards her wine glass.

'In the fridge,' Maggie replied sleepily. 'Bring it out, eh? Wouldn't mind a refill and it's far too nice to go back indoors just yet.'

Lorimer nodded. 'Aye,' he replied, looking up at the sky, the first vestiges of pink tingeing the slow-moving clouds. 'Think it'll be a cracker of a sunset.'

Maggie smiled and stretched. The sun reappeared from the drift of apricot-coloured clouds and she turned her face up, relishing the warmth.

It was good to have another warm evening in this crowded city, people spilling out onto the pedestrian areas where tables and chairs made for al fresco drinking. Music was everywhere, from the lone singer whose songs had made her stop and listen, his guitar playing better than she had expected from a street musician, to the rhythmic beat of dance music that floated from an open window high above the streets, and the taped sounds coming from inside the nearby restaurants. Juliana hesitated, the smells of grilled meats wafting from the open doorway. She was hungry but didn't wish to draw attention to herself by stumbling over the words needed to order a meal, the thought of actually sitting alone at a table more than she could bear.

For weeks she had been given food and clothing by the men who had kept her in that apartment, no need to think about where her next meal was coming from. But now Juliana Ferenc had learned to keep to the takeaways, her accent never once commented upon as she mumbled her order. Her feet took her along a now familiar street towards the big railway terminal and the chip shop where so many young folk hung around. The smell of greasy food hit her as she crossed the road but Juliana's eyes were everywhere, on the people streaming past, the youths shouting on the pavement, the *Big Issue* seller crouched against the wall.

She passed a Romany woman sitting on the street, headscarf on, hands reaching upwards, the obsequious expression in those dark eyes striking her heart. The girl wanted to stop, fling a few coins into the woman's plastic cup, but she dared not for fear that someone else might be watching. Sometimes those women were part of a bigger operation, Juliana guessed, their protectors hovering around to lift any money gathered and later the women themselves, spiriting them away to goodness knows what hovel deep within this city.

Uncle Pavol had said to wait for them here, in Glasgow. He would find her, he'd promised. But days were passing into weeks and Juliana feared that she was now alone here with no protection from the predators who sought a foreign girl like her. *We will meet at the station*, he'd insisted, *take a train to London then go home*. Home! Juliana felt tears start in her eyes as she imagined her own village, the sun setting behind the mountains, her friends calling for her to join them. They'd be running down the hill, hands linked, screaming with the carefree laughter of young girls who knew no evil in their lives. She pursed her lips. The things she had seen and done had destroyed any vestiges of her childhood; that old life now denied to her for ever.

She sat on the metal seat in the main concourse, eating chips and black pudding sausage from the greasy paper, watching the people come and go, occasionally looking up at the timetable board as if to check a particular arrival or departure. It was sensible to play-act, she'd learned. Juliana knew that there were police officers here, sometimes standing around in pairs, always watching the crowds coming and going. At first she had dreaded their glance but none had ever looked her way and gradually she had come to see them simply as young men and women in uniform, often chatting to each other, and, as she watched them, her imagination created relationships between them. They were there to help, not to hurt, she had decided after watching how they behaved towards the occasional drunk, smiles and consideration instead of the blows she had suffered at the hands of her captors.

Juliana crunched up the empty packet and strolled back out of the station to find a bin. She looked up at the velvety sky. Night would be falling soon and she must make her way back to the tiny hotel across the city where no questions had been asked, only nods as she paid the nightly rate and took a fresh towel from the receptionist's hand.

He wasn't coming, she decided. Something must have happened to Mario and Uncle Pavol and Juliana had no way of finding out what that was. The money he had shoved into her hand? Was it stolen, perhaps? And had he been caught? Juliana shivered, imagining the beatings an old man like Pavol could have received. But he'd managed to get her away before the raid began so surely he had escaped too?

'All right, hen?' A man leered at her, swaying towards her as Juliana stood at the edge of the pavement. She turned away, feigning disinterest so that he would take the hint, then, watching which way he crossed the road, she turned on her heel and walked swiftly in the opposite direction.

This money would not last for ever, Juliana told herself. And in all the months that she had been in this country there had only been two ways of earning more. She looked down at her bitten nails. Tomorrow, she promised herself. She would find a decent nail bar and have a manicure then ask if there were any openings. She was good at threading, something she'd learned from her aunt, so perhaps she could find a salon where that particular skill was in demand.

With that thought in mind, the girl walked uphill, towards her destination. She looked ahead, eyes on the evening skies streaked with crimson, promise of another fine day ahead.

As she crested the rise and turned west, Juliana spotted the full moon rising blood red above the horizon.

It was a bad omen, surely, a sign of danger to come. She shivered, hurrying onwards, glancing over her shoulder as her pace quickened, a sudden feeling that she was once more hastening towards her doom.

CHAPTER TWENTY-SEVEN

'Pop-up brothels,' the woman declared, swinging one leg across the other as she scanned the folder on her knee. Then, turning around as an elderly lady entered the room carrying a tray, she smiled. 'Mmm, chocolate biscuits. They are treating you well here, Superintendent!'

'Aye, an' so they should!' the tea lady declared, hands on hips. 'This yin's been through enough tae melt a dug's bone, so he has!'

'Thanks, Sadie,' Lorimer told the tea lady. 'Good of you to bring this up here.'

'An' here's yer Danish pastries fur afterwards,' the wee woman mumbled, surreptitiously passing a white paper bag to Lorimer before scuttling back outside.

Deputy Chief Constable Caroline Flint raised questioning eyebrows as she sat beside Lorimer in his Helen Street office.

'Sadie Dunlop,' Lorimer explained. 'The mother hen of divisional headquarters everywhere she can sell her home baking.'

'Ah.' Caroline Flint nodded. 'Special treatment, eh?'

'Sadie's always had a soft spot for me.' Lorimer grinned. 'Think I'm probably her best customer.'

DCC Flint returned his smile. 'Looks like you've settled in well at the MIT. And the team are behind you one hundred per cent?'

'Yes, they are,' Lorimer agreed. 'And it's all thanks to you that I'm here at all.'

She did not respond to this, merely nodded absently and continued reading the report, one hand reaching absently for a chocolate biscuit.

'This Molly Newton. Good officer?'

'One of the best,' Lorimer replied warmly. Of course, he remembered, Caroline Flint had been an undercover officer too, back in her Met days. 'Molly reckons they've been hiding in plain sight. Nail bars, street beggars, what have you; anything that catches the eye of a potential punter. Rent a room for a day and a night then scarper, taking their women to the next place.'

'Keeps them one step ahead of the law,' the DCC murmured. 'We've seen this pattern before, haven't we?'

Lorimer stifled a sigh. It was true that the people traffickers had grown cannier as they had built up their business. Sometimes whole gangs of labourers would descend on a building project, their gangmaster demanding cash in hand and getting it too. Undercutting the going rate was a common way of slipping under the radar and also saved the less scrupulous firms a lot in overheads. The women could be dispersed in shopping centres any distance from the city, hawking their freelance skills as nail technicians or eyebrow threaders with a view to proposing a whole other sort of service.

'So.' The DCC looked up at last and reached for her coffee cup. 'Think you can track them down? It's more than three weeks now since those raids in Aberdeen. Trail gone cold, do you think?'

'We've got several surveillance officers in and around the city as well as Molly,' he replied. 'The banks are also on the alert for any unusual transactions that could appear to be money laundering.'

'Goes hand-in-hand with that sort of game,' she agreed. 'They have to find somewhere to clean up their dirty money. Though lots of them appear to work on a cash basis, remember. Rolls of banknotes under the mattress.' She sighed. 'Well, I wish you luck, William,' she said, rising from her chair next to Lorimer's desk. 'Too old now to offer my own services,' she chuckled. 'Lucky DS Newton! Sometimes wish I was back in the field.'

Lorimer smiled as she shook his hand. DCC Flint had come to Scotland at a time when there had been a crying need for an objective eye on the management side of Police Scotland and she was already being hailed as the next Chief Constable when the present incumbent retired.

Molly Newton did not consider herself lucky in the least as she sat listening to the woman across the nail bar who was wittering on about her seven grandchildren and how clever they all were. She had been the third pensioner in a row and Molly was wondering if there would ever be a moment to listen to the girls in the back shop. But holiday time was approaching and the place was full of clients keen to have their talons in perfect order for whatever place in the sun beckoned them away from Glasgow.

She glanced up as the door opened and a dark-haired girl stood on the threshold, an uncertain expression on her face as she looked into the busy salon.

Molly caught her eye and smiled. 'With you in two minutes?' she called out, her accent deliberately affecting an eastern European drawl. She saw the girl hesitate then nod, walking towards the empty seat opposite Molly's space behind the nail bar.

There was something about her, Molly thought, noticing the way she curled her fingers into slack fists as though embarrassed about her nails. And she sat right on the edge of the chair, nervously glancing around as though making ready to flee at the slightest provocation.

Molly Newton's years of reading a person's body language told her many things and right now she was curious to understand why this young girl was here despite being very afraid indeed.

The screams from the man on the ground stopped suddenly as the figure over him plunged the knife downwards. No one would miss this piece of trash, the killer told himself, pulling out the blade and wiping it on the grass. He aimed a kick at the body, sending it tumbling down the cliff side. It landed in the water below with a satisfying splash. He stepped into the waiting car and leaned back, never once glancing at the driver. The big car roared away, a cloud of dust rising for a few seconds then settling on the patch of ground where, moments before, a man had been brutally killed.

He was glad that the driver had witnessed the scene. Max would be told about it and be pleased.

And they both knew that the boss did not tolerate the slightest deviation from his orders.

'Max wants us to find her,' the big man told his companion as he parked in a city centre multistorey car park. 'Take this.' He shoved a brown envelope onto the driver's lap. 'Half now and half when she's found. And I mean returned. Alive.' He grinned. 'We can have fun with her afterwards but Max gets her first. Okay?'

'Why does he think she's here, in Glasgow?'

'The old man told her to come here, didn't he? That was their back-up plan.' He grinned. 'Didn't reckon on being overheard by another Slovak, though. Or getting banged up in the Bar L.'

The driver opened the envelope and riffled the notes, tongue protruding between his lips as he counted.

'How do you know all of this?'

The hit man shrugged. 'Max told me. You know what he's like. Seems to know what goes on everywhere.'

The driver glanced at his companion, seeing the sudden shudder. It took a lot to put the frighteners on someone like this man but the power that the boss wielded was legendary.

'Right, I'm off. Got a shift coming up and need to keep an eye on that pair of Slovaks in case they're up to any more nonsense. Be seeing you.' He climbed out of the BMW and slammed the door. The sound reverberated off the concrete walls of the car park then, with a squeal of tyres, the car set off, taking the corner a little too fast. The hit man shook his head and sighed.

'Always in a hurry, that one,' he murmured. 'Come to grief if he's not careful.'

He made his way down the metal staircase, an old sports bag in one hand. For a moment it reminded him of the place he was heading but at least he would be out in a few hours, free to do the bidding of his real paymaster. It was just a matter of time before he'd be shot of the jail for good. Then there would be years ahead to sit back and enjoy all the money that was coming his way.

'Plum Tart?' Molly giggled as she showed the girl the shade of purple nail gel.

A quick upward glance gave her away immediately. That

strained look in her eyes, the way she snatched back her hands. Could this be the Slovakian girl that the MIT wanted to find? Juliana Ferenc? Molly thought hard, remembering all of the details. Maybe she could create a story, draw her in . . .

'Or how about this one?' she asked, pretending not to notice the girl's discomfiture, and bringing out a bottle of luminescent scarlet then turning it upside down to read the tiny label. 'An Affair in Red Square, it's called!' She gave another giggle and caught the girl's eye. But this time there was a smile of understanding that this was just a bit of fun between 'Sasha', the technician, and her latest client.

'Yes,' the dark-haired girl agreed. 'That one will be good.'

'Come far, have you?' Molly chatted. 'I love this city, don't you?' she went on, still smiling as she drew an emery board across the girl's fingernails.

'You from where?'

Molly shrugged, her mind casting around for a place to suggest, somewhere close enough to Slovakia that would give her an instant rapport with this girl. 'Nowhere special. You probably never heard of it. I was born outside of Timişoara but I've lived most of my life in Italy. Came here to study and got this great job.' She winked. 'Lots of perks, I can tell you!' She smiled and waggled her own pristine fingernails.

'I did work in a place like this once,' the girl offered.

'Back home? You're from Slovakia, right?' Molly concentrated on the girl's fingernails as though the question didn't matter.

The girl nodded. 'Yes, from a small village in the east. Not on many maps,' she added.

Molly tried to hide the growing excitement that she felt. It could be the girl that had escaped from that raid in Aberdeen. Her remit was to watch and see if the nail bar was a front for something altogether more sinister but perhaps she had unwittingly stumbled on another element of the investigation into the people-trafficking ring.

'I love your look,' she said, waving a hand at the girl. 'Gorgeous hair.' She sighed enviously. 'Maybe you'll let me take a photo for my client book once I've finished?'

There was a moment's hesitation so Molly rattled on. 'See, I've got loads already,' she insisted. 'It's a great salon, here. They encourage you to keep your clients as well. I can give you a discount if you like?'

The girl seemed lost in her thoughts but then she looked up and gave a shy smile.

'I wanted to see if I could find a ... job ... like yours,' she stammered. 'That is why I came.'

Molly took a silent breath. It had to be her. It just had to be.

'Let me see if I can persuade the boss to give you an interview,' she answered at last. 'There, first coat done,' she added, watching as the girl put experienced fingers under the gel-setting beam.

'When ... ?' The question hovered in the air, the expression on the girl's face anxious yet hopeful.

'How about coming back this afternoon? Say four o'clock?' Molly asked brightly. It would give her time to check back with the team, have someone ready to escort this Slovakian girl back to headquarters.

The girl nodded and Molly exhaled a sigh of relief.

'Right, hands up to your cheeks. That's right. Now, smile!'

Molly took several pictures with her smart phone and then put it carelessly into her bag as though it were a perfectly routine matter. The girl had seemed reluctant to be photographed at first but Molly's disarming manner had put her at ease.

'Okay. I'm giving you a special discount today. Can I have you name?' she asked briskly, pen poised over a pad of Post-it notes.

There was a pause. Then the girl shook her head. 'You can call me Julia,' she said at last.

Short for Juliana? Molly wanted to call out but for now that question had to remain unasked. And she wouldn't push for a surname lest she scare the girl off.

'Thanks, Julia.' Molly smiled, taking the twenty pound note and giving the girl five bright new pound coins in change. 'See you at four.'

She watched the dark-haired Slovakian girl leave the salon then sped into the ladies' toilets where she immediately sent the photos to her contact in Govan.

Think I've found the Ferenc girl, she typed. *Be here at 4.*

Juliana glanced at her reflection in the window of a shop. She could be taken for anyone in this city, an office worker on her lunch break, a tourist enjoying the sunshine. She looked at her perfectly manicured nails and stroked their smooth curves. Now she was ready to begin a new phase of her life. If that nice lady, Sasha, could find her a job, then surely she could earn enough to remain here until she had found Uncle Pavol and her beloved brother, Mario?

CHAPTER TWENTY-EIGHT

What if Rosie Fergusson was wrong? Kirsty heaved a sigh as she sat at her desk in Govan police station. There was some evidence to suggest that Dorothy Guilford had been murdered and now she felt that there were at least three people who might have wanted her dead. McCauley had decided it was the husband and, fair play to him, there was that tiny bloodstain on the man's old jacket. But what if that had been from a different assault? The poor woman certainly seemed like an abused wife from the injuries she had seen on her body during the post-mortem, despite no medical notes to verify that. But did Peter Guilford deserve to be tried for murder if he hadn't wielded that fatal knife? Some folk would say yes, Kirsty thought gloomily. The women who were hell-bent on getting revenge against abusers of any description.

But the law was there to protect the innocent, even when they had already done terrible things in the past. An image came to her of Guilford asleep in that bed, the rise and fall of the bedclothes, the whirr of machines attached to his body. Such a helpless human being he had seemed then! It was hard to reconcile that person with the one who had carried out numerous

attacks on his deranged wife. *Bastard deserves all he gets!* she'd overheard a colleague say when the news came in about the near-fatal attack on Guilford. But did he deserve such brutality? Did anyone? Had Dorothy been a difficult wife to live with? Her sister had drawn a picture of a nasty, grasping character but that alone was surely no reason for being killed.

Kirsty closed her eyes and drew a hand across her forehead. It was especially hot in the office today and she had a ton of paperwork to catch up on.

'DC Wilson?'

'Yes?' Kirsty looked up to see one of the senior officers approach. 'I was asked to give you this,' he said, handing her an envelope. Then he gave her a smile, adding, 'Good luck.'

Kirsty frowned as she slit open the envelope with a nail file and read the letter within.

You are invited to attend an interview ... the letter began. She grasped it tightly. It had not occurred to Kirsty that she might actually be considered for promotion just yet but nevertheless she had filled in the requisite form and submitted it to her divisional commander some months ago.

She felt her cheeks becoming hot. How ironic was this! Just when she had to decide whether or not she was going to accompany James to Chicago (if he got the job, she reminded herself) and give up her own career, here was yet another incentive to stay put. For a split second Kirsty wanted to tear the letter into pieces and throw them into the waste-paper basket but the thought of her father stopped her. How sad he would be if she were to give up the opportunity to further her career in Police Scotland! It had taken Dad a long time to reach the heights of DI before his retirement and, she thought, hadn't McCauley recently remarked that she might one day be addressed by her own colleagues as 'Ma'am'?

She read the letter again, making a note in her phone of the date and time that she was to present herself for interview.

This could change their plans completely. If she stayed here, would James try for a different job? She heaved a sigh. He'd already been turned down so often for jobs in Scotland that suited his skills and the Chicago one sounded just right. It wasn't fair. Here she was with the chance to climb up the promotion ladder and James was looking so much further ahead to a family life where she would stay home and bring up their babies. Oh, she wanted that too, she knew that she did. But was it so impossible to have everything?

'She can't have everything,' McCauley snapped. 'Either she gives her evidence for the Crown and keeps on our side of the court or we have to have a second opinion. After all, she's screwed up cases like this before.'

The woman across the desk nodded her understanding. It was policy to have two post-mortems in a case where there was genuine doubt as to the cause of death. 'All right,' she said. 'I hear what you say. But it will be at our discretion which pathologist performs the second PM.'

McCauley tried to hide his disappointment. 'Thought Jacqui White ...'

'Dr White is one possibility,' the depute fiscal replied. 'I'll let you know.'

McCauley grinned as he left the Fiscal's office and made his way back to the car park. He'd sown the seeds of doubt into the depute's mind. Fergusson was incompetent, that was his message, and he was certain that she would now be under added scrutiny. His tame reporter was ready and waiting for his signal to publish her piece on the consultant pathologist, just in time for the beginning of Guilford's trial, something that was definitely going ahead once the man had recovered sufficiently to put him on the stand. When it all came out about her earlier mistake then Fergusson was finished as a credible expert witness for the defence. And, if the timing was right, she's be trachled with a new bairn, too tired to concentrate properly, brain fogged by the post-baby state that all women seemed to get.

He chuckled as he drove back towards Helen Street. If Jacqui White was to be chosen as the Crown's pathologist then the odds were that she might even take over from Rosie Fergusson for good. The dark-haired beauty who had become a household name after her stint on television was waiting in the wings right now to fill the gap as head of Forensic Medical Science once Fergusson's maternity leave began. Alan McCauley had cosied up to Jacqui on several occasions, and not just because of this current business. She was a real stunner and he was a single guy with an eye for the ladies; smart ladies like Jacqui who could be persuaded to feather her own nest in return for a little muck raking.

It would all work out, he told himself. Another murderer would be banged up for life, he'd get a commendation and the satisfaction of seeing Rosie Fergusson make a complete fool of herself in court.

A frown crossed McCauley's face for a moment. It was a pity that young DC, Kirsty Wilson, was so friendly with Fergusson and her husband, Professor Brightman. Lorimer's fault, of course; the lot of them were thick as thieves. Wilson was a useful detective and he would need to see what he could do to bring her alongside in this particular business.

*

191

She saw Rosie heaving herself out of the office chair as she opened the door to the consultant pathologist's office.

'Jacqui, lovely to see you,' Rosie declared, coming forward and stretching up to give the taller woman a peck on her cheek.

'Great to be back in Glasgow again,' Jacqui White replied. 'And just look at you! How long to go now?'

'Too long,' Rosie grumbled. 'My due date's a few weeks yet but the way I feel I could go on leave right now. Thank goodness you're able to step into my shoes. The department needs someone with your experience, Jacqui. We're taking on a junior pathologist from Australia as well so you don't have to be overstretched. Daisy Abercrombie. She's a character.' Rosie grinned. 'Hope she'll stay once I'm back.'

Jacqui White returned the smile but kept her own counsel. She was tired of racketing about the country, even the smartest hotels had long since lost their appeal, and she wanted to settle down here in Glasgow and have a permanent job, possibly the one that Rosie Fergusson was about to relinquish for several months.

'I'd love to meet her,' she said. 'Now, how about you bring me up to date on the current workload? I'll be happy to start any time you feel I can come in, you know.' She affected a worried expression and nodded towards Rosie's bump. 'No need to wait till that little one decides to make an appearance.'

She heard the sigh, saw the woman shake her head and for a moment she was annoyed. Why couldn't Rosie just go home and put her feet up? Let *her* get on with running this department instead?

'Oh, you're always so dedicated, Rosie,' Jacqui said. 'But maybe it's time to put yourself first for a change.'

'Aye, well, perhaps you're right,' Rosie said doubtfully, shuffling back to her place behind the desk. 'I just need to sort a few things about this current case. Dorothy Guilford,' she added, lifting a file from the pile at her side. 'Here, it makes interesting reading.'

Jacqui White sat in the university library, hand on chin, poring through her colleague's notes. Alan was right, she decided. The case was shot full of holes. Rosie simply wasn't up to it any more. She felt a rush of sympathy for the woman who had seemed so weary sitting there in her office. It was always hard to juggle work and family, women constantly told her. But Jacqui White had decided long ago that kids were not part of her own plan and right now she wanted to see what she might do to persuade Rosie that staying at home for good was in everyone's best interest. Not least the good-looking detective inspector who had shared her bed last night, she thought, smiling a secret smile.

CHAPTER TWENTY-NINE

'White male, late twenties, no identity on him,' DS Jolyon, the scene of crime manager, noted.

Several people stood at the edge of the steep slope that ran down to the pool at the foot of the old quarry. The stink from the scum-covered water had been made worse by the recent hot spell and the officer wrinkled his nose in distaste.

The body had been spotted by kids, probably playing truant from school, their breathless phone call giving the location but leaving no names. A police diver in full wetsuit had retrieved the man and now his corpse was laid out on the grass, the team of white-suited SOCOs examining the terrain.

'Been badly beaten, by the looks of him,' Jolyon observed. 'We'll know more when ... ' He broke off as a car door slammed and a small blonde woman emerged, already dressed in protective whites. 'Dr Fergusson,' Jolyon called. 'Mind your step on these treads. Need a hand?' He watched anxiously as Rosie Fergusson stepped onto the first of the metal treads that snaked a path from where the patrol cars were parked to the body by the cliff edge. Having a heavily pregnant pathologist was just one more risk to assess, Jolyon's expression seemed to say as he came forward, one hand ready to guide Rosie forwards.

'I'm fine, really I am,' Rosie insisted. 'Who called it in?' she asked, stepping carefully but steadily along the row of treads.

'Some local kids. Wouldn't leave their names but the operator said they sounded genuinely freaked so we came to check it out. Turned out they were right. What they saw down there was a body floating in the water.'

'Phew, poor soul. What a niff!' Rosie exclaimed. 'Never mind,' she made a face at the DS, 'I've smelled a lot worse than this.'

The heat and the stink had brought swarms of flies and Rosie had to swat them away with her gloved hand several times as she attempted to examine the dead man. The wound from his throat was probably what had killed him, she decided, though a full examination back at the city mortuary would be necessary to determine that.

'Any idea when . . . ?'

Rosie looked up to meet DS Jolyon's eyes, giving him a *you know me better than to ask* sort of look.

'Just asking,' he sighed.

Rosie shook her head. 'Fairly recently, I'd say. A couple of days, maybe? Is there anyone fitting his description that's been called in as a missing person?'

'That's being checked out now, doctor,' Jolyon replied. 'The photographer's sent pics straight to divisional HQ. They'll be processing them as I speak.'

It was a change from the old days, Jolyon knew, when forensics could take days or weeks to determine certain details. And, once the post-mortem had been done and DNA samples and fingerprints sent to the lab, they would be able to see if this chap

195

had been on any database that might give them a clue as to his identity.

The detective sergeant stepped to one side, hand in the air to ward off a cloud of bluebottles. Only this morning he'd been extolling the fine spell of weather but here, at a crime scene like this, with the stench of putrid water floating upwards from the corpse and the drone of flies, he would have preferred a cold winter's day.

'Over here!' a voice called and Jolyon looked up to see two of the SOCOs bent down around a patch of ground.

'Blood stains,' one of the white-suited figures proclaimed as he came closer, careful not to disturb the area. 'Think this may be the place where they killed him.'

Jolyon looked to where the gloved fingers had parted stems of grass. The evidence would be bagged and sent for examination to see if it met the dead man's blood type but he was pretty sure that this was where he had drawn his final breath.

He looked up at the cloudless skies, one hand shading his eyes against the brightness, wondering if that was the last thing their victim had seen before he had closed his eyes for ever on the world.

'I could do the PM, if you like,' Jacqui offered. 'Give you a bit of a break.'

'Okay, I'll take notes, then. Thanks,' Rosie agreed. The double-doctor system this side of the Scottish border meant that one pathologist performed the surgery whilst another took notes, corroborating any evidence that would be required for the future.

As she watched her colleague, Rosie felt a sense of satisfaction that the department would be in good hands once she decided to begin her maternity leave. It wouldn't be long now, a couple of weeks perhaps, her due date early July. Perhaps, once Abby's nursery days were over, she could spend more time with her little girl, preparing for the new baby's arrival.

At last the body was wheeled back into the refrigerated drawer and Rosie could strip off her gown, another post-mortem completed.

'Not hard to see the cause of death, was it?' Jacqui remarked. 'That blade cut straight into his jugular.'

'They'd beaten him up first, though, hadn't they,' Rosie mused. 'And taking him all the way out there looks like they had a reason for that. Premeditated murder, wouldn't you say?' She had filled her colleague in with the SOCOs initial findings, two sets of footprints other than the victim's, leading the police to think that the dead man had been brought to that lonely spot deliberately.

'Yes. If I had to,' Jacqui replied. 'These marks around his ankles and wrists suggest that he had been bound up at some time before. Wonder why he hadn't been secured when they took him to that quarry? Especially if they had meant to kill him.'

'Maybe tox results will tell us more,' Rosie offered. 'See if the victim had been drugged.'

'Mm.' Jacqui White was non-committal. 'Anyway, you can forget all about this seeing as I'll be the one in court as expert witness.'

Rosie glanced at the woman, wondering at her confident tone. Would that really be the case? It was Dr Rosie Fergusson who had been at the scene of crime first, after all, so her name would be on the initial paperwork, but perhaps given that Dr White had performed the post-mortem, she could continue with the case should it ever come to court.

Rosie felt a familiar movement and smiled, glancing at her swollen belly. She'd have more important things to think about soon enough.

James Spencer paid the cab driver and looked around him. London in summer was a wonderful place to be, albeit just for the day. The trees in the adjacent park towered above him, then a movement caught his eye, making him stop as several bright green parakeets swooped overhead. Lorimer would have loved that sight. James grinned. It reminded the young man just how different things were a few hundred miles further south and how much more exciting life could be in another country altogether.

His interview with the American firm was in a little over an hour, plenty of time to have a quick coffee and look over his notes. It was as important to have questions of his own as it was to answer theirs, Solly Brightman had counselled. And James had agreed, wanting to know more about the life he and Kirsty might enjoy in Chicago.

The city appeared to have undergone a transformation, everything shining even more brightly than before in the early afternoon sunlight. Wherever he walked the pedestrian lights turned to green as though by magic to let him cross the roads. It was a day where nothing could go wrong, he thought, oblivious to people turning their heads and staring at him as James walked past, a huge grin on his face.

He'd done it! He'd actually done it! The job as an economist at the bank was his for the asking. All he needed to do was have a talk with Kirsty and let them know within the week if he was prepared to move to the US and begin his new career in Chicago. A generous housing allowance would be forthcoming, mortgage rates guaranteed, as well as a company car. He would have accommodation for two months initially, rent-free, in the company's own city centre flat until he found a home for them both. James clutched his briefcase and began to whistle, still oblivious to the stares of passers-by.

A flock of pigeons soared from the pavement near his feet and James felt his spirits lift with them as they flapped across the clear blue sky. Life was wonderful! Now he must hope that his lovely girl wanted to share this adventure with him and everything would be perfect.

The big man strolled along Gordon Street, turning into the shadows as the tall buildings in Hope Street cut off the sunlight. He blinked, the sudden change making him reach for the sunglasses, but his hand fell again. Better to keep them on, now that he'd spotted her.

He had followed her through Central Station, up one flight of steps from Union Street and across the concourse, watching as she hesitated and looked around. No Uncle Pavol, Juliana, he had thought, seeing her head droop with disappointment. Then, keeping a safe distance between them, the baseball cap pulled down across his brow, he had followed her out into Gordon Street and was now watching as she began to walk uphill.

'Juliana!' he called then watched as she spun around, her face alert, fearful.

'Over here!' He waved and grinned then watched as she retraced her steps and walked back towards him.

What did she see? he wondered as she hesitated, staying a couple of feet away, a look of concern on her face.

'Juliana? Juliana Ferenc? I've a message from your uncle,' he told her.

'Pavol?' The girl's face changed immediately and she took a step forward, no longer hesitant but eager to hear what this stranger had to tell her.

'Shh.' He looked around and motioned her to walk alongside him.

'It's okay, but we have to be careful. Never know who's watching us, do we? Here, down this lane.' He grabbed her arm and steered her around one of the cobbled lanes that criss-crossed the main arteries of the city. 'Got a car waiting. Take you to see him, okay?'

The lane was empty save for the big car and he pulled her roughly along, no longer the friend the Slovakian girl had hoped for but her captor.

Juliana struggled for a moment as he lifted her off her feet, mouth open in terror, a scream that never came.

*

'Where is she?' Molly Newton hissed at the two plain-clothes detectives who were standing outside the building.

'Didn't show, did she?' one of them said with a shrug. 'She changed her mind, I suppose.'

Molly frowned. 'I don't know,' she began. 'I was so sure she would be here at four o'clock. What if something happened to her?'

'Hold on,' he said sharply, holding his mobile to his ear. 'Hello, yes we're here.'

Molly watched as his face became serious.

'What is it?' she demanded.

'That was Transport. We've had them watching all the CCTV cameras in this area.' He began walking briskly down the hill, the others in his wake. 'Someone's lifted her,' he said quietly. 'Just down there on that corner.' He pointed to a lane two blocks down. 'Come on!'

They sprinted across the road, avoiding the oncoming traffic, ignoring the blasts from car horns.

'Where are they?' Molly ran, fists pumping by her sides. 'What's . . . ?'

'CCTV shows her with a big fellow, hard to see his face, wore sunglasses and a baseball cap. He took her around here.'

The three officers stood at the mouth of the empty lane, sunlight showing at its far end.

The detective held his mobile to his ear once more as another call came in, Molly watching him anxiously.

'They think he may have had a vehicle waiting. Traffic will have a record of every car and van that left this lane.'

'Any further signs of them?'

The detective shook his head. 'A few cars have been seen going down Renfield Street from that entrance in the last half-hour,' he told them as they walked swiftly to the end of the lane, glancing from side to side for any visible clues.

'So they're heading south,' the second officer suggested as they emerged into the sunlight once again.

'We don't even know what car she's in,' the first man sighed.

'Oh, dear God,' Molly groaned. 'We've lost her now. And who on earth has picked her up?'

'Has to be someone she knows. Or someone who knows her,' he answered darkly. 'Either way, she's in danger.'

CHAPTER THIRTY

O ne always had to think of their mothers. That was a per-
ennial consideration when the professor tried to create
a profile of someone who had strayed from so-called normal
behaviour into an area of darkness. The tabula rasa, or blank
slate, was what babies were born with, according to certain
philosophies, and Solomon Brightman also found it hard to
conceive of a tiny baby being born with inherent wickedness
in its soul. Yet, from his experience of life and humanity, that
was something he could not deny in some cases. The child that
tormented flies and birds then went on to target larger creatures
had more of a chance of becoming a killer of his fellow men.
Was there a genetic predisposition to kill? That was a question
both for the philosophers and psychologists that were students
of human behaviour.

Who was this man? Max, he was called, possibly his real name
but that was not something to be sure of either. Not a Slovakian
national and Europol had no record of a British criminal with
that name and answering the man's description on their list of
sex offenders or traffickers. An alias, perhaps? And, if so, why
choose that particular name? The word was redolent of power

and fame, *living life to the max, Maximilian, maximum* ... all sorts of connotations could derive consciously or subconsciously from that short syllable.

And why was he disposed to target vulnerable females? Power? That was possible. But money was also a strong motivator and this man had undoubtedly gathered some wealth from his trafficking if each girl was sold on for a cool ten thousand pounds. Had he deliberately selected these girls for their religion? Solly had considered this at the start but now he was inclined to believe that it was their sheer vulnerability that had made them this man's target. Juliana Ferenc, the missing girl, was a Romany, one of several taken from the small village in eastern Slovakia where their standard of living was achingly poor. Fruit picking, harvesting grapes and other seasonal work kept them from starvation and so the chance to find work in the UK was a life-changing opportunity for these young women.

Did this Max have any family links with the Slovakians? Solly did not think so, at least from the point of view of being related to them. There was a strong sense of family amongst many Slovakians and to deviate from that would be to break away from their Romany ties, something that the psychologist found hard to conjecture. Had he spent time amongst these people? That was a strong possibility, given that he undoubtedly spoke their language. And the face ... something that might make a woman shudder ... had it been hard for him to form relationships after whatever disaster had burned his features, leaving him with a mask of taut skin?

The fact that the gangmaster had subjected women to such terrors gave the psychologist an insight into his personality. The pictures he had seen on file showed scenes of torture and Solly wondered how anyone could have had the stomach to record them. But someone had and he suspected that it had been the gangmaster himself, relishing those women's screams. The accident aside, there were other things to ponder. Had his own mother been a cruel, unfeeling sort? Was he seeking revenge for a disturbed childhood? Solly had seen this pattern of behaviour in violent men before. Or, had he been abandoned as a child, lacking maternal nurturing in any form that would result in sensitivity towards womankind? Or, as he was beginning to think, was there some sort of hideous anger under that featureless face that wanted to punish or destroy the sort of young women who might have rejected or even mocked him?

An out-and-out psychopath of course had no empathy for his fellow man or woman and so this type of personality could never be ruled out either, which brought Solly back to wondering if Max's genetic make-up had been flawed from the start. *La mauvaise graine*, the pragmatic French called it; bad seed, as if somehow a child was fated to become a monster even before its birth.

The psychologist sighed. Needing to recapture the Ferenc girl gave him a small inkling of what Max was about, of course. He wanted to regain control of the youngster and, perhaps, to satisfy his own sexual needs before subjecting her once more to a life of prostitution. Besides that, there was the practical aspect of keeping her out of the clutches of the authorities in case she could tell them things that had to be kept under wraps. He shuddered, wondering what Juliana Ferenc's fate would be.

The CCTV images that he had been sent showed a glimpse of her terrified face as she was dragged out of sight along that shadowy lane. Did she know her abductor? Solly doubted that. She was young and fit, could easily have run along the busy street screaming for help. No, this Max had sent someone else to do his bidding, someone who had lured her away. The burly figure with the sunglasses and baseball cap pulled down was hard to identify. But it was not impossible for the experts at the Scottish Crime Campus at Gartcosh to create some alternative images in an effort to show what this man really looked like. Already there were images from Glasgow Central Station and, piecing them together, who knew what these clever men and women might discover?

His mind wandered to his own dear wife. Rosie was a loving mother as well as a dedicated professional and she would soon be here at home, nurturing her own newborn, settled happily in a calm environment away from the strains of her job. Their children would be given every chance to become decent citizens, the notion of caring for others instilled from an early age. For a fleeting moment he thought of the man he wanted to profile and felt a pang of sorrow. Had he been given such love and support? It was hardly likely, though those serial killers he had studied for years could sometimes seem to be quite normal, ordinary folk from outside appearances, family life behind closed doors telling a different sort of story.

Then there was Dorothy Guilford, Rosie's putative suicide victim, if that is what she really was. So many people with reasons to want her dead . . .

Her family situation had been a bit odd, too, according to Kirsty who had been updating them on her own private investigation. He sighed again, knowing that his brain was teeming with ideas and that it was probably time to wander into the kitchen and drink a restorative cup of camomile tea.

The door closed with a bang and Shirley heard the footsteps thumping along the uncarpeted hallway.

'You're here, then,' she remarked, not bothering to rise from her armchair as the man entered her living room. 'Suppose you'll be wanting some tea?'

There was no answer and Shirley smiled, pointing to the kitchen doorway. 'You know where the kettle is. Make some for yourself. Did you remember the biscuits?'

The man loomed over her, fists clenched by his sides, the expression on his face difficult to read. 'Yes,' he replied, though from the way his jaw worked it was obvious he wanted to say more. Then, turning on his heel he marched through to the kitchen as the woman's eyes followed him. She heard the gush of tap water, the clink of pottery mugs as he drew them from their old wooden pegs.

'Got what you want?' she called out but only a grunt of assent met her ears.

At last the tea was brewed and brought to her side, the man setting down a tray on the scratched table between them.

Shirley grabbed a handful of biscuits and set them on the arm of her chair, dunking them one by one and swallowing greedily as she looked over her mug of tea.

'Well, cat got your tongue?' she sneered. 'What happened?'

The man avoided her stare, stirring spoonfuls of sugar into his tea. Then, with a sigh, he nodded. 'I got it,' he told her. 'Lawyer wasn't happy about releasing it at first but when he saw who was asking I guess he had no choice.' A glimmer of a smile appeared on his face but disappeared again swiftly as Shirley rapped hard on the table.

'Did she sign it or didn't she?'

'Yes,' he admitted. 'Looks like she did.'

'And did you get to read it all? What did it say?'

The man shifted uncomfortably under her gaze. 'Look, you

don't need to know it all chapter and verse. "Assign, dispone and convey ... " Lots of legal words you wouldn't understand. I sat there and read it all, though,' he told her. 'There's absolutely nothing wrong with it as far as I can see.'

'But who was the beneficiary?'

The man paused to drink his tea, ignoring her for a moment, as if he was deliberately making her wait.

'Who gets it all?' Shirley demanded impatiently. She sighed and shook her head. It was hard going at times dealing with someone who considered himself her superior. He liked to torment her in little ways, she knew. So it took her a deal of patience to make him go out and do her bidding. And he would, knowing that in the end there was a great deal of money coming their way.

'We do,' he said at last, avoiding her eager gaze, the fat fingers grasping the edge of her grubby blouse.

Shirley blew out a sigh of relief. 'Well why not say so, then?'

'Got to go,' he said suddenly, draining his mug then picking up the biscuit crumbs with a damp finger.

'You'll call me if you need anything else, won't you?' Shirley asked.

'I will,' he replied. 'Just need to go and change now, okay?'

She heard the bedroom door opening and closing, the faint sounds of his feet as the man changed out of the well-polished shoes and smart suit he'd worn to visit the solicitor's office. He'd not uttered one word to reassure her, Shirley thought bitterly. It had always been the same, of course. Dorothy had been the favourite even with this particular man. But Dorothy was gone now and could no longer take his affection away from her.

'I'm off.' His face appeared at the doorway, glancing her way for a moment.

Shirley smiled up at him then opened her arms.

'C'mere, you big lump,' she said.

'It will take a while,' the woman at the Crown Office told Lorimer. 'We can't simply issue warrants for that. Not unless you have a bit more to substantiate your request. Are any of these men likely to present a danger to the public?'

The detective superintendent hoped that she could not hear his exasperated sigh. 'We don't know yet but one of them may well be guilty of the attempted murder of Peter Guilford,' he replied, knowing that this was something he had already explained and that his patience was running thin.

'Yes, well . . . ' She left her sentence unfinished and he could only imagine what she might have said.

Lorimer put down the phone after mumbling 'Thanks anyway', and drew the sheet of faces towards him.

If only he had been able to present them one by one then Guilford's reaction would have narrowed down these options. Lorimer cursed himself, knowing that it had been down to him to make that call. It just hadn't occurred to him that Guilford would refuse to identify his attacker. Still, there was the possibility of eliminating at least two of the men. McTaggart had been off duty at the time of the assault and Fairley off sick, so he was left with four prison officers whose shifts had coincided with the near fatal incident. It irked him that McSherry hadn't bothered to sift through these images and check who had been on a shift at the time of the attack. Still, he had to see the ones he was left with.

Raynor had been the officer first on the scene. He had taken charge of the prisoner and called for help. Would his assailant have done that? Endangered his own position? Perhaps he needed to talk again to the two prisoners who had found Guilford lying in that shower cubicle, see if they had noticed anything odd about Raynor's manner. Two of the other officers had also been quick on the scene: Whitehead and Grimshaw. That left Thomson unaccounted for. McSherry needed to let him know exactly where his officers had been at the time of the attack, something the prison governor had so far been reluctant to disclose.

He picked up the telephone again and dialled the number for HMP Barlinnie. This time he was coming in with his temper simmering under the surface and woe betide anyone who stood in his way!

'No, sir, I was in the library accompanying a visiting author,' Thomson told him.

Lorimer gritted his teeth, fuming inwardly. How hard would it have been for McSherry to tell him that?

'Thank you,' he said instead. 'Did you have much to do with Peter Guilford at all?'

The young prison officer thought for a moment then shook his head. 'Not particularly,' he said at last. 'In fact I probably couldn't have told you what he looked like. I tend to concentrate more on the newbies. Poor wee souls who are a bit lost when they come in at first.'

Lorimer smiled, believing the man. He seemed an open and honest type. Brian Thomson's background prior to becoming a prison officer had included some farm work and labouring jobs, though he had obtained a clutch of mediocre grades from high school that had given him the chance for further education at his local college.

Michael Raynor was next, the man that had been first on the

scene. Lorimer stood up as he entered the room. He was a big man, almost his own height of six four, but much broader across the shoulders, more like a rugby prop forward. He had examined all of these prison officers' CVs, something that a reluctant McSherry had handed over and, true enough, Raynor had played rugby during his spell with the army.

The man sat rigid, back ramrod straight, his eyes fixed unflinchingly to Lorimer's.

'You've been with the service for just a few months, Mr Raynor,' Lorimer began. 'What brought you to this particular profession?'

'Seemed a suitable thing to do, sir,' Raynor replied smartly.

He was from down south, Midlands, maybe, Lorimer guessed from the man's accent.

'Public service. Duty. All things we had to undergo as soldiers,' Raynor added. There was no trace of a smile, unlike the previous officer who had been quite affable. Had word spread about why the detective superintendent was here? Had any resentment at the suspicion one of them had attacked a prisoner filtered through to these other men? He hoped not.

'You were first to help the prisoner that was attacked,' Lorimer noted.

'Sir,' Raynor replied, nodding his affirmative.

'What did you think had happened?'

'Some toerags had a go,' Raynor said immediately. 'First thought that crossed my mind. Sir.'

Lorimer stifled a sigh. This one was hard going. If they had been standing then he'd almost have expected a click of heels at every salutation.

'You felt for a pulse?'

'Standard procedure, sir. All trained in first aid,' he said, his face perfectly immobile.

Perhaps inside this man was experiencing some turmoil of emotions Lorimer told himself, but outwardly his expression was completely impassive. Had he learned restraint under fire? It was possible. And a well-trained soldier could easily stand a barrage of questions without flinching.

'Did you think he was dead?'

Raynor's mouth worked for a moment then he shook his head. 'That's something I can't recall, sir,' he said at last. 'Everything happened so fast. Had to get help.' He shrugged then and Lorimer felt a modicum of sympathy for the man. If this was not Guilford's attacker but the man who had initiated his safe passage to hospital then he ought to be thanked. Still, there was no obvious way of knowing which scenario was real and he felt irritated that he had been given so little when the former soldier at last left the room.

Hugh Grimshaw was sweating as he entered the room, a hasty handkerchief stuffed into his trouser pocket. It was another hot day but the interior of the prison was cool enough and Lorimer reckoned that this prison officer was troubled by sweat of a different sort. He, too, was a big fellow, as broad as Raynor and undoubtedly fit enough to have manhandled a prisoner. Of course they all had to be strong, fit men to cope with the job. It was part of the reason that this was going to be a difficult process.

'They're saying you think one of us had a go at Guilford. Is that true?'

'I'm here to eliminate you from our enquiries, Mr Grimshaw.' Lorimer smiled, knowing as the man looked across that the prison officer was instantly reassured by his disarming expression.

'Also, I'd like your help.' He leaned forward as though to include the man in a little conspiracy.

The body language worked as he saw Grimshaw's shoulders relaxing right away and his breath exhaling in a sigh that might just be relief.

'Tell me, is there any way that your uniforms could get into the wrong hands?'

Grimshaw looked puzzled. 'Naw, cannae see it myself.' He shook his head. 'We've all got oor ain locker keys, like.'

'Nobody ever borrowed items of clothing? Boots?'

Grimshaw shook his head.

It was a useful tactic to make the prison officer think that they might be looking for someone outwith their own group. It set the man thinking away from the possibility that he was a suspect.

'What was Guilford like as a prisoner?'

'All right. Never gave any bother. Quiet type. Didn't have that much to do with him after the first day.'

'You were responsible for his orientation?'

'Aye.' Grimshaw shifted a little in his seat, a frown appearing on his brow.

'Was he upset at all?'

The man nodded. 'Aye, but that's common enough. Even with returning offenders.'

'You knew he had been in prison before?'

Grimshaw's face coloured a little. 'Word gets around, ken?'

Lorimer nodded, letting that remark pass. It was probably true enough. And perhaps it was wise to know who were repeat offenders, clued up to the prison system, unlike first-timers who might present the prison staff with other problems.

'No trouble between Guilford and any other inmates, then? His co-pilot?' he asked, using the term that was given by the officers for cellmate.

'Nope.' Grimshaw was leaning back, confidence in his manner now that the conversation had turned to the prison population. 'Nothing at all.'

The man had met Lorimer's gaze with a steady one of his own that made the detective believe him.

'Do you happen to know any of Guilford's family, Mr Grimshaw?'

The man sat up straight, alarm on his pudgy features.

'What?'

'Did you happen to know any of Guilford's family? Friends, maybe, or relatives?'

'No. What are you asking that for?' Grimshaw shook his head, frowning.

'You never saw any visitors for him?'

'Don't think he had any. But Raynor would know better than me. He . . . ' The man stopped abruptly, mouth shut in a sudden line.

You've said more than you want to, Lorimer thought, trying not to show the glint of excitement in his own demeanour.

'Oh? Raynor?' He let the question hang there for a moment, inviting a fuller response.

Grimshaw looked down at his hands, avoiding Lorimer's stare.

'Raynor would know better because . . . ?' Lorimer coaxed.

'He'd known about him before he came inside this time,' Grimshaw mumbled. 'Said he'd met the wife. The one he was inside for attempting to kill. You won't tell him I said this, will you?' He looked up, his eyes filled with trepidation. 'We all thought it was a load of pish, really. Didn't believe him.'

'Why?'

Grimshaw shrugged. 'He's always saying stuff. Like how he won the lottery. Why would he still be working in a job like this

213

if he'd hit the jackpot? Naw, he's wan o' thae fantasists.' He made a sign by his head, twirling a finger.

'So, let me get this right. You didn't believe him when he told you that,' Lorimer said slowly. 'How about after Guilford was attacked? Did you wonder if it was true?'

Grimshaw's chewed his lower lip. 'Cannae say that I thought anything about it,' he answered. 'He raised the alarm, didn't he?'

'That's all, Mr Grimshaw. You really have been very helpful and if there is anything more that you think we can do to apprehend Guilford's attacker you just have to call me,' he said with a smile, sliding his card across the table.

'You'll not tell . . . ?'

'Everything we have discussed is completely in confidence, Mr Grimshaw. You have my word.' Lorimer nodded, rising to shake the man's damp and sweaty hand.

'Can I talk to Raynor again?' Lorimer asked the prison officer who was standing outside the small interview room normally used for solicitors' visits.

'Gone off shift, sir. Soon as you'd finished with him he went home,' the officer told him.

Lorimer hesitated. To chase after Raynor and face him with further questions or remain here and interview the final prison officer whose face was on that sheet of six? He could surely find Raynor at home later on?

'Tell Mr Whitehead I'll see him now,' Lorimer decided.

Martin Whitehead was the oldest of the group, an experienced prison officer whose duties had seen him working in several of the male prisons over the years, including HMP Shotts, his previous posting.

He had had little to do with Peter Guilford, and, like Brian Thomson, preferred to deal with the newer prisoners on remand, those who had not experienced prison life before and needed a little more help in orienting themselves to its regime. The man was smaller than the others, too, possibly not someone that would have been able to inflict the injuries that Guilford had sustained. Still, you never could tell. The few questions that the man answered had the ring of truth about them and Lorimer was happy to eliminate this man from being Guilford's attacker.

It was with a heavy heart that Lorimer left the prison car park, wound his way through the Riddrie streets and headed back along the motorway. It was imperative that he find Raynor once again, see if Grimshaw's claim to have known Dorothy Guilford was true or not. The man hadn't struck him as a fantasist, more a disciplined ex-soldier who needed the authority of someone above him to carry out orders. But, if he had known Dorothy Guilford, was he the person who had set upon her husband in a mad moment of revenge?

There was no response from the flat in Maryhill that Raynor had given as an address. Lorimer gritted his teeth and was on the point of heading downstairs again when a door on the opposite side of the landing opened, an elderly man peering out from behind the security chain. The sound of a horse race could be heard in the background, the television probably turned up high.

'He's no' here,' the man said, his bony finger pointing across at Raynor's front door. 'No' bin here fur weeks.'

'Are you talking about Mr Raynor?' Lorimer approached the old man and held out his warrant card. 'He's been helping us with our enquiries,' he added blandly.

'Oh, aye? Well ye're no' like tae see him here. Buggered aff ages ago. Nae idea where he is noo,' he said with a cackle that became a cough.

'Would he have left a forwarding address with the landlord? The factor?' Lorimer asked, wondering if these flats were owner-occupied or rented, perhaps a mixture of both.

'Aye, mibbe. Sees a wee minute an' ah'll get ye a number,' the man agreed, shutting the door and leaving Lorimer standing outside. A few minutes later the door opened again and Lorimer was handed a scrap of paper with a name scrawled in the old man's shaky block capitals and a telephone number beneath.

'Thank you very much, Mr ...' he glanced at the plastic nameplate on the door jamb, 'Mr McPherson.'

'Aye, well, cannae help ye ony mair, son. Ta-ta the noo.' The old man grinned and shut the door once again, no doubt eager to get back to watching the horse racing.

'We need to find him,' Lorimer told the members of the team who were gathered in his office. 'Where did he go after he'd spoken to me? And why didn't the prison have his current address? He's not been with the service all that long so you would think they would have had his details up to date.'

'Unless he's got something to hide,' DCI Niall Cameron suggested.

'That's what I'm afraid of,' Lorimer replied gloomily. 'Find out where he'd been stationed in the army, what next of kin he had, anything that might tie him in with the Guilfords.'

216

CHAPTER THIRTY-ONE

He sat hunched over the edge of the bunk, eyes tightly closed, hands clasped, lips barely moving as he prayed. 'Lord, please let them find her,' he asked, the awful images returning inside the old man's head. 'Please, dear Lord.'

'Won't do you any good, pal.' A voice nearby made Pavol's eyes fly open, the prayer interrupted.

His cellmate stood over him, a look of pity in his expression.

'Naebody's listening,' the man declared. 'An', if thir is a Goad, how's he no' came doon an' sorted a' this mess oot, tell us that?'

Pavol looked at the younger man. He was a weasel-faced fellow, not much more than a boy, really, but already hardened against life.

'He did come,' Pavol said slowly. 'They nail him on a cross.'

'So what? He was deid, right? How come he nivver goat aff that cross and wiped the flair wi' them? Eh?'

Pavol reached out and took the young man's hand, drawing him to sit on the bunk beside him.

'Jimmy,' Pavol began, the effort of finding the words in English strangely less than usual, the mission woman in his village and her teaching coming back to his mind. 'Not part of his plan,' he began. 'He had to die.'

217

'How come?' Jimmy asked, a frown shadowing his thin face.

Pavol felt something stirring inside, a warmth as if hands had been laid upon him and a burden lifted. When he spoke again the words seemed to come from somewhere else as though he were merely a conduit for another's voice.

'A sacrifice. By God. To give his only son.'

'Eh?'

'The men of those times.' Pavol shrugged. 'Was what they did, made sacrifices to . . . ' he struggled for a moment, wanting the word, '*atone*,' he said, a glint of triumph in his watery eyes.

Then the words came tumbling from his lips as he told of the death and resurrection of God's only son and how anyone could ask for forgiveness.

'Like the thief next to him?' Jimmy asked. 'I 'member that bit.' He laughed and it was a hollow sound, more despair than self-praise for a distant memory about the crucifixion story.

'"Today you will be with me in Paradise,"' Pavol quoted, memories of the Easter story told so often at the Mission back home.

'An you think he's gonnae hear you when you ask him for stuff, eh? You're aff yer heid, auld yin,' Jimmy told him, getting up from the bunk and pacing up and down the narrow cell. Then he stopped and stared for a moment, slack-jawed. 'Here, how come ye're suddenly talking like this?' He looked a little scared as he shook his head, wondering at the change in the old man. It was as if a light shone on him, but, turning, Jimmy could see nothing that accounted for it. He shivered then muttered, 'Thocht your lot couldnae speak a loat o' English. Hiv ye bin kiddin' us all oan, like?'

Pavol watched his face, seeing the flicker of doubt that had been planted there. Jimmy, who had been so sure a few minutes ago, was now beginning to ask himself some rather big questions. And, if he noticed that his cellmate's command of English was better than he had pretended, he might wonder why Pavol had chosen to use it in this way.

The old man smiled quietly. 'He hears me' – he nodded, the certainty in his voice making Jimmy turn, open-mouthed – 'and he will answer.'

'No answer. It's ringing out but nobody's at home.' The big man turned, mobile in hand, and looked at Gid, the driver.

'Well, what are you going to do with her? We cannae leave her here till we know what Max wants done. An' how come he's no' answering his phone? Don't like that, so I don't. An' how come I huvenae been paid the second bit yet?'

Raynor ignored him, turning instead towards the closed door of the old deserted farmhouse, Gid scurrying at his heels. Nobody had been there for months and the flyblown windows were thick with cobwebs, one particularly large spider crawling speedily across the glass.

'She's no' makin' any more noise, anyhow,' Gid said.

Raynor grunted. It was just as well. He'd have slapped her around a bit more to make her shut up if she hadn't gone quiet. But Max had ordered that the girl be kept safe, or at least alive. What was the difference? Why keep this one in particular? They'd found her in Hope Street, heading for the nail bar. Just in time, apparently. She'd screamed blue murder, insisting that she had a job interview, that she was expected there by 'the other woman', whoever that might be.

'I'll try him again.' Raynor sighed, turning away and walking out of earshot until he came to a strip of cracked and broken concrete beside a disused outhouse. Gid was beginning to annoy him, harping on about when he was going to be paid, and Raynor wanted to talk to the boss without the driver hanging on his every word. At least there was a signal in this back of beyond place, he thought, clutching the telephone in his hand as he waited for the ring tone to stop. Outside, the shadows were lengthening and soon darkness would cover his steps. He sighed a long sigh, tapping his booted foot impatiently on the flagstones.

Then, at last, a familiar voice.

'Hello?'

'It's me. We've got the girl. Do you still want her where we planned?'

'Yes, make sure she cannot see anything before you take her inside. Understand?'

'Sure. Oh, and the driver wants his money. Said I'd mention that.'

There was silence at the other end and for a moment Raynor wondered if he had lost the connection. He thrust his hand into his trouser pocket, fingering the rolls of banknotes he had discovered in the girl's backpack. Finders, keepers, he had told himself at the time. Max could cough up for Gid's wages himself, no question.

'Hello?'

'I'm still here.'

'Right, well there's something else. It's the cops. They've been asking too many questions. I stayed away from the flat like you said but it's too risky to keep doin' the bed and breakfast lark. Too damned easy for them to trace me an' all so, the bottom line is, I need a place to crash.'

There was a pause and the man turned away from the sight of the driver who was looking his way.

'You can't come here.'

'Why not?'

'It's just a matter of time before they find out about us.'

'So?'

There was another pause then a sigh. 'You want us to have that money or don't you?'

'Think you already know the answer to that,' Raynor scoffed.

'Well, then,' came the reply. 'Here's what I suggest you do.'

Michael Raynor strolled back along the weed-infested path towards the parked car and jerked his head towards Gid Patterson.

'He says to take her inside,' he told the man. 'Then we head back to the city.'

'And just leave her there?'

'Max knows what he's doing,' Raynor replied. 'He wants her kept alive, remember.'

'She must be worth something,' Gid said at last. 'Max wouldn't want her unless she had money. Or *something*.' He leered and gave a dirty laugh.

Raynor did not reply. Juliana Ferenc was worth more than this thick fellow would ever realise. He'd ingratiated himself with the two Slovaks, asked questions about their plight, feigning a sympathy that he did not feel. And it had worked a charm: the old Slovak dropping the 'no-Engleesh' act and opening up to the kindly prison officer. And little by little the old man had told him, haltingly, about his niece. Juliana. She was meant to meet them in the railway station, Pavol had explained. Then he had looked crafty and tapped the side of his nose. *I not tell the policeman.* He'd grinned. *But I tell you.*

The prison officer recalled how his sleeve had been caught as the old Slovak had poured out his story: the trip from his homeland (thieving here and there as necessity demanded), facing difficulties at the border crossings as they headed north. And then, the final episode of meeting up with other Slovaks in Aberdeen where they had at last found the girl.

My jewel, Pavol had murmured, tears in his eyes.

'Well, she must be worth something,' Raynor murmured, echoing the driver. 'Max wouldn't make such a fuss otherwise.'

Juliana lay on her side on the dusty floor, only a ragged blanket between her body and the bare boards. She ached all over, the manhandling then the beating covering her with bruises. She'd heard the men whispering as they'd taken her away from the city to this place that smelled faintly of animals. Max had been mentioned and she'd shivered on hearing his name. Was that to be her fate, to face him once again? And was she to be punished for escaping? A special punishment that might be long and drawn out, as the gangmaster had promised?

There was no kindness in those men outside this room, but she was still alive and for that she must be grateful. She looked up at the window, set high against the sloping roof, and wondered what was outside. The sky was blue, the colour of speedwells before the wild hyacinths spread their purplish haze across the meadows and over the forest floor outside her village.

Juliana gave a shuddering sob. She wanted to go home. But it was so very far away.

The girl bit her lip to stop from crying but the tears fell silently.

Would she ever see the flowers there again?

CHAPTER THIRTY-TWO

Could there be something linking the attack on Guilford and the traffickers? Solly pondered as he sipped the pale green tea and looked out across the park. Glasgow in all its glory, he told himself, his eyes lifting to the city, its landmark buildings and the hills beyond. It hardly seemed any time at all since he had stood here looking at the snow-capped mountains to the west, and now summer was here, the trees partly obscuring that view.

The psychologist gave a happy sigh. By next winter he would have his family tucked up under this roof, the new baby gurgling in its cot, Rosie singing a song, as she had done when Abby was tiny; all her cares would be over for a time. At least he hoped so. This Dorothy Guilford case bothered him. The woman appeared to have been a strange mixture of spite and fear, a combination that could result in violence, as Solly knew from past experience. And the husband being targeted in prison was just one more marker against him, surely? Unless . . .

Solly drained the porcelain cup and laid it on the window sill, his eyes no longer seeing the landscape but the pictures he had been shown of the Aberdeen raid. One or two of them had found their way into the national press but most were kept within the confines of the MIT in Govan.

The faces of these distraught girls refused to leave him now that he had called them to mind once more. Juliana Ferenc had not been among them, her escape made good by the enterprising uncle and young brother who were still being held in Barlinnie Prison. Had the attack been anything to do with them? Was Peter Guilford involved in the trafficking to that extent? According to Kirsty his only sin was to have rented out vans to the traffickers, something the man insisted was completely out of his control.

'How would he know what they were being used for?' she had asked when they had discussed the case recently.

'He's the boss, anyway, surely it would be one of his under-lings that did the actual renting out?' James had chipped in. A reasonable enough remark, Solly had agreed, but now he was considering just what the system might be when one wished to rent a large van from a hire company. The officers from the MIT would know this, he told himself, checking his watch to see how long he had before the taxi came to drive him across the city. And perhaps at this next meeting he would be inclined to ask this very question.

The boardroom was crowded, windows open to allow some air to filter through, though the increased sound of passing traffic was the price they had to pay for this. Solly edged his way along the row of detectives until he found an empty seat and slipped in, hoping that he was not the last to arrive.

'Thanks for joining us, Professor Brightman,' Lorimer began. 'We need to take stock of exactly where we are with this case and see what actions are required from this point onwards.'

All eyes were on the detective superintendent at the centre of the table, his back to the windows. He was filled with a sort of restless energy, Solly thought, noting the man's body language, his back ever so slightly bent forwards as though he needed to have all of them heed his words, these blue eyes piercing anyone whose gaze met his. And yet, the deep crease between those very eyes betokened nights of sleeplessness, worrying about the apprehension of some killer whose ill intent made his job so difficult. He needed to see these people brought to justice, their victims given whatever peace lay beyond the grave. William Lorimer needed a holiday, he found himself thinking. That was what he would tell Rosie later on. He and Maggie should spend more time up in Mull, away from all of this.

The detective superintendent was speaking again, outlining the steps being taken to find the Ferenc girl. Then, to everyone's amazement, he began to tell them about Michael Raynor, the prison officer who had suddenly failed to turn up for his shift following his interview with the detective superintendent.

The room erupted in a torrent of questions until Lorimer held up his hand for quiet.

'I blame myself for not following him out right away,' he began. 'But nobody was to know that he'd done a runner. It was the end of his shift, so there was nothing untoward about him leaving the place.'

'Locker cleared out?' one voice asked and Lorimer nodded.

'He must have known he'd been suspected. And now, I think one of the first people I need to see is Peter Guilford.' He looked around at the officers who were nodding in agreement. 'And this time there is only one picture I'll be showing that man.'

The man in the bed turned his head away as soon as Lorimer produced the image, a blown-up head shot of Michael Raynor.

There was silence between the two men as Lorimer waited, stony-faced, for Guilford to look him in the eye.

A sigh, a pursing of the lips, then that imperceptible nod.

'You know him, then?'

Guilford glanced at Lorimer then looked away again, a pained expression in his eyes. 'I didn't know it was him when he attacked me,' he said at last. 'Couldn't see him for the shower spray.'

'When did you know?'

Guilford hesitated for a moment. 'I think he spoke to me,' he admitted at last. 'I recognised his voice.' He looked up. 'That English accent.'

'So, when you saw the picture you *did* know it was him,' Lorimer stated. 'Who is he, Peter?' he asked, his voice softening but his eyes still focused on the man in the bed.

Another sigh. 'Don't really know . . . '

'Come on, don't give me that!' Lorimer snapped, exasperated at what he felt was another lie.

'He knew Dorothy,' Guilford continued. 'Came to the house once or twice. Maybe more, I don't know. When I was out, possibly?'

'And . . . ?'

'And, nothing. She said he was a family friend from way back.'

'Can't have been that far back, Raynor's just twenty-nine, a good fifteen years younger than your late wife. What was their relationship?'

'I told you, I don't know,' Guilford insisted. 'Look, he turns up one day in his army uniform and Dorothy greets him like a long-lost son. Blethers on about how nice it is to see him again, blah, blah, blah. '

'You didn't enquire about the connection between them?'

'Thought he must be the son of an old friend from school, or something,' Guilford replied, deliberately avoiding Lorimer's gaze.

There was something he was not telling the detective; that was obvious. But were there any grains of truth in his story?

'She knew him well, then?'

Guilford shifted uncomfortably. 'All I remember was the way Dorothy treated them. I mean *him*. Like the prodigal son coming back home or something.'

Lorimer noted the stumble. Raynor had not visited Dorothy Guilford alone, then? But with somebody else?

'He was from down south?'

'Aye,' Guilford agreed. 'Maybe one of her pals had moved away there and she was wanting to make a connection again? I don't know.'

Don't know or weren't interested, Lorimer thought. Peter Guilford did not really seem to have cared much for his late wife or shown any interest in her, except for her wealth and the lucrative business her father had passed on to her.

'You didn't ask any questions then?'

'Too busy,' Guilford said. 'Never had much time for social chit-chat. I had a business to run.' A petulant note crept into his voice as though he were trying to make excuses for his lack of observation of the young man who had befriended his wife. A man who had tried to kill him.

'Why do you think he attacked you?'

Guilford sighed a long sigh. 'I've been lying here trying to work that out,' he said, avoiding Lorimer's eye. 'Can't fathom why someone I hardly knew would do that.'

Oh, yes you can, Lorimer told himself, his jaw clenching in sudden anger.

'Are you sure?' he asked softly, leaning closer to the patient and fixing him with a blue glare.

But Guilford had closed his eyes.

'Sure,' he mumbled. Then, 'I'm tired now. Please go and leave me in peace.'

'Michael Raynor was discharged from active service following a tour of duty in Slovakia,' Niall Cameron told Lorimer. 'We've got his record here. Was in the Royal Regiment of Scotland, funnily enough,' he said, a glint in his eye. 'Wonder if there was a connection? Anyway it says here that he was an exemplary soldier, even had a commendation for bravery when he rescued a chap from a burning building.'

The DCI from Lewis looked at Lorimer and smiled. 'In Slovakia,' he repeated, watching his boss's eyebrows rise.

'When was this?'

'About two or three years before he joined the prison service. Came back home to the UK when the regiment moved from Germany to North Yorkshire. It was shortly after that he left the army. Think he wasn't alone in that. According to the fellow I spoke to in Catterick, a few others seemed to have been disillusioned with the service once they were back home.'

'What was he doing in Slovakia?' Lorimer looked at his friend and colleague for a long moment and this time it was Cameron's grey eyes that registered a glimmer of interest.

'A connection with the Romany people way back then, d'you think?'

Lorimer nodded. 'Maybe. It all comes back to why Raynor wanted to kill Peter Guilford.'

'Something to do with the people trafficking?' Cameron mused. 'Maybe he fell in with the very people who were busy

228

making plans to have all these women taken from their homes and used in the slave trade over here.'

Lorimer exhaled ·a huge sigh and shook his head. 'No point in speculating,' he said. 'We need more evidence. And until we know where Raynor is and what his link was to Dorothy Guilford, we'll never be able to answer that question.'

But one question that had to be answered concerned the victim of that fire. Lorimer had a flicker of insight: a man with a burned face, a man called Max. Was this the same person that Michael Raynor had rescued? And, if so, where was he now?

CHAPTER THIRTY-THREE

Kirsty turned on her side and gazed at the tousled dark head on the pillow beside her. It was no use pretending any more, she thought. James was going to go to Chicago and begin a new life there. If she wanted to be part of that life then she had to make the sacrifice of leaving the police and abandoning all of her plans for promotion.

James had been so excited after that trip to London, eyes shining as he had told her about the sort of work he would be doing, the prospects that were his for the asking. He just needed to give them his decision within the week. What did she think?

Lying next to him, feeling that sense of utter contentment that invariably followed their love making, Kirsty thought that James Spencer was probably the best thing that had ever happened to her. *Don't let him go*, a small voice insisted. But was that inner thought saying that she should strive to keep him here in Glasgow while she pursued her own career, or that she must hold onto their relationship no matter what? Just at this moment Kirsty would have gladly abandoned her own job and followed her lover wherever he went. No worries about killers on the loose, no dangers to face in car chases or confrontations . . . Oh, hell, but she would miss all of that!

She grinned as she turned onto her back, images of past cases appearing like stills in the slide show of her mind. She'd be removed from the present intrigue, too, Kirsty reminded herself; her duty as a CID officer clashing somewhat with the private investigations she was carrying out on behalf of Rosie Fergusson. That wasn't all bad, though, she realised. It was fun finding out more and more about the background to Dorothy Guilford's life and meeting people like the grossly overweight sister, things that hadn't been part of the official investigation after Guilford's arrest.

She frowned as the memory of Lorimer's latest memo had reached her: *Michael Raynor has obviously had some sort of relationship with Dorothy Guilford. What that is we have still to discover.* The unspoken implication was that Kirsty ought to get a move on and find that out. She could go back and see the elder sister, she mused, see if the name meant anything to her.

With a sigh she cuddled into James's back and slid an arm around his waist. Later, she told herself; after all, it wasn't a matter of life or death, was it?

'You can't stay here,' Shirley told the big man standing in the middle of her living room. 'Told you already. The busies have been snooping around. Fine thing it would be if they found you in my house!'

The man did not reply, simply gave a sniff and nodded. 'What about the money?' he asked.

'It'll come our way,' Shirley promised. 'We just need to hold tight and wait. Don't you worry. Peter will never get out of that hospital, not if we can help it.'

'Okay,' he replied at last, looking at her with an impassive stare. Then he turned on his heel and left the room. Shirley listened as the front door opened then closed again.

Left alone once more, the woman breathed out a sigh of relief. Coming here had been a mistake. And she only hoped that he had the sense to stay away until they had everything sorted.

A shadow from the street outside fell across the room and Shirley glanced around, half expecting to see a figure at the window. But there was nobody.

Dorothy's presence seemed to hover over them still, she thought with a shudder. In life she had been a constant torment and in death she was still wielding some sort of power over them all. It was imperative that Peter should meet with a tragic end before he was whisked away out of their reach to another prison. She sat in the ancient armchair, thinking hard. Yet, no matter how many ideas came to mind, there was only one person that she trusted to carry out that final execution.

'Hello again, it's DC Wilson,' Kirsty announced brightly, smiling at the overweight woman standing on the doormat, a belligerent expression on her jowly face.

'What d'you want?' the woman snapped, arms folded across her heavy bosoms as she stood barring the way into her home.

Kirsty forced a smile. 'Just needed to ask you something,' she began, glancing over Shirley Finnegan's shoulders to see if she had any company inside the house; a reason for keeping the detective standing here on the threshold.

The door widened a little and the woman stepped back. 'Better come in,' she said grudgingly, slouching along the hallway leaving Kirsty to shut the door and follow her.

'How are you?' Kirsty asked, sitting on the arm of the settee that was covered in piles of laundry. Dirty? Or ready for ironing? It was hard to tell from the glance she gave them.

'I'm sure you didn't come here to ask after my health,' Shirley drawled, picking up a packet of cigarettes and reaching for a lighter.

'You didn't seem too well last time I was here ...' Kirsty began. 'But you're right, I did come here for a particular reason.'

She waited till the woman had lit up and taken a draw from the cigarette then caught her eye.

'Do you know a man called Michael Raynor?' she asked, watching intently to see Shirley Finnegan's reaction.

'Who?' The question was accompanied by a frown. But she still gazed into Kirsty's eyes, no flicker at all, no turning her head to one side.

'Michael Raynor,' Kirsty repeated.

Shirley shook her head slowly. 'Can't say I do,' she replied. 'Funny sort of name that. Never heard it before.'

'He's English,' Kirsty told her, as if that explained the man's surname.

'That right?' Shirley was clearly uninterested. 'So? Why would I know this person?'

'I think he might have known your sister.'

'Ha! That could well be right, Miss Wilson,' Shirley exclaimed. Then she leaned forward, the ash from her cigarette threatening to fall onto the stained carpet with its telltale burn marks. 'I hadn't seen my sister for years,' she hissed. 'So I wouldn't know what sort of company she kept, would I?'

Kirsty bit back a reply. There was more to that answer than Shirley Finnegan might realise. What sort of company? Was she implying that Dorothy had unsuitable friends? Or had some hidden extra-marital relationship? Shirley Finnegan knew more

233

than she was letting on, Kirsty thought. But her reaction to hearing Michael Raynor's name had thrown the young detective. Perhaps she genuinely knew nothing abut the man who had tried to kill her brother-in-law and Kirsty was wasting her time here.

'Sorry to have bothered you,' she told Shirley as she rose to her feet. 'I'll see myself out,' she added since it was quite obvious that the woman slumped in her armchair had no intention of performing that particular politeness.

Shirley Finnegan held the second cigarette to the smouldering embers of the first, puffing until she felt the hit of nicotine. Her heart hammered in her chest as she replayed the incident. 'A friend of Dorothy's ... aye, too bloody right,' she muttered. 'Maybe I'll see you both in hell!'

I hadn't seen my sister for years ... The phrase kept coming back to Kirsty as she drove back to Helen Street. And every time she repeated the words she wanted to add *until* ...

Had Shirley Finnegan seen Dorothy in the days running up to her death? She was not what Kirsty would call a reliable sort of person and she still suspected that some of the things she had been told were outright lies. Had she been in the house in St Andrew's Drive that night? Had *her* podgy fist wielded that kitchen knife? There was sufficient animosity against the younger sister to believe that she could have killed her in a moment of temper ... *I hadn't seen my sister for years until* ... what?

There was something nagging at her, telling her she should be looking in a different place to find that answer but her mind kept drifting back to the cleaning lady, Margaret Daly, and what else she might have to tell about the two Pettigrew sisters.

CHAPTER THIRTY-FOUR

olly Newton glanced up as the big man entered the salon
and then disappeared into the back room that doubled
as an office. She tried hard not to let the black gel drip onto her
client's finger as she painted the long curved nail. 'An' I says tae
her, get a life, will ye?' The client babbled on about one of her
work colleagues, Molly barely listening but nodding from time
to time, a fixed smile on her face. She was desperate to finish
this job, grab her mobile, dash downstairs and call HQ. That was
Michael Raynor who just walked in, she thought, heart drumming with excitement.

'Just put your hand under there ... great,' Molly said, switching on the gel dryer. 'Just need to nip out for a wee moment ...'
But, as she began to rise from her place behind the nail bar, the
man emerged once more and stopped, looking around at the
girls busy with their clients. His gaze came at last to Molly, who
turned away a little, letting her long hair fall across her face.

'Och, it can wait,' she told her client. 'What did that woman do
next?' she asked, pretending interest in the story that had been
unfolding a moment before.

She did not look up as a shadow fell across the table, grinning and nodding as she busied herself with tidying up the bottles of lotion and gel, faking a concentration on the other girl's words. Molly felt the sweat gather along her hairline, conscious of the man standing, staring at her. It would be unnatural not to look up, she thought.

Her lips curved in the sweetest smile as she caught his eye.

'Hello, can I help you?' she asked. But he merely continued staring then shook his head, moved away and walked back out of the salon.

'Funny sort of guy, eh?' the client remarked, her own eyes following the man as he left.

'Oh, we get all sorts in here,' Molly told her cheerfully. 'Never a dull moment.' She was conscious of her heart thudding and wondered if Michael Raynor would be waiting for her at the foot of the stairs.

At last her client paid and left and Molly rushed into the toilet, whipping out her mobile and pressing the number.

'It's me,' she said breathlessly. 'Michael Raynor just walked in here. He went into the office, came back out and hovered over me and my client then left. What do you want me to do?'

The woman felt a sense of relief when she was told, *Do nothing.* But that relief was tinged with a sense of foreboding. He knows who I am, she thought, as she gathered up her bag and unlocked the toilet door. Should she follow orders and stay put? Or was it time to creep out after the fugitive and see where he went?

'Hope Street,' the radio call went out, giving time and source details. Soon there would be other people following up Molly Newton's call, searching the city streets for the ex-soldier who had attacked Peter Guilford. A description had already been circulated to every unit in the country, surveillance cameras being monitored all the time, intelligence officers combing the information to catch a glimpse of the wanted man. But, after an hour, it seemed that Raynor had disappeared as though by magic.

'He has to be holed up somewhere,' Lorimer fumed. 'People don't just vanish in a city like Glasgow!' His frustration was etched on his face, the cleft between his eyes deepening as his frown darkened. Where was he? Had he spotted Molly Newton, guessed that she was a plant in the nail bar? Just how much did Michael Raynor know about Guilford's business and was that tied up with the sex trafficking? Is that why he had tried to kill Guilford in Barlinnie Prison? There were too many questions going unanswered. Perhaps it was time to put more pressure on Dorothy Guilford's husband, Lorimer decided, looking out at the clear blue skies and wondering how much information he could squeeze out of the man.

'Don't.' Cynthia bit her lip as Peter dropped her hand. 'Why . . . ?'

'Shh,' he whispered, glancing across the room to the open door where a uniformed police officer sat. 'They watch us all the time, you know. If they suspected . . . '

'What? That I love you? That I miss you? Dear God, Peter.' Cynthia shook her head, her eyes widening.

'Keep your voice down, will you?' Peter hissed. 'If they think we're more than business colleagues, what do you imagine the prosecution will make of it when the trial begins? Eh?' He leaned closer towards her. 'They'd say we wanted Dorothy dead, wouldn't they? And you, my dear, would be implicated, wouldn't you?'

Cynthia drew back at the malicious expression on Guilford's

face. 'Stop it, you're frightening me!' she told him, her voice barely a whisper.

'You can't keep coming in here,' Guilford told her. 'Now go away, Cynthia, do what Frank said. Keep things going at work and stay away from here, d'you hear me?' His voice rose a little, enough to alert the officer sitting with his newspaper folded across his lap.

The woman gathered up her jacket and stood, ready to leave. For a moment she hesitated, wanting to lean forward and kiss the man in the bed, but a jerk of his head made her turn away and walk swiftly out of the room, past the cop and past two men standing talking in the corridor, hardly seeing them for the tears that were blurring her eyes.

Cynthia paused for a moment by the nurses' station.

'Please,' she began as one of them looked up to see her standing there. 'You're his dedicated nurse, right?'

'Mr Guilford? Yes, I am. What is it?' the nurse asked, rising from her seat and coming around to take Cynthia by the arm. 'Are you okay?'

Cynthia fought back the tears. 'It's just . . . I don't know when I will see him again. Please . . . ' She gulped. 'Please can you do one thing for me? Let me know the moment anyone comes to take him back to prison? I couldn't bear it if . . . ' She choked back the sobs.

'Well, I don't know,' the nurse replied doubtfully.

'Please,' Cynthia begged. She scrabbled in her handbag and pulled out one of her business cards. 'Look. Here's my number. Just ring me. Please?'

The nurse took the card that Cynthia held out and slipped it into her pocket.

'Oh, all right, but I hope this doesn't get me into any trouble,' she muttered.

Cynthia shot her a grateful look then walked swiftly away, head down, too blinded by tears to notice anyone else passing her by.

'Oh, I would say he's making a good recovery, Superintendent,' the consultant told Lorimer. 'Better than we could have expected after the protracted period when he was in a coma.' Mr Ahasan shrugged. 'The brain is a fascinating organ, and the human skull is far more robust than most people suppose it to be.'

'When might he be fit for discharge?'

The consultant pursed his lips and thought before answering. 'Ideally we would like all of his functions to be back to normal. His blood pressure is still giving a little concern. Fluctuates.' He nodded. Then he gave a little smile. 'Most probably when you come to visit, I'd say.'

They stood aside as a thin, dark-haired woman rushed past them and hurried along the corridor.

'That's his ... secretary,' Ahasan told Lorimer as the two men followed her with their eyes. 'She seems quite upset, doesn't she?'

'Has he had any other visitors?' Lorimer asked, though in truth he knew the answer to that, the on-duty police officer keeping a close watch on the man who was still under suspicion for murdering his wife.

Mr Ahasan's dark eyes twinkled. 'Just the ones you already know about,' he smiled. 'That lady ... from his business,' he remarked tactfully, though the raised eyebrows told Lorimer that the consultant saw more than he was letting on. 'Then of course there have been visits from his solicitor and the prison governor.'

Lorimer nodded. They had kept a close eye on Cynthia Drollinger, the whispers that had passed between the patient and his secretary appearing more than merely business talk. Kirsty's impression was that Drollinger and Guilford had been in an intimate relationship and this seemed to be true. And her obvious distress might just be the perfect time to confront Guilford and ask some more awkward questions.

'You again.' Guilford's words were accompanied by a glare of resentment. 'Cannae leave me in peace, can you?'

'Michael Raynor,' Lorimer began. 'He wasn't always a prison officer, was he?'

Guilford turned his head away, refusing to meet the detective superintendent's eyes.

'A soldier for a good few years before that, wasn't he?'

Guilford shrugged, still looking away from the tall man's stare.

'Let me tell you a little about him,' Lorimer continued. 'Humour me for a few minutes, will you? I'm sure you know all of this already but let's see, shall we?'

He could hear Guilford's sigh as he let his head sink into the pillows, saw the tightening jaw and wondered if he was wasting his time here with the man.

'Michael Raynor was brought up in Huddersfield, father was a soldier and his two younger brothers also went into the forces.' He paused for a moment but there was no flicker of interest in Guilford's expression so he plunged on. 'Michael had an unblemished service record, even received a commendation for bravery when he was out in Slovakia.'

He stopped. Was that a muscle moving in Guilford's face? And was that ripple beneath the bedclothes a fist suddenly clenching? Perhaps.

'Slovakia,' Lorimer repeated. 'Bit of a coincidence that the people to whom you rented your vans came from there, isn't it, Peter?'

Guilford turned and looked at the detective. 'So what?' he sneered. 'Told you already, I never knew what the clients did once they rented my vehicles.'

'That right?' Lorimer mused. 'Maybe Ms Drollinger had a better idea of their ultimate use than her boss. Perhaps I should ask her?'

'Leave her alone!' Guilford snapped. 'Cynthia is just an administrator. She does a good job and that's all.'

'Is it?' Lorimer left the question hanging and for a moment their eyes met, Guilford looking away first.

'Peter, I've asked you this before, but this time I want the truth. What do you know about Max?'

The man turned his head away then Lorimer heard another sigh.

'Tell the nurse I need to have a rest,' Guilford said at last. 'You've tired me out again, Superintendent. Not good for a man in my condition.' He turned back and looked at Lorimer through narrowed eyes.

'A man in your condition?' Lorimer replied quietly. 'You were never meant to get up from the floor of that shower. It's only by sheer luck that he didn't finish you off when he had the chance.'

Guilford's brow furrowed.

'Two inmates came by, disturbed him,' Lorimer explained. 'He pretended that he was trying to help you and had to raise the alarm. Otherwise . . . ' He shook his head meaningfully.

Guilford looked away again but this time Lorimer could see that the colour had drained from the man's cheeks. Perhaps he was genuinely tired? The emotion caused by his previous visitor would have taken its toll, too. But this was no time for pity, not when there was a killer on the loose and the lives of so many trafficked women were at stake.

'You will be taken to Low Moss and kept in a secure unit,' Lorimer told him. 'Then you will go for trial.'

Guilford turned his head back swiftly. 'How many times do I have to tell you people? I did not kill my wife!' His fist thumped the bedclothes. 'She was fine when I came to bed. Then the next time I saw her was down in the kitchen, covered in blood.'

The man glared at Lorimer, his jaw clenched tight and the detective could see a pulse throbbing in the man's neck.

'The forensic evidence . . .'

Another silent thump on the bedclothes.

'Can they no' tell the difference between an old stain and a fresh one? I havenae worn that jacket for years!' Guilford exploded, his Glagow accent thickening as the question burst from him.

'How do you know about the jacket?'

'Frank Dawson's been keeping me up to date with developments,' Guilford told him through gritted teeth.

'If it is a particularly old stain then perhaps that can be shown in court. Your defence will make sure of that,' Lorimer mused.

'That's what Frank said.'

Lorimer sat looking at the man for a long moment. 'Let's say you are found not guilty of Dorothy's death,' he began, choosing his words carefully. The word *murder* might not apply if Rosie Fergusson's theory was correct, after all. 'What then? You go back to work, you are asked to hire out vehicles again . . . and perhaps one day the client who comes to your premises turns out to be Michael Raynor. A man who evidently wanted to see you dead.'

'Then, Superintendent, your lot better make sure and find him before that happens,' Guilford replied.

'Why did he want to kill you, Peter?' Lorimer asked softly, leaning as close to the man as he dared. But Guilford had turned away and closed his eyes, one hand already on the buzzer to alert his dedicated nurse.

Margaret Daly had been hard to track down again, her different little cleaning jobs taking her all over Pollokshields where the owners of so many big houses required her services. Kirsty stood at the woman's own door and rang the bell. The sound of Big Ben played out on chimes made her smile. This would be a perfect home, she guessed, with all of the frills and furbelows exactly right, no speck of dust permitted anywhere.

'Aw, hen, it's you again!' Margaret Daly beamed at Kirsty and the detective smiled back as she was ushered indoors in marked difference to the frosty reception she had received from Shirley Finnegan.

Kirsty's smile broadened as she entered the sitting room, her guess about Mrs Daly's home spot on. A glance showed her that each cushion on the armchairs and twin settees was balanced on its points, the sweeping curtains held back with decorative bronze holdback arms and a cluster of tiny crystal ornaments arranged on the well-polished side table by the window, the sunlight glancing off their facets in rainbow hues.

'Well, now, nice tae see you, lassie. But I 'spect you've come on business,' Margaret Daly said, sitting down next to Kirsty and affecting a serious expression. 'Is it about pair wee Dorothy, then?'

Kirsty smiled and shook her head. 'Only sort of,' she told the cleaning lady. 'We have another investigation that impinges on this one,' she said.

Margaret frowned and Kirsty decided it was best not to explain 'impinged' but leave the word hanging. Sometimes being deliberately obscure was the best way forward.

'I wanted to ask you about a man,' she continued. Then, bringing out a folded sheet she smoothed it out and laid it in front of the older woman.

'Oh, aye, I know that face,' Margaret exclaimed. 'It wis yon Michael that came to see Dorothy,' she said. 'Lovely big fellow, so handsome in his uniform. But then,' she gave Kirsty a playful nudge with her elbow, 'I've always had a soft spot for a man in uniform.'

'So, you know him?' Kirsty asked.

'Not *know* him, exactly, dearie, I just met him the times he was in the house when I happened to be cleaning, that's all. Oh!' Margaret's hand flew to her mouth. 'Don't tell me something's happened to him! Poor boy! And him that brave to help yon other one, too!'

'Other one?'

'Aye, never said much, pair sowel.' She leaned forward and whispered conspiratorially, 'Maybe a wee want. His face . . . dear God, what a sight! All burned away and skin grafted back on. Gave me the willies, so it did!'

Kirsty's heart seemed to miss a beat. 'This other man. Do you remember his name?'

Mrs Daly shook her head. 'Sorry, hen. But I 'member Dorothy was real kind to him. Funny, that. She wis never that soft tae onybody else. Och, I've no' bin much help, have I, lass? And . . . is it something serious?'

Kirsty patted her arm reassuringly. 'Nothing to worry about, Mrs Daly,' she soothed. 'We just need to find Michael and speak to him about something, that's all.'

'Thank Gawd for that,' she sighed. 'I thought you were going to tell me some bad news. Poor Dorothy doted on that pair o' laddies. I could see that. Came from not having any of her own, I suppose. But then you can always fall for a nice face and a smart turnout.'

'Dorothy fancied him?'

'Get away with you, it was nothing like that, lassie. She jist . . . ' Margaret Daly stared into space as though trying to find the right word. 'Dorothy needed to be the lady bountiful, I suppose. Took them under her wing.'

'How did they meet?'

Margaret Daly shrugged. 'I don't know and that's Gawd's honest truth. One day the laddies just turned up and then the quiet one wid be there sometimes, not often, mind. But I got the feeling . . . '

'Yes?'

Margaret Daly screwed up her face in concentration. 'I think she must have known him from way back,' she mused. 'But I don't know how. He was English, you see. Like Michael. And the Pettigrews had no family in England far as I know.'

Kirsty nodded. 'Thanks, Mrs Daly. That's been a big help. We might find Michael Raynor through some other channels . . . '

'Raynor?' Margaret Daly looked up, surprised. 'Wis that his name?'

Kirsty nodded.

'Well, if you say so. My memory's that bad nowadays it's a wonder I can remember ma own name at times!' she chuckled. 'I get names all mixed up nowadays. Maybe I'm thinking on that ither one, the one with the burns . . . oh, what was his name now?'

Kirsty waited patiently but it was evident the old lady was struggling to remember.

Raynor had certainly been the name given by his regiment and was on his UK passport as well as his driving licence and so perhaps the cleaning lady was simply mixed up, Kirsty decided as she rose to leave.

'Have you any idea when Dorothy's funeral will be …' Margaret Daly asked as she showed Kirsty out. 'Only I was hoping to pay my respects.'

'Sorry, her body won't be released for burial just yet,' Kirsty said. 'But if you give me a mobile number I can text you when there is some news?'

'Aye, here it is,' Margaret said, fishing in the pocket of her cotton dress and bringing out a slightly dog-eared card: *Daly's Cleaning*.

The woman had the grace to blush as Kirsty looked at the card. It was supposed to be a few wee jobs on the side, but maybe the cleaning lady raked in more cash than she was letting on. Still, she was doing the police some favours so Kirsty would keep this to herself. After all, if she did quit the force, who was to know what this kindly woman did in her own time? And besides, perhaps she did pay tax on all of her extra income.

The walk back along by Bellahouston Park gave Kirsty time to reflect on her visit. Above, the trees were waving in a gentle breeze, their lime green still fresh before the humidity of the coming months. Margaret Daly had seen a lot of changes in that family; the disgraced Shirley banished from the house, Dorothy's parents passing away and now this tragic death. How, she wondered, had it affected the visiting soldiers? Had he lashed out at the prisoner because he had held some affection for Dorothy Guilford? She frowned. Was it a mere coincidence that Raynor had been a prison officer at Barlinnie when Guilford was there on remand? There was certainly nothing to show to the contrary. Often, the young detective knew, people took advantage of situations that gave them opportunities. And, if this Michael Raynor had been someone special in Dorothy Guilford's life, then why hadn't they heard about him before? And who was his quiet friend? It was a puzzle.

A figure striding towards her put all thoughts of the case aside as she stopped, the detective superintendent returning her wave.

'Hello, out for a breath of fresh air? Have to admit I needed a break myself,' he told her as they fell into step, heading back to HQ.

'We have had a possible sighting of Raynor,' he told her. 'Out past Shawfield Stadium. Could be nothing, but we're following up everything right now.'

Kirsty studied the tall man loping by her side. He looked careworn and she wondered if that would be how she might appear to others if she climbed the promotion ladder and spent her days and nights ferreting out society's ne'er-do-wells. For a moment the idea made her grimace. It wasn't what she wanted, was it? To become like some of the other female officers, hardbitten and cynical in their outlook, always trying to show that they were as good as if not better than their male colleagues.

'James has been offered a job in Chicago,' she blurted out suddenly, making Lorimer stop and stare at her.

'Wow, that's a big step, isn't it?' he remarked. Then, a frown on his face, he added, 'Where does that leave you, Kirsty? Thought you had your sergeant's interview coming up?'

Kirsty looked away and shrugged. 'I'm not sure,' she admitted. 'I still have to decide. But if I do leave the police then it will be for good reasons, I promise.'

She felt his hand clasp her and give it a squeeze.

'I know, lass. Some choices are harder to make than others. But at the end of the day I am sure you will do what's right for yourself.'

'I hope so,' she told him.

'What do your mum and dad think?' he asked.

It was a reasonable question. Lorimer had known her parents for years, her dad having been his DS at Stewart Street for long enough, and they looked on Lorimer as a family friend as much as anything else.

When she looked at the ground and didn't reply, he shook his head and sighed. 'You haven't told them?'

'They know about the promotion possibility,' she mumbled.

'But not about Chicago?'

'It's a big thing,' Kirsty insisted, then spread out her left hand, the engagement ring sparkling in the sunshine. 'They'll want him to make an honest woman of me now. But I don't want a big fancy wedding, just family and friends around us.'

Lorimer grinned but kept quiet and Kirsty laughed. 'Okay, so we probably will change our minds about that. Can't see Mum being done out of her daughter's big day, can you?'

'You are their only child, lass,' he told her.

'Aye, aye,' she sighed. 'Oh, well, I suppose it will all turn out okay. Anyway, how are things going upstairs? Any news of the gang boss?'

Lorimer made a face. 'Absolutely no progress on that front though we do have some operatives working in various parts of the city, keeping an eye on several likely places. Trouble is, these prostitution rackets are everywhere and anywhere; not like Aberdeen where they had these old rented flats. This is harder to pin down.'

'Pop-up brothels?'

Lorimer nodded. 'Pop-up everything these days. Makes it hard to keep track of even legitimate businesses.'

'There something I wanted to tell you,' Kirsty began. 'It's about the two—'

She was interrupted as Lorimer's phone rang out.

'Sorry, I have to take this,' he told her, stopping abruptly and putting his mobile to his ear. Stepping away from her, he spoke into the phone, his back turned so that Kirsty could not hear what was being said but she could see from the way his shoulders stiffened that something was up.

'So sorry, I have to go,' he apologised again. Then, quickening his pace, he glanced to left and right and sped across the road, Kirsty watching as he practically ran back into the red-brick building leaving her curious to know what had made him race off so suddenly. She frowned. Pity that Lorimer hadn't asked her to be part of the MIT; she would loved to have known every detail about the ongoing operation, not just the bits that he had chosen to reveal to her.

CHAPTER THIRTY-FIVE

'Where is she?' Lorimer demanded as he rushed into the DCI's room.

Niall Cameron shook his head. 'We don't know. Molly's phone just suddenly stopped responding so we sent one of her colleagues to the salon.'

'And ...?' Lorimer's face was twisted in anxiety.

'She was told that Molly had left, just that. Nobody knew where she had gone or why. She had clients waiting to be taken ...'

'Dear Lord!' Lorimer exclaimed. 'You don't think she's gone off on her own? She was told to stay put!'

Cameron shook his head. 'Molly is pretty good at keeping in touch. Hasn't ever been known to do a Lone Wolf stunt before ...'

'But you think maybe she has this time?'

'It's possible. Or else someone was waiting for her if she nipped out of the salon?'

Lorimer's face blanched. These people were ruthless. And, if Molly Newton's cover had been blown, they might find the undercover operative's body floating in the Clyde.

*

Molly struggled against the hands that held something soft and sweet-smelling against her face. Then she felt herself falling, falling into a dark and endless void.

When she awoke it was to see a pair of eyes looking down at her, shining in the darkness. Was it night? Or had they put her in some underground room where no light could penetrate? She felt a wave of nausea creep up into her mouth then she swallowed hard, forcing it back down. She would choke, Molly told herself, trying to remain calm. But her hands were secured behind the wooden chair where she was seated, her shoulders a dull ache, a strip of tape across her mouth.

'Sasha? Are you all right?' a voice in the darkness asked, a voice she recognised.

Molly looked up at the girl and saw concern in those frightened eyes.

'It will hurt,' Juliana told her, lifting her hands and letting them fall in a gesture of apology.

Molly stared back and nodded.

Then, as the strip was yanked off, she stifled a scream, the pain searing across her face.

Juliana held up the tape in front of her face and Molly could see something dark dripping from it. Her face must be a mess, she thought, the pain burning around the delicate tissues of her lips and cheeks where the tape had been stuck fast.

'Can you untie me?' she whispered but Juliana shook her head.

'I tried,' the girl told her. 'But it is hard ... too hard ...'

Molly wriggled her wrists and felt the plastic ties cutting into her flesh. Flexing her fingers, she strove to make sense of how she was bound. It felt as though a circlet of hard plastic was wrapped around each hand, linking them together with another ridged tie. Unless the girl had a knife or something equally sharp, there would be no way to cut her free.

'Where are we?'

Juliana glanced at the wall and Molly blinked, just now making out the shape of a doorway.

'I don't know, Sasha,' she confessed. 'When you came they brought me down here too.'

Molly bit back a reply. If Juliana still thought that she was a nail-bar girl named Sasha, then perhaps her captors would think that too?

'Drugged?' she asked.

Juliana nodded. 'I was sick,' she told Molly. 'What they gave to make me asleep . . . '

'Is there any way we can get a light?' Molly asked, gazing around at the space, blinking hard as if that would illuminate the pitch-black room they were in.

'I don't think so,' Juliana replied. 'It always like this. I don't know if it night or day,' she said, then began to cry softly, hands covering her face.

Molly struggled a little more, wishing she was free of her bonds and could take the Slovakian girl in her arms to comfort her. But the plastic ties only cut into her more and she could feel a slither of wetness crawling down her fingers that was either blood or sweat.

'Has anyone been here since they locked you in?'

Juliana nodded and wiped her face with the back of her hands. 'Just to give me water and . . . ' she turned and indicated a bucket that was hardly discernible in one far away corner, '*that*,' she added, wrinkling her nose.

'No food?'

The girl shook her head.

Molly thought hard. It was like terrorist tactics, keeping your prisoners in darkness, denying them food. What next? She shivered, her imagination creating scenes of unspeakable horror, the sorts of things she had read about in missives from overseas, things that the general public seldom got to see. She was just one of the officers who had read the dossier about the traffickers, had seen some of the horrific pictures of women being tortured ... women tied to chairs ... Then a thought occurred to her.

'Did this happen to you before, Juliana? When they took you to Aberdeen?'

There was a momentary silence then the girl came closer and stared at Molly.

'How do you know about that?' she asked, mouth open in astonishment.

'Never mind how,' Molly said quickly. 'Are these the same people who took you before?'

Juliana nodded, head bowed. 'They came for me to the village,' she said slowly. 'Thought I had been picked because I was clever, learned to speak English at school. Not like my poor brother, Mario. He hated the lessons,' she added sorrowfully. Then, bit by bit, in her halting English, the story unfolded. How the promise of work in a fish processing plant had made her eager to leave for Scotland, her friend Alysha with her.

'After we come to England I never see her again,' Juliana said sorrowfully. 'She was taken away ...'

'Pretty girl?' Molly guessed.

Juliana nodded.

It was more than likely that the other Slovakian girl had been sold as a bride, Alysha's European passport like gold dust for the Asian man who had purchased her.

Molly listened as Juliana recounted her journey to Aberdeen, the filthy flat where she had been forced to have sex with all manner of men, the tiny salon where she painted nails all afternoon, often too tired to care about trying to escape.

'But you did?' Molly asked.

'Yes.' Juliana's face lit up for a moment. 'When Uncle Pavol came with Mario it was like a dream. They said not to talk, to pretend I not know them,' she said.

'And you got away before the raid?'

Juliana nodded again. 'Uncle Pavol gave me money . . . lots of money,' she said quietly. Molly bit her lip. Perhaps that was one reason these men had sought the girl. It would have been better for both of them if Juliana Ferenc had been caught during these raids and repatriated. Now, there was no knowing what would become of either of them.

'Listen, Ferenc, this is of the utmost importance,' Lorimer told the Slovakian prisoner. 'We think that Juliana has been taken again, probably by the same men as before.'

When this was explained to him by the third man in the room, Pavol Ferenc put his head in his hands and uttered several words, moaning in his native tongue. But Lorimer didn't need a translator to hear the man's obvious distress.

'Tell him we need to know everything. If he's been keeping things from us then it will hinder our ability to find his niece again.'

Lorimer watched as the older man's eyes flitted back and forward from the translator to himself. Then he gave a huge sigh and nodded, eyes cast down as if ashamed to look the detective in the eye.

The speech came haltingly, hand gestures showing a degree

of apology for keeping secrets. *After all*, his expression seemed to say, *whom could I trust?*

Then the story unfolded, the old man speaking without further need for the translator. Max was the big boss, not often seen but always to be obeyed or else. Or else what? People disappeared, he said solemnly. Never to be seen again. Ferenc accompanied this statement by swiping a finger across his throat.

'And, who is this Max that makes people afraid?' Lorimer wanted to know.

'Bad, bad man,' Ferenc said gloomily. 'He takes away the girls, takes them far away.' He waved a hand expansively.

These Romany folk were poorly educated, Lorimer had been told, and so Max might have gone to the UK in any direction; Hungary, Austria, the Czech Republic, Poland or even the Ukraine if he had wanted a roundabout route.

'Do you know anything else about Max?'

Ferenc shook his head. 'He speak English and other languages,' he said. 'Lured our girls away with promises of riches. Spoke to them slowly in words they could understand. But the women were afraid of him, even then.'

'Why was that?'

Ferenc shrugged and spread his hands across his cheeks.

'He had a scary face. It frightened them to look at him. None of them wanted to sleep with him. But he could talk well and they listened to his stories of Scotland and how wealthy they would be if they came with him.'

Ferenc paused as if to consider his words. 'He was like a professor. Or a schoolmaster, the sort you could trust.' The old man shook his head sadly. 'They were afraid of him but they do what he tell them,' he added.

A man who spoke many languages, Lorimer thought to

himself. That might help Solomon Brightman as he created the man's profile. Where had he picked that up? Was he a university graduate in languages? Or had he a different sort of background that had given him the chance to travel around, picking up other languages as he went, something a clever man with a good ear for speech might well do?

'Now, Pavol,' Lorimer bent closer to the man, making sure that he caught his eyes, 'what did Max look like?'

A conversation followed and Lorimer jotted down some notes but even as he did so he knew that they would only be marginally helpful. A man of medium height, strongly built like a boxer, shaven head. No, he didn't remember his eyes. He'd worn sunglasses most of the time as if the light hurt his eyes. But maybe they were blue? His face . . . the Romany man stopped and shook his head. 'Not a face I will ever forget,' he began. 'A face like a mask . . . smooth and without expression.'

'When did you last see this man?'

A mutter and a shrug followed.

'They aren't good with remembering years and dates,' the interpreter told Lorimer. 'Some of them don't even know their own ages,' he scoffed.

The detective ignored the slight against the Slovakian man and his people. The interpreter was clearly miffed that his services were not needed any more, the Slovakian's command of English surprising them both. Perhaps his remark about the Romanies' disregard for dates and times was true enough, however. And, if so, it certainly wasn't going to be helpful in establishing details about past events like this accident. There were other ways of finding out about this gangmaster, however. Meantime, they would concentrate on finding the two missing women and putting these Slovakian men somewhere safer.

256

'We are going to transfer you and your nephew to a different place,' Lorimer said at last. 'We've applied for a Home Office order to have you kept in a detention centre instead of Barlinnie but meantime we have permission to move you both to Low Moss. There's more accommodation there and other Slovakian prisoners too, so that might help you feel less isolated.'

The old man looked up at Lorimer, sudden tears in his eyes, then he reached out and grasped the detective's hands in his, a torrent of words pouring from his mouth. But, before the interpreter could translate, Ferenc spoke once more in English.

'Bless you, sir,' Ferenc said. 'And, please, find our Juliana.'

CHAPTER THIRTY-SIX

'Won't be long now,' the nurse told Rosie cheerfully, snapping off the disposable gloves and dropping them into a bin. 'Everything nicely in place, what we like to see. A textbook pregnancy, Mrs Brightman.' She beamed at Rosie as she helped her off the bed and handed her the slip-on shoes that the pathologist wore all the time now.

'Thanks,' Rosie replied. 'And I'm grateful that you made me your final patient of the day.'

'I take it you've not stopped work?' the nurse asked and Rosie shook her head, avoiding the woman's eyes.

'Not quite,' she admitted. 'Just doing a few things in the office. No more surgery though. I can hardly get near the operating table now.'

What Rosie did not mention was the pile of files that she had brought home from work, mainly concerning Dorothy Guilford. If she was going to end up in court as a witness for the defence in Peter Guilford's trial then she was determined to be prepared.

It was more difficult than ever to strap herself into the Audi so Rosie had come to the health centre on foot and was now preparing to walk back along Woodlands Road and through the park.

Midsummer night was almost upon them and the late afternoon sun still burned brightly in a blue sky with wisps of cirrus clouds floating high above the city. A summer baby, she thought, running a hand across her belly. He was asleep now, possibly glad of the rhythm of his mother's measured footsteps. Night-time was this little one's time for play, she thought with a wry smile. Bet he keeps us up all night once he's here.

A pain low down in her back made Rosie stop and glance around for the nearest bench. There was one just along this path and she sank into it gratefully. Just normal twinges, she knew from experience; nothing to worry about.

It was nice to sit for a while, watching the world go by, lads on their skateboards heading for the skate park, mothers with toddlers, their eyes on the little ones' staggering steps, tense with anticipation lest a tumble bring them back with a cry. It would be like that soon enough, Rosie thought: sleepless nights, changing nappies, the exhaustion after giving birth something she only dimly remembered. Should she decide to change her lifestyle? Take over from Morag, their wonderful nanny, and become like one of those young mothers gossiping as they pushed their buggies past her?

One of them stopped and caught Rosie's eye for a second, a warm smile as she saw the bump. Mother to mother. Could she live like that? Talking only about babies day after day? As the woman passed, she saw the usual clutter of baby paraphernalia in the bottom of the buggy but something else caught her eye; the cover of a book that Rosie had been meaning to read for ages, one of last year's Booker shortlist. Maybe, she thought, gazing after the group of women, maybe that could be her one day? Perhaps there could be a nice life waiting for her after this baby? A chance to step back from her role at the department?

For a moment Rosie closed her eyes, enjoying the warmth of the sun on her bare legs, the idea taking hold. Then, as another pain made her wince, she remembered the hands that had clutched that Laguiole knife and the mystery surrounding Dorothy Guilford.

No, she told herself. You've been given this task. It's yours to finish. Then we'll see about coming back to work. But, as she closed her eyes again, Rosie knew that she had already made her decision. The baby would be fine in Morag's care, just as Abby had been. And Dr Rosie Fergusson would continue to lead her department as before.

'When do you suppose it might happen?' McCauley asked the Fiscal.

'His consultant thinks that Guilford will be fit to leave the Queen Elizabeth in a couple of weeks' time,' she told him. 'He'll be transferred to Low Moss and kept in the hospital wing there until he can take the normal routine, but that could be months away.'

'So the trial could be postponed for that long?'

'Not at all. If Guilford is deemed medically fit to stand trial he can come from Low Moss hospital wing on a daily basis. Not a problem as far as we can see,' she told him.

'So, how long . . . ?'

'No,' she smiled. 'Impossible to put a date on the trial just yet. Might as well ask me how long is a piece of string.' She sighed.

DI Alan McCauley whistled as he left the Fiscal's office. It was a perfect night for meeting up with Dr Jacqui White and unless his phone rang and called him to another job, the evening was theirs to enjoy. He had already spoken to his friend at the *Gazette* and she was happy to do a double page spread on the woman who would be replacing Fergusson. Jacqui White had a glamour that Fergusson lacked, he told himself. And her TV background made her that much more attractive to a readership. He grinned to himself as he shifted the sun visor, tilting his head a little as the rays of the sun dazzled off the car next to his on the motorway.

It would all work out fine, McCauley thought. Fergusson would go off and have her baby and by the time she returned, the trial over and the press hounding her for comments about her mistakes, her reputation would be in tatters.

CHAPTER THIRTY-SEVEN

The email came through just as Lorimer was heading towards the stairs.

He stopped and read the message then read it again just to be certain that his eyes were not deceiving him.

Max is not who we thought he might be. (We know this, at least, thought Lorimer.) *Sources confirm he is a UK national originally born in Scotland.*

Not just British, then, but actually Scottish?

The email was signed with a code name, none of the Europol officers taking chances that their computers might be hacked. This was a delicate operation that was being conducted from both ends of the continent; the Slovakian police hunting for any clues that might help locate the missing women, and the MIT in Scotland doing their best to round up the perpetrators of this trafficking ring. So far the sweep at Aberdeen had allowed more than a score of women to return to eastern Slovakia but many more remained unaccounted.

Lorimer closed his phone and looked out of the window at the side of the house where the sky had now turned a velvety cobalt. It was too bright here with street lights along his road to see many stars but he could discern one or two that might be planets. Somewhere this man was under those self-same stars, planning his ruthless campaign. And he was Scottish. Could he be closer than they had thought? That was something to chew over.

Thanks to Pavol they had learned Max was a British national, but they knew little more than that. The man they sought was a home-grown trafficker, but one who had links with a particular area of Slovakia. How had the Englishman, Raynor, come across him? Had the former soldier been the man to rescue Max from fire or was it something here, in this country, that had tied them together in the trade of human trafficking? First Aberdeen, now Glasgow . . . What, he wondered now, would Solomon Brightman make of this news? They already had an inkling that Max was multilingual and had assumed that he was a person that travelled widely and picked up languages accordingly. How else would this man have acquired his language skills? That was something else for the Major Incident Team to ferret out.

Lorimer crept upstairs, unwilling to waken Maggie who was no doubt asleep, worn out with waiting for him to come home, but his place was mostly at HQ for now, coordinating the various strands of this operation.

He slipped into the upstairs lounge, a bright and airy room that overlooked the garden. There was much work to be done now, messages to write, calls to make and this email to answer.

It would be a good while before he saw his bed tonight, he thought with another sigh.

Molly was certain that it was night. Her body clock appeared to demand that she close her eyes and settle back against the high-backed chair but the strain on her arms made it too painful for

263

sleep and she needed to stay awake in case an opportunity to escape presented itself.

The Slovakian girl was curled against the far wall, her jacket, a dark shape folded beneath her head. Molly's vision seemed to be stronger now, her eyes adjusting to the blackness. Whatever drug she had been given had worn off and she felt more alert than she had been hours before.

The shape of the chair at her back was something that had begun to command her attention. She could feel the curve against her neck, the twin knobs on either side of her head, and knew from the way her wrists were tied that she was not actually secured to the wooden struts. If she leaned forward far enough it might be possible to raise her arms as high as she could and stand up, pulling herself free of the chair, though the danger of falling over and crashing down on the stone floor was a distinct possibility.

The lack of light actually helped in an odd way, Molly realised, as her sense of touch appeared to be heightened. She closed her eyes and felt the chair against her shoulders then pressed harder, learning the shape with her body.

She could do it.

The pain in her wrists and shoulder muscles almost made her cry out as she bent her elbows and began to ease her weight forwards.

It was important to keep her balance, not to let the chair tip over as she began to raise her wrists upwards, the plastic tags cutting deeper into her broken and bloody skin.

Molly felt her arms like wings of pain as she raised them higher and higher behind her back. Then, the world seemed to tilt and she gasped, fearing that she was about to fall.

With a sob she sat down once again.

She heard a faint moan from the girl on the floor, then, as

though that tiny sound had given her some additional strength, she heaved her arms backwards as far as they would go. Now, if she could just stand up . . .

The chair teetered then fell backwards and Molly sprawled away from it onto the floor, hitting her head as she landed.

'What . . . ?' Juliana gave a cry.

'Shh!' Molly told her. 'Stay still. Don't move.'

The room was silent as Molly listened, darkness all around. Good. Nobody had heard that noise. There were no running feet coming to investigate.

She needed to have her hands in front of her again. Molly thought hard, visualising the contortions of pulling her tied wrists under her bottom and looping them over her feet. But, could she do it?

She sat upright, wriggling her backside, feeling the space between her wrists where the plastic ties had been fastened. If she could just push herself through that gap, make it bigger somehow? Her clothes were an extra layer that would impede the struggle to achieve this objective, Molly realised. There was only one thing for it.

'Juliana,' she whispered. 'Come over here, I need your help,' she hissed.

'What can I do, Sasha?'

'Pull off my trousers,' Molly told her. 'I'm going to try and get my hands free.'

There was a moment's silence as the girl thought about this command.

Then, 'I see . . . ' Juliana whispered back and knelt to do as the older girl had asked.

Molly felt the chill of the stone floor against her panties as she wiggled free of the trousers; one less impediment to releasing her arms. Calling up a blessing for the genes that had given her a slender shape, she began to pull her wrists towards her hips, biting her lips to stop screaming as the plastic bit deeper into her flesh.

Her arms ached as she pulled and pulled. Then with one final thrust, she felt the backs of her legs. Panting to make her muscles relax, she rolled onto her back, pointed her toes and gave one last heave.

Something deep within the woman's shoulders seemed to tear and she slipped sideways, unable to stifle the moan of pain.

'Sasha, Sasha, are you all right?'

Molly felt the girl's breath on her cheek as she lay beside her, hands now nestled on her lap.

'I'm okay,' she whispered. 'But my shot-putting days are probably over,' she joked.

'Here, put them on again. It is cold,' Juliana said, squatting at Molly's feet, the trousers in her hands.

She let the girl ease her into the trousers, grateful for her help, her own arms trembling with pain and fatigue. Then, sitting side by side, Molly felt the soft touch of the girl's fingers on her upper arms and closed her eyes as her muscles responded to the light massage. She would need some rest, Molly knew, but soon the next stage of her plan must be put into action. She ran her tongue across her teeth, feeling the healthy gums. In a few hours they would be bleeding and swollen, in a punishing effort to bite through the hard plastic. Yet she could see no other way to free them.

'Who are you, Max?' Solly murmured into his bushy beard. It was a puzzle that he wanted to solve, a puzzle with very few clues. Yet there were perhaps sufficient to make some progress. Now that they knew the man who sold women for sex was a British national, he could wander down certain pathways in his mind, seeking this elusive figure. Max was multilingual too. Did that imply a peripatetic lifestyle? Had he worked overseas? Been a languages graduate, perhaps? Or, and here, Solly stroked his chin thoughtfully, had he been in the forces? Like Michael Raynor? The link between Raynor and Guilford was a difficult one. But what if Guilford had more to do with this human trafficking than he was letting on? What if his wife's sudden death had absolutely nothing to do with any nefarious business that had used the vehicles he hired?

The psychologist sat at the bay window in the darkness, oblivious to the city twinkling below him. Raynor had attacked Guilford, evidently meaning to kill him. Then he had calmly talked to Lorimer and walked out of the prison, never to be seen there again. Why? A man that had been commended for bravery had gone on to the prison service but then had brutally attacked an inmate.

Where had that happened? Solly lifted the notes on his lap and peered at the pages. One foot reached out and stepped on the light switch of the standard lamp, a halo of brightness enclosing him where he sat. Shuffling through the file, he came at last to the lines he had almost forgotten. Ah, he thought, nodding sagely. So was that where it all began? Too much of a coincidence, surely, to pull a man out of a burning building in the very village where Pavol Ferenc and his family had lived for generations. And the man? Well, a little more detective work was necessary to establish his identity. But, if Solomon Brightman's deductions were correct, then that may well have been a fellow soldier, an officer perhaps, with a facility for languages. And who could tell what rewards had been promised as a result of saving that man's life?

CHAPTER THIRTY-EIGHT

'Max Warnock,' Lorimer told the assembled team. 'Major Warnock by the time he quit the army. Medical discharge after the accident in Slovakia.'

'Do we have a police record for him?' one of the DIs asked.

'Nothing. Clean as a whistle. Which is a pity as something on file would have helped to identify him. Nevertheless, we now have this photograph.' Lorimer turned to the screen behind him and flicked a switch on the overhead projector.

The image of a young man appeared, his thin face turned slightly at an angle to the camera, shadows cast against his temples, the sphenoid bone flat against his head as though his face had been chiselled out of stone. His eyes were staring at the camera, unsmiling, full lips slightly parted as though he wanted to speak.

'This is Max Warnock as he was when he joined the army,' Lorimer told them. 'We have obtained a few pictures from the hospital where he was initially treated after the fire but there are no up-to-date images either for his British passport or driver's licence.' He tapped the edge of the screen. 'This is the one he has used ever since the accident.'

'What can you tell us about that?' Solly asked from the back of the room. Several heads turned towards the psychologist as he waited patiently for Lorimer to proceed.

'Happened in a brothel,' Lorimer told him. 'Several of the men had been in the habit of frequenting it and Warnock was one of them. We have no information about how the fire began or who else was involved, just the army's own records of the incident and the victim's medical notes.'

'Was he taken back to the UK?' someone asked.

'Not initially. He was kept in a burns ward for several months then sent back home. Supposedly for plastic surgery,' Lorimer said with a meaningful look at the men and women seated around the table.

'So we have no idea what he really looks like now?'

The detective superintendent nodded his head. 'Exactly. Max Warnock could look like any burns victim, depending on the level of treatment he had when he left Slovakia. And our intelligence suggests that he may have travelled to the US for facial reconstruction. His passport records show several lengthy spells across the pond.'

'What made him turn into a people trafficker?' one female DS asked aloud.

'Whatever happened back in Slovakia changed not only Max Warnock's appearance,' Lorimer suggested, 'but his outlook on life. Would you agree, Professor Brightman?'

Solly cleared his throat before he began. 'I would like to know a lot more about the man he was before,' he said. 'But I do agree that something as traumatic as that life-changing event may well have affected his outlook. And,' he added, 'his behaviour.'

What Solly did not add was the thought that creating brothels in his own country and bringing young women and girls from the very place that had scarred him so badly might be a twisted form of revenge. And, if he could begin to build up a picture of this man's personality, perhaps he might find a vulnerable area in his present life that could lead to his whereabouts.

'We have had this breakthrough thanks to the vigilance of one of the detective constables from CID,' Lorimer explained. 'Some of you will remember DC Kirsty Wilson?' He looked around, gratified to see several heads nodding.

'She found that Michael Raynor and a man answering Warnock's description had been occasional visitors to the Guilford home.'

A murmur broke out as the members of the team reacted to this news.

'What is more interesting is that Raynor and Warnock came to see Dorothy Guilford. The cleaning woman who has known the family for decades recalls them being particular favourites of the dead woman,' Lorimer continued.

'That might explain Raynor's attack on Peter Guilford,' DCI Cameron chipped in.

'Could be. But we have to find out more about Warnock,' Lorimer insisted. 'Mrs Daly has given a statement to the effect that they both spoke with English accents. But intelligence tells us Warnock was born in Scotland. We need more, and we need it fast. This is a highly dangerous individual who exploits women for his own gain.' He looked around the room at each and every one of them. 'I don't need to tell you that with every hour that passes we have less chance of finding DS Newton and Juliana Ferenc alive.'

Molly lay in the girl's arms, her teeth jarring with the effort of biting through the bonds that had held her fast. But now it was

270

over, her hands and feet free, her whole body aching with the effort of straining down to her ankles, her mouth cut in several places as she had chewed the plastic ties like a dog.

Tears of relief trickled down her face, mingling with the blood, but Molly was now too exhausted to care, the gentle caress of the girl's fingers on her hair soothing her agony.

'We must take them by surprise,' Molly told the girl. 'But for now, I need to sleep. If anyone comes into the room they will have quite a shock when they see that we have disappeared,' she said, trying not to smile.

The two women were seated side by side, next to the doorway, ready to flee the moment that it opened. Taking their captor by surprise was the only way, Molly had insisted. She would fell him with the chair then they would slam the door shut, hoping that the key had been left on the outside.

'Then?' Juliana asked, a tremble in her voice.

'Then you will be safe with me,' Molly told her, hoping that the confidence in her voice was enough to cover the inner fear that escape might be far more difficult than she had told the young girl.

It must be morning, Molly thought, blinking in the darkness. She had slept against the wall, her head and Juliana's together for pillows and now every muscle seemed to protest as she took stock of what her body had endured a few hours earlier. There was definitely some damage to her shoulders and she would need anti-tetanus jabs, for sure, once they got out of this hell-hole. The wounds on her wrists were beginning to harden already, the body's own defences quick to begin the healing process.

The scenario had been gone over again and again before the pair had fallen asleep at last. As soon as the door opened and their guard entered the room, Molly would hit him over the head with the chair, the sudden and unexpected attack giving them sufficient time to carry out their escape.

But, as the minutes became hours and the day wore on, Molly Newton began to wonder if they had been left there for good with no chance to carry out her plan.

CHAPTER THIRTY-NINE

The light had faded from the skies and, although the room was shrouded in inky shadows, the woman sat staring at the window, unmoving. A television set in one corner of the room displayed shifting scenes from the ten o'clock news but the remote was turned to mute as if Cynthia Drollinger craved silence but not solitude.

The buzzer sounding made her start and rise to her feet. In two strides she was across the lounge, hand stretched out to lift the security telephone.

'Yes?'

Anyone observing the woman at that moment would have seen a change in her face; the mouth becoming smaller, the jaw tightening.

'I need to talk to you about your friend, Peter,' a man's voice told her. There was a silence as she hesitated.

'You'd better come up,' she said at last, replacing the telephone and activating the entry switch.

For a moment Cynthia returned to her seat but rose again almost immediately, pacing up and down between the door to the hallway and the window that overlooked the landscaped gardens below, one finger placed between her teeth, the gesture of anxiety hidden for the moment from prying eyes.

When the doorbell rang a few minutes later, she all but ran along the hall and opened the door, admitting the man who stood on her threshold.

'Come in, quick,' she commanded, letting him enter before stepping out onto the balcony and looking one way and the other, lest her visitor had been noticed by anyone loitering around. But there was nobody on this summer's night and she breathed a sigh of relief then closed the door behind them.

There was no sign of her visitor until Cynthia came back to the lounge and there he was, sitting in the chair she had recently vacated. For a moment she felt a spasm of annoyance at the stranger's cavalier attitude but that disappeared the moment he turned his gaze to her.

'Better sit down,' Michael Raynor told her. 'We've got a lot to discuss.'

It was nearly midnight when Cynthia Drollinger closed the door again and leaned against it, heart still thudding as she replayed the man's words in her head. The big man had not introduced himself, never given a name, but perhaps that was just as well after what he had told her. Whoever he was he seemed to know a great deal about Peter, the van-hire business and about her own part in it. She'd shivered as he'd mentioned facts and figures: this was a dangerous man who had sat talking to her. And yet she had hung on his every word.

They were going to set Peter free. And she was to be a crucial part of their plan.

*

'Did she buy it?'

Raynor grinned at the man sitting next to him in the van, its tinted windows denying any passer-by the possibility of seeing who sat inside.

'Course she did. She's as desperate to get hold of him as we are,' he chuckled. 'Even better, she's talked his nurse into phoning her the moment the screws come for him.'

'Everything ready?' his companion snapped.

'Of course, sir.' Raynor stiffened as though he were still in uniform taking orders from his superior officer. Then he grinned. It would be just like old times; weapons at the ready, nerves taut with anticipation, the smell of cordite in the cold night air.

'And she'll tell Guilford we'll be coming for him?'

'Yes,' Raynor replied, then began to snigger. 'Just doesn't know what we intend to do with him once we've sprung him, though.'

The man beside him did not share his laughter. Perhaps those wasted facial muscles were no longer capable of responding to mirth. Or, more likely, the thought of what fate awaited Dorothy Guilford's widower suited an expression that was both cold and grim.

'Good news,' the nurse told him as she bustled in with a trolley covered in the usual paraphernalia of items that Guilford had become used to: blood pressure kit, thermometer, that small plastic cup of pills. She bent towards him, fixing the cuff around his arm to take his latest blood pressure reading. 'Looks like you'll be leaving here in a day or so,' she confided. 'That's good, isn't it?'

Peter Guilford shot her a dark look. What was good about that? He was already heavily guarded by police officers in the Queen

Elizabeth University Hospital and would continue to be as he was transferred to Low Moss Prison.

Here in hospital he had experienced the only real sense of freedom he'd known since that DI had arrested him for Dorothy's murder, the nurses and doctors treating him like an ordinary human being.

It was madness. Nothing had turned out the way he had wanted it, her death cheating him of everything he had planned ... The nurse was prattling on, reassuring Peter that he would be missed and congratulating him on such a good recovery.

'Now,' she said at last, pulling the trolley away from his bedside, 'that's you all set for your visitor.' The woman beamed and tilted her head towards the glass door.

Peter followed her gaze where a familiar figure stood. Cynthia! For a moment Peter felt the old surge of delight at seeing his mistress then his face fell. She would not be seeing so much of him any more once he was taken to Low Moss prison. Once a month, if they were lucky.

He waited until the room was quiet, noting that the uniformed officer outside in the corridor was drinking tea and chatting to one of the nurses before nodding in her direction.

'Thought I told you not to come back,' he began as she approached his chair, but his face had creased into a smile, his expression belying the words.

'I had to see you, Peter,' Cynthia whispered. 'It's important. Someone came to see me ... '

'Shh, keep your voice down,' Peter scolded. 'What is it? What's happening?' he asked, conscious of the eager look on the woman's face.

'They're going to get you out,' she whispered. 'You won't be spending the rest of your life in prison, not if they can help it.'

'How?' Peter shook his head, stunned at her words. 'What are they planning to do?'

She glanced behind to ensure that nobody was within earshot, then, taking his hand in hers she bent towards him, her voice low, her gestures aimed to appear like a woman making assurances to her lover.

Peter Guilford kept his face close to hers but his expression changed as Cynthia told him of what the stranger who'd visited her had planned, a smile of satisfaction softening his features. At last she finished and looked up at him.

'Thank you, my love,' he said, taking her hand to his lips and kissing her fingertips. 'We'll make a fresh start, you and me, just wait and see.'

CHAPTER FORTY

She blinked, rubbed her eyes and read the report once again. The results from the post-mortem of the man found in that quarry had not given him a name but had turned up some surprising information instead.

'Well, well, well,' Rosie murmured, reaching for her phone. Lorimer needed to know about this right away. Forensics had thrown up DNA evidence from that crime scene that matched material taken from Michael Raynor's flat. Whoever had stayed there most recently (and she supposed it must have been the prison officer himself) was now in the frame for the brutal murder of their latest victim.

Rosie screwed up her face as she heard the recorded message. She hesitated for a moment then spoke a few words to let Lorimer know the basic facts. Jacqui White might be taking over that particular case but it now looked as if there was a link to Dorothy Guilford.

Solly had filled her in after the meeting at Helen Street and she had listened as he had passed on the information about Raynor and his visits years before to the big house in St Andrew's Drive. He'd been seeking revenge for Dorothy's murder, they thought. But, Rosie reasoned, how could that prison officer be so certain that it really was murder? She heaved a sigh. Ought she to give in now, let them pass judgement on Peter Guilford? He'd been a wife beater, for sure. But had he actually killed Dorothy in a moment of rage? Surely his intention had been to grasp all of that lucrative insurance policy? And if so, wouldn't he have taken pains to cover his tracks, not simply lash out at his defenceless wife?

No, she thought, that old stubborn streak coming to the surface. She would not give up on her own position of seeing Dorothy Guilford's death in terms of suicide. There were still too many unanswered questions and Alan McCauley didn't yet have a monopoly on the right answers.

It all came back to Dorothy. And, she supposed, it should really be her husband digging deeper for the truth about the woman's death. After all, he was the man who could sometimes give answers to the questions beginning with 'why'.

Her thoughts were interrupted as the dark-haired pathologist entered the room.

'Rosie,' Jacqui began, a strange, eager look on her face that was overshadowed by a frown. 'Something you need to see.'

A pot of tea accompanied by some reassuring, if inane, words then Jacqui White was gone, leaving Rosie still trembling with emotion. McCauley had pushed for a second post-mortem on Dorothy Guilford and the Crown had advised that Dr White would undertake this if she were willing.

Willing? Rosie clenched her teeth as she thought of the expression on Jacqui's face. She was dying to do it; that was something even a good actress like Jacqui couldn't fail to hide. And, if her findings contradicted Rosie's? What then? Jacqui had been quite matter-of-fact on the surface, but Rosie was not fooled for one minute that the other pathologist might see this as her chance to shine.

She recalled a conversation they had had together recently, Jacqui wondering if Rosie had ever considered being a stay-at-home mum. Was that something she hoped would happen? Two wee children and a career break? And Jacqui White taking over not just as a locum but as a permanent member of the department, possibly setting her sights on the top job, Rosie's job.

It was more important than ever to find out the truth behind Dorothy Guilford's death. And, Rosie told herself, looking down at her swollen belly, she had to make sure that happened before this baby entered the world.

'You all right, boss?' The sing-song Aussie accent told Rosie at once that Daisy had entered the room. 'Hey, something's upset you. C'mon, what's up?'

Whether it was the kindness in the younger woman's voice or the arm slung about her shoulder, Rosie would never know, but she found herself pouring out her troubles to the Australian doctor as they sat together in her office.

'So, you think she might shaft you? That what you're saying? Hey, can't let that happen. Look. How about I keep an eye on things while you're gone? Make sure that nothing goes on that you don't know about?' Daisy grinned. 'I'll be your eyes and ears. How about it? Got the feeling I'd rather work for you long term than Miss TV personality out there.'

Rosie smiled up at her. 'Golly,' she laughed. 'What a lot of intrigue!'

'Yeah, but sometimes you need to be one step ahead of the ones who are looking to overtake you,' Daisy claimed. 'I saw it happening back home once or twice. Guys taking advantage of a woman on maternity leave. She comes back and finds herself out of a job. Told to do part time or job share, know what I'm saying? Jeez, this glass ceiling, won't it ever crash down on them?'

'Well, this is a bit different here,' Rosie reminded her. 'We're not talking about gender issues.'

'No, that's true enough. Scotland doesn't seem as bad for that as back home. Why I want to stay, partly,' she admitted.

'The issue here is one of trust,' Rosie said gravely. 'And I'm not at all sure I can trust this colleague any more.'

'Don't you worry, Dr Fergusson,' Daisy soothed. 'I'll keep a watch on her every move.'

Rosie sighed as Daisy left the room, closing the door behind her. Why did this have to happen? She was a shrewd enough judge of character to suspect that Jacqui was planning things behind her back whilst making a show of being her friend. Yet her instinct told her to let Daisy, a young woman she hardly knew, be her spy in the department both now and later when her maternity leave began. Did Daisy Abercromby have a hidden agenda? Was she making sure that her own future was secure by keeping in with the head of department? Perhaps, but Rosie felt a whole lot better right now knowing that the Australian was on her side.

She gasped suddenly as a pain shot across her abdomen. The baby. She must remember the baby. Probably nothing, she told herself, just one of those muscular spasms that happened from time to time. Nothing to worry about. Anxiety induced, more than likely.

Still, Rosie glanced at her watch to take note of the time that this particular pain had hit her. Just in case.

'We're getting there,' Lorimer muttered to DCI Cameron as he entered the room. Then he turned his back on the man, intent on adding the message from Rosie onto the whiteboard at the far end of the room, a blue pen line now linking the names of Michael Raynor and the victim whom they had called 'Quarryman' meantime until his identity could be established. Dark haired and swarthy, Lorimer suspected that the dead man was in fact a Slovakian national and they had sent as much information as possible to their counterparts in Bratislava.

It was late in the day now and yet he and the team would remain here for hours more, working through the documentation about these traffickers, looking constantly for intelligence that might bring some news about Molly Newton and the missing girl.

His phone rang and he put it to his ear.

'Lorimer.'

Watching the detective superintendent, Niall Cameron noticed the clenched jaw and the slight nod of his head as Lorimer listened to the caller.

'That was the governor of Low Moss,' Lorimer told him. 'Guilford's being released into their custody tonight.'

Cameron breathed out a long sigh. 'One less for us to worry over then,' he observed. 'And lets us have our officers back.'

Lorimer nodded slowly. There were so many pressures, so much to think about, not least the ever-present worry over manpower and where best to deploy it.

He glanced out of the window at the summer evening sky. What he would give to be home in the garden with Maggie! And yet, that pleasure would be denied him for a while longer. Time was against them to find their undercover officer and the Ferenc girl, precious time that needed his presence here.

Was Molly Newton somewhere looking at that same pale blue sky? Was she even alive?

CHAPTER FORTY-ONE

'But we haven't had any word . . .' The nurse backed off as the two prison officers stood at the desk, their papers offered for her to see.

'Oh,' she said, reading the official letters that concerned her patient. 'I see. Well, this is unexpected. And in the middle of the night!'

'Security,' one of them muttered. 'We need to make sure that nobody is outside watching his transfer. Press boys would love to get hold of this.'

'Aye.' The other shrugged. 'And see there, your consultant Mr Ahasan has countersigned the permission.'

The nurse nodded as she turned the page and saw the familiar scrawl. It was all in order. 'All right, then, I suppose you will have a police escort?'

'Oh, yes, there are officers waiting downstairs with the ambulance,' he assured her.

'Okay, just wait over there,' she said, turning away and fingering the pocket of her uniform.

One quick call; that was what she had promised the woman, remembering her stricken face as she had begged for this favour.

Slipping into an empty side room, she dialled the number and waited.

'They've come for our friend,' she said then cut the call. A wee favour, the woman had begged. And surely that couldn't do anyone any harm? Yet she shivered as though that thought was a premonition of something bad.

Too many nights, she told herself briskly, shaking off the sudden feeling of gloom. It would be better once she'd had a break and was back on day shift. Then, summoning up her professional self once more, she walked towards the room where Peter Guilford lay sleeping.

'Peter,' she said, folding back a corner of the bedclothes and tapping the man's shoulder, 'wake up.'

Peter Guilford looked about him. The lights everywhere were dimmed at this time of night, the silence only broken by the sound of a trolley being wheeled along the corridor. He trembled a little as the porter came towards his bed. Had they forgotten him after all? Was this a ploy from HMP to effect his transfer to Low Moss without a chance for him to escape? Or was it all an elaborate plan by those people who had spoken to Cynthia?

The porter did not make eye contact with him as he helped Peter from his bed to the hospital trolley. Was this a genuine hospital employee? Or one of the people Cynthia had said would help him get away? He pulled the cotton waffle blanket around his shoulders as they headed along a corridor, round a corner and stopped at a bank of lifts.

From out of the corner of his eyes Peter could see the shadowy figures of the prison escorts and the officer whose shift had kept him outside his room that night. Three burly men plus the porter against . . . how many out there to help him get away?

As they entered the lift and he felt it begin its descent, Peter wondered what awaited him at the end of this short journey to the ground.

He tried to sit up as they left the lift and crossed the huge concourse that led to the main entrance but firm hands pushed him down again and he lay back, watching the upper floors disappear as they walked him steadily past shuttered shops and coffee bars.

A swish of doors then he felt it; a fresh blast of air, warm enough to breathe in deeply, the night sky above pierced with lights from the buildings around. He heard the wheels of the trolley trundle over tarmac, felt the difference from the smooth floor to this harder ground beneath his body and glanced across at the waiting ambulance.

There were mere yards now between him and the vehicle and his heart sank in despair. Cynthia had been played for a fool! There was no plan to spring him after all, or else it had all gone awry.

A pair of green-jacketed paramedics came and shifted Peter yet again from the hospital trolley onto their own gurney, strapping him in securely.

'Worried I'll run away,' he muttered as one of them bent to buckle the straps.

'Standard procedure, mate,' the paramedic told him. 'We do it for all our patients. Just like you'd strap on a safety belt in a car, see?'

Peter did not reply but let himself be hoisted up on the stretcher and carried into the waiting ambulance. The interior was full of equipment on each side, high-tech-looking stuff, a blue covered seat below.

'Right, pal, that's you,' the man said as he made sure that the gurney was comfortably in place.

Any moment now these doors will close, Peter thought, gazing out at the hospital building. And the next thing I see will be the inside of another prison.

But, before anyone could come and slam the doors shut, a shot rang out and he heard a scream.

'Man down! Man Down. Get—' someone shouted, then another volley of gunfire rang out, bullets pinging off the metal side of the vehicle.

'What the . . . ?' the paramedic began, crouching down beside his patient, mouth open in shock.

Peter sat up. They were coming to set him free! Just as Cynthia had promised!

His fingers fumbled the straps loose in his desperation to be rid of the restraints. Then, throwing the bedcover aside, Peter Guilford stood up.

He could hear the sound of feet thumping across the ground outside and more screams as people fled the scene.

Crouching low to avoid detection, he headed for the doorway and freedom.

Somewhere in the distance he could hear police sirens. There wasn't much time now, he had to get away!

He clutched the door of the vehicle and leaned forward, preparing to jump down, when another shot rang out.

At once he was thrown backwards, pain searing his shoulder.

Bright lights flashed before him, only to be suddenly extinguished as he fell into total darkness.

Lorimer had been woken by the telephone and in minutes he was dressed and gunning the Lexus away from his house towards the Queen Elizabeth Hospital.

As he approached it from the motorway his mouth grew grim.

In the darkness he could see just why Glasgow folk had nick-named it the Death Star, its resemblance to the mighty edifice in the skies uncanny. Yet this night would surely reinforce that moniker? Three, maybe four dead, he'd been told and even now he was hearing reports through his earpiece.

What the hell had happened?

He was soon to find out as he parked the car behind a line of police vehicles and strode over to the officer in charge who quickly updated him on the situation. Lorimer listened, his face grave.

By the time the police reinforcements had arrived there were three bodies lying on the tarmac, he was informed; one of the paramedics and two prison officers. Lorimer walked carefully across to the scene where white-suited figures were already at work. Guilford lay sprawled and bloody, across the steps of the ambulance, the blue light beating across his face. Up above he could see faces peering from scores of windows, no doubt wondering at the tumult beneath them. He imagined nurses chivvying patients back into their beds, whilst trying to catch a glimpse of what was happening on the ground below, the curios-ity of human nature at work. All too soon word would spread and the newspapers would have people here asking questions.

Officers in high visibility vests streamed across the tarmac, some of them already armed. Of the gunmen who had carried out this atrocity there was no sign though Lorimer knew well that every CCTV camera in the area was already being closely monitored.

He watched as the bodies of the victims and those who were injured were removed and taken inside the hospital, several figures in blue scrubs accompanying them. But it was to the ambulance where Guilford lay, a doctor now kneeling by his side, that Lorimer focused his attention.

287

Someone had wanted that man dead. Wanted it badly enough to cause this carnage. But why? What was so important about the man who had simply hired out his vehicles to these ruthless people? Looking down at Guilford, Lorimer shook his head. Well, it looked as if they'd succeeded at any rate.

'A goner, then,' he murmured.

The doctor turned at the sound of his words.

'Who are you?' He frowned.

'Detective Superintendent Lorimer. We've been investigating the previous attack on this particular victim,' he said.

The man in blue scrubs gazed up at him and shook his head. 'Victim? You can't call him that. Not yet, anyway.'

Then Lorimer was aware of other men beside him, a trolley ready to transport Guilford inside the hospital once again.

The doctor touched his sleeve, motioning him back from the medics who now lifted Guilford's bloody body from the ambulance steps.

'This man isn't dead.'

It was not just a physical cordon that surrounded the scene now, Lorimer thought to himself as daylight began to show along the city's horizon. He had enabled a different kind of security to surround the place, here, where Guilford's life still hung in the balance. *Let them think he is dead*, he'd told a select group of men and women earlier. Guilford would no longer pose a threat, the hospital and staff safer to go about their business, he'd argued. But, underlying that decision was the scheme to keep one step ahead of these dangerous gunmen. The press were going to have a field day reporting on the carnage that had taken place, innocent people caught up in the whole bloody business. It was going to be hard to dissemble right now and so the best thing to

288

do was say absolutely nothing to them. For, what could he tell them? That Peter Guilford had been shot whilst attempting to escape? Or had in fact been the target of those gunmen all along?

He was in a small room high above the continuing bustle on the ground, looking towards the city. The familiar shapes of Glasgow could be seen beyond; the university tower, the Hydro like a half shell gleaming in the morning sun, a glint of gold from the Sikh temple over in Finnieston ... emblems of a city that was itself a multifaceted place. A seat of learning that had once earned the title of knife capital of Europe; a place that could be riven with sectarian violence yet had played host to the legendary Garden Festival back when he was a boy, and more recently to what had been described as the best ever Commonwealth Games. A city proud of itself and still humbled in shame by those seeking their own ends through violent means.

He was a tool, that was all, Lorimer thought. A man striving to make this city work a little better. And, if he could succeed in that then perhaps it would be sufficient to say that his had been a life well lived.

He turned away from the window, heading for the door. The morning was still young and today would bring many people asking difficult questions. The time for such thoughts would come later, once he had succeeded in tracing the people who had carried out this city's latest atrocity.

CHAPTER FORTY-TWO

Cynthia sat trembling, her hand drawing out to take the glass. But it was empty. She had drunk the last of the bottle hours ago, anxiety of waiting replaced by the knowledge that she would never see him again.

The TV news report was still playing on the screen before her, sound turned to mute, the newsreel strip endlessly telling her the facts.

He was dead. That was surely the only fact she needed to know, yet still she sat, watching the words revolve as if somehow they might change and make everything different.

Why had they come here? Why had she been gulled into making that telephone call, letting these mysterious people know the moment Peter was going to be taken away? If she hadn't done that . . . Her brain refused to continue, tears flowing once more as she howled in anguish, a raw animal sound.

It was her fault, hers and hers alone. Not the men who had fired these deadly shots. Guilt consumed her as the images on the television screen showed the pictures once more: the hospital concourse, now a scene of crime with police vehicles in attendance, aerial shots that panned in on the place where it had happened, the ambulance still there, its sides pitted with bullet holes. Then these faces, dead men just doing their job, a paramedic who had been there to take care of Peter and two prison officers; strangers who had nothing to do with Cynthia Drollinger except that she'd been responsible for their deaths.

Really she should be dead too, but all through the night Cynthia had baulked at the idea of swallowing a handful of pills even to end the misery that had overwhelmed her. The coward's way out, she'd told herself. Yet it was not a warped sense of pride that had stopped her but the knowledge that she deserved to suffer as she was suffering now. No eternal hell could possibly be as bad as this.

Outside, the sounds of the city waking up did nothing to make Cynthia leave her place in front of the television. Her bags were still packed and waiting in the hallway, the notion of departure with Peter uppermost just a few hours ago. Whoever came into the office would find that Ms Drollinger had not arrived to open up and eventually someone would call to find out why. But Cynthia did not care about things like that any more

When the doorbell rang she ignored it. They would go away eventually, she decided. But then the hammering began and shouts of 'Police! Open up!' made Cynthia jump from her place, hand to her throat. It was no more than she deserved, she thought, heading for the door, not bothering to check the spyhole first.

Shaking fingers drew the chain aside and unlocked the door. Standing there were two large figures of men, one who stepped forward with a grin on his face.

'You—' she began, but Cynthia Drollinger's words were cut off for ever as the man thrust forward, the deadly knife plunging into her body.

*

It was sheer bad luck, Kirsty thought, looking at the letter in her hand. Her interview had been brought forward and now she would be asking herself some serious questions about what sort of future she really wanted. James had given her until Friday lunchtime to make up her mind, stressing how he had to give the US firm an answer. *They're five hours behind us, pet*, he'd told her. *But I think they'll want to know our decision when they come into work Friday morning.*

Our decision, James had said. He would not go away without her if she decided that her career meant so much.

Should she tempt fate? Decide to stay if she received that promotion? Go with James to Chicago if she was passed over? It was like tossing a coin and really, that was unfair on James, who deserved better for his patience with her.

The events of the previous night cast a dark shadow over everyone today, Kirsty knew, glancing around at her colleagues. All talk was about the shooting and the latest reports from the Queen Elizabeth Hospital. She bit her lip, feeling guilty for even thinking about her own personal problem when somewhere across the city families were weeping for the loss of loved ones.

'Who would benefit from Peter Guilford's death?' Lorimer asked, looking around at the MIT officers assembled once more in the Helen Street building.

'No children from his previous marriage?' one of the officers in the room asked.

'No. And no siblings either,' another replied.

'So, on the event of his death who inherits the Guilford business plus the house and Dorothy Guilford's estate?' a female DS queried. 'Must amount to a pretty penny.'

Lorimer nodded at the woman. 'Take that as your immediate

action. We can't rule anything out, even if there appears to be no connection to this current attack.'

They had concentrated mainly on Guilford's links to the traffickers, something they all now believed was far more than simply supplying vehicles. The paperwork obtained from his city centre offices was all above board, of course, and Lorimer was certain that anything incriminating would have long since been shredded by his faithful secretary.

He gave a sigh. 'We're still keeping quiet about Guilford,' he told them. 'And I think our next step should be to bring in Ms Drollinger.' He glanced around, seeing looks of approval from his fellow officers. 'She is to be under the impression that her lover is now dead and gone. So let's see what she might be willing to tell us.'

Lorimer stood at the doorway, a feeling of nausea rising in his gullet. He would never know what part this woman had played in the carnage at the hospital but her body lying here was testament to some involvement in that story, of that he was sure. The officers who had been dispatched to bring the woman to Helen Street had found her there and even now it looked as if they had been just an hour or so too late. The body had been still warm when they had examined it, showing that death had occurred not long before their arrival.

He stepped alongside the bloodied corpse, noting the blood spray across the wall by the open door. Something for forensics to add to the story of what had taken place.

Her cases were stacked along the hallway, evidence of a decision to escape, something that had been thwarted by her killer. Lorimer moved carefully on covered feet, his gloved hands touching nothing, aware that his very presence could contaminate the scene. They had suited up in the landing outside the row of flats, watched by a neighbour from a window around the corner until a uniformed officer had intervened and asked her to talk to them instead. Nosy neighbours could be a source of information, even those that seemed mere voyeurs.

Leaving the forensic team to carry out their task, Lorimer walked along the short corridor and entered the main lounge where a television set was switched on, the sound turned to mute. He took note of the empty whisky bottle and the glass sitting on the coffee table between the television and the settee, a pile of crumpled tissues stuffed under the cushion where she had been sitting.

The story here was easy enough to read: Cynthia Drollinger had been sitting watching the news as it came in with the latest tragedy to hit their city, a tragedy that now included the woman herself. She must have believed that Peter was dead. And that would have been to Lorimer's advantage had he been able to question her, something that would never happen now.

But why had she been about to leave? He glanced down at the settee and saw a large tan leather handbag propped open to one side. It was the sort of designer bag he'd seen in glossy Sunday supplements and appeared to be brand new.

'A new bag for a new beginning?' he murmured aloud. Perhaps its contents might add to whatever Cynthia Drollinger had been planning before she had been halted by the attack at the hospital.

He laid them out on the laminate floor one by one: her phone, a purse stuffed with banknotes (some of them euros), a wallet full of credit cards and her passport as well as a small leather diary with GUILFORD VEHICLE HIRE embossed in gold lettering. A set of keys had been placed in a side zipped pocket (the office keys, perhaps? Or did they fit the house in St Andrew's Drive?). A pack of mint chewing gum, a Chanel lipstick and a small perfume spray, a glass nail file in its plastic sleeve and another set of keys with a leather Volkswagen fob that would no doubt match one of the cars in the underground garage.

Already Lorimer's mind was allotting actions to different members of his team: the phone would tell them something once it was examined and calls traced, but right now he took the diary in his hands and opened it.

Had she ever suspected that the hands of a policeman would open these pages, Lorimer doubted that Cynthia Drollinger would ever have written upon them.

He began by flicking back to the date when Dorothy Guilford had been found dead. There, in red pen, underscored were the words:

free at last!!!

Alan McCauley would love this, Lorimer thought grimly, though in truth there was nothing incriminating about expressing such a sentiment. Counsel for the prosecution would have made mince of the woman, though.

There were dates circled in red, sometimes with the letter P in bold, surely a sign of the times when they had met? The frequency of the letters had diminished, naturally, after Guilford's arrest. Yet there were occasional dates underlined when she had visited him in hospital; once a scribbled note: *bring more pyjamas*, the sort of wifely thing that a woman in love would do.

The final entry had been made the day before but what it meant Lorimer could not fathom. A series of numbers, possibly a telephone number, but certainly not anything within the UK. That was also something for one of the team to follow up, he thought. Who had she known overseas? And was it connected to the atrocity at the hospital?

He flicked back to the weeks before the death of Dorothy Guilford, noting more circled dates and, yes, there it was again, the same series of numbers but this time with a name beneath: *Simon*.

Lorimer frowned. Was this some sort of code? Simon in the New Testament had also been known as Peter. But then he noticed the mark above the letter *i*. Not Peter Guilford, then, but someone from Europe called *Símon*. He tapped the edge of the notebook thoughtfully. He'd seen numbers like that before, hadn't he? And, if he was correct, what he was looking at was a telephone number somewhere in Slovakia.

CHAPTER FORTY-THREE

When her phone rang she saw straight away that it was a text from Rosie.

Can we talk? At home? Are you free today?

Kirsty glanced up at the other officers in the room. She had several actions on a house-breaking case to follow up but it was all paperwork. Could she find the time to slip out? Nobody had asked for her to do anything more specific today and McCauley was out of the office.

Can make time. Say over lunch? 1 at yours?

The reply came back saying yes and Kirsty closed her phone, curious to know why she had been summoned by her friend.

When Kirsty drew up at the parking bay near the Brightmans' flat she spotted Rosie and Solly sitting on the front door steps with Abby between them, enjoying the sunshine.

'Well, this looks nice,' Kirsty told them. 'No work on a Monday for you three?'

'Nursery finished last week,' Rosie explained.

'And I don't have classes this late in the year,' Solly reminded her. 'Rosie likes to come back home for lunch.' He looked across affectionately at his wife.

'Though it's taking me longer to walk back from the office every day,' she joked.

'And we're off to see the ducks, aren't we,' Solly said, patting Abby's curls. Kirsty gave a small frown. Nice and all as it was to be in their company, the text from Rosie had seemed to convey a sense of urgency and she only had a limited amount of time to spend away from her own place of work. Besides, she had actually planned to mug up on some details for Friday's interview during her lunch break.

'Ah.' Rosie smiled as a grandmother wheeling a large pram, a small toddler in tow, passed them by and headed into Kelvingrove Park, a teenage girl walking beside them, her hand devoid of any rings resting on the side of the pram. 'How times have changed! Nice to see a mum so willing to help her own daughter like that.'

'Sally Gardiner is as proud as punch to be a grandmother,' Solly murmured as they watched their neighbour walk along the path. 'Loves these chidden to bits and doesn't give two hoots about her girl being a single mum.'

'Poor Shirley Pettigrew never had that sort of mother's love,' Rosie said.

'Who?' Solly asked.

'Shirley Pettigrew, Dorothy Guilford's older sister,' Kirsty chipped in.

'I thought her name was Finnegan,' Solly said. 'Did she marry the lad, then?'

'That must have been later,' Rosie replied as Kirsty listened, intrigued to know where the conversation was heading.

'I was told that the baby's father fled the scene almost at once. Shirley was left to fend for herself.'

'She married Finnegan years later,' Kirsty explained. 'I looked it all up to check. She divorced him a fair while back. Kept too much to the wrong side of the law for Shirley's liking, I suppose.'

'What happened to the child?' Solly asked.

Both women gave a shrug as Abby began to squirm in her father's arms. 'Ducks, Daddy!' she protested.

He laughed. 'Okay, let's take a walk to see your ducks, my girl.'

'Sorry about that, Kirsty, I thought we'd be alone for a while. Come on up and I'll put the kettle on. Solly made enough sandwiches for an army!'

As she prepared lunch, Rosie explained about the second post-mortem and that it would take place soon.

'I need to be sure that have all my facts right,' she confided in the girl. 'It's so vital that we understand the truth about what happened to Dorothy.' She gave a sigh. 'I know I seem stubborn and obsessed about this,' she continued, putting out a hand and touching Kirsty's arm, 'but I want to know what she was thinking at that moment.'

'Only the dead really know. You must have had that thought umpteen times,' Kirsty replied. 'So, tell me, how can I help?'

'If Dorothy took her own life then she must have had a reason.'

'Maybe she thought she was terminally ill?'

Rosie shook her head. 'I've spoken to her GP and it couldn't have been that. Dorothy was a regular visitor to the practice. But she did telephone her old doctor,' she explained. 'And he told me that Dorothy was terrified that Peter Guilford was planning to kill her.'

'So, let me get this straight. If she thought that then why not just scarper? Find a refuge for battered wives?' Kirsty demanded.

'It's not always as easy as that,' Rosie replied. 'Ask Solly and he'll tell you numerous stories about women who stay in the marital home for all sorts of reasons. It takes a sort of bravery to just get up and leave and lots of these women have had all the courage knocked out of them.'

'Okay, so she stays and expects to be murdered?' Kirsty screwed up her face in disbelief.

'Where would she go?' Rosie asked. 'She's estranged from her only sister, there are no other relatives we know of . . . '

'And it looked to me as if Guilford held the purse strings,' Kirsty mused, thinking of the dowdy clothes hanging in that massive wardrobe in St Andrew's Drive.

'Exactly. Did she have a single soul on earth she could confide in, apart from her doctors?'

'Is that what you'd like me to find out?' Kirsty asked, the reason for her visit becoming apparent.

Rosie nodded. 'You've met the cleaning lady. Did she give any indication that Dorothy used to chat to her? Who else might be her confidante?'

'Women often talk to their hair stylist or spa therapist but I doubt if poor Dorothy ever indulged much in that sort of thing,' Kirsty mused.

She cast her mind back to the day when she and DS Geary had traipsed in and out of the rooms of the big empty house looking for evidence that might suggest a murder had taken place. The bedroom with its tidy surfaces, the prescription pills in the bedside cabinet . . .

300

'Wait a minute!' she exclaimed. 'I *do* remember something. The blueys.'

Rosie shook her head, clearly puzzled.

'Blueys, that's what Dad used to call them when my cousin Ruaraidh wrote from his posting overseas. The blue airmail paper,' she explained. 'I found a bundle of them in Dorothy's bedside drawer, all tied up. Took them and bagged them as a production.'

'What happened to them?'

'Nothing, as far as I know. Geary found the insurance papers then DI McCauley reckoned that was enough to pinpoint Peter Guilford to the murder.'

'So, you don't know who sent them or whether it was someone Dorothy might have written to on a regular basis?'

'Someone she could tell about her fears?'

'Exactly,' Rosie concurred. Then the pathologist smiled a winning smile. 'Don't suppose you could take a look at them for me, DC Wilson?'

Solly watched as Abby threw handfuls of crumbs into the pond, the ducks gobbling eagerly and approaching them without the least fear.

'Now, ducks, be good,' Abby was telling them. 'Don't be so greedy,' she scolded in a tone that made Solly want to laugh, she sounded so like Rosie. 'It's good to share.' She nodded at the quacking birds that were now gathered at their feet. 'Here, that's it aaa-ll gone,' she sang, flinging the last handful into the air and stepping back as the ducks rushed forward.

Solly took his daughter's hand in his and felt its warmth as they strolled along the path. They would walk as far as the bridge, see if they saw a flash of turquoise down below: kingfishers had been spotted there last week, the Bird Man had told them. But the psychologist's thoughts was not really on these or any other birds but on the questions that had gathered in his mind since that conversation back on his front door steps.

What had happened to Shirley's child? Had she kept him after her marriage to Finnegan? And if so, where was the boy now? Solly blinked as a pair of pigeons swooped low overhead, making Abby dance on the spot with glee. He'd be much older, surely? The woman had been thrown out as a teen, and was middle-aged now. And, what had happened to the child's father? The old doctor had told Rosie that he had fled the scene and joined the army. Michael Raynor and Max Warnock had been soldiers, too. Was this a link that hadn't yet been made?

'Abby,' Solly kneeled down and took his daughter's hands in his, 'would you like to come with Daddy to visit a different park?'

'Are there ducks?' Abby asked, her eyes widening.

Solly smiled, wondering if Maxwell Park was going to prove a disappointment or not. 'I don't know, darling. Shall we take a taxi there and see?'

Donald John McDougall was going to be at home and yes, it was no trouble to bring the little girl, he assured Solly. The old doctor put down the telephone and looked into the distance. The celebrated psychologist wanted to talk to him about Shirley Pettigrew and her background, particularly about her son. Could he help?

He hadn't said why but Donald John guessed it had more to do with the death of Dorothy Guilford than the birth of her nephew.

*

302

Abby was asleep by the time the taxi drew up outside the house and Solly had difficulty paying the driver as he struggled with the little girl against his shoulder.

'Professor Brightman ... oh ... ' Donald John stepped aside as he saw the bearded man, the child fast asleep in his arms. 'Just lay her on the settee,' he whispered, beckoning Solly to follow him through the house and into a bright conservatory.

He handed a fleece rug to Solly who tucked it around the sleeping child then the two men stood, regarding one another.

'Professor ... '

'Solly, just call me Solly,' he said.

'Donald John,' the doctor replied, giving the psychologist a firm handshake. 'I'm bursting with curiosity to know what's behind all of this.' He lowered his voice in case he woke the professor's daughter. 'Please, take a seat.'

'It concerns Shirley Pettigrew's son,' Solly told him, sitting next to Abby. 'I wondered if you could tell me what became of him.'

Donald John's bushy white eyebrows lifted for a moment as he considered the question.

'Well now,' he began. 'He was a healthy enough baby. And I should know.' He chuckled. 'Delivered him myself. Local hospital had what they called a GP Unit back in those days.'

'And she kept the boy?'

'She did, though it can't have been easy for her. On benefits, in a rented flat near Ibrox, nobody to give her a helping hand. It was shocking, really, the way those people washed their hands of her,' Donald John remarked. 'Even back then being an unmarried mother didn't carry too much of a stigma. But they were fiercely against anything that smacked of immorality, that pair.'

'The Pettigrews?'

'Aye.'

'And Dorothy? Didn't the girl want to see her sister's baby?'

Donald John's eyes clouded for a moment. 'Hard to say. Most wee girls want to be around babies, don't they? But I was never sure about Dorothy. She was always a strange one, even as a child . . . '

'They were still your patients, even when they moved to Ibrox?' Solly asked.

'Oh, yes. She kept the boy with her. Married that ne'er-do-well, Paddy Finnegan, some time later. Moved away to Castlemilk once the boy upped sticks and left home.'

'So you don't know what happened to them after that?'

Donald John grinned. 'Oh, that's where you're wrong. Finnegan was a right waster. A drunk. Died of cirrhosis eventually and Shirley moved back nearer home. She told me all about it. The boy was long gone by then, Shirley completely on her own.'

'Do you know what happened to the son?'

'It was a sad story. But all too common. Finnegan resented the child. He was a bright wee lad, clever at school, apparently. Left home as soon as he turned eighteen. He joined up,' Donald John mused. 'Just like his father before him.'

'And did he ever come back to help his mother?'

The doctor shook his head. 'Not as far as I know. Think he resented the fact that his mother had chosen the Finnegan fellow over him. Strange boy, as I recall. Very bright, as I've said, but quite intense.'

'And you never saw him again after the father's death?'

The old doctor shook his head. 'He may have been reconciled with Shirley, who knows? She's a poor creature herself, these days,' he continued vaguely.

Solly simply nodded. It would not be professional of the doctor, retired or not, to comment on the medical history of one of his patients.

'Ach, who knows what good it would do her anyway to have Maxwell back into her life,' Donald John said at last, shaking is head wearily.

'Maxwell?'

'That's what she called the child,' the doctor chuckled. 'The local gossip was that he had been conceived one night in Maxwell Park. Of course,' he went on, unaware of the psychologist staring at him intently, 'we just knew him as Max.'

Solly and Donald John strolled around the edge of the pond, Abby clutching their hands, sometimes asking to be swung off her feet. It had been a rewarding afternoon, Solly thought as they circled the pond, a few mallards swimming in and out of the water lilies that were opening up to the sunshine. The doctor had remembered Archie Warnock, one of his own patients, when his parents had come to live in Glasgow for a time. He'd been an only child, a bit spoiled, Donald John remembered. But it was interesting that Shirley had given her baby his name, despite the fact that he'd abandoned her.

The sound of a diesel engine made both men look up.

'Think that's our taxi,' Solly said, letting go of Abby's hand for a moment and shaking the outstretched hand. 'Thank you for all of this. It's information that may be crucial to an ongoing police investigation.'

'Oh, that's all right.' Donald John smiled. 'Happy to make a proper statement if it helps. I've enjoyed our little chat. And seeing you, young lady.' He nodded at Abby.

'Say bye-bye and thank you for the biscuits,' Solly told her.

'Thank you.' Abby smiled shyly and ducked her head against her father's legs.

'Say hello to that wife of yours and make sure she rests,' Donald John told Solly as he waved them off.

Solly looked back as the figure became smaller and smaller, the man silhouetted by the brightness behind him, one arm aloft in a farewell salutation.

CHAPTER FORTY-FOUR

Max Warnock might have agreed that he was a patient man. It had taken years now for his idea to become a reality and he was not one to let it slip through his fingers too quickly. He had them now, both of them in fact, the girl and that interfering woman from the nail bar. It had been a risk keeping the place open for so long but it had worked in the end and the Ferenc girl was now his to do with as he liked. The moment they had taken the other one the whole place had been shut down, of course, the other girls sent packing to different parts of the city.

Michael had made a good job of that, Max told himself, grudgingly. He might be big and brawny but Mike Raynor had one other outstanding quality: obedience. It was an admirable quality in some situations but it would prove to be the man's undoing once he had outlived his usefulness. At least he had managed to finish Guilford off this time, he thought, though the peripheral damage was going to mean far more police interference. No, despite what he had done for him, Raynor had to be sacrificed. He knew too much and was already showing signs of wanting more than his promised share.

His mind turned again to the fire. The crackling sounds had

been almost as fearsome as the heat and the pain. She'd held him tightly, screaming in his ear, trying to save herself, he remembered. If he'd managed to shake her off, perhaps he might have escaped . . . The memory faded but the pain lingered, a stiffness in his face, an inability to perform like a man . . .

Let her rot in hell! Maybe she was in a place where fires burned her for eternity.

His mouth twitched a little, an excuse for a grin.

Soon he would have his revenge and it would be all the sweeter for knowing how it would have hurt her.

The first sign that they were no longer alone made Molly sit up suddenly, ears straining to hear more. There was the sound of a car engine, then silence as though it had stopped close by the building. And, was that voices? She pressed her ear to the crack in the doorway, listening. Men's voices.

She turned to Juliana and drew her closer, nodding.

It was time.

Somewhere a door banged shut and then footsteps came downstairs, closer and closer.

Molly gripped the chair, ready for whoever was coming.

The sudden light streaming into the darkness let her see the figure entering the room; it was the same man who had grabbed her in that lane.

She raised the chair and heard it crashing down on his head, knocking him to the floor.

'Run!' she yelled and Juliana dashed past her, heading for the stairs.

The man was getting back onto his feet, one hand to his head, feeling the blood. Then, with a roar he launched himself at Molly.

Years of practice made her quicker on her feet than this lumbering man.

She ducked then side-stepped, pushing past and slamming the door fast behind her. It was with a steady and determined hand that Molly Newton turned the key, hearing it click as it locked.

Inside the darkened room she heard the yells as he beat his fists against the door.

'See what it's like being a prisoner, now,' Molly whispered grimly, blinking as the unaccustomed daylight hit her eyes.

At the top of the stairs she met the girl crouched against a wall, shivering with cold or fear.

'We need to get out,' Molly told her urgently. 'But there may be other men around. Can you remember if there was a back door?'

Juliana shook her head so Molly took the girl's hand and led her through the deserted house, creeping softly, keeping as close to the walls as they could.

Soon they entered what appeared to be a huge kitchen, the sort that Molly remembered from farmhouse holidays in her childhood. Old pots and pans dangled from hooks in the ceiling over a large wooden table where a drawer was half open, revealing an assortment of kitchen implements. There might be something worth grabbing there, she thought, a knife, perhaps? But no blade glinted amongst the tools.

The noise of a car door banging made them both stop and stiffen.

'Someone's coming . . . ' Juliana began.

'Shhh,' Molly implored. Then she moved swiftly, pulling out the drawer a little more and grabbing a white marble rolling pin.

She motioned the girl to follow her to the space behind the kitchen door then waited, one fist grasping the makeshift weapon.

There was a sound of heavy footsteps on the flagstone floor. Then the door where they hid creaked open a little more.

'Raynor? Have you got them yet? Which one am I having?' a voice called out.

As soon as he entered the room, Molly swung the marble baton across the man's skull, felling him.

Juliana grasped her sleeve. 'Have you killed him?' she gasped, looking up at Molly with shock in her eyes.

Molly shook her head though in truth she did not know whether the inert figure sprawled at her feet was dead or alive.

'We need to get out,' she hissed. 'Come on!'

The back door to the kitchen was unlocked and opened easily. Molly stepped outside, head forward, listening intently, looking all around. Wherever that car was parked there was no sign of it at this side of the house. Straight ahead was a patch of shrubbery across a grassy path, overgrown rhododendrons with trailing branches.

'This way,' she whispered, pulling the girl along. She crouched down and on all fours scrambled under the bushes, creeping on the damp earth, desperate to hide from any prying eyes.

The tangled branches made an ideal refuge, full bushes hiding them perfectly as they made their way deeper and deeper into the undergrowth.

The ground rose a little as they crawled and Molly felt the softness of turf under her fingernails as she inched slowly forward, desperate to keep as silent as possible. Then the leaves parted and she could see the sky above, a bowl of shining blue.

They had climbed higher than she had realised as they emerged from the bushes and looked back down on the old building, probably a deserted farmhouse. A car was parked to one side, its front door open. Molly sat absolutely still. She could see but not be seen, peeping through the topmost leaves of the extensive shrubbery. Rhododendrons might be an invasive species, she thought with a wry grin, but their sprawling habit had saved them from detection.

She turned to look at Juliana as the girl tugged her arm.

Then, at that moment a figure emerged from the back of the car and she ducked down again, a warning finger to her lips. From their position up here it was impossible to tell who he was but Molly watched as he walked around the car then opened the boot and took out a heavy object.

'That's him,' Juliana whispered. But one look from Molly silenced her, both women now concentrating on what was happening below.

Max Warnock was carrying a can in one hand, the weight of it making him lean slightly to one side. Then he disappeared out of sight.

Now was the moment to flee or remain motionless, hidden deep within the bushes. Silence would be their friend, Molly decided, motioning her companion to stay as still as possible.

For several minutes nothing happened. Had he found the other men? Was he even now kneeling beside the one she had whacked? He would surely be aware that they had escaped, so sitting tight was definitely their better option; to make any noise would alert him to their hiding place.

She frowned, puzzled, as he appeared beneath them and paused outside the back door, evidently locking it up. But why? Didn't he know the other men were inside? Had he not found that the prisoners had made their escape?

Her heart beat loudly, the questions making Molly stare silently as he walked around the side of the farmhouse and out of their sight.

Waiting was the hardest thing to do but all of Molly Newton's training told her that she should stay still and not move a muscle until this man presented no further danger to them.

The smell was what hit them first, a pleasant woody whiff of smoke. Then a crackle as a fire began somewhere out of sight. But not for long.

Molly's eyes widened as she saw the flames rip up the side of the old farmhouse. Where was Warnock? And had that been a petrol can in his hand?

The figure of a man running made her stiffen in fear. But he headed for the car and she watched as it drove off along the rutted track, then stopped, fifty yards or so from the house. She saw a glint of sun shining off the window as he rolled it down and realised with a sudden shock that he had stopped to watch the fire.

He had heard a distant drumming of fists against the cellar door and grinned. These women would be trying to fend off Raynor and his driver, a man whose name he had never bothered to learn. Then, without even looking inside, Warnock had turned the keys in the lock. The front door was also secured and then the fun part began as he walked slowly around the side of the house where an old woodpile was stacked. It had been one of the first things he'd seen all those weeks ago, the grain of his idea planted. Wood and fire, smoke and death . . .

Max watched as the fire caught hold, imagining the screams of the men and women inside, trapped by the smoke, unable to move.

He knew exactly what that was like, didn't he? One of the lucky ones, they had called him afterwards, the pain searing like molten metal through his entire body. One of the lucky ones? Raynor had pulled him out and over the years Max had shown his gratitude, but Raynor had become a liability and no debt lasted for ever.

He began to laugh as a sudden whoosh caught the side of the house, engulfing it in flames that shot upwards. The women would be frantic now, yelling their heads off, battling against smoke and flames, maybe even begging their captors to save them.

Max remembered her cries as the flames had licked his flesh, her arms holding him down, keeping him from the half-open doorway. He could have been whole, free, not this sad excuse for a man burned almost to death, if she'd let him go.

Well, she was dead and her bones left to rot beneath the charred sticks of that hell-hole and now her daughter was learning what it was like to suffer the same fate. He lifted his phone and looked through the viewfinder, snapping image after image . . . memories that would last a lifetime.

The smoke drifted towards him, stinging his eyes so that he rolled up the window and looked around. The place was obscured by trees and acres of shrubbery climbing up to the hills but he knew that eventually the smoke would rise higher and someone would make a call that would bring others here to find what had happened.

Max Warnock gave a great sigh and turned the steering wheel, letting the car head away from the roaring flames, away from the scene of his triumph.

What the hell was happening down there? Molly could no longer see for the smoke and Juliana had begun to cough as it rolled up towards them.

'We need to get away,' Molly urged. 'Climb, now, as high as we can. Come on!'

No longer afraid of being spotted, she pulled the girl by the hand and crashed through the shrubbery, the sounds of their flight impossible to hear against the noise of falling timbers as the fire took hold.

At last they were high above the old farmhouse and only wisps of smoke drifted past as they flung themselves down on a grassy plateau. Molly took long breaths of the clean, sweet-scented air before turning onto her knees and gazing around, wondering where on earth they were. The sun was high in the sky so it was possibly just after the middle of the day with plenty of daylight left. That could be to their advantage, so long as they were no longer being hunted.

She looked at the Slovakian girl who was sprawled on the ground beside her, her shoulders shaking as she wept.

'It's okay, Juliana, we're safe now,' Molly whispered.

But the girl continued to sob, muttering something that Molly could not understand.

'What is it? What's the matter?' she asked, putting a comforting arm around the girl's shoulders.

'My mother . . .' the girl sobbed, then shook her head and would say no more.

CHAPTER FORTY-FIVE

The team had worked tirelessly through the night following the attack at the Queen Elizabeth Hospital and the discovery of Cynthia Drollinger's body. The search of the woman's flat had resulted in detailed scrutiny of her phone records – both landline and the mobile Lorimer had found in that designer handbag. Someone had called her for about two seconds just before Guilford had left his ward, their identity still a mystery.

He had added several notes on the whiteboard at the end of the room with lines that now intersected Cynthia Drollinger's name and those of Max Warnock, Guilford and the mysterious Símon.

Further searches had pinned down the location of that Slovakian telephone number to a residential property in the heart of a small village near the place where the Ferenc family lived. *Gypsy town*, he remembered the interpreter at Barlinnie calling it, though its real name was Streda nad Bodrogom.

Calling the number had resulted only in hearing the phone ringing out, the conclusion being that nobody was at home. Further investigation with the Slovakian police was ongoing and the members of the MIT were hopeful that a name and address might soon be emailed to the Glasgow office.

Lorimer rubbed his eyes and wondered if he would manage to last through the day without falling asleep. The telephone on his desk rang out and he lifted it automatically.

'Lorimer,' he said shortly, then sat up a little straighter as a heavily accented voice spoke at the other end.

The detective superintendent listened, one hand scribbling furiously on his notepad, the other clutching the handset as though it were a lifeline to a drowning man.

At last he responded to the Slovakian policeman's message.

'I can't tell you how grateful we are. That intelligence is going to make a great deal of difference to us. Thank you.'

'Just get him for us, okay?' the Slovakian officer demanded.

Lorimer grinned as he nodded. 'We will do our best, I promise,' he told him, crossing his fingers. There was no way he was about to divulge the fact that Peter Guilford, a man wanted for questioning by the Slovakian police, was at this moment hanging between life and death.

After the call ended, he sat still for a moment, reading the notes in front of him.

There was a big house in the village of Drobný-Bodrogom, a village of many big houses, the Slovakian police officer had said, his voice implying that there was something less than healthy about the place. Its owner was a Scottish person, Peter Guilford, a man who owned several of the houses in this small village. Most of them were empty all year round but sometimes there would be parties in the summer months, men and women descending in droves, all intent on having a good time. They came in buses, straight from the airport, then left several days later, only the housekeepers staying on to clear up the mess.

One of his officers had been dispatched to the house in question, the telephone number for which had appeared in Cynthia Drollinger's diary. Nobody was at home, Lorimer was told, but a big transit van with the sign Guilford Vehicle Hire was parked to one side.

'And no mention of Max Warnock,' he said to himself once the call was ended and he was alone again in his room. 'Where do you come into all of this, Max?'

He closed his eyes for a moment, drifting between waking and sleeping, tempted to doze. They had all assumed up until now that Warnock was the gangmaster, trafficking women from a base in Slovakia to Scotland, but now the information suggested that all along it had been Peter Guilford who had been pulling the strings. Or had he simply been bankrolling the entire operation? Was that what it was all about after all? Greed for money: one of the oldest motives in the book. With both Dorothy and Peter out of the way, had Max Warnock seen himself as the legal heir to what now looked like the Guilford empire? True, Dorothy had kept ownership of both the house and the Scottish side of the business but it was now obvious that Guilford had invested heavily in property in this tiny village near Gypsy Town.

With this latest information Lorimer could now see a shape to the tangled mess that had given him a headache for weeks. It was like a spider's web with Max Warnock at its centre, weaving his strands of evil.

He opened his eyes and sighed, feeling his shoulders and neck rigid with tension.

Somewhere out there Juliana Ferenc and Molly Newton were at the mercy of a very dangerous man and Lorimer was determined to hunt him down.

*

Molly stopped and listened to the sound of a tractor somewhere quite close. A tractor meant a farmer and a possible farmhouse nearby.

She took Juliana by the hand and pulled her along, keeping to the shade of a copse of trees for cover. The sun had shifted and Molly estimated that they had been walking for around three hours, her bare feet now cut and scratched with thorns.

The girl had not spoken a word since they had left the burning building where they had been kept imprisoned.

Molly glanced at her from time to time, recognising the shock on the girl's face. *My mother*, she'd cried out. Had that been a natural cry for help? Or was there something more to the Slovakian girl's pale face and refusal to meet Molly's questioning gaze? Trauma could result from the what-might-have-been moment when Juliana had pictured them both burning in that building together, something that figure watching in his car had intended.

She'd recognised him, hadn't she? Molly glanced again at the closed face, a curtain of dark hair obscuring her features. There were questions to be asked, but right now it was more important that they find a place of safety.

The sound of lambs baaing made her look down the slope as they crested the hilly plateau. There beneath them was a field full of sheep, lambs now rushing to be with their mothers as these two unknown humans stumbled into their territory.

She clasped Juliana's arm and pointed. 'Look!' she said, and grinned. A little further on she could see a red-tiled roof beyond a stand of conifers. 'Must be a farmhouse.' She urged the girl forward. 'We can ask them for help.'

But Juliana remained rooted to the spot, terror in her eyes.

'What if . . .' she began.

Molly flung an arm around the girl's shoulders. 'It'll be all right,' she soothed. 'Farmers are decent folk. Besides, we need to phone my colleagues and they'll come and take us back home.'

Juliana looked at her quizzically for a moment and Molly cursed herself. Where was this young woman's home? And, once they were back in the city, where would she be taken? Some detention centre perhaps? Or could she make a case for keeping the girl with her until she was properly repatriated to her own country?

'Come on,' she coaxed. 'Stay with me and everything will be all right. I promise.'

Mrs Sunter had never imagined playing hostess to a pair of barefoot strangers who had lost their way, especially when one of them turned out to be a police officer. She had sat them both down at her kitchen table, letting the taller one use the telephone whilst piling a plate full of freshly made pancakes and switching on the kettle. Tea, the universal panacea for all ills, all situations, though in truth this pair had looked as though they needed more than that.

Later, the farmer's wife had watched the squad car taking them away, that young foreign lass and the one who seemed to be known to the plain-clothes policemen who had greeted her like a long-lost friend. Detective Constable Newton, they had called her. Who'd have guessed it? And what on earth was the story behind their bedraggled appearance?

'We'll be in touch, ma'am,' one of them had told the bemused woman as he had turned to leave. 'Most grateful for all your help,' he had added, though Mrs Sunter had not the least idea what he meant. She had gathered up the empty plates, nodding with satisfaction that every one of her pancakes had been eaten.

CHAPTER FORTY-SIX

Lorimer looked up as the door opened to admit a familiar bearded man.

'Solly?' He rose to his feet as the psychologist came forward and clasped his hands.

'I've found out about Max Warnock,' he began. 'You are not going to believe this, Lorimer,' he said slowly. 'He's Shirley Finnegan's son.'

'What?' Lorimer sank back into his chair, mouth slightly open as the news hit him. 'When did you find this out?'

Solly explained about his visit to the retired GP. 'I was curious about the child, Shirley's baby.' He shrugged. 'Families can bond together at the birth of a child but sometimes . . . well, in Shirley's case it split the family asunder, made her a pariah in their eyes.'

'So Max Warnock began his days only a few miles away from here,' Lorimer said, whistling under his breath.

'Grew up in Glasgow then left to join the army.'

'Where he met Michael Raynor,' Lorimer continued.

'Yes, strange, though, don't you think? An officer and a private?'

'Raynor was the one to save him from that burning building,' Lorimer reminded him.

'So, you would think that Warnock would be in the man's debt ever after, yes?'

'Yes.' Lorimer frowned. 'But Raynor seems to have been the one to do the dirty work. Attacking Guilford in prison and, if we're correct, murdering that unknown man whose body is still lying the mortuary.'

'What if he's not unknown to the Slovakians?' Solly murmured. 'Any chance of showing a post-mortem photograph to them?'

Lorimer raised his eyebrows. 'It's worth a try,' he began. 'You think he was part of the gang? A falling out amongst the ones under Max's control?' That number in Cynthia Drollinger's diary might begin to make some sense now.

Solly remained silent. It was an unanswerable question, after all; one that would remain a puzzle until they discovered the whereabouts of the main leaders in this affair.

'Good work, Solly.' Lorimer grinned faintly. 'You see things that other people sometimes don't and that's brought us a lot closer to finding out what's going on here.' He rose from his chair, his mind turning to the undercover officer and the Slovakian girl. The relief that they had been found alive was immense. They were even now on their way back here and soon Lorimer and the other officers at the MIT would find out exactly what had happened to them both. Meanwhile, the team were working all the hours that God sent them, the attack on the hospital complicating matters and deploying officers more thinly than he would have liked. Still, every new piece of information had its value and this one from the professor was pure gold.

'Think it's time we had a little chat with Shirley Finnegan, don't you?'

'Yes, but first I'd like to share my thoughts about that lady, if I may.'

Lorimer listened as the psychologist formulated his theory: a story about envy, loss and the bitterness that could have swollen into a torrent of hatred across the years.

The debriefing was to take place shortly but Molly had insisted that Juliana be kept with her meantime. 'She's still in shock,' she'd told Lorimer. 'And I think she'll tell us a lot more if I'm there beside her.'

Their reception at Helen Street had been nothing short of a celebration, hugs given to them both, much to the surprise of Juliana who had gazed wide-eyed at the men and women who had crowded around and cheered at the sight of them.

The feel of warm water coursing over Molly's tired body had been bliss, the aches on her shoulders throbbing, though the cuts and scratches on her legs and feet stung under the shower's spray. Now what she craved more than anything was to sleep for as long as she wanted. But first there had to be a period of sitting and talking to the detective superintendent and the rest of the team.

When she emerged from the shower cubicle, Juliana was already dressed in the clothes that one of her fellow officers had conjured up from somewhere.

A fresh summer dress and a pair of open-toed sandals made all the difference, Molly realised, watching as the Slovakian girl twisted her wet hair into a knot. She had to make do with someone's spare uniform, but that was okay, though she left off the boots, preferring to wear just the pair of socks that had been laid out on the bench for her.

'You are a police . . . ' Juliana asked, a frown on her face.

'Yes,' Molly admitted. 'I was sent to find you and make sure that you were safe.' Then she shook her head. 'Didn't make a very good job of that, did I?'

Juliana came forwards and touched her arm. 'You saved me,' she said simply. Then, stepping forward, she flung herself into Molly's arms and wept at last.

Lorimer looked up as the two figures entered the room. The Ferenc girl was wearing a white cotton frock with blue polka dots, looking for all the world like an overawed schoolgirl who had come for a tour of the police station. She was accompanied by the tall woman in uniform who met his eyes with a smile; Molly Newton, whose disappearance had caused him several sleepless nights. He rose to his feet and came around the table to greet them.

'Miss Ferenc,' he said, giving a nod to the dark-haired girl. 'We are so pleased to have you here safe and sound.' He took her hand and shook it. 'Your uncle and brother have been informed of your arrival and you'll see them later,' he told her.

'Uncle Pavol?' The girl's eyes lit up.

'Yes, I've met him,' Lorimer told her. 'He has been helping us,' he added as though to assure this young woman that she was now on the side of law and order.

'DC Newton,' he turned to Molly, 'we have lots of questions for you so please bear with us for a while longer.'

The pair sat down side by side at the big table, several of the team taking their places quietly, Solly looking at the women with an expression of pity in his dark eyes.

'Max Warnock,' Lorimer began. 'We know rather more about him than we did before your disappearance. He was in the army, a major no less, and stationed in Slovakia.'

He saw the Ferenc girl's head rise. Was it the mention of

Slovakia or did the name Max Warnock mean something to her?

'Moreover, it has been established that he was Dorothy Guilford's nephew, her sister Shirley's son by a local boy.'

He saw Molly Newton's expression of amazement but mentally commended her for keeping quiet as he continued. 'So far as we can ascertain he was in some sort of arrangement with Peter Guilford who has property in a place called Drobný-Bodrogom.'

He heard Juliana's gasp and turned to give her a smile. 'That is close to your own home, is it not?'

She nodded, eyes wide, but said nothing, gazing up at him.

'Now, we have to find this man, Max. Can you help us with that, Miss Ferenc?'

Juliana nodded and glanced at Molly as though for reassurance.

'Go on, tell us whatever you know,' the policewoman urged.

'It was Max who—' She broke off, biting her lip.

'Yes?' Lorimer asked gently.

Juliana looked away from him and turned to Molly instead as she answered.

'It was Max back there,' she began. 'He was the one who set the place on fire. He wanted us to die there like—' She stopped suddenly, a sob wrenched from her throat.

'It's okay,' Molly said, 'take your time.'

'My mother . . . ' Juliana began again. 'She died in that other fire. My papa, too. When I was a baby . . . ' The girl swallowed hard and took a deep breath, every officer around the table intent on her words.

'Max was burned in that fire but he came out alive,' she said. 'The story was told about a miracle . . . ' She shrugged a little. 'I don't know, it was like a . . . what do you say . . . something to be told to a child out of a book?'

'A fairytale?' Molly suggested.

'Maybe,' Juliana said. 'We heard it sometimes. Then one day he comes back.' She gave a shudder and Lorimer watched as Molly put a comforting hand on the girl's arm.

'They all said he was changed. His face ...' She tailed off and shook her head. 'It was all smooth and ... and ... he did not know how to smile,' she stammered. 'But they were happy for me to go away with him in the big bus, all of us girls off to Scotland to find work ... make lots of money ...'

Juliana looked around at the faces regarding her solemnly, turning at last to Lorimer.

'I was there,' he told her. 'In Aberdeen. I saw what they did to you.' He remembered the frightened face of the child he had wrapped in that grubby blanket. 'We rescued many of the girls, perhaps some from your village. But you were not with them.'

Juliana hung her head for a moment. 'No. Uncle Pavol, he gave me their money. Lots of money ...' she whispered. 'I came to Glasgow and tried to find him but there was nobody at the place where he told me to go ...'

There was silence as the girl sat, staring into her lap.

'Then you met me,' Molly said, encouraging Juliana to continue her story.

'I was hoping for work, proper work. But they took me away before I could return to see you,' she told Molly. 'I thought you were somebody else, you said your name was Sasha ...'

'What happened after you were taken?' Lorimer asked, turning his attention to DC Newton.

Molly described the darkened basement room and her attempts to escape, though Lorimer knew she was probably glossing over many of the more lurid details.

'They came in a car, three of them,' she said. 'We managed

to lock one into the cellar.' She stopped and shuddered suddenly. 'I knocked out the second man and left him lying on the floor ...'

Lorimer watched as she closed her eyes for a moment.

'And the third man?'

'We couldn't believe it,' Molly said slowly. 'He had a petrol can ... then he set fire to the house as we watched from our hiding place high above, in a mass of rhododendrons.' She turned to face the officers around the table. 'He meant to kill them. And us. Who was he? Why did he do such a terrible thing?'

The voice that answered did not come from Lorimer but from the Slovakian girl.

'It was Max,' she said simply. 'I saw him. In that car, the one that took me away. He wanted to destroy me in another fire just like the one that burned my mother to death.'

Professor Solomon Brightman looked out across the waving trees as a breeze blew amongst the lime green leaves. All of the pieces of the puzzle had come together at last, despite the knowledge that Max Warnock was still out there somewhere, a dangerous man hunted by scores of officers from Police Scotland.

Mothers, he thought. Shirley Finnegan, the Ferenc mother, the Pettigrews ... all different people with children who had gone astray in one way or another.

He breathed in deeply, glad to know that one mother at least was safe from the fall-out of this case. Rosie had made the decision to go on maternity leave now and was at this moment resting at home, Morag, their beloved nanny, staying with her to look after Abby.

CHAPTER FORTY-SEVEN

Shirley was folding the last of the bed linen when the knocks came on her door, making her blood run cold for a moment. Only two sorts of people knocked loudly like that and right now she didn't wish to see either of them.

Then, to her horror, the sound of the letter box flapping and a male voice called, 'Open up. Police.'

Dropping the sheet in her haste, Shirley almost ran along the hallway and slipped on the door chain before unlocking her front door.

Two strangers stood there, one very tall and dark, the other a foreign-looking bloke with a bushy beard and horn-rimmed spectacles.

The warrant card thrust forward made Shirley drop her gaze and read the name. Lorimer. She looked up again.

'May we come in, Mrs Finnegan,' the tall one asked. It was not a question, Shirley realised, her hand already slipping off the chain.

'Sorry 'bout the mess,' she muttered, standing aside and letting the strangers into her home, a feeling of dread creeping into her very bones as she followed them into the living room.

*

Lorimer's eyes took in the untidy room. There were bundles of laundry piled up on every spare piece of furniture, black plastic bags and cardboard boxes lined up against one wall. It looked at first as if someone had been packing but then he saw the piles of folded linen and the freshly laundered towels packed into open bin bags and a faint smile tugged at the corner of his mouth.

'You take in washing, do you, Mrs Finnegan? Sorry to bother you when you're so busy,' he began, his voice both polite and apologetic. He saw the colour heighten in the woman's face. If his guess was correct, Shirley Finnegan was part of the entire scheme. Someone had to take care of the laundry for these pop-up brothels; a dry-cleaning business was too easy to trace and it probably saved them money keeping it in the family. His eyes scanned the rest of the room for any sign of another person living there, but it looked as if Shirley Finnegan was on her own.

'Max keep you busy then, does he?'

Shirley put one hand to her mouth and sank into the nearest armchair.

'You see, we know that Max Warnock is your son, Shirley,' Lorimer said softly, leaning forward so that he could catch the woman's eye, hold her there as he spoke. 'And we know that he's been back here in Glasgow,' he continued. His gaze flicked across the floor where the discarded sheet lay in a heap, then back to her face. 'What's all this then? Fresh laundry for his . . .' he hesitated, watching the woman's tongue run across dry lips, '*businesses*, shall we say?' He folded one leg across the other. 'Yes, let's call them that for the moment, shall we? Not brothels. Not nail bars. Not these sorts of words.' He leaned forward further, making the woman shrink back into her chair. 'No, we don't want to call them that, do we, Shirley? Because that would be too hard for you to hear, wouldn't it? Your only son mixed up in nasty stuff like that?'

He let the question hang in the air. Watching the terror in the woman's eyes.

He saw her swallow hard then her eyes left his and flicked across to where Solly was standing.

'No idea what you're talking about,' she said, her voice cracking. 'Not against the law to do some washing, is it?' But the man with the beard did not answer and she turned back to her inquisitor.

'Max Warnock,' Lorimer repeated. 'Where is he, Shirley? We need to find him before anyone else gets hurt.'

She gave a shrug. 'Don't know,' she said, clasping her arms together across her stomach in a defensive gesture.

'Oh, I think you do, Shirley,' Lorimer declared. 'Max left you to join the army, didn't he? Turned up with his friend, Michael Raynor.'

Lorimer noticed the tightening of the woman's jaw, the narrowed eyes.

'But not here, perhaps? At his Aunt Dorothy's big house in St Andrew's Drive.'

The flash of anger on the fat face was answer enough. He'd guessed correctly. And so had Solly. 'Did that hurt you, Shirley? Did it make you jealous that your boy preferred the company of his Aunt Dorothy?'

For a moment there was a silence then a snake-like hiss issued from the woman's lips.

'You'll never find him,' she declared at last. 'He's far cleverer than any of you lot! Just wait and see.'

Lorimer stood up and signalled to Solly to do the same.

'Get your jacket, Shirley, you'll be gone a while,' he told her. He watched while the woman heaved herself up, grabbing a pack of cigarettes from the arm of her chair and shoving them into an open handbag.

'I'll take that for now,' Lorimer told her, glimpsing the mobile phone inside.

She shot him a venomous look and shoved past him, not caring that he followed her out of the room.

They would take her into custody, try to wring the truth out of her, but as they escorted the woman from her shabby home, Lorimer had grave doubts about whether this particular mother would yield up any more information about her son.

CHAPTER FORTY-EIGHT

She would have to sign for them; it was the only way. If the chain of official signatures was broken then any case coming to court could be called into question. Every piece of evidence from a crime scene had to be bagged and tagged then written up and left in the secure room down in the depths of the Govan police building, a civilian in charge of entering the data and handling the items. And there had to be an official reason for Kirsty to take the pack of airmail letters and read them at her desk. Just asking DI McCauley might work, she thought. But he was so obsessed with the thought that the case was done and dusted, Guilford dead and gone, so the station rumour-mill had it, that she hesitated to ask.

Besides, there was her sergeant's interview at the end of this week and she needed to be squeaky clean going into that. Tampering with any of the evidence would result in instant dismissal, she reckoned. No, she would have to do this properly.

Just then DS Geary passed and dropped her a wink. 'Looking serious, young Kirsty. Anything I can do?'

'Well, sir, as a matter of fact, there is.' Kirsty looked up at his friendly face bending down towards her. 'D'you remember when we went to the Guilford house in St Andrew's Drive?'

Geary grinned. 'Not likely to forget that place in a hurry,' he said. 'What about it?'

'I bagged a pack of airmail letters that I found next to the victim's bed.' She drew a quick breath. 'Any chance I could retrieve them and have a look?'

Geary stood up and frowned. 'What for? McCauley's pretty well closed that case as far as he's concerned.'

Kirsty bit her lip. 'Lorimer ... ' she began.

'Ah, something going on upstairs, is it?' Geary winked at her. 'You being seconded again, kiddo? Won't do your interview any harm if that's the case, eh?' he laughed. Kirsty smiled and said nothing. It was true that she had been seconded to the MIT on a previous case but her investigation now was purely on the sidelines and certainly not along official channels, even though she might have had Lorimer's blessing.

'I'll nip down and sign them out for you, shall I?' Geary offered. 'I can make a note that this particular production is needed for background material, that do?'

Kirsty exhaled a sigh of relief. 'Oh, yes, thank you,' she said. 'Thank you so much.'

'Nae bother, first pint's on you once it's all over and you can spill the beans, right?'

He gave her a slap on the shoulder and strolled off, whistling, no doubt anticipating a friendly get-together in the local pub where he could hear all about whatever was happening upstairs in the MIT, police gossip and stories being meat and drink to most officers everywhere.

'Oh, sir ... ?' Kirsty was on her feet now and following the DS. 'Any chance I could have them today?'

Geary looked at his watch. 'Get it for you later unless there's a particular hurry?' He looked at her anxious face. 'Ah, like maybe yesterday was soon enough, that the way it is?'

Kirsty nodded.

'Okay, give me half an hour and I'll see what I can do.'

Kirsty imagined the DS stomping down the flight of stairs that led to the dimly lit basement where huge shelves of evidence were kept stored, the grim-faced woman in charge like the gatekeeper of Hades. Geary would be kept waiting while she retrieved the particular box he needed, watched while he signed out the packet of letters and dated it all in her ledger. Always hard copy, she'd remind them, although every single transaction was written up on her computer and stored in an alternative basement somewhere in the ether where neither moth nor worm could damage them.

The half-hour had stretched into forty nail-biting minutes before Geary appeared again, a packet in his meaty fists.

'There you are,' he told her. 'Sign below my name and don't forget to obtain further signatures from anyone else who handles them, okay?'

'Thanks.' She beamed. 'I mean, really. I owe you one, sir!'

'Aye, too right, but maybe you won't be calling me that much longer, eh?'

And he walked off, leaving Kirsty with a feeling that his words were strangely prophetic. Perhaps by Friday they would be on equal terms, detective sergeants both. Or perhaps she would be contemplating her resignation from the force?

Dear Aunt Dorothy,

Life here goes on just as normal, if you can call this normal. Not the sort of life you'd be accustomed to, I bet. Anyway, let me tell you a bit about the countryside around the little town where we're billeted.

Kirsty read on, lines describing the gypsy town and the people that Max Warnock had met. No names but pen portraits of dark-haired folk and their different ways.

He was a good letter writer, she'd give him that, Kirsty thought as she put down the first bluey, noting that the date had preceded the fire that had damaged Warnock's face.

Dear Aunt Dorothy,
Sorry to leave this for so long but life here has been pretty full on. Met a nice girl and have taken her out a few times to a local bar. She seems quite keen on an officer in uniform. Must remember to wear mine when I come on leave to visit you.

There was more about day-to-day life but no mention of Michael Raynor or anything that the military were actually undertaking in that part of Europe. No, Major Warnock was far too astute to let fall any crumb of information.

Every letter was signed off in an affectionate tone:

Your loving nephew,
Max

Kirsty sighed. Was this all a complete waste of time, after all? Had Max Warnock just written some casual stuff to entertain his lonely aunt? She flicked through the pack of letters, looking at the dates. Then she frowned. There was a huge gap between the first few letters and the rest. Looking at the dates, her eyes brightened.

'After the fire,' she whispered under her breath.

Sure enough, several of the airmail letters bore a US mail stamp. Kirsty's eyes gleamed. This would tie in with Warnock's medical trips for reconstructive surgery.

These letters were shorter and the style less chatty, the handwriting shaky as if the letter writer had difficulty in holding a pen.

Dear Aunt Dorothy,
Wish you were with me right now. Could do with a friendly face to keep me company. Can't say much, just that I will not be back home for quite a while.
You can write to me c/o the above address.
Your loving nephew,
Max

Dear Aunt Dorothy,
Please don't worry. I had a bad accident overseas but everything will be okay, I promise. Sorry to hear that you've not been well. Is Peter doing all right with the business? Tell him to look after you.
Your loving nephew,
Max

Dear Aunt Dorothy . . .

Kirsty read on and on. Gradually the content of each letter increased and the handwriting became stronger, reflecting the recovery of the badly burned soldier. It was interesting, she thought, how often the man had asked questions of his aunt: What sort of vehicles did Peter hire out? Did she feel better this week? Why was she thinking so much about death? Once he'd even joked . . . I was close to it myself but I'm still here . . . Don't worry so much.

And often he'd assured her, I'll come and see you, I promise. Nobody's going to hurt you . . .

Kirsty rubbed her eyes, aware that she had been peering at the pages for hours now and the light in the room was becoming dimmer. It was like hearing a one-sided conversation and trying to fill in the other person's words. What on earth had Dorothy Guilford written to her nephew that had elicited such questions about death and dying?

She turned over another letter and saw that the next one was dated more recently. Lorimer would need to see these, she told herself. No doubt the MIT officers had some sort of a timeline for Max Warnock's activities. But these looked as if they had been written long after his medical discharge. Had Dorothy assumed that Max was still in the forces? Had he conned her into thinking that his visits were to be few and far between? And only when it suited him, Kirsty thought suddenly. She squirmed restlessly in her seat, anxious to be off and present these to the man who had originally inspired her to become a police officer. But there were still several more letters to be read.

As she scanned the lines on the final blue pages, Kirsty gasped. What on earth had Dorothy Guilford written to evoke such a response? Her gloved hands trembled as she read the words again.

336

It made sense now, of course it did. Rosie needed to see these letters. But first she had to show them to Lorimer.

'Sorry, the boss is unavailable right now,' the female officer told Kirsty. 'Can you come back tomorrow?'

Kirsty bit her lip anxiously. 'I've got a production from the Guilford murder ... ' she began. 'I think it's relevant to the trafficking case.'

'You know about that?' the woman asked.

Kirsty nodded. 'I've been doing a bit of background ... er ... research.'

'Moonlighting?'

Kirsty reddened. This sort of talk would do her career prospects no good whatsoever. 'No, not really. Superintendent Lorimer asked me to help a little seeing as I was one of the officers at the scene of crime in St Andrew's Drive,' she explained.

'Ah.' The door to the room was opened and the woman stood aside. 'Better come in then, DC Wilson.'

There was an air of tension in the room, explained by several officers who were gathered around a glass wall at one end.

'Want to see where he is right now?' The woman smiled and gestured for Kirsty to sit next to the others.

The wall was slightly above the room where Lorimer sat across a table from the figure Kirsty recognised as Shirley Finnegan, the officers able to see through the glass partition wall but not be seen. Lorimer's back was towards them but Kirsty could see the big woman's face.

'What's going on?' she asked quietly but hands flapping and shushing noises from the assembled officers made her turn towards the scene instead.

*

Below them, apparently oblivious to the watching eyes and listening ears of his team, Lorimer stared hard at the woman opposite.

Shirley Finnegan bore no traces of similarity to her dead sister whatsoever, the grey permed hair and puffy face quite at odds with photographs of Dorothy Guilford. There was something hugely unattractive about her bloated body; some fat women were motherly types whose large laps were made for small children to snuggle into, others made a constant joke about being overweight, as if shaking with laughter like a wobbly jelly was part of their fun. But this woman simply looked malevolent: her piggy eyes were sunk into folds of flesh, swollen arms folded under enormous bosoms, the chair she sat on plainly too small for her spreading frame. How had she become so obese? He'd wondered this as they'd left her home and travelled back here an hour ago. Had it been comfort eating? Food a substitute for an affection she craved?

And how had Shirley Finnegan felt when her son had returned, no doubt demanding that she help him? These, and other questions, had been on Solly's lips before they had confronted her in her own home.

The preliminary questions had been asked, date and time noted for the video recording, and now Lorimer was shuffling some paperwork at an angle so that only he could see what was written there.

'Max was pretty successful in his career, wasn't he?' he murmured, as though the documents before him contained information about Shirley's son.

'So?' The woman edged one fat shoulder forward dismissively but there was no mistaking the toss of her head, a fleeting look of pride in those eyes.

338

'His reconstructive surgery seemed to go well enough, too,' Lorimer continued, still examining the notes almost as if he was speaking to himself.

Shirley Finnegan frowned and sat back, folding her doughy arms with a sniff as though this tall police officer was simply wasting time with inane comments.

'A lot of people have been killed,' Lorimer went on, suddenly changing tack as he extracted several photographs from the folder, placing them on the table so that the woman could see them.

Each picture showed the victim at a scene of crime, the grim details clear to see. The Slovakian men whose bodies had been found in Aberdeen had now been identified but the Glasgow murder victim was still without a name. The paramedic and the pair of prison officers . . . Cynthia Drollinger . . . He pushed each picture towards her slowly, willing her to look at each one in turn.

'Max was responsible for this,' Lorimer said, in a tone of voice that neither condemned nor condoned the murders. It was something those listening had heard before: talking to a suspect in a neutral tone was simply to disarm them. Shouting could make them clam up, cajoling make them sneery.

'The people-trafficking business was lucrative,' he continued. 'So I don't understand why you are still living in such conditions, Shirley. Didn't Max give you enough money for your help?' He glanced up but the woman sat silent, a mulish expression on her face.

'Not what one would expect from a wealthy son, is it? I mean, most kids like to repay their parents for all the good things they experienced during their childhood. Wouldn't you agree?'

A shrug was his only answer, Shirley Finnegan's eyes drawn

from time to time to the lurid photographs like a voyeur trans-fixed by pornographic images.

'Just became his laundry woman. A washerwoman, some call it. Not very kind, is it, Shirley? But, perhaps you were expecting more? Is that it? Had Max promised you something, maybe?'

The woman glanced up and Lorimer caught something in her eyes, a flicker, just for a split second, but he was certain that she had revealed something with that knowing look. He'd hit a nerve, that was for sure, but it could wait for now. He'd come back to that later, by a different route.

'Dorothy's home was once yours. Am I correct?'

'Yes,' Shirley sighed. 'You know fine it was.'

'And you still had a set of keys for the property?'

She shifted a little in her seat, but gave no reply.

'Do you or do you not have keys to the house?'

'S'pose I do,' she replied. 'What of it?'

'So you could access your sister's home any time you liked?'

'I could but I didn't,' she sneered.

'Or you could have given them to someone else, couldn't you?'

The woman's mouth closed tightly as though she were afraid to utter another word.

'Let me set a proposition before you, Shirley,' Lorimer began, leaning back in his seat and putting one hand over the folder. 'Let's say that you lent your door key to a certain person who wanted access to your sister's home. Let's say that person entered and was disturbed by Dorothy. A scuffle breaks out and in the heat of a moment Dorothy is killed.'

'I didn't—'

Lorimer put up one hand to silence her. 'Let me continue. I haven't finished the story yet,' he said mildly. 'Now. The person to whom you gave your key panics, leaves and locks the door behind him.' He gave a faint smile. 'See what I did there, Shirley? I gave you a clue. *Him*,' he repeated. 'Now, let's give him a name, shall we? Let's call him Max.'

'I never gave him my key,' Shirley snapped. 'This is all a load of tosh. How can you say that? He wasn't even in Glasgow when—'

'So you knew whereabouts he was, is that what you're telling me, Shirley?'

Her eyes flicked to one side where the duty solicitor sat, impassive, giving no hint to what his latest client ought to say.

'Don't know anything,' she muttered, gazing down at her clasped hands then fidgeting as if suddenly fascinated by the state of her fingernails.

'You don't know or you won't say? Fair enough. You are his mother, after all, and it is understandable that you want to protect him. Did he hope that Dorothy would leave something to him in her will?'

The sudden change of question made Shirley Finnegan's head snap up and she opened her mouth as though to protest.

'Have you seen Dorothy's will?' Lorimer asked, shuffling his papers again and glancing downwards as though he had the details there in front of him.

'She left everything to Peter,' Shirley blurted out. Then, as if she had made a mistake in speaking, she shrank back, frantically looking from the tall policeman to her solicitor who was leaning back in his chair, arms folded, refusing to meet her gaze.

'And nothing to poor Max?'

'She hardly knew him. Why would she leave anything to a nephew she'd never seen in years?'

'Ah, but that's where you're wrong,' Lorimer corrected her, his tone like that of a teacher keen to assist a reluctant pupil. 'You see, Max used to visit Dorothy every time he came home on leave. Didn't he tell you?'

341

Shirley Finnegan's eyes darkened but she did not rise to Lorimer's bait.

'Please.' Kirsty stood up and turned to the other officers watching the interrogation. She lifted the plastic bag full of letters. 'I've got something here he needs to see. Something that is crucial to what's going on right now!'

It was several minutes later that the officers upstairs saw the interview room door opening and one of the team beckoning Lorimer out.

'What is it?' Lorimer loomed over them, a dark look in his eyes.

'Sir, DC Wilson wanted to give you this,' the officer explained, handing him the sealed production bag.

'Kirsty? Where is she?'

'Here, sir,' Kirsty said, making Lorimer whirl around to see his young friend appear from around the corner of the corridor. 'It's Dorothy's letters from Max,' she told him. 'I think you really need to read them before you talk to his mother any more,' she said.

There was a sharp intake of breath from the other officer, as if this young DC advising the detective superintendent was sheer effrontery.

But Lorimer did not react as expected, simply took the packet and examined it. 'Where did you get this?'

'Dorothy's bedside cabinet, sir. It's been with the other productions since DS Geary and I found the dead woman's will. I just read them for the first time today,' she explained. 'And it's pretty enlightening stuff.' She raised her eyebrows and gave Lorimer a grin.

*

342

Shirley Finnegan sat beside the solicitor, mouth shut tight. Had she already said too much? Surely they couldn't hold her here? After all, what wrong had she done? There was absolutely nothing that they could arrest her for. Unless ... She thought back to the moment when Frank Dawson had called her with the news about Dorothy's death. She had felt an enormous sense of release then, hadn't she? And, with Dorothy out of the picture, it had been easy enough to persuade those that mattered to see just how to capitalise on that event.

But what if they actually thought that she had murdered her own sister? Was all of this storytelling nonsense a sort of double bluff? Did this Lorimer fellow think that *she* was capable of killing Dorothy? Those other cops had asked about an alibi for the time of Dorothy's death, hadn't they? And, Shirley realised with a feeling of nausea swelling in her stomach, she had none to give them.

The clock on the wall ticked on, its hands recording one hour then two as Shirley Finnegan sweated under the artificial lights of this small room. Tactics, she told herself. Deliberately leaving me here to make me talk. She shifted her glance at the solicitor who was tapping away at his smart phone. Well, she'd show them. Keeping silent was maybe her best defence right now. And, besides, wouldn't it annoy that good-looking detective who'd spoken to her as if they were discussing her bank overdraft and not a matter of several murders?

'It's hard to believe,' Lorimer said at last. 'The woman must have been out of her mind.'

'He was feeding her ideas,' Kirsty agreed. 'See that last one?' She pointed to the final letter from Max Warnock to his aunt.

Dear Aunt Dorothy,

Yes, I think about death a lot too. Coming back from the dead was not what I had expected. The pain, especially the pain, was the worst thing. So, if death is what you really crave, death by your own hand and not his, make certain that you do it properly.

Lorimer nodded, reading on to the end.

One thrust to the heart, like the soldiers of old, falling on their swords. A mark of glory and a way to stop your endless torment for good. No one can cheat death but you can cheat HIM out of anything he's got planned for you.

'That says it all, doesn't it?' He heaved a sigh. 'That poor impressionable woman, caught between a brute like Guilford and a villain like the nephew she adored.'

'She wasn't in her right mind by then, surely?' Kirsty ventured.

Lorimer shook his head. 'No, the Fiscal's verdict on this will probably be suicide while of an unsound mind.' He left his thought unspoken for now that Max Warnock had one more death to answer for. 'Well, Rosie's going to be off on maternity leave feeling one hell of a lot better about the future now, isn't she?'

Kirsty grinned. 'Can I tell her, sir?'

'Not just yet, DC Wilson,' he replied. 'We need to present this to Mrs Finnegan first, see what she might tell us. Besides, I have a notion that Rosie might appreciate hearing it from somebody else.'

Kirsty looked crestfallen but she nodded in agreement.

'It ought to be DI McCauley who tells her, don't you think?' Lorimer said. 'After all, he was the SIO in the case.'

There was something fitting about Lorimer's idea, she agreed. Alan McCauley would be instructed by the detective superintendent from the MIT and the Fiscal would then decide what was to happen to Peter Guilford. If he survived, Kirsty thought. She had been taken into Lorimer's confidence about that, as would DI McCauley, partly because it impinged on the trafficking case and the MIT's dual operation with the Slovakian authorities. The need to keep the truth about the man was paramount. Any leaks to the press would find their way back to the DI, she thought.

There was a sense of anticlimax as Kirsty drove slowly out of the car park and headed towards the Clyde Tunnel. Her part in all of this appeared to be over now, even bringing the news about Dorothy Guilford and those airmail letters was denied to her. What next? she wondered as the traffic slowed down, the two lanes in front of the tunnel entrance crammed with commuters crossing the city.

James would be waiting for her. Waiting to know what decision she had come to. And suddenly, with a clarity that surprised her, Detective Constable Kirsty Wilson knew exactly what her future was going to hold.

CHAPTER FORTY-NINE

She had been permitted to go to the lavatory, escorted by a female officer, then back to the claustrophobic interview room where cups of tea had been offered. But no biscuits, a fact that had made her simmer with resentment.

Shirley looked up as the door opened again. At long last the tall police officer had deigned to return. Part of her wanted to ask what had kept him, but her warier self simply watched as he seated himself opposite once more.

There was no apology for keeping her waiting. Nothing. She gritted her teeth as he flicked through the same damned folder, unable to see what he was reading but keeping her eyes fixed on the pages nonetheless.

'Max Warnock was in regular contact with your sister,' he began, glancing across at her then back at some pages in his hands. 'From the time he entered the forces right up till she died, in fact.' He looked across and met her eyes with his own. Shirley felt them staring at her, like a hypnotic force field, a blue gaze that refused to let her go.

'You didn't know that, did you, Shirley?'

She said nothing. The question was rhetorical, after all. And he was correct. Of course she hadn't known this. Bile rose in her throat, the old fury against the sister who had beguiled Shirley Finnegan's only son. She tried hard not to speak while the policeman's fingers flicked through a pile of blue airmail papers.

'Max appears to have had quite an intimate relationship with his aunt. He gave her advice, wanted to help her with her illness ... actually told her how she might find release from her predicament ... '

Shirley frowned. Illness? What illness? Dorothy had pretended to be unwell all through their childhood. She remembered it so clearly: a pile of comics and a hot water bottle given to the sickly little sister whenever she wanted a day off school ... the cuts to her arms bandaged up ... that triumphant look in her eyes that had been reserved for Shirley alone. A look that said, *See the power I have over them and you don't!*

'Was she really ill this time?' Shirley blurted out the words then immediately regretted them.

'It was an illness of sorts, I suppose,' the man agreed, his tone so neutral that Shirley decided that Dorothy didn't really interest him at all. It was Max they were after. 'And Max, your son, Max, was the one who helped take care of her.'

'How?' Shirley demanded, the bitter pain of betrayal making her throw caution to the wind. 'How did he help her? He wasn't even there ... '

'No, he wasn't there, was he, Shirley? Not in person. But, yes, he helped your sister all right.' He leaned forwards and for the first time Shirley could see the tightened jaw, the changed look in those blue eyes as he lifted one of the airmail letters in his hand, waving it slowly in the air between them.

'You see, Shirley, he showed your sister how to take her own life.'

*

After that, the woman had crumpled and the whole story had come out. How Max had promised to get the big house back for his mother, the family inheritance coming to Shirley once both Dorothy and Peter were dead.

Only she had not reckoned on Peter Guilford being charged with his wife's murder. That had thrown a safety net around the man: he was safe from Max's murderous intentions, safe in prison. But the choice of Barlinnie had been to their advantage as Michael Raynor was already working there following his discharge from HM forces. The plotters had lured Raynor into their net, Max's guile working its old bewitchment on the man who had saved his life.

In due course Lorimer had turned the interview to the trafficking and watched as Shirley had shrugged it off. Max was just doing a job, she'd told him, as though operating a trade in human misery was something to be admired. It brought in lots of money, she had told him, and Lorimer had squirmed at the unmistakable glint of pride in Shirley Finnegan's greedy little eyes.

But she had sat back, arms folded, refusing to meet his eyes, refusing to say another single word as Lorimer had asked that final question.

'Where is he now?'

They could hold her for a while longer, charged with conspiracy, of being part of this international trafficking gang, though Frank Dawson had protested about that. *What are you going to charge her with? Washing dirty laundry?* he had scoffed.

The solicitor's remark had got Lorimer thinking, though.

'Who collects the laundry?' he wondered aloud as he sat in the DCI's room with Niall Cameron. 'Certainly wouldn't be her son. More likely to be one of his minions.'

And then he sat up. 'Do you think that Shirley would cooperate with us if we say she is going to be allowed out on bail?'

'Will she get bail?'

Lorimer shrugged. 'Who's to say?' The kernel of an idea had occurred to him, a risky idea to be sure, but then he had never been one
to shy away from situations that might cause him some difficulties.

Shirley Finnegan shrugged her shoulders. 'Can't see why not,' she
said, feigning an indifference that was at odds with her body language. Her head was held a little higher and there was a new gleam
in her eyes that Lorimer recognised. Hope. The mere chance that
she might escape the law had evidently occurred to the woman. She
had been given the chance to cooperate with them, help them to
identify one of the traffickers; the chap that collected the laundry
from her house. Would she stumble into their trap and unwittingly
give away the whereabouts of her renegade son? She had intimated
that they would never find him. Did that mean he was already far
away? Or had Max merely put that thought into her gullible head?

Lorimer sat next to her as they drove along the short distance
from Helen Street to the dingy flat that Shirley Finnegan had
transformed into a laundry for the various brothels hidden in the
city. The smell of body odour was strong and he felt a sudden sympathy for this enormously obese woman who had spent so many
hours stuck inside a police interview room. He glanced down at
her hands, fat fleshy fingers that were stained with nicotine.

'Do you need to stop for anything, Shirley? Cigarettes?'

She shot him a venomous look but then her mouth opened a
fraction as she realised he was serious and not mocking her.

'Don't have any money on me,' she muttered, looking away.

'That's all right. I'm sure I can afford a packet of . . . what is it
you smoke?'

He made a show of searching in his pockets as though to be sure that he had some change to hand.

'Silk Cut,' she said, turning to look him up and down.

'Anything else? Some chocolate biscuits to go with that cup of tea you promised to make me?'

Shirley opened her mouth to protest. 'I . . .' then her expression softened as she realised that Lorimer was gently teasing her while actually inviting himself into her home.

'S'pose so.' She nodded. 'Aye, and while you're at it a loaf wouldn't go wrong. White, plain. None of your healthy stuff,' she added.

Lorimer looked away. Did she really imagine that after today she would be free to go about her business? That was not what the Fiscal would have wanted. Twenty-four hours, that was all he had until Shirley Finnegan was back in custody; a day's grace to identify the people behind this trafficking scheme and to land the biggest fish of them all in his net.

They were travelling in a white van, unmarked but with enough horsepower under its bonnet to outrun even the latest top of the range sports car. Lorimer had given the driver a note of what to buy then settled back beside Shirley Finnegan. Now they were almost back at her house.

'It will be worth your while sticking to what we agreed,' he murmured, trying to catch the woman's eye.

'Less time inside, you mean,' she sniffed.

'You don't want a murder rap added to whatever else we can throw at you, do you?'

'It wasn't my idea to kill Peter,' she muttered.

'But you were happy enough to think you could inherit everything once he and Dorothy were dead,' Lorimer insisted. 'And a jury will see it that way, I can assure you.' He turned to the woman as they rounded the corner of her street and slowed down.

'If you help us to track down the traffickers, find the women who are being kept like slaves, then any judge is going to go easy on you,' he insisted.

There was no mention of Max, though he was certain that Shirley Finnegan's son was at the forefront of both their minds. Would she go through with their plan? He hoped so, otherwise what direction would they take next? Officers were scouring the city for the invisible folk who had melted away after that nail bar had closed. Areas where the immigrant population was high were being searched meticulously: Govanhill in particular since the BMW that had taken Juliana Ferenc had been caught over there on CCTV.

The van parked a few yards further along the street and Lorimer stepped out, taking the woman's arm as though he were helping her along the street; by anyone watching them it might be construed as a random act of kindness to a big woman who found walking a little difficult.

Once inside, Shirley Finnegan made for the bathroom and Lorimer could hear the sound of water running. She was bound to be desperate to freshen up, he thought. But that was all right. Her mobile phone was in his own pocket; there was nothing she could do to contact Max without Lorimer knowing.

'All right?' he asked as Shirley emerged, her face looking a little pink from being rubbed with a flannel, hair combed back and tucked behind her ears.

'Tea first,' she grunted and waddled off in the direction of the kitchen.

Ten minutes later Shirley Finnegan sat back, fag in hand, regarding Lorimer with a baleful expression in her eyes.

'It's time, Shirley. Just do it, okay?'

She put out her hand as he offered her the mobile.

'The speaker's turned on so we can both hear him,' Lorimer reminded her.

Heaving a sigh, she flicked the ash onto a saucer and laid down her cigarette, Lorimer watching her every move.

'Danny? It's me, Shirley. You need to send someone round to get the laundry. It's bloody piling up here. Cannae move for the stuff. Need to be right now, d'you hear me?'

There was a pause as they both listened to the voice on the other end.

'What d'you mean right now? There's nobody here to take care of the girls except me. Raynor and Gid haven't appeared and there's been no sign of Max. What's going on?'

'Just do as I'm telling you, Danny,' Shirley sighed. 'Just turn the key in the door and come over in the van, okay?' She looked at Lorimer as though for reassurance that she was acting well and he gave her a nod.

'That's an order,' she added sternly.

'Okay, okay, I hear you. I'll come over as fast as I can. Twenty minutes tops,' he replied, then the line went dead.

'Wee scruff,' Shirley muttered, looking at her mobile as though it were enabling her to see the man called Danny.

Lorimer stretched out a hand as Shirley made to put the phone into her cardigan pocket.

'I'll take that, thanks,' he said and, with a sigh, she handed it over.

It was less than twenty minutes when the officer across the road alerted Lorimer that a van with GUILFORD VEHICLE HIRE emblazoned across its side was drawing in to the kerb.

'That's him, Shirley. Right. You know what to do,' Lorimer

told her, slipping into the kitchen. 'I'll be listening to every word you say, mind.'

Shirley Finnegan nodded, her mouth a small hard line. The wire she'd been fitted with back at HQ allowed them to hear her at all times and record the conversation she was to have with the delivery man.

The door was knocked a rat-a-tat then she walked as fast has her heavy legs would carry her along the corridor.

'You took your time,' she huffed at the driver.

'Gie's a break, missus,' the man retorted. 'Came as fast as I could. Right, gimme they boxes and I'll be oot o' here in double quick time, so ah will.'

There was much heaving and shoving as Danny lifted the boxes full of linen and transported them from the house to the open doors of his van outside.

Back and forward he went, lifting and shoving them into the van, oblivious to the fact that he was being watched by a police officer from across the road, listened to by Lorimer and other members of the MIT.

At last he had carried every black plastic bag and cardboard carton and with a slam the van doors were shut.

Lorimer heard the front door close and emerged from the kitchen where he had been viewing the business from a crack in the door.

'Well done, Shirley,' he told her, putting a hand on her shoulder that she immediately brushed off with a glare.

'What now?' she muttered, preparing to pick up her handbag.

'Tea and toast and a smoke before we head back to Helen Street?' he suggested.

Shirley raised her eyebrows in surprise. 'Okay, fine with me,' she agreed.

Lorimer watched as she entered her kitchen for what was probably the last in a long time. Shirley Finnegan wasn't to know that the white van they'd arrived in was at this moment tailing Guilford's vehicle back to wherever the captive women and girls were hidden, nor that a different form of transport would be arriving to take her back to Helen Street police office.

CHAPTER FIFTY

It was all over by the time he arrived in Govanhill, reinforcements lining the street, scores of women and girls being ushered into the waiting vans. The Guilford vehicle was parked there as well as the white van that had tailed Danny from the Finnegan home. But his eye was caught by another car; a BMW. Surely this was the one that Juliana had told them about? And did this mean that Max Warnock was somewhere close by?

Lorimer looked up at the tenement building, the clear blue sky above a contrast with the dark red sandstone and the grey pavement where he stood. It was a rerun of the raid in Aberdeen, he thought, without the seagulls screeching and the bitter wind racing along from the sea. He gave a brief nod to the DC from the MIT who was standing guard at the close mouth and left the brightness of the day as he entered the building.

The old stone stairs were worn, some cracked in places, the handrail at the top of the second flight of stairs held together with binder twine. As he climbed higher the smell of curry wafted upwards, reminding Lorimer of the melting pot that was Glasgow; its ethnic diversity something he had grown up with and taken for granted. Nowadays the Asian community was well established, the more recent newcomers Eastern Europeans.

355

The women he had glimpsed down at street level, many looking hardly older than teenage girls, could well be Slovakian, though that was still to be confirmed.

He passed a female officer escorting a youngster who was weeping and holding a bundle of clothes close to her chest; one more story to be told, one more child to be cared for by the Scottish services. At last he was at the topmost landing where yet another of his DCs stood at the open door.

'All done here?' he asked.

'Not quite, sir,' the man replied. 'One more to come. She's gathering things up in the kitchen. DCI Cameron's with her.'

Lorimer walked down the dingy hallway. His feet felt sticky against the faded linoleum and the bare walls on either side were grubby with countless fingermarks. It smelled bad, as if too many unwashed bodies had congregated in this flat. A breeding ground for germs, he thought grimly, putting a hand up to his nose.

The kitchen was barely more than a scullery with a walk-in larder, an ancient stone sink, some dark wood cabinets and one four ring electric stove, blackened with grease and grime. A bare light bulb hung from the ceiling but most of the light came from a single window, barred like a prison cell.

A dark-haired woman turned with a start when she saw him.

'It's all right, this is Detective Superintendent Lorimer,' Niall Cameron assured her. 'He's here to help you all.'

The woman bobbed her head in a sort of bow, large dark eyes looking at him solemnly.

'This is Elena,' Cameron said, by way of introduction.

'You'll be safe now,' Lorimer told her. Then, as she made to move away, he caught her eye.

'Elena,' he began, 'can you help me? I want to find Max. Do you know where he is?'

The woman froze at the sound of the name. Then, without a word, her eyes drifted upwards to the ceiling and she nodded.

Lorimer pointed and she nodded again then scuttled out of the room like a frightened rabbit, Cameron following.

Lorimer stared at the square shape above his head. It was the top flat, of course, and so any attic space would be accessed from here. Was this woman, Elena, actually telling him that Max Warnock was holed up there?

Lorimer saw the metal ring and the fresh scratch marks against the faded paintwork of the trapdoor, signs of recent use. He looked around for a pole of some sort to open it up but at first could see nothing. It was an instinct to open the larder and find the hooked pole placed firmly between two metal clips fixed to the back of the door.

In moments he had inserted the hook into the metal ring and was pulling hard against the trapdoor. With a sudden heave, the wooden square opened and a set of metal steps was revealed above his head. Lorimer stepped to one side, looking up and listening but there was no sound at all.

Taking the pole once more, he fixed it into a hole on the metal stair and pulled hard. The staircase came down with a metallic screech, and stopped in mid-air, its steps doubled up for storage. One more pull brought the entire thing down to the floor with a thump.

Lorimer looked up at the dust motes swirling in the fetid air. If Warnock was up there then the detective superintendent had announced his arrival, all right. He began to climb, aware of the darkness above him, wondering already what sort of space he would find in this tenement attic.

Each step took him further into the gloom and he blinked as the gritty air smote his eyelids.

It was impossible to see much except the beams above his head, the dim light from the kitchen giving a little indication of head height. He would be on his hands and knees, crawling, that much was evident.

Taking a deep breath, Lorimer plunged into the shadows like a swimmer launching himself forward. His hands felt wooden boards and he knew a moment's relief that the roof space was floored at least. There would be no danger of falling through a ceiling.

He began to crawl away from the trapdoorway, inching forward, listening for any sounds that might indicate that there was another person up here. But so far there was nothing, just the sound of his own breathing and a dull ringing in his ears as the old sense of claustrophobia began to grip him.

The feel of warm metal told Lorimer that he was passing the water tank then, still on hands and knees, he moved into the inky blackness. For a few moments all he could sense was the hard flooring against his fingers then he felt something soft, the edge of a blanket, perhaps?

He sensed the presence of the other man without actually seeing him. Was it the exhalation of a breath? Or an impression of something defiant ahead, a belligerent force that was waiting in the darkness? Lorimer put one hand into his pocket, drawing out his mobile phone.

He crouched beneath the oppressive beams and then clicked it open.

The light showed him a face, just feet from his own. But it was the face from a nightmare. Smooth, without texture, its eyes blinking in the sudden glare from the tiny screen, it was a hairless creature staring at him, one hand raised to ward off the light.

'Max?'

The word was scarcely out of his mouth when the creature lunged at him, hands scrabbling at Lorimer's throat.

He felt fingers pressing hard and struggled in the confined space to get a grip of his own.

Then, with a mighty effort, he shook his assailant free and made a grab for his leg as it kicked out.

Suddenly Lorimer had the advantage, his greater weight pulling Warnock along the floor and backwards towards the open space.

It was only as his back met the edge of the opening that Lorimer realised his danger.

With one great effort, the man pulled back then heaved at the policeman with all of his strength. One push would see Lorimer tumble down the ladder.

In the attic space there was no room to duck but here, by the door, he moved sideways, twisting his body away from the metal ridge.

It was the man's own momentum that made him leap into the void, but Lorimer made a grab, clutching at Warnock's clothes, feeling the weight pulling him down.

He heard the scream, a thin eerie sound as Warnock's face hit the metal treads, then Lorimer was pulling him back up and shouting out for help.

But no one seemed to hear.

Warnock was slipping from his grasp now as Lorimer tried to find a foothold on the lower steps. Then, with an unearthly cry, the man slithered to the floor with a thump.

Lorimer scrambled down the staircase just as Warnock got to his feet.

He saw the flash of the blade in Warnock's hand, heard the snarl as he rushed forward.

It was a split second instinct to make a grab of his wrist but even so, Lorimer felt a sharp pain score against his forearm.

Then the sound of feet running. And the cry of a wounded man as Warnock was grappled to the floor and cuffed by two of Lorimer's men.

'You all right, sir?' Niall Cameron asked, pointing to the blood trickling from Lorimer's arm.

'Aye, just a scratch. Get him up,' he demanded, turning to the man struggling on the ground. 'Max Warnock, I am arresting you for the attempted murder of Peter Guilford—' he began.

'*Attempted?*' The man's first words came out as he stood there, mouth open in shock.

'Aye, he's not dead yet,' Lorimer answered grimly. 'And there will be several more things to add to this charge. Get him out of here,' he said wearily, the desire to leave this stinking place and breathe fresh air suddenly paramount.

CHAPTER FIFTY-ONE

Maggie Lorimer smiled at the man sleeping by her side. Exhaustion had overtaken him at last as well as a desperate need to recover his strength. It had been months ago now that her beloved husband had succumbed to a depression that had threatened to take him away from the job that he loved. More and more was being written in the newspapers about the difficulties police officers faced in the line of duty and she, more than anyone, knew all about this. Living with a man who was driven to seek justice above all else had taken its toll on her, too. But that time had passed and she had found a certain solace in writing her little story.

When the time was right she would tell him her news.

Bill had talked all evening about the case, about Molly and the Slovakian girl turning up in some farmhouse out by Fintry. Forensics had been too late to do anything about the burned-out building but the fire service had recovered two charred corpses, burned beyond recognition. Maggie shuddered. Real life was pretty gruesome so perhaps it was no surprise that she had found refuge in writing tales about an imaginary ghost, a little fellow who was beyond any harm and who could look down on the world with compassion.

William Lorimer muttered something incoherent, flinging out a bandaged arm then settling onto his side, some dream or other disturbing his sleep.

Tomorrow, thought Maggie. I will tell him tomorrow. A new day would dawn and their future together would take a slightly different turn. Yet she was certain that come what may, the man slumbering at her side would always want to be part of the force for good.

Rosie woke with a small cry of surprise. First a sharp pain then a warm sensation as the waters began to stream into the bedclothes.

'Wake up!' she said.

'Mmmm?' Solly rubbed the sleep from his eyes as he turned towards her. 'What . . . ?'

'It's started,' Rosie told him with a smile. 'Can you get me a pile of towels, please? I've wet the bed, I'm afraid.'

It was daylight by the time they arrived at the hospital, the taxi driver ushering Rosie out carefully.

'Okay, missus, you take care now, eh? Good luck.' He grinned as the bearded husband thrust a pile of money into his hand.

He glanced back at the couple before driving off, the man with one arm around her shoulders, the other carrying a holdall, the small blonde woman walking slowly but steadily towards the entrance. A new life about to begin, the driver thought, that was something good to happen amongst all the news of misery. He'd seen it all, heard it all, yet still each time he drove an expectant mum to hospital he had a tingle of anticipation that diminished every bit of his world weariness.

*

Solly sat outside the ward, knowing that he was, for the moment, surplus to his wife's requirements. The nursing staff had made that quite clear. He could go home for a while or come back in half an hour once his wife was settled. It would be a while yet, he was assured.

The professor of psychology sat still, thinking of all that had taken place in the past few days. A major incident at the hospital, the burned-out farmhouse with two charred bodies found beneath its rubble, then the raid on that Govanhill flat and Lorimer's apprehension of Max Warnock. It had been a stressful time for them all but now the case appeared to be coming to a satisfactory conclusion. He had still to hear the final outcome of their interview with the former army major and his part in the human trafficking scheme. Meanwhile, Peter Guilford hung between life and death, still evidently on the critical list. Would he be one more statistic to add to the crimes committed by Max Warnock and his foot soldiers? Solly hoped not. Guilford had done some terrible things but nobody deserved to be murdered for them. Besides, he was certain that with the arrest of Warnock Lorimer would be able to prise the truth from Peter Guilford at last.

He looked up as a nurse came through the double swing doors.

'You can stay with Mrs Brightman meantime,' she told him. 'Just don't tire her out. She's going to need all her energy for later on.'

Max Warnock looked different in daylight. Lorimer could see the younger major still in those chiselled cheekbones, the shape of his bald head. The man had been permitted to wear sunglasses in his prison cell but now, in this interview room where the sun barely filtered through the small window, Lorimer motioned for him to remove them.

363

The difference in his appearance was immediately evident. Those small, eyes, blinking against the natural light, did indeed make Warnock look like some alien creature, the unnaturally smooth skin adding to the effect. Once, William Lorimer might have pitied the man but now, having seen the misery that Max Warnock had inflicted on his numerous victims, he hardened his heart. Yes, Major Warnock was himself a victim, Solly had reminded him, but the thought of those young women taken from their homes and thrust into prostitution sickened the policeman. Besides that, there was the insidious preying on the mind of an already deranged woman as he had sought to tempt Dorothy Guilford into taking her own life. And the deaths of several more were doubtless down to this man, his own friend, Michael Raynor, amongst them.

Lorimer looked across the table for a long moment and noted with a small sense of satisfaction that Warnock could not meet his eyes but dropped his head like countless small-time thieves and bigger criminals had over the years when confronted by the detective superintendent.

He began the interview as he usually did, establishing the man's name and other essential details for the video recording. Warnock replied hesitantly, clearing his throat each time before he spoke, making Lorimer wonder if he had a problem. Had smoke inhalation caused permanent damage of a different kind? There was a plastic beaker of water on the table for the man who took frequent sips. It would need replenishing at some point, but perhaps that could be used as a lever to make him talk, if need be?

'Maxwell Warnock.' He hesitated, shuffling the papers into a different order. 'Sometimes known as Símon Farkas.' He looked up at the man opposite. 'Simon, the Wolf,' he added. 'The name

364

you took in Streda nad Bodrogom. The Slovakian authorities have identified you.' Then, picking up a sheaf of light blue air-mail letters, he waved them in the air. Warnock tried to disguise his surprise, his facial expression bland, but Lorimer saw the beat of the pulse in his throat.

'We have read all of your correspondence to Dorothy,' Lorimer told him. 'Their contents appear to be a matter for a separate charge.' He watched as Warnock looked up suddenly, a defiant cast to his mouth. 'Grooming a victim for a nefarious reason can be a criminal offence,' he told him. 'But we can come back to that. What I would like you to tell me is why you wanted to target Peter Guilford himself? After all, he was your business partner, wasn't he? You set up this trafficking operation years ago after you found that Dorothy had married Guilford, a man with as few scruples as yourself. A very useful man to have with that fleet of vehicles to hand whenever you wanted transport in a hurry. And someone that was only too keen to put capital behind what he saw as a money-making scheme. Like you, he didn't care too much about the lives you were both ruining.'

Warnock said nothing but the insolent shrug as he reached out yet again for water made Lorimer see how indifferent this man was about taking the life of another person. Had it been more than the fire that had inured him to this? Had his military experiences made him feel that killing was nothing particularly significant?

'Guilford isn't dead,' Lorimer said, looking at Warnock steadily. 'Your shot didn't kill him.'

'That wasn't me, that was Raynor. Stupid fool had his chance and blew it. Twice,' he spat disgustedly.

'That why you had to get rid of him? Burn him in that derelict farmhouse? Raynor, the man who saved your life?'

365

'That debt was paid long since,' Warnock said quietly, avoiding Lorimer's stare once more.

'I've spoken to Guilford, you know,' Lorimer said. This was true, of course, but nobody had been able to see let alone speak to the severely injured man since the barrage of bullets had left three other men dead at the Queen Elizabeth Hospital.

'What did he tell you?' the man sneered. 'That he was the big shot? That I was just the one who did his bidding? Did he tell you that?'

It was Lorimer's turn to remain silent but a slight raise of his eyebrows made Warnock leap to the wrong conclusion.

'It wasn't Guilford pulling the strings,' he spat. 'I came up with the idea in the first place.' He thumped his chest with a closed fist. 'Me, yes, me! I might look like this but I can still think and plan and make people do whatever I want!'

'The evidence we have gathered pretty much substantiates that,' Lorimer agreed. 'The Slovakian authorities have given us plenty to back this up. However ...' he paused and sat back, arms folded, index finger tapping his lips as though he were considering a new fact, 'there is also the matter of planning to take the life of your uncle, Peter Guilford, in order to inherit your aunt's estate, not to mention the properties back in Slovakia.' He made a pretence of consulting the notes in front of him. 'Little Bodrogom, is that what you call it?'

Warnock's jaw moved slightly so that Lorimer guessed he was gritting his teeth, a sign of annoyance or frustration. But there was no reply to his question.

'Sorry to be the one to tell you, but a murderer cannot inherit the estate of his victim under either British or Slovakian law,' he said.

'My mother will get it ...' Warnock told him, chin lifted in defiance.

'No, she won't.' Lorimer shook his head. 'Your mother is presently in custody awaiting trial for her part in your nasty little plan. Do you want me to tell you how we knew where to find you?' he asked, leaning forward and fixing the man with his blue glare.

'She didn't!' Warnock yelled. 'She wouldn't!' But doubt was clearly etched across these bland features now.

'How do you think I came across you in that attic?' Lorimer taunted him.

'She wouldn't betray me!' Warnock cried, thumping both fists on the table. But then his shoulders slumped and he began to sob, loud heaving sobs that were more like those of a wounded animal than a human in distress.

'They all made me like this,' he whimpered. 'All of them ... bloody, bloody women ...'

There was more in this vein as Max Warnock recounted the horror of the fire in which he had been disfigured for life and left impotent, his weakness building up such a well of bitterness that it had spilled out as revenge against the gypsies of Streda nad Bodrogom and the Ferenc girl in particular. There was satisfaction in having caught Warnock, whose plans now lay in disarray in this small Glasgow room. Yet Lorimer knew a fleeting sense of pity for this man.

Warnock's admission about setting up his henchmen to attack the ambulance taking Guilford to Low Moss was the only moment when the man's defiance returned.

'I never handled any of the guns, though, your forensics can't pin that on me!' he'd claimed. His was the mind behind it all, however, and that was something Lorimer would try to prove.

'Was that why you needed to dispatch Raynor and Gideon Patterson?'

'Who? Oh, was that the driver's name?' Warnock answered carelessly.

'Gideon Patterson was identified as the driver of a BMW registered in Michael Raynor's name,' Lorimer replied. 'A vehicle you were seen to drive after setting fire to a deserted farmhouse near the village of Fintry. There are witnesses who can testify that it was you.'

Warnock crossed his arms and tossed his head back in a sudden laugh.

'Don't believe you,' he said. 'You're making this all up.' He shook his head. 'Can't pin that one on me either,' he crowed.

Lorimer did not reply but merely gave a slight nod to the uniformed officer standing at the door.

There was complete silence as he sat holding Warnock in his gaze. The man flicked his eyes across to the door as it opened again. Then Warnock rose to his feet, knocking over his chair with a clatter.

'Nooo!' The cry was ripped from him as the two women stood in the open doorway.

'It's okay, you can go now, but thank you both for being here,' Lorimer told Molly and Juliana, the latter cowering beside the policewoman as she stared into the room to see Max Warnock's face once again.

'Thought you'd killed them both, didn't you?' Lorimer mused, once the officer had placed his hands on Warnock's shoulders, forcing him to sit down again.

That was when Warnock began to yell and beat the table with his fists, the blood-curdling screams of a madman torn from his damaged throat.

CHAPTER FIFTY-TWO

Kirsty stood up and shook the man's hand.

'Congratulations, Detective Sergeant Wilson,' the senior officer said, giving her a smile that was quite at odds with the grilling she had undergone over the previous hour.

Jim Geary was waiting in the corridor outside.

'Well? What do I call you? Wilson or Kirsty?'

'I did it, Jim!' Kirsty told him gleefully. 'Or should I still call you sir?'

'Well done, lass. I knew you would.' He clapped Kirsty on the back. 'And one day I'll be calling you ma'am. Just you wait and see.'

There were celebrations in the form of fizzy drinks and cream cakes bought in specially from Greggs bakery in the CID muster room. Kirsty gazed around at her colleagues, savouring the moment of her triumph. Her dad would be delighted, of course. Alastair Wilson had made it to detective inspector not long before his retirement and had faith that his only child would emulate that rank at least. She could imagine his grin already and her mum's 'Well done, Kirsty!'

But first it was James she wanted to tell and there were still hours to go before she could speak to him face to face.

Kirsty slipped away from the impromptu party as the other officers went back to their work, her phone in hand. She would text them, she decided, let them all know that she had gained her sergeant's rank. Then it was a matter of talking to James, telling him that she had made that all-important decision at last.

Solly watched, entranced, as the baby slithered into the hands of the waiting midwife, Rosie's final scream of pain dying away.

Behind his mask he mouthed the words 'I love you', gazing into his wife's eyes as she struggled to sit up, see the baby for herself.

'It's a boy,' the midwife proclaimed. Then, as if on cue, the tiny cries of the newborn infant began to fill the room and Solomon Brightman burst into tears of gladness.

Afterwards, when Rosie had been made more comfortable, the professor of psychology sat beside her, cradling their little son in his arms.

It was as if a magic bubble contained them all at that moment, some unseen membrane encapsulating the precious trinity of father, mother and child, the little one gazing with dark eyes into his face.

'Benjamin,' he whispered. 'Our little Ben. Welcome to the world.' Then a tiny finger curled around his finger and Solly began to laugh and cry at once, the sound of pure joy as love joined all three of them together.

It was the sort of day when traffic had impeded her at every set of lights but now Kirsty was parked outside their flat in Barrington Drive and climbing the steps to their front door. Her key was hardly in the lock when the door opened and she was suddenly in his arms.

'Well done, my lass!' James spoke into her hair. 'Never doubted for a moment that you would get it,' he murmured. He hugged her long and hard then let her go, looking at her wistfully. 'I suppose his means that all our plans to move away are over and done with?' he asked. 'You'll want to stay here and pursue your career with Police Scotland, I guess? That's all right. I'll find another job somewhere nearer to Glasgow.'

Kirsty swallowed hard. Such love this man had for her that he was prepared to sacrifice his own burgeoning career! And it was his love that had helped her to make the decision at last.

'No,' she said, clutching his arm. 'That's not what I've decided at all, James. I want to come to Chicago with you, start a new life there together. But only on one condition.'

James shook his head, eyes wide with astonished delight. 'Anything!' he declared, swallowing hard.

'We get married here in Scotland first,' she said firmly. 'Mum would never forgive us otherwise.'

Maggie Lorimer was waiting for the sound of his car, something she had been doing for all of their married life. Perhaps she would not always be at home first, she mused. Once things began to take on a life of their own she would need to travel around the country, promoting her debut, the agent had warned her.

She sat in the garden, face tilted up to the sunshine. It was midsummer now and soon school would be over for another session and they would be free to go to their beloved cottage in Mull. Chancer brushed against her bare leg, his soft fur making her fingers reach down to caress the cat's head. He reared up on stiff legs and landed on her lap then began to move slowly around, settling himself down to sleep.

Maggie closed her eyes. The Guilford case was over, the

Woman Who Killed Herself headline news for a day, soon overtaken by columns devoted to the trafficking scheme, lurid pictures of women and girls forced into unspeakable situations, the perpetrators all imprisoned. Life was full of changes, she mused. There they were, Rosie and Solly with two lovely children; Abby and baby Ben, the Lorimers' little godson. Kirsty and James were full of wedding plans, Betty Wilson no doubt putting her culinary skills into baking her finest wedding cake ever. Bill had been surprised at the news that Kirsty was leaving the police force but Maggie Lorimer had simply smiled and nodded when she had been told. Finding the love of your life was the most important thing of all and holding onto it was a greater joy than any career could offer.

She heard the car door slam then the front door opening. Chancer slumbered on in her lap and she stroked his fur as she waited for her husband to come out into the garden. Perhaps her own new venture would bring changes, give her a different perspective? There was to be a nationwide book tour next year, the publisher had promised when they had spoken earlier today, their marketing department welcoming Margaret Lorimer into their ranks of children's authors.

She looked up as he approached then turned her face up to receive his kiss.

'Hi, gorgeous,' he murmured, caressing her hair before standing up again. 'Want something to drink?'

'Mm,' Maggie replied. 'There's some champagne chilling in the fridge. That would do nicely.'

'Champagne?' His expression made Maggie laugh out loud as she caught hold of his hand.

'Yes,' she said. 'I've got something to tell you.'

ACKNOWLEDGEMENTS

There are so many people to thank for helping me with writing this, the fifteenth in the Lorimer series. All of the team at Little, Brown deserve big hugs for their marvellous support (and flowers!) particularly Cath, Lucy, Thalia and Steph but most of all my dear David Shelley who has been with me almost from the beginning. I have the proud boast to be his longest standing author, at least for now. Among so many others, my editor, Lucy Dauman, and Jenny Brown, my dear friend and agent, gave me support and encouragement when things were tough and illness made it look at one stage that I might never finish this book on time. Bless you both.

As ever, Dr Marjorie Turner gave me insights into the pathology that I needed to know, particularly for the first death in the story. Imagination is one thing, bringing it into a credible fashioning of reality is quite another! Detective Sergeant Mairi Milne was also there to help me with details on a regular basis. Hard to remember when she was a wee lassie in my Second Year English class and I was her teacher. Seems the other way round nowadays!

I owe a huge debt of gratitude to Detective Inspector Steven

McMillan who gave me his time and insight into the sex trafficking case that was a joint operation between Slovakia and Glasgow. Listening to his stories as we sat together at Gartcosh, the Scottish Crime Campus, was a real privilege. (Imagine making up a story then finding its real counterpart happening practically on my doorstep!)

Thanks to Chris at the Apple Store, Braehead, who fixed my Mac when I was in despair: you were efficient and kind in equal measure.

Writing this book has given me different insights and reminded me of the important things in life: my friends, my family (John, the real Bird Man; Suzy, who shares my passions for words and gardens) and most of all, my beloved husband, Donnie. Thanks, my love, for sticking with me all this time!

Alex Gray, 2017

Now turn the page for your bonus Lorimer short story,

The Bank Job

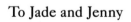
To Jade and Jenny

'Get down! Everyone on the floor!'

Kevin Patterson's mouth opened but no sound came from his lips.

As the tall man brandishing a sawn-off shotgun came rushing towards him, customers and bank staff threw themselves onto the ground in sudden panic. A second man was standing in the middle of the room, his weapon describing an arc of menace over bodies lying stiff with terror.

'You! Put your hands up where I can see them. No funny business,' the gunman added in a hoarse voice.

Kevin stared at the figure and felt his hands begin to tremble.

Was it so obvious that his fingers had been drawn towards the panic button on his desk?

The man came closer, watching the teller, his blue eyes like chips of coloured glass behind the black balaclava.

Kevin froze. Even as he stared back he knew these eyes would be the stuff of nightmares for months to come.

'*You*. Get me the money. All of it.' The man jabbed Kevin with the tip of the gun, making him whimper.

'Now!' The shout came like a bullet from the open mouth,

causing one of the women on the floor to cry out in alarm.

Kevin had been told often enough what the drill should be in such an event. Press the panic button and fall to the floor behind his desk. But nothing in his experience had prepared the fifty-year-old for this sudden rush by a masked gunman. Or for the threat in those mesmerizing blue eyes.

The teller gazed at the snarling mouth, terror-stricken. *Move*, his brain was insisting, *do what he says*, yet when he tried to stand his legs seemed to have turned to jelly. Another look at the barrel of that weapon coming towards his face and Kevin was scrambling to the door behind his desk. His hands shook with fear as he attempted to tap out the code on the security keypad, aware every second of the gunman breathing down his neck. *Don't make a mistake, don't hit the wrong numbers*, he thought, watching his quivering fingers.

How had they known when the delivery of money came into the bank in central Glasgow? And who had told them that it lay in the vault right behind *his* desk until the following morning when the bags of notes would be sorted by the cashiers and distributed among the rest of the tellers?

He felt the cold metal against his back, propelling him into the tiny room.

'Get it out of there! You know what to do!'

Kevin fell to his knees in front of the safe, a band of pain circling his skull. *Don't take one of your dizzy spells*, he told himself, hands fumbling with the combination. *How did they know that I was in charge of this money?*

His fingers felt like lead weights as he pulled out the bundles of banknotes, those eyes boring into him, the gun now pointing at his chest. Trickles of perspiration coursed down his forehead, a sudden heat suffusing his whole body.

Was he going to die? Would that gun be fired into his heart? Would his life (the life he'd grumbled about to his wife over breakfast) suddenly be finished?

He jumped at the sound of an old canvas sports bag flung down by his side.

'In there! Get a move on,' the gunman growled.

He shoved the money into the empty bag, glancing at the serial numbers. Would these notes be traceable?

Suddenly, as if at a signal, the gunman snatched up the holdall. 'Down on the floor!'

Kevin cringed as he lay on the dusty carpet, waiting for the crack of a rifle butt against his balding head.

He screwed his eyes shut but all he heard was the sound of running feet, then . . . silence.

As swiftly as they had burst into the premises, the gunmen were gone, leaving the bank teller to crawl back into his chair, white-faced and shaking, his fingers almost lacking the strength to press the panic button at last.

William Lorimer whistled as he crossed Union Street and headed for work with the steady stream of commuters from Glasgow Central station. There was something satisfying to the student about being part of this crowd of folk who spilled out of the concourse and were intent on making their way to offices all over the city. A nine-to-five job that paid well wasn't a bad thing at all, especially as it wasn't going to last for ever.

He paused mid-stride to admire the Ca' D'Oro building. His History of Art studies had given him a new perspective on his home city, its architectural gems frequently making him smile with pride. *Always look up*, his tutor had told him. And now he did just that, seeing an expanse of blue beyond the decorated rooftops. The summer's morning was already warm, and he resented having to stay indoors in the stuffy cash room all day, but the thought of picking up his first pay cheque had put a spring in the young man's step. The work at the bank was deadly dull and his colleagues were not exactly the sort he'd choose to accompany on a night out but the rewards for a student holiday job were there all right. Besides, there was rugby training after work and he was looking forward to the exercise as well as sinking a pint or two with the lads in the Students' Union.

The blue and white police tape across the entrance to the neoclassical façade of the bank stopped William Lorimer in his tracks. Glancing up, he noticed that the solid wooden doors to the banking hall were shut fast, its grand marble floor hidden from sight. It wasn't his usual way in to the building but he stood and stared nevertheless.

'Sorry, sir, they're closed for business this morning.'

William's six-foot-four frame might have towered over the uniformed officer barring his way but the look of authority in this cop's expression made him take a step backwards.

'I work here,' he said, shifting his sports bag from one shoulder to the other.

The officer looked him up and down for a moment.

'Got any ID on you?'

William rummaged in his trouser pocket for his railcard and flipped it open. The officer squinted at it and nodded.

'Round the side door. There'll be one of the staff to check you in,' he said shortly, looking thoughtfully at the tall student.

William nodded back, curious. The side entrance was the one he usually used. The banking hall was where the tellers worked, not the sort of people he saw on a day-to-day basis.

'Worked here long, have you?' the policeman asked.

'Just a month,' William shrugged. Then he gave the officer a tentative grin. 'First pay packet today. What's happened anyway?' He glanced past him at the front door closed to the public. 'Someone rob the bank?' he joked.

The police officer shot him a strange look. 'You'll find out soon enough, son,' he replied.

Then, as William Lorimer strode off, the policeman spoke into a radio handset, his eyes following the student around the side of the building until he disappeared out of sight.

William was no longer smiling as he sat at his place in the cash room, fingers counting the dirty banknotes that lay in banded bundles on the curved counter. All around him staff were whispering about the raid.

'Happened just before closing time last night,' he heard one of them say.

'Wonder why it wasn't on the news?' another ventured.

Nobody had spoken to him at all this morning, William realised as he secured a pile of notes with an elastic band and placed the counted bundle at the back of his table. Mind you, it was pay day and he knew that the woman who sat to his left thought it unfair that a *student with no previous experience* should be on a better scale than most of the *hard-working folk* in this room just because he had a decent clutch of Higher Certificates. Ethel was large and stout, with several chins that wobbled as she munched her way through a daily packet of digestive biscuits. She had never offered even one to the young man by her side.

'Lorimer!'

All talk stopped as the cashiers turned to see the bank manager enter the long narrow room, his clipped moustache bristling with suppressed indignation as he scanned the seated figures.

'This your bag?' Mr Pringle held up William's sports bag with two fingers as though it were full of smelly, unwashed kit.

'Yes, that's mine. Why?' William began to rise out of his seat.

'Come!' Pringle ordered, holding the door open with one well-polished shoe. 'My office.'

William felt the row of eyes staring at him as he followed the bank manager out of the room and up the dark wood-panelled staircase. What was going on? Why had the manager brought his sports bag from the staff cloakroom? His stomach began to churn, reminding him of the hasty single slice of toast that had been breakfast.

'Close the door behind you,' Pringle barked at him as he took his seat behind the large mahogany desk, leaving William to stand, legs apart, fists bunched by his side as though on parade, looking down on the smaller man. In the silence that followed, William noticed a fly buzzing at the window, trapped behind the hot glass, the sun shining onto the manager's balding pate and a faint whiff of something with lavender undertones that might have been furniture polish.

Outside the restaurants and cafés in Royal Exchange Square would be open for business but all that William could see from where he stood were the ornate carvings on the rooftops.

'You bank with us.' It was a statement, not a question, and William nodded, not quite knowing what to reply.

'Knocked off early last night?'

'We all did, sir. Mondays begin an hour earlier because of the weekend cash coming in from all the other banks,' William said, wondering as he did so why the manager was unaware of the working hours of his own staff. Perhaps he was too far removed from the goings-on of the cashiers, those lowly creatures who worked day after day thumbing banknotes in that claustrophobic basement room, windowless for security reasons.

'This *is* your bag?' Pringle pointed to the holdall where he had dropped it beside his desk.

'Well, I think so. It looks like mine,' William said, frowning. Then he spotted the frayed handles and the D-ring where his locker key from school had been fixed. 'Aye, I'm sure that's mine,' he added, nodding.

'You'll know why we have closed the bank this morning,' Pringle said, glaring at him.

'Someone said there had been a raid?'

Pringle leaned forward. 'Two masked gunmen carrying a sports bag,' he said slowly, never taking his eyes off William's face. 'One of them particularly tall. With piercing blue eyes,' he added.

Then an accusing finger pointed in William Lorimer's direction.

'*You* fit that description,' he hissed between uneven little teeth. 'And now the police want to speak to you.'

He didn't want to do this.

'It'll be all right,' the police officer assured him, clapping a heavy hand on Kevin Patterson's shoulder. 'Just walk along slowly, take your time. There's no need for a snap decision.'

Kevin took a crumpled handkerchief from his jacket pocket and wiped the sweat from his brow. His shirt was sticking to his back, its armpits soaked through.

He had already been shown the sports bag. 'I . . . I really can't be sure,' he'd stammered. 'It *might* be that one. I didn't really take too much notice.'

The police officer had smiled encouragingly. 'Don't worry about it, Mr Patterson. It's easy to forget details when you're under that sort of pressure.'

But they *wanted* him to remember, Kevin knew that. What if

he got it wrong? What if he couldn't correctly identify the man they had arrested for the robbery? Would he track Kevin down?

'You need to look closely at every man in the line-up, Mr Patterson,' the policeman told him. 'When you are certain that you know the right one, simply tap him on the shoulder. Can you do that?'

He was a coward. Kevin knew that even as he nodded. *I'll never forget the look in his eyes*, he'd told them afterwards. And they had written that down, asked him to sign the statement.

And it was true. He'd woken up several times in the darkness, that nightmare figure looming over him, the shotgun close to Kevin's face.

There were five men already standing in a line, all staring straight ahead, when William Lorimer was escorted into the room at Police Headquarters. The student rubbed sweating palms against his trousers as he took the vacant space between two of the men.

They thought he was the bank robber! William's stomach lurched uneasily. How could this be happening? He stared curiously at the others, dressed in two-piece suits, just like himself. They would be police officers or ordinary men brought in off the street – wasn't that how it worked? He hadn't a clue, really. Just what he'd seen in TV dramas. Not one of the others in the line turned to look his way. Was that a bad sign? Did *they* all think he was guilty of the robbery?

'Please keep looking straight ahead, arms by your side,' a voice commanded and William stared at the glass wall in front of him, wondering, even as his heart thumped within his chest, if it was actually a two-way mirror, unseen people watching his every move.

A door on his left opened and he resisted the temptation to turn his head. Somebody was walking slowly past the assembled men and, as he passed by William, the student saw the man hesitate, staring into his face as though searching for something.

For a moment their eyes met and William could see fear in the older man's eyes.

It wasn't me! he wanted to blurt out. *You've got the wrong man!*

Then an unexpected sense of pity came with the sudden thought: what a terrible ordeal this poor soul must have suffered in that armed raid.

The old chap blinked and moved on.

William held his breath. Would he come back along the line? Pick him out once he had looked at all the others?

Time seemed to stand still as the man walked out of his vision.

'That's the man!'

William's heart leapt. Was he pointing at him?

He tried to swallow but his mouth was dry.

'All right, sir.' The CID officer who had brought him into the room was suddenly holding William by the elbow, hustling him quickly away.

'What? Where are we going?' William tried to turn and look at the older man who had walked past him, wanting to explain, but he was taken firmly by the elbow and led round a corner, away from the room with the glass wall. He heard the sound of a door closing behind them and shivered. Was it releasing him or shutting him in?

'Well done, Mr Patterson!'

Kevin felt the clap on his shoulder. He rummaged for his handkerchief to blow his nose, a sudden urge to burst into tears now that it was all over.

'So pleased you managed to identify him,' the officer beamed at Kevin. 'Such a difficult thing to do when he'd been wearing a balaclava.'

Kevin nodded. It hadn't been as easy as he'd expected it to be but once he spotted the tall man with the ice blue eyes he knew.

'Cup of tea, sir?'

'Yes, thank you,' Kevin replied, though what he really needed more than anything was to sit down somewhere before his legs gave way beneath him.

'Think that manager of yours had you tried and convicted already,' the plain-clothes police officer told William as he ushered him along a narrow corridor, past a row of interview rooms and round a corner. The student glanced as a uniformed officer passed them by, a bunch of keys dangling from his belt. Was this where the police cells were located? Was that his destination? William hesitated, gripped by a claustrophobic fear of being enclosed in a tiny dungeon.

'Just along here, sir.' The man by his side held out a hand indicating a set of double doors.

William looked at the men and women he could see sitting around tables. Several were in uniform, many dressed in suits or even jeans and T-shirts. Off-duty cops? Undercover officers? William Lorimer's eyes were everywhere, seeking out some clue as to who these people were.

'Sorry you had to go through that, Mr Lorimer. The description our witness gave ...' The officer smiled and shrugged, ushering William to a table.

'You mean there was a bank robber who looked just like me?' William's eyebrows rose in astonishment as he sat down in the police canteen.

'Well, we had a pretty good idea who it was when we brought him in for questioning,' the man chuckled. 'Can't say more than that.' He tapped the side of his nose.

William returned his smile, the tension ebbing away. *What an idea*, he thought. *I look like a bank robber, or a bank robber looks like me. Appearance and reality*, he mused. And, as he looked around him, the student understood that this was what these ordinary-looking men and women must do for a living: identifying and seeking out criminals who preyed on the innocent folk in society. Studying History of Art suddenly seemed tame stuff compared to the sorts of work these people undertook on a daily basis.

'What's it like?' William asked, his curiosity aroused. 'Being a police officer, I mean?'

The detective looked amused by the question. 'Do you really want to know?'

He turned slightly and pointed at a recruitment poster on the wall.

'There's one way of finding out, young Lorimer,' he grinned. 'Ever thought about it?'

C ᴡ